Midnight

Christi J. Whitney is a former high school theatre director with a love for the arts. She lives just outside Atlanta with her husband and two sons. When not spending time with them or taking a ridiculous number of trips to Disney World, she can be found directing plays, making costumes for sci-fi/ fantasy conventions, obsessing over Doctor Who, watching superhero movies, or pretending she's just a tad bit British. You can visit her online at www.christijwhitney.com or connect on Twitter (@ChristiWhitney).

Also by Christi J. Whitney

The Romany Outcasts
Grey
Shadow

Midnight

CHRISTI J. WHITNEY

Book Three of the Romany Outcasts Series

HARPER
Voyager

Harper*Voyager*
An imprint of HarperCollins*Publishers* Ltd
1 London Bridge Street
London SE1 9GF

www.harpervoyagerbooks.co.uk

This Paperback Original 2017

First published in Great Britain in ebook format by Harper*Voyager* 2017

A catalogue record for this book
is available from the British Library

ISBN: 978-0-00-818153-6

Typeset in Sabon by Palimpsest Book Production Limited,
Falkirk, Stirlingshire

Printed and bound in Great Britain

MIX
Paper from
responsible sources
FSC
www.fsc.org   FSC™ C007454

This book is produced from independently certified FSC paper
to ensure responsible forest management.

For more information visit: **www.harpercollins.co.uk/green**

To my love

1. Josephine

'They're putting Sebastian on trial.'

I stopped walking and stared hard at my brother, trying to wrap my head around his words. Fifteen minutes ago, Sebastian and I had been on our way back to the Circe de Romany from our picnic. Then Quentin and his Marksmen met us at the gate, and turned everything upside down.

'What are you saying, Francis?' I demanded. 'Putting him on trial for what?'

'We have to go, Josephine. It's starting.'

My brother took me under the arm and hurried me through the opening of the red and gold tent. I couldn't believe my eyes. Our entire clan had gathered in the Circe's large Holding Tent. People stood along the canvas walls or squeezed themselves onto the long benches, talking in low, questioning voices.

A table had been set up on the far side of the tent and our father, Nicolas Romany, sat blank-faced in the center. I recognized the men positioned on either side of him. They were judges, appointed by each family in our clan to preside

1

over a trial. One of them was Andre, my Circe partner. And another was Quentin.

My heart dropped like a heavy weight inside me.

Francis followed my gaze, and his green eyes mirrored mine. His jaw tightened. 'Father called the kris a half-hour ago and ordered everyone to be present. We've been waiting for you to get back from your trip to Copper Mountain.' My brother nodded towards the entrance. 'Both of you.'

'Francis, what—'

'It's not good, Josephine,' he said, cutting me off. 'It's really not good.'

I allowed him to lead me through the center of the tent. I felt eyes on me from every direction, like bugs crawling all over my body. I held my chin high and kept my face wiped clean of any expression, but my insides churned.

I took my place, standing behind the table next to my mother. She didn't look at me. Francis stayed on my other side, his shoulder pressing comfortingly into mine. Leo, the head judge, stood up from the table and motioned to the Marksmen standing on either side of the tent door.

'Bring it in.'

My stomach clenched with nausea as the guards opened the flaps and Sebastian was shoved forcefully through the opening. He went down on one knee, but only for a moment before he was yanked to his feet. I winced at the sight of him. They'd strapped his gigantic wings to his back with tight cords, and their clawed tips dragged along the ground behind him. His arms were also pinned behind him, heavily chained across his wings.

Sebastian stumbled to the center, looking weak and disoriented. He shook his head several times, like he was trying to clear whatever it was away. His pewter hair fell across his *forehead. Marksmen forced him down onto his knees, but he looked up sharply, his strange, silver eyes focusing on the people at the table. And then, his gaze landed on me.*

Sebastian's expression held no anger, only confusion. He blinked once, slowly. Immediately, I felt his emotions, deep inside my chest, as strongly as if they were my own. He was concerned about ... me. My breath caught in my throat. I could only stare back at him, praying he felt my emotions the same way. He gave me one last blink, then pushed himself determinedly to his feet.

Quentin also rose and stepped around the table. He was dressed in his normal Marksman outfit, perfectly fitted from head to toe. Once, I used to love the way his tall, trim figure looked in the uniform. Now, it just made me feel sick inside. He smoothed his sleek black hair, the way he did when he was feeling confident about something.

Sebastian ignored him, turning to my father instead. 'Nicolas, I don't—'

'Chain the creature,' said Quentin.

I watched in helpless horror as four of our largest guards descended on Sebastian. They pushed him backwards to the middle of the tent, to the thick center support beam. Metal chains were flung across his chest and yanked taut. Sebastian grunted as one Marksman adjusted the manacles and fastened them with a lock that clicked ominously into place.

'What's going on?' demanded Sebastian.

I heard the telltale growling sound seeping into his voice, though I could feel him trying his best to stay calm. My eyes pricked with hot tears, but I forcibly blinked them away.

My father answered. 'It's not your time to speak, Sebastian Grey.'

One of the Marksmen – a man named Jacque, who I'd

known since we were children – stepped forward and raised his fist towards Sebastian. I opened my mouth, but Quentin yelled out a command, and Jacque lowered his arm.

My father stood. The crowd went instantly quiet. Nicolas Romany was our bandoleer, and no one from our clan would dare speak over him.

'We've called this kris because what happened tonight affects the entire clan – and not just us, but everyone in our kumpania.'

I searched frantically for my brother's hand. Francis felt my touch and looked down at me. I saw the light of fiery anger behind his eyes. That tiny glimmer steadied me. My brother had supported Sebastian from the beginning, even when so many others had been unwilling to trust him because of what he was.

'What's happened?' I whispered to him.

Francis turned his eyes towards our father. 'I don't know,' he said tensely, through clenched teeth. 'I heard there was another chimera attack.'

I froze. Had those demonic beasts we'd fought on Copper Mountain infiltrated the Circe while we were gone? Were people blaming Sebastian for not being here to protect them? If so, then it was my fault. I'd been the one to ask him to come with me. Guilt twisted my lungs like a tourniquet. All I'd wanted was some time with Sebastian alone – a moment of peace away from the business of the clan. It was the Marksmen's job to patrol the Fairgrounds.

How could they blame Sebastian for this?

Leo, the head judge, addressed the crowd, turning his old withered face to the benches full of people. 'The purpose of this kris is to determine the guilt or innocence of the accused.'

My throat seized up. Accused?

'Nicolas!' Sebastian's voice suddenly rang out from the center of the tent. Jacque took a swing at him with his fist, but Sebastian ducked his head out of the way. 'I demand to know why I'm here.'

Leo's head snapped around. 'You will speak only when directed to, gargoyle!'

'I have the right to—'

'You have no rights in this court,' said Andre, cutting him off.

I felt my stomach sink even lower. Andre was my Circe partner. It wasn't a secret that he was wary of Sebastian, but the malice in his voice took me by surprise. All around me, people were murmuring. People I'd always considered my friends – or, at least, people I'd always liked. Now, it was as though someone had poisoned the entire room with dark thoughts.

Quentin leaned across the table. 'Leo, for the benefit of the court … and the accused, of course … why don't you state the accusation?'

'Very well,' said Leo, drawing up his wrinkled face. 'Sebastian Grey, you are on trial for the murder of Karl Corsi.'

The crowd exploded around me. I gasped and dug my fingers into Francis' arm. Karl was dead? A cold shiver went down my spine. Karl had been more than just our circus trainer. He'd been like a grandfather to us all.

At Leo's accusation, Sebastian slumped forward, as through someone had punched him in the stomach. The life went out of his inhumanly silver eyes. He looked sick. My heart wanted to burst.

'No,' I said loudly. Francis pulled on me, but I broke out of his grasp and rushed to the table. 'That's not possible. Sebastian was with me all day.'

As soon as the words were out of my mouth, Quentin went rigid all over. He turned his piercing eyes in my direction, and I saw the familiar set of his jaw that meant he was furious with me. But I didn't care. What they were doing was wrong. It was all wrong.

My father was also staring at me. 'We'll cover the details in time, Josephine,' he said slowly. 'Go back to your place.'

Though his voice sounded relaxed, his expression wasn't. I felt the tension between us, and I knew I'd come dangerously close to overstepping my bounds. At this moment, I wasn't Nicolas Romany's daughter. I was a member of the Romany clan, and he was my bandoleer.

Every part of me screamed inside. But the authority of the kris was absolute. I was bound by it, the same as anyone else. With a huge amount of effort, I managed a stiff nod at my father. I felt Francis guiding me back to my place. He took my hand in his, holding it tightly.

'There's nothing you can do,' he said quietly in my ear.

I watched with mounting dread as Leo regarded Sebastian with a frigid look and crossed his arms expectantly.

'Well, gargoyle,' said Leo. 'What is your plea?'

Sebastian pushed himself up as straight as possible against the support pole. The clanking of his chains echoed eerily in the silent tent. Trickles of purple-black blood ran down his hands from the metal cuffs. His gray skin looked oddly pale, but his expression remained resolute. Sebastian looked steadily at each and every man at the table, and his silver gaze fell lastly on me. He took a deep breath and said in a voice loud enough for the entire room to hear:

'I didn't kill him.'

*

The neon sign of the *Gypsy Ink* flashed, ripping me from the memory. The horrible scene of the last few hours vaporized, and I found myself staring at the black door of the Corsi tattoo parlor, the place where Sebastian had spent most of his life. My chest ached.

How was I going to tell them about Sebastian?

I took a deep breath and flung open the door. A group of heavily tattooed men turned to face me. I looked around the room, trying to catch my breath and squash my nerves at the same time. I clutched Quentin's keys in my fist, wondering how long it would be until he realized his SUV wasn't there.

'Where's Hugo?'

The three men gaped at me, then turned their heads simultaneously towards a narrow hallway. I heard the clamp of heavy, steel-toed boots approaching on the tile floor. I squared my shoulders and pulled my robe tighter around my Circe costume as Hugo Corsi, the leader of the Corsi clan and Sebastian's foster brother, stepped into the room.

'Josephine.'

Hugo's voice was rough and harder than concrete. The voice of someone used to being in charge and giving orders. The tone in which he said my name demanded answers to questions he hadn't even asked.

'I'm sorry,' I blurted out, my nerves getting the best of me. 'I tried to come sooner, but I couldn't get away.' I felt utterly ridiculous in my stage outfit and makeup. My Circe life was so different from Sebastian's world – the world I was standing in now. 'My father's been watching my every move since it happened.'

'Since what happened?' Hugo punctuated every word.

His dark eyes shifted to the door and back. 'What are you doing here? And where's Sebastian?'

I glanced over Hugo's head, at the skull-and-crossbones clock hanging on the back wall. I had less than an hour until our show began. Andre, my routine partner, would realize I was missing the second he came by my dressing room to fetch me.

'Sebastian's gone,' I answered.

Hugo tossed his cleaning rag aside and stormed around the counter. The muscles beneath his neck tattoo bulged, and the ink seemed to come to life across his skin.

'What do you mean he's gone?'

Before I could reply, a huge man standing on my right reached for me, his touch surprisingly gentle on my arm. He gave me a small smile. 'Why don't you start over, from the beginning?'

A man with red hair and a lip piercing shoved a stack of magazines off the couch and motioned for me to sit. I barely knew the Corsis, but I could pick them out from Sebastian's descriptions. The red-haired man was Vincent. The stocky, thick-shouldered one was Kris, and the massive man with the gentle demeanor was James. Then, there was their leader Hugo Corsi. His expression was scary, intense.

'From the beginning,' I repeated. I inhaled through my nose and breathed out slowly through my mouth, as though preparing for a stunt in one of my acts 'My clan held a *kris* last night.'

'A trial,' said James, frowning heavily. 'Why?'

'Last night, Karl Corsi was found dead in his trailer.' I spoke quickly, pushing my raw feelings aside. 'All the evidence pointed to him being killed by a shadow creature.

They accused Sebastian of murdering Karl and taking all his books with information on the shadow world.'

I paused, gauging their reactions. I didn't know how close they'd been to Karl, but he was a Corsi, and clan ties were stronger than blood. James looked visibly shaken, but the others remained blank and silent, which was somehow worse.

'Our council was deadlocked,' I continued. 'They couldn't find Sebastian guilty or innocent, but because of everything that had happened, they refused to release him.'

'That's ridiculous,' said Kris, crossing his thick arms. 'If they couldn't find him guilty—'

'Everything was out of control,' I said, cutting him off. 'People were scared. There were reports of shadow creatures in the woods, and a lot of people were convinced Sebastian had called them there. The Marksmen ordered everyone to stay in our trailers, and our clan was demanding a verdict. My father had no choice but to defer to the High Council in Savannah.'

'A convenient action,' snarled Kris.

'But it's the law,' said James. 'Whether we like it or not. If a decision can't be made in a *kris*, then it has to go before the High Court. Nicolas was only doing his job.'

Hugo studied me. 'Why haven't we been told?'

'My father didn't want other clans getting wind of what happened, especially after all the rumors of shadowen attacks and clan feuding that have been coming out of the north. He thought it would only cause panic.'

'Karl may have worked with you, but he was from our clan,' said Vincent from the other side of the room. His face turned as red as his hair. 'Your family had no right to keep this from us.'

Christi J. Whitney

I looked away, feeling awful. 'I know.'

'We will mourn for Karl in our own time,' said Hugo, addressing the others. 'He was a Corsi, but he belonged to the Circe. They will do right by him. For now, Sebastian needs to be our focus. If we start making preparations now, we can leave before—'

'Wait,' I said. 'That's not all of it.'

I closed my eyes, forcing my thoughts to go back, to return to the last time I saw Sebastian, almost seventeen hours ago. To make myself see the old animal cage at the back of the Circe property where he'd been held. To relive the moment I'd lost him.

'Right after the trial, Augustine showed up at the Circe.'

At the mention of the man who'd been banished from Outcast Gypsy society, the Corsis immediately bristled with hatred and fury. But, they kept silent, letting me continue.

'Augustine is actually my uncle Adolár.' The words burned like acid in my throat. 'I never knew it until last night. I was too young when he left the Circe to remember him.' I shuddered. I didn't want to dwell on my relationship to the former Gypsy anymore than I had to. 'Augustine told my father he was on his way to Savannah to meet with the Queen. He had somehow found out about our *kris*, and he offered to escort Sebastian there.'

'So, Augustine has my brother,' said Hugo, in a deadly tone. 'That *marimé* traitor with a grudge against every clan in this *kumpania*, and Nicolas just lets him waltz out of the Romany camp with your guardian?'

'It happened so fast,' I replied, rubbing my palms together until my skin stung. 'My father couldn't spare a Marksmen escort, but the High Council was already expecting Sebastian. Augustine said that if he personally delivered Sebastian to

10

the Court, he'd be able to get an audience with the Queen.'

'Why would he think that?' huffed Kris. 'He's *marimé*. He's lost his Gypsy blood and every right he had under our law. It's not like he could even get anywhere near her.'

'Unless he had an extremely important reason,' Hugo said, sarcasm heavy and dripping. 'Unbelievable. Nicolas let Augustine use my brother like some kind of bargaining chip to see the Queen.'

'My father had no choice,' I replied, feeling caught between my family and Sebastian and sickened by the whole thing. 'Augustine threatened to tell the other clans we were harboring a murderer. The Marksmen made Sebastian look like some merciless killer. Half the troupe already believed he was guilty. But then, when they let him out of that cage ...'

I dropped off. A cold chill poured through me.

James touched my shoulder again, gentle and non-threatening. 'What happened when they let Sebastian out?'

'He wasn't himself,' I said quietly.

'What do you mean?' asked Hugo. He sat on the other end of the couch. I felt the tension coming off him like the heat from an engine.

'I've seen what Sebastian can do.' I paused, trying to find words to describe the change that came over him, but everything sounded wrong in my head. 'What I mean is, I know how he can be when he's forced to act as a guardian, when he has to protect me ... or anyone else. But he's always snapped back before. It was different this time. He was vicious, and his eyes ... his eyes were just ... empty.'

Like an animal's, I'd nearly added, but stopped myself. No, he wasn't the creature Quentin accused him of being. In that brief moment – just before he'd gone so wild – he'd

11

asked for my forgiveness, and in his eyes, I saw the sweet, strange boy whose life had intersected with mine. He wasn't a beast.

Something had happened to him.

Hugo's gaze traveled to the window. It had grown dark outside, and the glass reflected the room. The corner of his mouth tightened. 'Do you believe he killed Karl?'

'Absolutely not!' I leapt up, suddenly shaking with a fury that caught me off guard. 'He would never do something like that. You're his brother. You should know!'

'He's not the same kid you knew in school. He's a gargoyle now.'

'He's my guardian,' I snapped. 'I don't care what he looks like or where he came from. He's still Sebastian. He has the best heart of anyone I've ever met, and he would never … ever …'

Hugo rubbed his eyes. 'I'm not saying it was intentional …'

'He didn't murder Karl!'

I pressed my hand against my mouth. I would not cry. Not in front of them. As my fingers brushed my lips, I remembered the impulsive kiss I'd given Sebastian after the trial. How he'd stared at me, so shocked and wide-eyed with that unearthly silver gaze, that it felt like my heart was going to leap through my chest.

'Okay,' said Hugo, after several moments. Both his expression and his voice were softer this time. 'I just wanted to hear it from you.'

Hugo walked to the front window, his hands shoved deep into the pockets of his ripped jeans. The others watched his movements the same way people in our troupe watched my father.

'This was Augustine's doing, from the very beginning,'

said James. 'He had his shadow creatures kill Karl, then he took his books.'

'And framed Sebastian in the process,' added Vincent.

It felt like the temperature had dropped ten degrees. 'But why?' I questioned. 'My uncle ... I mean, *Augustine* ... had his own collection of shadowen books. I remember his library when I was a child. It was mostly fairy tales and stories, same as Karl's.'

'I think Karl had more information than we knew,' said Hugo.

A moment passed. Then another. The four tattoo artists locked stares with each other. The veins in Hugo's neck bulged. Goosebumps rose along my arms.

'Whatever Augustine took from Karl is the least of our problems,' said Hugo at last. He ran his hands through his wiry hair. 'Maybe he's using my brother to gain safe passage into Savannah, but he wants Sebastian for himself.'

'Sebastian's sealed to me.' I clutched the dandelion pendant at my neck. Though I hadn't believed it at first, there was no longer any doubt in my mind. He was my guardian. I was his charge.

'I know,' said Hugo, sounding resigned. 'But Augustine has wanted Sebastian from the start. After everything that went down last autumn, I thought he'd given up his quest. But it looks like I was wrong. Augustine knows there's something special about him.'

My stomach rolled uneasily. I'd known Sebastian was special, even before he'd become a gargoyle. I'd never met anyone like him before. But the way Hugo used the word sounded different. Ominous. 'What is it?'

James sighed heavily. 'We don't know.'

All my scared feelings funneled back into anger. 'Well,

what *do* you know, then? I came here because I thought you could help Sebastian. You're the ones who turned him into a gargoyle in the first place.'

'People don't *turn* into gargoyles, Josephine,' Hugo replied. 'Shadowen have to be created. Their bodies are carved from special stone and then brought to life with *prah*.' Hugo paused, as though working over several thoughts in his head. 'You know what Sebastian looked like when you first met him, and how he is now. There's something unique about him.'

Vincent pounded his fist against the wall. 'Now, Augustine has him.'

'Augustine was ordered to take Sebastian directly to the Court of Shadows for trial,' I said. 'If he had failed to show up, the Council would know. And so would my father.'

'Josephine's right,' said Hugo. He moved behind the counter and stared at the wall calendar near the register. 'The High Council is scheduled to meet in three days. That gives us time. But we should leave tonight.'

'When?' asked Vincent.

'Midnight,' Hugo replied. Then he turned back to me. 'Thank you for letting us know what's happened. I'm sure you're being missed right now. You'd better get back to the Circe.'

'No. I have to get to Savannah.'

Hugo frowned. 'What good would that do?'

'I'm going to testify on Sebastian's behalf.'

'So tell your father to take you.'

I hesitated. I hadn't been allowed to set foot inside our primary Gypsy Haven since becoming the Queen's successor. But I couldn't tell the Corsis that. 'Look,' I continued quickly,

14

'I have to get to Savannah before Sebastian goes on trial. I'm a Romany. The Queen has to see me.'

'Josephine.' Hugo's voice was firm. 'I get where you're coming from, I really do. But you're not coming with us. Besides, what do you think would happen if Nicolas discovered you just took off and left the Circe without permission?'

I met his gaze without blinking. 'I'm going to Savannah.'

'No, you're not.' Hugo lifted me to my feet, not forcibly, but enough for me to know he meant business. The guys crowded around me, herding me towards the door. 'Thank you for coming here to tell us. I know it was a risk. But let us handle it from here.'

I grabbed hold of Hugo's shirt, desperate now. 'Hugo, please.'

James opened the door and stood aside.

Hugo took my hands in his. 'Things are complicated enough as it is. You being there would only make things more difficult. The sooner we get to Savannah, the sooner we clear this up and get Sebastian back.'

'But—'

'Go home, Josephine.'

Hugo ushered me out of the *Gypsy Ink* and shut the door behind me.

2. Josephine

It was sweltering underneath the stage lights. My thick tights clung damply to my legs, and sweat tickled the back of my neck. As I eased carefully into a headstand, balancing on Andre's shoulders, my sequined costume scraped against my arms.

Once I made it through the routine, the show would be over, and I would be free. I tried to focus, to keep myself in the moment of our performance, but the Circe continued to fade around me ... my mind traveled, the crowd blurred ...

The Holding Tent emptied quickly after Sebastian's trial. The benches were abandoned and the space was eerily quiet. Except for one sound – the sound of labored breathing, the sound of someone in pain.

He was still chained to the center support pole, just as he'd been during the kris. *I stared at Sebastian in sickened shock. His jeans were ripped in several places with long tears. There were gashes in his arms, covered with his strange, purple-black blood. A deep slash cut across his* chest. It had ripped the fabric of his t-shirt away. His jaw was discolored, his gray skin turning an unsettling shade of indigo.

My eyes rose to his face, and his eyes met mine.

I ran across the room.

'Sebastian!'

'Josephine,' he answered. His voice was hoarse. 'What are you doing here?'

I studied his wounds. 'Oh, God, what have they done?'

'I'm fine,' he said, smiling.

He kept his lips closed, as always. But how could he smile right now? I tried to laugh, but it felt like I was choking. 'You suck at lying, you know.' I suddenly remembered the Marksmen. 'Are they still here?'

'They're in the woods,' he answered. He shifted his body, trying to loosen the chains around his middle. I could see pain flicker behind his silver eyes. 'What's going on?'

'A handful of grotesques near the back gates.' I looked away, hating to say it out loud, to admit the next bit. 'And two chimeras.'

Sebastian growled. The sound was inhuman, threatening. But it wasn't directed at me. It was for himself. I saw the glimmer of sharp teeth as he started to speak. 'I should've—'

I pressed my fingers against his mouth. 'Don't go there. I'm the one who told you to leave Anya and Matthias. The Marksmen will deal with them. Even if you had killed those chimeras on the mountain, it wouldn't have prevented all this from happening.'

I removed my hand, and I saw him swallow back another growl. His eyes, which had taken on a fierce gleam, softened again. I felt a kind of unspoken communication pass between us, wrapping around me like a blanket, familiar and comfort-

able. We were in this together, no matter what happened next.

Sebastian's wings suddenly shuddered against the cords, and he winced. He maneuvered his body, trying to find a comfortable position, but the Marksmen had done their job well.

Quentin's Marksmen.

Anger licked across my stomach as I remembered how nonchalantly Quentin had withheld casting a vote in Sebastian's verdict – a decision that could've set him free. Quentin's hatred of the shadow world was fierce. I'd once seen it as noble. But after this …

'They're wrong about you,' I said, placing my hand against Sebastian's neck. I felt him tremble. 'I should have challenged my father and the kris. *I should have forced Quentin to change his decision. You're innocent.'*

'There's nothing you could've done,' Sebastian replied, giving me that same, gentle smile that made me feel all kinds of things. 'Not even your father can go against the ruling, you said so yourself. I don't know much about your people's laws, but I saw the power of the council tonight. They'd already made up their minds.'

My shoulders slumped under invisible hands, pushing me down. 'I know my words wouldn't have changed anything but, believe me, I'm not done trying. There has to be another way.'

I stared into his eyes, and a powerful, electric silence fell between us. He leaned forward, but the chains prevented him from going very far.

'Thank you,' he said softly. 'For believing me.'

'I've always believed you, Sebastian.' I raised my hand to his face and pressed my palm gently against his right

18

cheek. His skin was cool to the touch, like a stone plucked from a mountain stream. I felt my heart beat faster as our eyes met. 'You're the only one I can believe.'

Applause roared around me. I jerked to the present. My legs wobbled in my pose. The chair Andre was balancing on teetered underneath his feet, but he adjusted so fast, no one in the audience would've noticed. But he did. I came out of my handstand. He offered his hands and I dismounted beside him.

'What's in your head?' Andre hissed in my ear. 'Focus!'

I sprang onto his broad shoulders again for our next pose, the most difficult of our combinations for the routine. His hands wrapped around mine, giving me a cue with one firm squeeze. I pulled myself up again, this time, balancing on one arm. My body quivered. Just a few more seconds. I tried to block out the crowd, the lights, and the pressure. But my mind …

Sebastian …

I said his name like a plea.

Sebastian …

He turned his silver-moon eyes toward me. Guilt, like a massive explosion, struck me from the inside out. I strained to reach him through the bars of the cage. I couldn't. He was too far. I'd come too late. All I could do was whisper the same phrase, over and over again.

I'm so sorry … I'm so sorry … I'm so …

I over-rotated. Andre's hand clamped tighter, but I couldn't straighten. My body wouldn't obey. I clenched my teeth and willed all my strength into my muscles. My stomach burned as I held on. It was only skill and hours of practice that kept us together. We morphed fluidly into another pose and I managed a smooth dismount without missing a beat. Applause erupted from around the Big Tent.

My cheeks burned as Andre took my hand and we faced the audience. We took our bows and hurried out of the circle as the lights dimmed on the stage space. We slipped behind the curtain separating the Big Tent from the backstage.

'What was that?' Andre snapped at me. 'That's the worse we've ever done that routine.' We stopped in front of our dressing areas and he looked me over, his close-set eyes scrutinizing me critically. 'What's going on? Are you hurt?'

'No,' I said, pulling back the separating curtain. I didn't want to look at him. I just needed him to leave me alone so I could change out of my costume and be finished with the performance for good. 'I'm fine, Andre. I just had an off-night, that's all. It's been a long day.'

'When is it *not* a long day around here?' he said.

'I know—'

'It's about that gargoyle, isn't it?'

I froze, my hand on the curtain. I saw the judgment written across Andre's broad face, along with his scathing disbelief. He'd formed his own opinions, just like Quentin – I knew it the second I saw him sitting at the table for the *kris*. I felt a slow, cold anger seep through my bones, pushing away my guilt and shame.

'His name's Sebastian,' I said.

And I shoved the curtain closed between us.

*

I stripped down as quickly as possible, relieved to put away the sequins and glitter. I'd spent most of my life hiding behind the show glam, disappearing within the elaborate makeup and bright clothes. It gave me a sense of peace. Now, I suddenly felt stifled by it.

The curtain rustled. I finished buttoning my jeans and sat down to pull on my shoes.

'Come in.'

Francis slipped inside my small dressing room. My brother was dressed all in black, but it was the uniform used by the Circe crew, not the Marksmen. He plopped down in a chair opposite me, giving me a crooked smile, but his eyes were clouded.

'Are you sure about this, Josie?'

I stood and grabbed my duffel bag, hastily cramming a few outfits inside it, along with items off my dressing table. 'Yes, I'm sure. It's the only way. I've already worked it out. Claire is going to take over for me for tomorrow's show. I talked to Father and told him I need a short break, so I can clear my head.'

'I still can't believe he's giving you permission to spend the entire weekend away from the Circe,' said Francis. 'It's totally not like him at all.'

'Father's a lot of things, but he's not heartless.' I zipped up the duffel bag, then shrugged and looked away. 'And he knows how much Sebastian—'

Means to me.

I didn't complete the thought, but I didn't have to. Francis already knew what I was going to say. He was my twin, after all. His eyes narrowed into a knowing look, and he pursed his lips.

'You're taking a big risk, you know. You're not allowed

21

anywhere near Savannah, you remember that, right? What with you being the secret successor to the Queen and all.'

I almost smiled. 'It's kind of hard to forget that.'

'Okay,' said Francis. 'Just checking. As your brother, I feel it's my obligation to let you know that your plan is both dangerous and ridiculous.' He crossed his arms over his chest. 'Which is why I'm behind it, one hundred and ten percent.'

I reached for his hand. 'Thanks.'

Francis smiled. 'So, you ready?'

'Almost.'

I pulled open the top drawer of my makeup table. Inside was the small, leather-bond book Esmeralda Lucian had given me the day before, when Sebastian and I were in her cave home under the bridge. I ran my fingers over the worn cover. Esmeralda, my high school teacher, who I'd only recently discovered was a banished guardian, had instructed me to keep the book safe. So it had to come with me.

I stuffed the book into the back pocket of my jeans and hoisted my bag over my shoulder. 'Now, I'm ready.'

My brother and I slipped out of the Holding Tent and headed towards the back of the lot, where our vehicles were kept. It was quiet around the Circe. Most everyone had retired to their trailers for the night. My nerves dissipated as we climbed into Francis' pick-up truck and he steered us out the back gates of the Fairgrounds.

My fingers tingled with nervous anticipation. I'd told Sebastian after the trial that there had to be another way to help him. Earlier this evening, I'd thought that way was with Hugo and the Corsis. But it wasn't. They'd pushed me out.

Which meant, I was going to have to do this on my own.

22

We crossed the churning Sutallee River and headed through the woods in the direction of town. Francis stayed uncharacteristically quiet for most of the ride. We'd never been ones to try and talk the other out of things, but I could tell by the way he gripped the steering wheel that he was wary.

Ten minutes later, we pulled into the front entrance of a well-manicured neighborhood. We passed several houses before turning into the long, winding driveway of a beautiful three-story home. Francis put the transmission in park, and then reached across the cab and wrapped his arms around me.

'I should go with you,' he said.

I hugged him back. 'You know you can't.'

His voice was muffled against my shoulder. 'Josie, just be careful, okay? Just get down there and testify, and then come straight home. If you're not back by Sunday night, Father's going to be suspicious that something's up.'

'I know.'

'Alright then,' Francis said suddenly, pushing me away. 'Stop wasting time. You get Sebastian out of there and bring him home, you hear me? He's gone through enough crap already.'

I nodded and climbed out of the cab. 'Bye, France.'

My brother put the truck in reverse, foot still on the brake. He surveyed the large house looming in front of us. 'And what makes you so sure she's going to go along with this?'

I couldn't help smiling. 'Because it's Katie.'

*

23

I pressed the doorbell, but I didn't have to wait long.

Almost immediately, the door swung open, and Katie Lewis threw her arms around me, squishing the air out of my lungs. 'Oh my gosh, you're here!'

'Hey, Katie,' I said, breathless. 'It's so good to see you.'

She pushed me back, holding onto my arms. 'Of course it is,' she said. 'I should totally be pissed at you right now, though. Don't think I didn't know you've been in town for weeks.'

Katie herded me inside. I paused, looking around the vast entryway. I never got used to houses this big. The high ceilings, the giant rooms – nothing like our small trailers back at the Circe.

'I'm really sorry,' I said, following her through an extensive kitchen and down a hallway. 'My father wouldn't let any of us away from the Fairgrounds this trip. Our schedule has been crazy. Plus, I knew you were in New York.'

'Only for two weeks,' she said, ushering me into her spacious bedroom. 'It's okay, being at my dad's, but I was so ready to come home. I'm in desperate need of some lake time and a serious tan.' She shot me a disgusted look. 'Not all of us were blessed with skin like yours.'

'Runs in the family,' I said with a shrug.

'Speaking of your family, how was the show tonight? I'm totally planning on coming to see you just as soon as I can get everyone together.'

'It was fine,' I replied, trying not to think about how I'd nearly botched our last routine. 'Just a few first-night jitters. I'm sorry to come by so late. The show ran longer than expected.'

Katie laughed. 'Well, I just got off work, and my Friday night plans involved some major television binge watching, so no worries. I've missed you like crazy, by the way. So, how's your summer been so far? Did you get your graduation certificate? Oh, and how's Quentin?'

'He's fine,' I replied, feeling suddenly cold. 'It's all … fine.'

I looked around Katie's bedroom. Like everything else in the Lewis home, it was huge. Everything matched perfectly, from the pastel walls, to the puffy bed pillows – even the frames of all the pictures lined across her desk. I picked up a photo of Katie, posing with a group of friends, and standing beside her was …

Sebastian.

I barely recognized him. His skin was a normal shade, his hair dark brown and wavy, flopping across his eyes. Not the luminous silver eyes I'd looked into so many times. They were simply hazel. No darkened lips or sharp teeth. And he was smiling, bright and full, as though he'd been halfway through a laugh when the picture was taken.

The guilt I thought I'd released taunted me again, savage and heavy. Sebastian told me he'd always been a gargoyle, and I had to believe him. But his life seemed so normal before all of this. Before he met me.

Katie took the picture out of my hands. 'Josie, I've been totally patient with you, but I'm about to freaking blow up if you don't tell me what's going on.'

I glanced up, startled. 'What?'

Her eyes narrowed into blue slits. 'In all the time I've known you, you've never once spent the night at my house. Like ever. And then, suddenly, you're asking to come over, like immediately? Something's up, and you'd better spill.'

Katie plopped on the bed, sending her mound of stuffed animals exploding in all directions. She looked at me expectantly.

I tried smiling, but my face didn't know what to do. I wondered how Sebastian had managed to keep the truth of what he was from Katie and his friends for so long. Those first months during his change must've been horrible. But deep down, I knew he'd kept his secrets the same way I'd kept mine.

He'd lied.

Keeping my family's Outcast Gypsy roots hidden was something we had to do – it was for our protection; it was how we preserved our heritage. But secrets like ours came at a constant cost. They built a wall between our world and the outside one. But it was a divide I was going to have to tear down.

'Katie,' I began hesitantly. 'I'm not here for a slumber party. I came here because I need your help. But first, there's a lot I have to tell you.'

'No problem.' She leaned forward eagerly. 'I'm all ears.'

A lifetime and a very long past pulled on me. I respected our Outcast traditions, but I also valued my friendship with Katie – more than I even realized until now.

'I guess I should start by telling you that I'm a Gypsy.'

'Well, yeah,' she replied, staring at me as though I'd told her the sky was blue. 'I mean, what with your last name and the whole circus thing you've got going on. Not to mention the fortune tellers and folky music and stuff.'

'No, you don't understand,' I said. 'It's not like that. We're Roma. The entire Circe troupe. We make up part of the Romany clan, and my father's the head of it.' I fiddled with the bracelets on my wrist. 'It's not something we tell outsiders. Letting non-Roma into our world isn't allowed. It's one of our laws.'

'Whoa.' Katie uncrossed her legs and slid off the bed. 'For real?'

'Yeah.'

'Oh my gosh! Actual Gypsies?'

'Not all my people like using that name, but in my *kumpania* – in my group – we don't mind. It's what we are. Outcast Gypsies.'

'Outcast from where?'

'From Europe, from our original clans, two hundred years ago. My ancestors wanted to start a new life in America so we could follow our own ways.'

'That is so unbelievably cool!' she exclaimed, practically bouncing in front of me. Her brows lowered suddenly. 'But wait, if you're not allowed to go around telling people who you are, then why is your family so open with all the Gypsy stuff at the Circe?'

'People don't make the connection between our stage shows and our real life. My father says it's using an old stereotype to our advantage. The Circe gives us freedom to live like we want and travel where we like, but without anyone knowing who we are.' I shrugged. 'It's not like we're the first circus to use a theme.'

'So it's a gimmick,' Katie said. 'You know, it's kind of like what Sebastian's brother does with his tattoo shop.' She stopped abruptly, and I literally saw the wheels click into place behind her eyes. 'Hang on. Is Hugo a Gypsy, too?'

An unsettling sensation pricked at me. I wasn't betraying the Corsis, I told myself. I didn't have a choice. 'Yeah, he is. Everybody that works there is part of his clan.'

'No freaking way,' Katie exclaimed. 'What about Sebastian? Is he—'

'Sebastian's not a Gypsy.' I glanced away. 'He's … something else.'

'What's that supposed to mean?'

27

Conflict pulled inside me, tighter than acrobat robes. This was worse than telling a *gadje* about my heritage, even if that *gadje* was Katie. My gaze drifted to the picture Katie had replaced on her desk. The image of his smiling face made my stomach ache. 'When was the last time you saw Sebastian?'

'My graduation party. Why?'

'How did he seem to you?'

Katie huffed. 'Honestly, I was surprised he even showed up. Something major's been going on with him, and he's been totally distant, in a really weird way. I don't know, I guess it's the trauma from the accident with his van or something, but whatever it is, Sebastian's just not the same. I mean, we text sometimes, but he won't talk to me on the phone, and my party was the first time I'd seen him in weeks. But he was acting all freaked out. And totally paranoid. He wouldn't even come inside the fence.'

I paused to take a long breath. 'You're right Katie, something has been going on with Sebastian the last few months. But it's not what you think.'

'If you're about to tell me he's on drugs—'

'No, it's nothing like that.'

'Good, 'cause I wouldn't have believed it anyway. I mean, it's Sebastian we're talking about here. In case you haven't noticed, he's not really the rebellious type, which is why I always found it so hilarious that he wanted to be a tattoo artist.' Her eyes widened. 'Not that they're rebels, I mean. His brother's totally cool. They all are. It just never seemed like Sebastian's thing.'

'What did you picture him doing after high school?' I asked. I was stalling, but I couldn't help it. Talking about him made it feel like he was still here, waiting for me back at the Circe with that soft, apologetic smile of his.

'Gosh, I don't know,' she said. 'His brother wanted him to go to college.'

'That would've been nice. He deserved that.'

'Josie.' Katie crossed to me and gripped my shoulder. 'You're talking about him like he's dead, and it's starting to freak me out. Is Sebastian okay?'

Her question shook me to attention. Without Katie's help, I'd never be able to get away from the Circe. I'd be stuck here – trapped, with no way to help the person who mattered most. I still didn't know how to define my feelings, if there were even words, but one thing I knew for sure: without him, nothing else made sense anymore.

'He's in trouble,' I said quickly. Katie opened her mouth, but I kept going before she could interject. 'He didn't do anything wrong, and it's not his fault, but he's been sent to Savannah by my people.'

'Savannah,' Katie repeated, letting go of my arm. 'What are you talking about? Is he okay, or isn't he? You're not making any sense.'

I felt stupid for thinking I could get away with only telling Katie what she absolutely needed to know. But this wasn't my secret … it was Sebastian's. I turned the dandelion pendant between my fingers, pressing the cold glass against my skin. He'd kept this from Katie on purpose. Once I crossed this line, there would be no going back.

'Katie, there's something about Sebastian, something that's happened to him, but I don't know how to say it without sounding like I'm insane.'

'Too late for that,' she replied. 'So just spit it out.'

I saw the rising irritation in Katie's eyes, but behind that, the fear. Suddenly, I hated secrets, more than I ever had in my life.

'There are these creatures,' I said quickly, before I could change my mind. 'My people brought them to life a long time ago. He's one of them. Hugo's parents brought him here, and he looked normal, but he didn't know the truth, and when my family came to Sixes, stuff began happening to him, and he's different now.'

'Creatures?' Katie's mouth quirked. 'Seriously Jo, you're making it sound like Sebastian's not human.'

'He's not.'

'Josephine,' said Katie, drawing my name out slowly. Her expression turned hard and skeptical, and the tension between us instantly rose. 'What's really going on?'

My throat was so dry I couldn't swallow. It was too late to stop now. This went deeper than just acquiring her help. This was about truth and trust. Katie was Sebastian's friend.

But she was also mine.

'Sebastian's a gargoyle.'

For a moment, I didn't think Katie had heard me. She just stared, blank-faced. I chewed on my fingernail. I couldn't remember the last time Katie had been at a loss for words. I saw her jaw clench, and then she stood slowly from the bed.

'I want every single detail. And you'd better not leave anything out.'

*

I told Katie everything.

Everything that had happened since the day my family had arrived in Sixes last autumn. How Sebastian was my guardian and how we were sealed the moment my pendant, my *sclav*, and his dandelion tattoo touched – and how we were now connected through that bond.

30

I'd never said so much about my life to anyone outside the Circe, but now I'd spilled my guts, and there was nothing to do but wait for Katie's verdict. She paced back and forth across the plush rug in the middle of her room. At last, she stopped and faced me with a heavy, drawn-out sigh.

'Seriously, Josie, I don't know what you expect me to believe.' She shook her head fiercely. 'I mean, yeah, I remember how weird Sebastian got during the school play, and him getting sick, and then, there was that thing with his hair.' Katie pulled a face before continuing. 'And you're telling me it's all because he's some creature from your people's fairy tales. You get how that sounds, right?'

'Yes.'

'Do you, *really*?'

'I'm not making this up, Katie.'

'Okay.' She walked to her desk and studied the same photo that had held my attention. 'If he's really this ... shadow creature you say he is, then show me a picture of him.'

'It's not something I'd put on my camera roll, Katie. No Gypsy would ever risk exposing the existence of the shadow world, the good or the bad. It's for *gadje* protection as well as our own. Besides, Sebastian would never have let me take a picture of him.' I winced. 'He hated ... hates ... the way he looks.'

Katie flopped on the rug. 'That night at my party, I was talking to Sebastian about his back brace, you know, the one he was wearing because of his car accident.' She saw my look and frowned. 'That's what he told me. Anyway, I tried to look at it, and he jerked away from me, like he was totally scared of me getting close to him. But I swear, I saw something.'

'What?'

'I'm not sure.' She rolled her eyes. 'Maybe it wasn't anything.'

'Katie—'

'Listen, I'm way ticked off right now,' she snapped. 'Okay, so maybe I can forgive you for not telling me because it's like your people's rules and everything not to talk about stuff, but why would that idiot not say anything to me?' Katie's eyes turned an icy shade. 'I thought Sebastian and I were friends.'

'You are,' I said. 'But he couldn't—'

'Couldn't tell me he thinks he's a gargoyle? Yeah, I can see why not.'

'He doesn't *think* he is,' I said.

She grimaced through a bitter laugh. 'Yeah, okay.'

'Katie, I don't blame you for not believing me.' I sat beside her. 'I wouldn't believe me, either. But I still need your help. Hugo and the Corsis are leaving for Savannah tonight. I have to get there, too. But I don't have a car. My father only let me leave the Circe because he thinks I'm spending the weekend with you.'

'So you want me to drive you to Savannah.'

'It's four hours away. You could be back before morning. After I testify, I can find my own way home.' I started to reach for her hand, but held back. 'Please, Katie. I have to do this.'

She drummed her fingers rapidly against her leg as her gaze went around the room. 'But I'm ... whatever it was you called me.'

'*Gadje.*'

'Yeah, that. I thought you weren't supposed to associate with us.'

'It has nothing to do with hanging out with you. It's about not telling *gadje* all about us. My father trusts that I will do what I've always done – keep my heritage a secret.'

'Well, you obviously suck at that.'

Katie didn't smile, but the iciness melted from her eyes.

'I guess I do,' I said.

We sat in silence in the middle of Katie's room, surrounded by stuffed animals. I closed my eyes. Memories immediately sprouted to the surface. The *kris*, my uncle, Sebastian locked up. If Katie didn't agree to this, I didn't know how I was going to make it to Savannah without my father finding out.

A door suddenly squeaked. I opened my eyes to find Katie rummaging in her massive closet. She began tossing clothes into the center of the room and then dragged out a small piece of luggage.

'What are you doing?' I asked.

'Look,' she said, stopping long enough to glare at me. 'This does not mean I believe your ridiculous creature story, because I don't. But if you think Sebastian's in trouble, then I want to help.'

'But you don't have to—'

'Yes I do. Your father can still think you're staying with me for the weekend. But I'm not leaving you in Savannah alone, not after everything you've just told me. So you're gonna have to deal with that.'

I really smiled for the first time all night. 'I'll help you pack.'

3. Josephine

'Hey mom,' said Katie, knocking on the door. 'You awake?'

'Yeah,' came a muffled voice from inside.

Katie motioned for me to follow her into her mother's bedroom. Nicole Lewis walked out of the bathroom wearing a fluffy bathrobe, her face covered in a green-tinted facial mask.

'Hey, Josephine,' she said pleasantly, opening the top drawer of her dresser as she smiled at me. She was an older, mirrored image of Katie, right down to the bright blue eyes. 'I haven't seen you in a long time. How's everything going with the Circe?'

I smiled back. 'It's been busy.'

'Mom, can we switch cars this weekend?' asked Katie.

Nicole sat on the edge of the bed and proceeded to file her nails. 'Why, is something wrong with yours?'

'No, it's just that Josie and I just decided to take a girls' weekend to Savannah. They're having a food and craft festival tomorrow, and Josie's in serious need of a break from the Circe for a couple of days. You know your car's a lot more reliable than mine on long trips.'

I glanced sideways at Katie, but I didn't say anything. Nicole finished one hand and turned the emery board over to start the other. 'When are you leaving?'

'Right now.'

Nicole paused and looked at her nightstand clock. 'It's 11:30.'

'We want to get an early start in the morning,' I jumped in, still smiling. 'I have some family in Savannah that don't mind us staying with them for a few nights.'

'Please, Mom,' said Katie. 'I promise I'll bring your car back home with a full tank. This is the only weekend Josie's free all summer.'

Nicole looked at me for a few seconds, and then puckered her lips in a sympathetic way. 'Well, I suppose so. My keys are on the kitchen table. Just don't forget to leave me yours.'

Katie rushed forward and hugged her mom. 'Thank you!'

Nicole laughed and wiped a smudge of green facial off Katie's cheek. 'As long as you promise me you'll call when you girls get there. And let me know when you're coming home. Okay?'

'I'll make sure she does,' I replied.

We backed out of the room quickly and retrieved our things. Katie swiped the keys off the table on our way to the garage, rolling her suitcase behind her. I threw my duffel bag in the back seat of her mom's Lexus and slid into the passenger seat.

'Why are we taking your mom's car again?' I asked.

Katie adjusted the mirrors. 'Because Hugo knows my car.'

I felt a surge of surprise. 'I hadn't thought of that.'

'Which is exactly why I'm coming with you.'

The tension in Katie's tone was palpable. She pulled the car out of the garage and headed down the long driveway.

We didn't say anything as we drove through town. Katie was even quieter than Francis had been. I felt a knot form in my stomach. Finally, I couldn't take it anymore.

'Katie—'

'You know,' she said, stopping me with a wave of her hand. 'All these months, I thought Sebastian was the one who'd gone completely nuts. But you're telling me a man was killed at the Circe, and then some crazy guy hauls Sebastian out of Sixes in a cage, and no one even called 911?'

'You know we can't do that,' I said slowly.

'Why, because you'd have to explain your *monster* story?'

I leaned back in the seat and stared out the window. 'Katie, maybe I shouldn't have told you ...'

'No,' she said. 'I asked for it. I did.'

'Okay,' I said, and left it at that.

Maybe I'd crossed the line by telling Katie the truth, but I couldn't help feeling grateful she was here with me; relieved not to have to pretend with her anymore – whether she believed me or not.

Katie put on her blinker as we waited to turn into the small strip mall that housed the *Gypsy Ink Tattoo Parlor*. 'So, what's the plan?'

'Park on the far side of the lot,' I replied. 'There's a convenience store that's still open. We can watch the shop from there. We'll wait for them to leave, and then we'll follow behind.'

'Can't you just map out the directions on your phone?' asked Katie as she turned into the parking lot. 'Why do we have to follow Hugo?'

'It's not about directions. I want to know what the Corsis intend to do when they get there. I haven't been to our

Haven in years. I'm not even sure the High Council still meets in the same place. I need the Corsis' help, but this time, they won't be able to push me out.'

Katie chose an empty parking spot near the road, but one that faced towards the tattoo shop. She turned off the car, and we settled in to wait. I glanced down to check my phone. It read 11:50.

'Hey, isn't that Ms Lucian?' said Katie suddenly.

I peered through the shadowy lights of the parking lot. A woman was making her way quickly across the empty space, carrying a small bag. She was dressed in jeans and a t-shirt, and her red-tipped black hair blew across her face as she walked in the direction of the *Gypsy Ink*.

'Yes,' I said. 'That's her.'

'What's our drama teacher doing here, and this late at night?' Katie leaned over the steering wheel, watching with narrowed eyes as Esmeralda Lucian walked into the shop and closed the door behind her. 'Oh, do you think she's getting a tattoo?'

I glanced over my shoulder at my duffel bag in the back seat. I could just see the outline of the small, leather-bound book, where I'd placed it in the side pocket. If Ezzie was here, it could only mean one thing: she was going with Hugo and the Corsis to Savannah.

'There was something I left out when I was telling you everything,' I said, turning to Katie. 'Ezzie sort of works with the Corsi clan.'

'Ezzie?'

'Ms Lucian … Esmeralda Lucian … is a former gargoyle.'

Katie shot me another suspicious look. 'What is that supposed to mean?'

'I don't know all the details,' I said, looking back towards the tattoo shop. Everything was still quiet. 'A long time ago, when she was a gargoyle, Esmeralda had a charge. His name was Markus, and he died. Apparently it was her fault, and she was turned human as punishment.'

I could see Katie processing. I assumed it was about Ezzie, but her question caught me off guard. 'So, does that mean that Sebastian could be cured of whatever this is?'

'It's not a disease.'

The words snapped free of my lips harsher than I'd intended. But I didn't regret them. My stomach turned over again as I saw Sebastian's face in my memory and heard my name as he said it, gentle and full of warmth.

'I didn't mean—'

'I know,' I said quickly, studying the flashing neon sign of the *Gypsy Ink*. 'Ms Lucian still has a lot of shadowen abilities,' I continued, preferring to switch the subject back to Ezzie. 'And her senses are really good. Plus, she's still really protective of the Corsis.'

'Why do the Corsis need protecting?' Katie asked.

'We all do,' I replied.

'From what?'

'I told you, from the shadow creatures.'

Katie slumped in the driver's seat with a heavy, exasperated sigh. 'Yeah, yeah. The monsters that have been after your people since the Dark Ages. I heard everything you said back at my house.'

I didn't have the energy to reply, not that there was anything else to say. After listening to my outrageous story, Katie had still chosen to come with me. Could I really expect anything more?

The shop's neon sign went dark.

I checked my phone again. It was five minutes past

midnight. After a few moments, three motorcycles rounded the side of the building from the back of the strip mall. It was easy to make out the figures of James, Kris, and Vincent, even underneath the sickly light of the street lamps. An old pick-up truck followed them through the empty lot. As the vehicle slowed to pull out into the street, I caught a glimpse of the occupants: Hugo driving and Ezzie in the passenger seat.

'Okay,' I said, buckling my seat belt. 'Let's go.'

Katie kept a considerable distance from the Corsi caravan as they took the main road leading out of Sixes, just enough to keep Hugo's brake lights in view. Neither one of us spoke as we turned onto the Interstate. I leaned against the window, staring at the darkened road and the occasional white lights from oncoming cars.

'So, what are we going to do when we get there?' asked Katie.

'I'm still working on that.'

I massaged my temples with my fingertips. I would testify before the High Council on Sebastian's behalf. I would do everything in my power to make sure he walked free. But my head ached with uncertainties, questions that went deeper than his being framed at the *kris*.

What information did Karl's books contain that was so important Augustine would be willing to murder for it? And why was he still after Sebastian, as Hugo believed? But there was one question that bothered me the most: what had happened to Sebastian when he was in that cage to turn him so wild?

'Josie, did you hear me?'

I jumped in the seat. Katie threw a sideways glance at me as she drove.

'I'm sorry, I was thinking.'

'About Quentin?' she asked. Her tone was level and pointed. 'You do realize you haven't said one thing to me about him this whole time.'

I felt cold again, and I wrapped my arms around my stomach. 'He went with Augustine last night, on my father's orders, to make sure Sebastian was delivered safely to the High Council. I'm sure he's probably on his way back home by now.'

'You don't know?'

'He hasn't texted. But he usually doesn't when he's working.'

Katie's curious stare burned into me. But I didn't look at her. I knew Quentin had been pleased with how things had turned out in the *kris*, despite the sweet words and consoling hugs he offered me. He'd never liked Sebastian, never even gave him a real chance. And I knew I was going to have to confront that head on. But right now, I had Sebastian's trial to think about.

*

'We have to stop for gas,' said Katie.

'What?' I bolted out of my half-slumber and yanked out my phone. We'd been on the road nearly three hours. I stared at the black road stretching out before us. There were several red taillights, and I wasn't sure which one was Hugo's anymore. 'No, we can't. We'll lose the Corsis.'

'My refuel light's been on for the last twenty miles,' said Katie. 'We won't make it there on this tank. Besides, I really have to pee.' She glanced pleadingly at me. 'I promise, we'll be really quick. But I'm seriously going to wet myself if we don't stop now.'

40

'Okay,' I said, trying to manage my frustration. 'Just hurry.'

We took the exit ramp and stopped at the first gas station. I filled up the tank while Katie went inside to use the facilities. She came out a few minutes later carrying two sodas. I finished paying, but as I reached to take one of the bottles from her, a cold breeze whipped across my face.

The garish white lights from the gas station only reached the edges of the parking lot, leaving everything beyond in shadowy darkness. The air felt warm, but the breeze was noticeably colder – a sensation I'd felt before. Goosebumps sprouted up my arms.

'What is it?' Katie asked, frowning at me.

'This was a bad idea,' I said, moving towards the car. 'We aren't anywhere near an Outcast Haven. We don't have any Marksmen with us.'

'What are you talking about?'

I opened the back door and reached for my bag. I retrieved the diamond-coated knife Quentin had given me – the one I'd used on Matthias when Sebastian and I had been attacked on Copper Mountain. The blade caught the light and glittered. Katie stared at it as though I'd pulled out a jar of scorpions.

'It's a Marksman knife,' I said as I surveyed the parking lot. It was empty and still. Poster advertisements covered the front windows of the tiny convenience store, preventing me from seeing inside. 'Diamond-coated weapons are the only things that can kill shadow creatures.'

Katie's shock morphed into irritation. 'And we're back to monsters.'

I ignored her comment as I eased cautiously around the front of the car. I'd gotten so used to having Sebastian by my side the last few weeks, that I'd almost forgotten what it felt like to be afraid, genuinely afraid. But he wasn't here, and all I had to defend us was one small knife and my limited fighting experience.

The cold breeze swirled bits of trash across the concrete.

'I should've known,' I said, peering upward. 'It can smell me.'

'*Smell you?*' Katie took a step backwards, her jaw hung open in disbelief. 'Okay, you know Josie, I've been giving you the benefit of the doubt all night, but this is just too much to swallow. I'm starting to think you might be delusional or something.'

A dark form swooped through the air, just over one of the streetlights. I heard the leathery flap of wings. Fear worked its way up my throat with prickly fingers. I brandished the knife, though I couldn't see anything against the cloudy, starless sky. Why had I been so reckless?

'We need to get in the car,' I said.

Suddenly, a vehicle came screeching into the parking lot from the road. Katie sprang back, and I spun on my heel as Hugo's truck roared up beside ours and slammed to a halt. Hugo and Esmeralda flew out of the truck. I didn't like the look on either of their faces.

'We're being tracked,' said Hugo.

Three motorcycles rumbled in behind him. James, Vincent, and Kris leapt off. Their faces were tense as they spanned out and searched the sky. Hugo scowled at me.

'How did you—' I began.

'A discussion for later,' said Ezzie. She tilted her head and sniffed the air. 'We must get out of the open.' She gestured to a thin line of trees running parallel to the parking lot, just outside the glow of lights from the station. 'It will reduce their advantage.'

'Can't we just outdrive them?' asked James.

'Only to have them follow us to the next stop and attack there?' hissed Ezzie. Her eyes glittered dangerously. 'No, we must deal with them here.'

Katie suddenly chucked her soda into the trash and whirled on us with a half-crazed expression. 'Are you serious? You guys believe all this stuff, too? I can't even … it's like some freaking shared delusion!'

'There is no time for this, Katie Lewis,' snapped Ezzie, flinging open the door of Hugo's truck. Her hazel eyes flickered silver. 'You are not Roma. They will leave you alone. Stay here and do not open these doors.'

The color faded from Katie's cheeks. 'Josephine …'

I grabbed her hand. 'Just do what Ms Lucian says.'

'But—'

'And stay low,' I said as I closed the door after her.

We hurried into the trees, Esmeralda leading the way and the Corsis bringing up the rear. My heart pounded. Marksmen were the ones equipped to kill these things, not us. And Esmeralda, though intimidating, was human, not gargoyle. I said a quick prayer under my breath.

We crouched behind a group of shrubs. Ezzie sniffed the air again, and I sensed her frustration. I knew she retained bits of her old shadow creature abilities, but I didn't know how well they worked.

'I cannot tell how many,' Ezzie whispered. 'Two, I believe.'

Hugo reached down and wrapped his fingers around a fallen branch the size of a baseball bat. He caught Ezzie's look. 'Yeah, I know. It won't kill 'em, but it'll still hurt.'

James, Kris, and Vincent found their own pieces of wood. We waited. I kept anxious eyes on the truck, praying that Katie would stay put. Ezzie leaned forward in her crouch, fingers splayed wide against the ground in a posture that reminded me of Sebastian. I clutched the knife tighter.

Ezzie closed her eyes and took in one smooth breath. Then, her eyes snapped open. She pointed with both hands, at two different trees directly above us. A wild snarl erupted from a cluster of branches. Something dropped to the ground. Ezzie shoved me aside.

The thing hissed, shuffling into view. I cringed in disgust. A grotesque. It was at least the size of a horse. A body and head like some medieval serpent, with black liquid dripping from its venomous-looking fangs. It scrambled closer, moving on multiple legs.

From out of the darkness, a winged creature slammed into Hugo from behind. He kicked at the beast as James bashed its scaly head with his branch. Kris and Vincent jumped into the fray, but my attention snapped immediately back to the shadowen in front of us.

Ezzie made a snarling sound, and inky mist appeared around her body. The creature lunged. Ezzie reappeared in another clump of mist several feet away. The grotesque roared in fury, its solid silver eyes gleaming, as it whirled around. It backed me up against a tree.

Out of the corner of my eye, I saw Esmeralda move into view. The creature reared back like a coiled snake. As it went for my head, I ducked and rolled to the side. With accuracy I'd learned over years of Circe training, I tossed the knife in Ezzie's direction. She caught it and stabbed the creature, right in the middle of the back. The blade buried itself in the grotie's flesh, all the way to the handle. The creature shuddered and dropped to the ground.

'Ezzie!' yelled Hugo.

Ms Lucian spun and aimed my knife at the other

grotesque. It screeched and went down. Hugo wasted no time. He yanked the blade free from the creature's wing and plunged it into the thing's scaled chest.

Both shadowen collapsed, dead.

I leaned against the tree, gasping for breath. Hugo pried my knife free from the winged grotesque just as its body solidified into stone. Within seconds, both shadow creatures became nothing more than statues lying on the leaf-covered ground.

'Is everyone okay?' Hugo asked.

Suddenly, panic gripped me. 'Katie!'

I rushed back to the truck. I could see her tear-stained face pressed against the window. I wrestled open the door, and she stumbled out, shaking all over. She stared at me with enormous eyes.

'I believe it,' she whimpered, clutching my arms. 'I believe all of it.'

Then she was sick all over the tops of my shoes.

*

James and Kris hid the bodies of the grotesques in the brush, while Hugo supervised. I waited anxiously next to the car, with Katie by my side. She took small sips from a water bottle James had given her. Her face was pale, and she was unusually quiet.

Hugo emerged from the trees, wiping his hands off on his jeans. The others followed behind. His face grew darker as he approached us, and he sized me up with one long, penetrating stare. I met his gaze, unblinking, though inside, I felt close to crumbling.

'How much does she know?' Hugo asked me.

'Everything,' I replied.

Hugo paused long enough to give a definitive huff. Then he turned to Katie and held out his hand. 'Well Katie, I guess you're in.'

Vincent's mouth gaped open.

James grabbed Hugo's shoulder. 'I don't think that's a good—'

'No arguments,' said Hugo brusquely. 'If Josephine trusts her with our secrets, then so do I. Katie Lewis, consider yourself *diddikoi* from this point forward.'

'Friend of Gypsies,' I said, for her benefit.

Katie shook Hugo's hand with the confidence of someone handling a snake.

'How did you know we were following you?' I asked.

'It was Ezzie,' he answered, watching as Ms Lucian walked the perimeter of the gas station, her head tilted upward. 'She saw a couple of girls in a shiny SUV, hanging out in the back of our parking lot before we left. It didn't take a lot of brainwork to put the rest together. Ezzie's had the scent of groties on our tail for the last hour. When you two pulled off the Interstate, I got worried.'

I felt heat rise to my face. 'Thanks for coming back.'

His expression softened somewhat. 'I don't reckon Sebastian would forgive me if I let you get yourself killed,' he replied. 'And since you're obviously not going to listen to our advice about staying home, I'm offering you a place to stay in Savannah. The Corsi clan owns a B&B in the Victorian District. That's where we're heading.'

I nodded as Ezzie approached, ending our conversation.

'Anything?' Hugo asked.

'No,' she said, her attention still on the dark trees beyond the lights. 'I don't sense any other shadowen in the area.

46

But we should be on our way. I've never seen grotesques so bold before. To attack Roma in public as they did is highly unusual. I fear this was not simply an isolated incident.'

'Agreed,' said Hugo. He turned his sharp eyes towards Katie. 'Since you've been following us for three hours, I'm sure it won't be too much trouble to continue on into the city.'

Katie nodded weakly.

'I'll drive,' Ezzie said to her. 'If you don't mind.'

Katie dropped her car keys into Esmeralda's outstretched hand without the slightest hint of argument. I looked at our former teacher curiously, but she only smiled, an oddly tight expression.

'Try and keep up,' said Hugo wryly. 'And no more pit stops.'

We pulled out onto the Interstate once more, Hugo in the lead. The rest of the guys maneuvered behind us on their motorcycles. Katie took the passenger seat, and I retreated to the back. I didn't try and explain anything more to her. She'd seen enough by now to be convinced– at least of everything that mattered at this point. But there was nothing I could do to make it any less horrible.

I turned the diamond-coated knife over in my hands. The grotesque's black blood had cleaned off easily, but nausea lingered in the back of my throat. I hadn't wanted Quentin's weapon – he'd only given it to me to protect myself against Sebastian – but now I was glad I'd brought it. His weapon had saved our lives.

A lump of conflicted emotion rotated in my stomach. My feelings for Sebastian, however new and undefined they might be, weren't going to change. But neither, I hated to admit, were Quentin's. In his eyes, he was a Marksman and

Sebastian was a shadow creature. There was no middle ground.

'Josie?'

I leaned towards Katie. 'Yeah?'

'Does Sebastian ... look like that?' She shuddered visibly. 'Like them?'

'No,' I said firmly. I focused on the windshield, finding myself once more at a loss for the right words. 'I mean, not exactly. It's like I told you before, he's still Sebastian. Mostly. Just different.'

'Different,' she repeated numbly. Katie rubbed her eyes. Her mental conflict and exhaustion were etched clearly on her face. She was still pale, even through her rosy-pink makeup. 'So why did they attack you?'

It was Ezzie who answered. 'Roma blood. Grotesques smell it. The scent draws them in, like a predator seeking its prey.'

'Prey?' said Katie. 'You guys are their *prey*?'

Ezzie gripped the steering wheel. But she didn't answer. Instead, she frowned through the rear-view mirror at me. 'Josephine, did you bring the book I gave you?'

It was at that moment that I realized why Esmeralda had insisted on driving our car. She wanted to talk.

'Yes, I packed it when I left the Circe.'

'Good,' she replied. 'Markus' book may be of use to us in Savannah.'

Pain flickered behind Ezzie's eyes when she mentioned her charge by name. I felt my own pain welling up inside of me. Maybe it was only a fraction of hers, but the source was the same. What if I couldn't save Sebastian? What if I failed?

Katie looked between us. 'What book?'

'One similar to those stolen from Karl Corsi,' answered Ezzie. 'Markus believed it to be important to the future of the shadow world when he entrusted it to my care. I must confess, I had not thought of it until Sebastian's awakening last autumn. I have felt a strong upheaval in the shadow world the last few months. The increase in shadowen activity and the timing of Sebastian's awakening cannot be treated as mere coincidence.' She paused as she checked the side mirrors and changed lanes. 'His difficult adjustment as a gargoyle has concerned me. I can't explain it, but Sebastian is not the same to me as other shadowen. Even the way he smells—'

Katie made a sound in the back of her throat.

'His scent,' Ezzie continued, flashing a silvery glare at Katie that made her cringe. 'Since his transformation I have been at a loss to figure it out. It is my hope that Zindelo and Nadya will be able to answer our questions.'

'Hugo's parents? But I thought no one knew their whereabouts.'

Esmeralda almost smiled. 'That's not entirely true.'

I swallowed past a sudden lump in my throat. 'What does Hugo think about Sebastian?'

'He denies anything openly,' Ezzie replied. 'But Hugo Corsi is an intelligent man. Unfortunately, I believe his attachment to Sebastian as his brother clouds his clarity.'

'What about you?'

'I am a guardian,' she answered. 'Or at least, I was. Guardians do not form attachments outside of our charges.'

'That's not true of you,' I said. 'Or Sebastian.'

Esmeralda paused. 'No, it's not.'

I stuffed the diamond-encrusted knife into my bag and closed my eyes. I wasn't sure when I drifted off or how much time passed, but the sensation of slowing down woke me up. Katie had also fallen asleep; her head resting against the window and her mouth slacked open.

The skies were still dark, with dawn at least another hour away. I nudged Katie awake as we passed the Savannah city limits sign. We entered the coastal city, surrounded by palm trees and large oaks dripping with Spanish moss. Even in the darkness, it felt like we were passing into another world. Hugo led us down several roads, driving by numerous hotels and restaurants, before we ended up on a small cobblestone street lined on either side with eclectic, Victorian-style houses. He pulled into one and drove around the back.

'Whoa,' Katie breathed. 'This is seriously gorgeous.'

The brick house was three stories tall, with a massive porch, lined with white columns. There were even balconies on the second and third levels with several brick chimneys sticking out from the roof. Thick trees, their limbs heavy with clumps of moss, populated the courtyard.

'Josephine, Katie,' said Esmeralda, turning off the car. 'Welcome to *The Dandelion Inn*, headquarters of the Corsi clan in Savannah.'

4. Sebastian

Rocking.

Like a boat – Katie's boat, out on the lake. Out with her family. Waves lapping the sides. Dipping in and out. Up and down. Sideways. Lulling and sleepy; a lullaby without song. Constantly repeating.

Repeating ...

Repeating ...

My body awakened with a start. Every sense was flooded – with an overwhelming, pinpoint clarity that still shocked me. Noises and smells exploded inside me full force, and I registered exactly where I was before I even opened my eyes.

The cage.

I coughed out a mouthful of hay and pushed up onto my elbows. The paralyzing Vitamin D I'd been injected with was out of my system, freeing me to move again, but the rush of blood to my head made me dizzy. I blinked, using my gargoyle night vision in the darkness. My cage had been loaded into one of the Circe's equipment trailers. Heavy locks clanged against the bars as we moved at a decent speed down the road.

'Brilliant, Sebastian,' I muttered. 'You really thought this one through.'

It had seemed like the best solution – allowing myself to be taken by Augustine to keep Josephine safe – but now doubts crept along the edges of my vision. The separation from Josephine felt like a constant throbbing ache, a wound that wouldn't heal.

The pang intensified as I began to fully realize the deal I'd made with Augustine and what it had cost. This was far from over. Coming up with a decent plan on an empty stomach, however, wasn't going to be easy. Now that I was conscious again, hunger ate not only at my stomach, but also at my mind. I squeezed my eyes shut and shook my head to clear it.

'Stay focused,' I whispered.

The wheels of the trailer came to a stop, and an engine shut off. My heart thrummed nervously. I was having serious second thoughts about everything. I didn't regret getting Augustine away from the Romany camp, but I had no idea what to do next.

The heavy trailer door slid open and clanged into place. Faint light from the highway spilled through the opening, and my eyes instantly adjusted. Cold ice lodged in my chest, and a nasty burning smell singed my nostrils. Quentin Marks walked in. He was still in head-to-toe black, typical Marksmen attire, but his bow and quiver were gone. A snarl played across my lips. He stopped at the door to my cage, and it was at that moment another scent hit me.

Meat. Dried and spiced.

My mouth instantly watered. I curled my body into a tense crouch to keep from moving forward. Quentin smiled – thinly tight, like a piece of stretched rope. He pulled out a pouch of jerky and tossed it through the bars to the far side of the cage.

It took everything inside my head to force myself to stay where I was. My claws, my teeth … everything strained for the meat. The hunger was very close to controlling me completely, and it was disgusting. Utterly and thoroughly disgusting. I hated being under the command of this thing, this dark, murky part of me. I managed to turn my head away.

'No thanks.'

'Oh, you're going to want to eat,' said Quentin. 'We're still a couple of hours out of Savannah, and from what I hear, you don't fare well on an empty stomach.'

I glared at him. 'So why are you feeding me, then?'

'It's not my call,' he answered. 'I could care less if you starved. But Augustine wants you coherent when we arrive.'

Coherent.

Augustine not only knew about my gargoyle weaknesses, but also about my particular appetite as well. The knowledge of that made me feel sick. 'And if I refuse to eat?'

Quentin leaned closer to the bars. 'Trust me, you don't want to do that.'

He leapt from the trailer and the door slammed shut again. I waited until we were moving again before I scrambled across the cage and ripped the meat free from the plastic wrapping. My instinctive reaction was embarrassing, and I was thankful no one was here to watch, especially Josephine.

Josephine.

Her name was like a punch in the gut.

I didn't want to imagine what she thought of me now. I clamped my teeth together and shoved Josephine from my thoughts. But the farther away we drove from the camp, the more off-centered I felt. I didn't know how I'd function separated from my charge, but I had to find a way to manage. She was safe in Sixes, and that's what mattered.

The meat's tangy scent was overwhelming. I wiped dribble from my chin. Eating would lighten the cloudy brain haze, but the thought of doing anything Quentin told me to was downright revolting. I gripped the package so tightly my knuckles burned. The jerky was probably tainted with something. That would explain why they wanted me to eat. No, I'd keep my head clear – not by eating their food, but by using my own force of will. I was not going to be Augustine's pet.

I summoned my strength and flung the meat as far away from me as I could. The package thumped against the trailer wall and landed unceremoniously in a pile of old woodchips.

My stomach hated me immediately.

Underneath the thick manacle on my wrist, the dandelion tattoo burned. I tried prying my claws underneath the metal, but the spikes lining the inside of the cuff ground deeper into my already raw skin. The shadowen-proof diamond coating had zapped my energy and rendered my limited shadowing abilities useless.

'Karl,' I whispered. 'I'm sorry.'

My stomach twisted, but not from hunger. If I'd listened to the old circus trainer more, if I'd managed to get past my trepidation of what I was, maybe I could've done something to save him. I'd failed him, and I'd failed the Corsis.

The Corsis.

I reached for my jeans pocket before remembering I no longer had my phone. Would Hugo realize something had happened if I didn't answer his texts? Would he even text at all? Our communication had gradually waned the longer I'd been at the Circe, sometimes going a week between calls.

Josephine.

She didn't have any more control over this situation than I did. Besides, I'd seen the way she'd clung to Quentin after I went completely nuts. I saw the horrified look on her face when they carted me away. Even if she *had* felt something for me, it meant nothing after tonight.

I leaned my shoulder against the metal bars of the cage. A year ago, I'd been a senior in high school, looking forward to the freedom of graduation. Now, freedom sounded like a foreign word. My head dropped heavily to my chest. I had no idea what kind of Gypsy trial awaited me when I got to Savannah, but I was going to have to face it alone.

*

The next hour slogged along. The cage rocked and jolted as we made various turns. I lay on my stomach, my face pressed into the rotting hay. I rolled my shoulders and cringed. My old set of nylon straps may have been uncomfortable, but they were nothing compared to the thick cords the Marksmen used to bind my wings. Each time I moved, all the muscles along my back cramped.

At last, the trailer rolled to a stop. I rose as the door opened once more. I smelled Quentin's unpleasant scent, but after that, came the smell of saltwater, moss, and stone. We were parked in an alley of some kind. Streetlamps shone between branches weighted down with Spanish moss.

55

Quentin ascended the stairs and sauntered around the cage without acknowledging my presence. Then he knelt beside the pile of woodchips and retrieved the beef jerky. He held it between two fingers, as though it were contaminated.

'Just like he said you would,' Quentin remarked.

I snarled as another scent reached my nose.

'Not very wise, Mr Grey.' Augustine entered the trailer. 'I know for a fact it's been at least six hours since your last meal. Very likely even longer than that, since I can only speak in regards to my arrival at the Circe. I assumed you understood your shadowen needs by now.'

I clutched my stomach as a wave of nauseous hunger slammed into me. My legs wobbled, and I found myself on my knees, gritting my teeth, fighting against the thickness in my head. I had to keep my rational thoughts, no matter what.

'Yeah, I'm hungry. But if you think I'm going to trust anything you give me, you're delusional.'

'I'm just trying to help you,' Augustine replied.

'I'm fine,' I growled.

'Well, then. Suit yourself. We've just arrived in Savannah,' he continued. 'But before we begin this next part of our journey together, let's go over a few ... expectations I have for you.'

I wrapped my fingers around a cage bar and hoisted myself to my feet. My upper lip twitched uncontrollably. I felt the jagged edges of my teeth; the hideous things could make short work of a rib-eye steak but remained stupidly ridiculous to talk around.

'Like what?'

Augustine pulled a wooden stool from the corner of the

trailer and set it down with a loud bang. The sound stung my ears. 'Well, I can't exactly bring you any further in this cage. It's a bit conspicuous. So I am going to need your cooperation. When they come to escort you to the Court of Shadows, I expect you to go calmly, quietly, and without a fuss.'

I stared back at him.

'The Court of Shadows is the hub for all Outcast Gypsy activity, not only in Savannah, but for the entire *kumpania*,' he explained. 'Its location is a carefully guarded secret, so we must take precautions.'

'Since when did you care about keeping secrets?' I demanded. 'Or care about anything to do with the Roma.'

'You misunderstand me,' Augustine answered, propping his elbows on his knees. 'Despite my current status among the Outcasts, I continue to have a deep respect for our traditions, and for our very rich and unusual past.'

'No offense, but that's not really coming across.'

Augustine chuckled. 'It's a shame we won't be having many more of these conversations, Sebastian.' He stood and tapped the corner of my cage. 'I've quite enjoyed them.'

As soon as he left the trailer, Quentin approached. I caught sight of a long knife tucked through his belt. The diamonds glinted like deadly sparks – a grim reminder that he knew exactly how to end my gargoyle-y existence.

'Time to go,' he said.

'Don't guess you're going to tell me where.'

Quentin whistled sharply. Thomas and Ian, my Marksmen guard dogs since the *kris*, stomped into the trailer. Ice exploded in my gut, but my blood heated in my veins. Quentin pulled out a key. I stared hard at the lock as it clicked. Instincts skittered up my spine like a colony of ants.

Red seeped into my vision, but I ground my teeth even harder, pushing it away.

Augustine was desperate to see the Queen. If I went quietly, maybe I could find out what was going on. I blinked everything into focus as the cage door swung open. Besides, even if I could fight them off, where would I go?

Thomas clamped a short chain to my manacles, pinning my arms in front of me. A long cloak was thrown around my shoulders and the hood was pulled up to obscure my face. The three Marksmen surrounded me, keeping my form hidden as we stepped from the trailer into the night.

5. Sebastian

The narrow street where we'd parked was deserted. Streetlights cast a yellow sheen on the cobblestone and drew long shadows from between the close-set buildings. I tilted my head and glanced up as we stopped at a three-story brick storefront. A dark-green canopy stretched across the length of the ground floor. Printed on the canvas flap were the words *Tea and Spice*.

Augustine came alongside me. 'May I remind you, if you want Josephine to remain safe, you will behave yourself. We have many loyal to us within the Marksmen ranks. It would only take a word from Quentin, and her circus career would be finished. Accidents are unpredictable that way.'

I flashed my teeth under the hood. 'Don't you dare.'

'Don't give me a reason to,' said Quentin.

'See now?' Augustine's broad smile made me want to retch. 'We all have an understanding. None of us wants my niece to come to harm, and she doesn't have to. Let us simply conduct ourselves in an orderly manner, and all will be fine.'

White-hot anger boiled inside me, heating up my protective instincts. I grit my teeth until the sensation cooled enough to answer. 'Alright.'

Quentin approached the green painted door with a CLOSED sign in the window. He rapped on the wood in a series of short and long knocks. I sniffed the air, catching the smell of another Gypsy. After a few seconds, the door opened. An elderly Roma woman motioned us inside.

Floor-to-ceiling shelves lined every wall of the sparsely lighted store, filled with assortments of cooking spices and various loose teas. The aromas made my sensitive nose burn, and mixed with the pungent scent of Marksmen, added to my headache. I switched to breathing through my mouth.

The Gypsy woman walked purposefully behind the counter and took a long, skeleton-looking key from a peg on the wall. Without saying a word or even giving my heavily cloaked self a second glance, she pushed past the group to a door marked PRIVATE in the back of the room. She unlocked it, and Quentin pushed the door open, which was thicker and heavier that it appeared.

Beyond was a decent-sized storage room with more shelves. A man sat at a circular table, playing a game of Solitaire with a grungy set of cards. He nodded at the woman. She stepped outside and closed the door behind her. I heard the lock click into place.

The man shoved back his chair and stood. 'We've been expecting you,' he said. He was tall, with a large nose and a buzz cut. He was dressed like a Marksman. 'It's good to see you, Quentin.'

'And you, Donani.'

My brows lifted in surprise, until I remembered that all Marksmen were from the same clan. It made sense they would know each other – something Quentin seemed pleased with as well.

The Marksman named Donani turned his attention on me. 'So this is the gargoyle.' He gripped my hood and yanked it back. My shoulders flexed, but I kept my eyes on him and breathed in slowly. Controlled. He smelled like charred wood. 'Interesting,' he said, regarding me with a calloused expression. He returned to the table and retrieved a belt full of weapons from the chair. He strapped it on and drew out a particularly nasty-looking blade – sharp, diamond encrusted, and probably capable of slicing me up like a block of cheese. 'We'll take the creature from here,' he continued. 'You and your Marksmen are welcome to join us, of course.' Donani kept his eyes on Quentin. 'Oh, and tell your *marimé* companion that we will return for him tomorrow.'

'But,' started Augustine, visibly ruffled, his gaze settling on the blade. He hesitated, then clamped his mouth shut and straightened, arranging a smile that mirrored Quentin's.

It seemed this turn of events wasn't exactly what he had planned.

Donani clapped his hands once. Two Marksmen appeared from behind a single shelf, where they'd been stationed, I supposed, all along. They took hold of the shelf and rolled it out of the way. Behind it was a paneled door made of ancient-looking planks held together with rusty metal braces.

A weird, uncomfortable sensation took up residence inside me as they unlatched the door. Just beyond, I saw stone stairs, leading downward in a spiral, concealed by a brick wall.

Augustine gripped Quentin by the shoulder and pulled him aside. My gargoyle hearing picked up their conversation.

'Do not forget all we've spoken about, Marks.'

Quentin shrugged him off. 'I won't.'

Donani made his way down the stairs. Quentin, Thomas, and Ian went after. I followed, after being kindly persuaded by a spear in my back from one of Donani's men.

The staircase wound in a circular pattern, weaving down farther than I would've thought possible. It smelled damp and pleasantly earthy. I shifted my body sideways as my bound wings scraped against the narrow walls. After descending in silence for a full minute, we reached the bottom. It opened into a circular tunnel, several feet taller than my head and lined with packed dirt and cobblestone. A heavy gate of the same shape barred the entrance.

'It is with God I have arrived,' said Donani.

A bearded man peered through the gate. 'It is with God you are received.'

The gate opened, and we made our way along the tunnel for several yards before it suddenly veered left and opened into a gigantic room. The chamber could have easily held several hundred people. The jagged stone ceiling loomed twenty feet above us, and a railed balcony ran the length of a second level.

This had to be the Court of Shadows.

The Marksmen pushed me hastily through the room and another, shorter tunnel. On the other side was a smaller room, filled with long tables and benches. Soft light filtered through the space, provided by a mixture of electric and gas lanterns.

At least a dozen Gypsies chatted noisily around me, drinks in hand. Food and spiced smells perfumed the air. Donani increased his pace, and we swiftly passed through another room. I felt the stares of the inhabitants, and I was glad for the cloak and hood the Marksmen had provided as my disguise. From the next room, corridors broke off in many directions. The entire underground area must've taken up three blocks of the city above.

But the tour wasn't over yet. Donani led us down eight stone steps and an extremely narrow passage. My nose wrinkled. It reeked of mold, dirt, and stale air. Even before we entered, I knew I wasn't going to be a fan of the next room. Barred walls lined each side of the corridor, separated into individual cells, like an old, underground prison.

The Marksmen prodded me into the nearest one. The dirt walls absorbed the clanking of the metal as the iron-gate door slammed shut after me.

'Could I request a different room?' I asked. 'I'm not really feeling this one.'

'Ah, it speaks,' said Donani.

'Unfortunately,' Quentin replied.

Donani leaned on his spear. 'Well, listen up, gargoyle—'

'The name's Sebastian.'

'—I suggest you behave like a good little beastie and shut your mouth.'

It seemed Marksmen were pretty much the same, no matter where.

'Or what,' I shot back. 'Let me guess, you're going to beat me up and throw me in a cage. Oh, wait.'

He rammed his blade through the bars, just missing the side of my face. 'Trust me,' he replied. 'I could make it worse.'

The laughter of the Marksmen echoed down the passage.

'So what now,' asked Quentin.

'Now, we get some breakfast,' Donani replied. 'This gargoyle's not going anywhere for a while.'

Quentin smiled at me. 'Enjoy your stay.'

I'd lost track of the amount of times the two of us had stared each other down between a set of metal bars, but it had gotten old a long time ago. I'd been ignoring my hunger and pulsing adrenaline. Now my nerves and my will were both on the verge of snapping, but I wouldn't give them that satisfaction.

'Enjoy yours,' I said, forcing every word. 'While you can.'

6. *Sebastian*

I really missed lying on my back.

If I was honest, I missed a lot of things from my old life, but I refused to dwell on any of them at length. Instead, I put my energy into finding a comfortable spot along the wall to prop myself against. My jeans and shirt were filthy. I smelled of blood, dirt, and sweat. My eyes burned hot when I closed them, and my stomach felt deeply hollow in a way I hadn't experienced before.

What would happen when it was time for me to stand before the High Council? Would they let me speak, or would they kill me on the spot? I didn't know the rules and laws for the Outcasts, much less the shadow world.

There was no possible way this was going to go well.

Something wet fell against my cheek and I reached up to brush it away. Tears. I hadn't even realized I was crying. Now, I was conscious of them rolling down my face, one after the other.

I thought of the stares I'd gotten the day I arrived at the Circe. The way people avoided me when I approached. The way I'd just been hustled through the Court of Shadows like I had the plague.

I scared people. I scared myself. Maybe I really was the demonic abomination so many Gypsies feared. But as I sat on the dirt floor, shackled and trapped, I just felt like a helpless little kid; frightened, alone, and ...

Hungry.

Visions of meat scrolled behind my eyelids. I struggled to concentrate on something else. On anything else. But I was too tired, and nothing worked. My teeth throbbed beneath my gums. I groaned inwardly and let the feelings cloud my head, turning my thoughts to unintelligent jumbles, diminishing my sense of time.

*

Ice solidified in my stomach, jerking me from the incoherent haze. I sniffed the air and sighed. They were back. Donani and Quentin were alone this time. I noted the Romany's head Marksman had resumed his full arsenal of weaponry, complete with a full quiver of arrows strapped to his back.

I also caught the smell of meat. My stomach lurched greedily. I licked my dry lips, pricking my tongue on my jagged teeth and tasting blood. As the Marksmen neared my cell, I shuffled to my feet.

'Listen guys,' I said, stretching as much as I could. 'I really need a bathroom. Seriously, this hotel sucks.'

'Still running your mouth,' said Donani. He pointed to the rudimentary latrine in the corner. 'Your accommodations are better than you deserve, demon.'

Quentin produced a brown paper bag. I tried not to sniff, but I couldn't help it. Instantly, my brain registered hamburgers. I swallowed several times as my mouth began to water uncontrollably. The Marksman thrust the bag through the bars.

'I brought you dinner.'

I moved aside, putting as much distance as I could between us. 'You know, I was really craving some pancakes, so I'm afraid I'm going to have to pass. Thanks for going to all this trouble, though.'

Quentin's usually composed expression suddenly cracked. He threw the bag into my cell. 'You idiot,' he said, spittle flying from his mouth. 'Do you think starving yourself will do you any good? Why won't you eat?'

I gave him a steady look. 'Because you want me to.'

'I'm trying to keep you functioning. Do you wish to stand trial as nothing more than a slobbering beast, or do you want the capacity to defend yourself to the Council?'

'What difference does it make to you?'

'I want the Council to hear from Sebastian Grey, the proclaimed guardian of the Romany clan. And then I want them to see that you're no different than the rest of your brethren, despite all your protests: a gargoyle who would and did kill someone of Roma blood.'

'And me scarfing down a couple of burgers is going to prove your point?'

'There isn't an Outcast Gypsy in our *kumpania* who hasn't witnessed the destructive nature of the shadow creatures. Grotesques and chimeras are an evil curse, a scourge to our existence. But gargoyles.' He stepped closer, his voice lowering as he continued. 'Your reputation as guardians has kept you safe over the decades. But the loyalty the Old Clans held for gargoyles is long dead. And soon, the same thing will happen among the Outcasts. You're not guardians.

You're a threat. But when you're convicted of murder, I promise you, it will be open season on all of your kind.'

'That's why you're working with Augustine.'

'We have an arrangement.'

I tried to smile, to keep the conversation going so that I could think clearly. 'Well, since I'm doomed anyway, could I at least brush my teeth and take a shower? I want to look my best before my trial.'

Quentin's black eyes narrowed. 'Sorry, but that's not on the agenda.'

Suddenly, the smell of exotic flowers wafted through the passage. For the briefest instant, I thought it was Josephine. As soon as the thought crossed my mind, it was immediately negated. The scent was similar, but definitely not her. I moved to the front of the cell for a better look.

A tall woman stood at the passageway entrance, with Augustine at her side. I knew at once it was Josephine's aunt – which meant I was staring into the face of the Queen of the Outcast Gypsies. She wore a multicolored dress and an elaborate head wrap that concealed her hair. Heavy makeup outlined her eyes, and gold jewelry sparkled at her neck. Just behind her, four men, armed with diamond-coated spears, lined the inside of the corridor.

The woman scrutinized me with eyes like cold emeralds.

'This is the gargoyle.'

'Yes, *Rani*,' said Augustine. 'Just as I—'

'Silence,' said the Queen. 'You are not to speak directly to me. *Marimé* is *marimé*, no matter the bargain that was struck with the Council. If you wish to address me, you will speak through the Marksman.'

Their eyes met for a single, tension-saturated moment. I glanced between the two. If Augustine hadn't told me his family connection to the Romanys, I never would've guessed he and the Queen were siblings. She reminded me of Nicolas. But Augustine shared nothing with them, apart from his tall, lean frame.

The Queen turned her attention back to me. Something within me felt her Roma authority in a way that hummed through my guardian blood. Before I even realized it, I had bowed my head respectfully.

'Very well,' said Augustine, his tone curt. 'Quentin, if you would tell the Queen that I have brought this gargoyle to be placed on trial for the death of Karl Corsi, of the Romany clan, as requested by Nicolas Romany.'

She continued to look at me – not with fear, disgust, or pity as I was accustomed to, but with something that bothered me a lot more. Something emotionless.

'The gesture seems honorable,' she said. 'But the man once known as Adolár Romany has no honor in him and does nothing without seeking his own gain. So why is he really here?'

Augustine rolled his shoulders back in a slow, fluid motion. Only the hardened edges around his eyes betrayed his irritation. 'Quentin, if you would please relay to the Queen my request for a private audience with her.'

The strange emphasis he put on the woman's title sparked my curiosity. It was heavy with a meaning I didn't understand, but one that seemed to heighten the tense air between them.

'I have already given the *marimé* access to the Court of Shadows, which is against our highest law. And yet, he still has the audacity to ask for more.'

'The Queen will benefit greatly from this meeting,' said Augustine.

Quentin repeated his sentence. The Marksman's expression hovered somewhere between smug and annoyed, however he kept his eyes lowered respectfully. The Queen hesitated, turning her gaze from me to the ceiling.

'Because I am in an amiable mood,' she said finally, 'I shall grant the *marimé* a thirty-minute audience with me, but he must be accompanied by my Marksmen and an appointed liaison to speak through.'

'Surely I could have an audience with you alone, for only—'

'If he speaks to me again,' said the Queen, 'he shall have nothing.'

Augustine dipped his head. 'Quentin, if you would offer the Queen my sincere apologies. Her offer is gracious, and I will accept it.'

The Queen moved down the corridor, glancing sideways at me. She carried herself much the same way as Josephine's father did, all authority and confidence. Whatever she thought of me, I couldn't tell, but she'd scored major points in my estimation for the way she'd treated Augustine.

She snapped her fingers. 'Release the gargoyle.'

Donani dipped his head. 'But *Kralitsa* …'

'Now.'

The Marksman removed the padlock and slid open the heavy door. I watched him warily. His weapons remained sheathed, but I had no doubt he'd be fast to draw them. My wings felt like stone slabs attached to my back, and my head was so heavy I could hardly lift it. I willed my feet to move and stepped out of the cell. The Queen assessed me steadily.

'He looks half-dead,' she said to the Marksman at her right.

'Only because he is being stubborn,' said Augustine, his gaze moving past me to the untouched bag of hamburgers on the cell floor and then meeting my eyes once more. 'It is, unfortunately, his loss. Now, Quentin, if you would kindly repeat all this to the Queen.'

'The *marimé* traitor tests my good will,' said the Queen.

The pompous expression I was used to seeing on Augustine's face returned with a vengeance. His smile stretched the white scar at his cheek into a thin line. 'Allow us to demonstrate what this creature is capable of.'

Warning vibes tingled down my spine.

'Please, Your Majesty,' I said softly. The phrase sounded weird, but I didn't know how else to address her. The Queen's forehead wrinkled in surprise, and I hurried to speak before she could respond. 'I don't understand what's happening. Nicolas sent me here because the *kris* was deadlocked. I didn't kill anyone. I only want the opportunity to defend myself and show you the truth.'

'The truth is precisely what I desire,' she replied. She stepped back. 'Take the gargoyle to the Stone Chamber.'

Quentin and Donani took up positions on either side of me as I was escorted down the hall and out of the dungeon area. We moved through an intersection of corridors and descended several more steps before reaching another room. The cavernous space looked two stories high and void of anything – save an enormous cage.

It was octagonal in shape and made of chain-link fencing on all sides and along the top. The floor was spread with a thick mat. It looked like something out of a professional cage-fighting match.

'You can't be serious,' I said.

Quentin undid the latch. 'Get in.'

71

Donani stripped off my cloak. The straps around my wings were cut, and the chains linking my manacles together were removed. The Marksmen's spears made sure I complied with Quentin's order. Once I was inside, the door of the cage was shut and bolted. Adrenaline seeped into my blood, turning my breaths shallow. I grabbed hold of the chain-link wall, my eyes searching for the Queen.

'What about the trial?' The pleading in my voice mingled with a growl.

'You shall have your trial,' she said. 'After I know what manner of creature I'm dealing with.'

A hissing sound reached my ears. I lifted my head and sniffed the air. Instantly, I wanted to gag. Grotesques. I recognized the smell, thanks to the one that had infiltrated the Romany camp the evening I'd arrived. My heart beat faster, pushing the adrenaline through my veins.

Screeching metal reverberated off the walls. Another door on the opposite side of the cage opened. I recoiled as several Marksmen rolled two large containers inside. The lids lifted and two shadowen leapt into the cage. One was a feral cat, large and mutated, with razor-sharp claws. The other was almost twice my size, a terrifying mixture of reptile and bird.

A snarl quivered against my lips. I backed away, unfurling my wings and taking to the air. The muscles along my shoulder blades and wing joints ached from being pinned so long. I hovered, using most of my energy to keep my wings pumping.

The reptile bird spread its gray-feathered wings and launched itself at me. I rolled in the air. The grotesque streaked by me and circled around the cage. I countered, keeping plenty of distance between us. My blood felt hot in my veins, burning me from the inside out. I clenched my fists.

Below me, the cat creature paced, its solid silver eyes narrowed into slits and black ooze dripping from its fangs. The bird beast screeched, readying itself for another charge. There was no way I could escape them, in the air or on the ground. The edges of my vision blurred crimson.

'I'm not going to fight for your sport,' I called down.

'It's not sport,' said Augustine. 'It's evidence.'

I was a guardian. I was supposed to defend Gypsies from the nasty creatures circling the cage below me, but I had a feeling that wasn't the kind of evidence Augustine was looking for.

I dropped to the mat, crouched low, wings expanded to their full length. The cat dove at me, teeth catching my shoulder. They pierced my skin like knives, and I cried out. I clamped onto its body with my claws and stripped it off me, flinging it against the chain-link wall.

I retreated quickly, retracting my wings.

Stop.

The word came unbidden into my mind, and I wasn't even aware that I'd spoken telepathically at first. But the cat creature hesitated, the gleam in its silver glare fading. The bird-snake landed opposite me, tilting its head. Its beak opened and closed. A fragment of hope kindled inside me.

Groties were dumb beasts, according to Karl. They relied purely on instinct, driven by their need to kill. Only chimeras and gargoyles could communicate. But maybe these creatures could understand basic commands. I closed my eyes and fired off another telepathic order.

Get back.

For a fleeting second, I thought the creatures might actually obey as they regarded me with unblinking, silver-orbed eyes. The enormous cat suddenly shook itself off, hissed, and dropped into an attack crouch. The bird-snake snapped its gray feathers. Both came at me, full speed.

I took flight. The winged shadowen pursued. I saw the Gypsies out of the corner of my eye, watching intently. Anger clawed its way up my spine. I didn't want to fight. I just wanted to go home; to see Josephine again and go back to the way things were at the Circe.

But the thing inside me: the guardian or monster or whatever it was, wouldn't let up. It welcomed the threat and longed for action. It pressed on the back of my skull. Controlling. Demanding. Unrelenting.

'Please, let me out,' I yelled.

My voice had turned to gravel and growls.

Donani flashed a wicked grin. 'There's only one way out, gargoyle.'

I changed direction and streaked downward, knocking the feline shadowen off its feet. It hissed as I came back around. Then, I was knocked off course. I slammed into the chain-link wall, the bird-snake creature on my back. Talons ripped my flesh.

Instinct and rage forged into one.

Everything went red.

*

When I came back to myself, I was lying on my side in the middle of the cage. My wings were splayed wide. Black blood spattered the floor. My shirt was gone, the remnants shredded into pieces a few feet away from me. My own purple-black blood dripped from claw wounds on my shoulders.

Both shadowen lay on the ground on the opposite end of the space. The bird-snake's wings were bent underneath its body. The cat was huddled in a crumpled mass. I gasped in horror and struggled to sit up. Disgust and loathing churned in my stomach.

'Oh no …'

Then, I realized, neither creature had turned to stone. Relief surged through me. If they weren't stone, it meant the shadowen were still alive! I collapsed, breathing a thankful prayer. I didn't want to kill them, no matter how much my instincts told me to.

A sudden wave of ferocious hunger lit into me. I gasped again and pushed myself into a crouch. My arms shook. I peered through the cage to find the Gypsies staring at me. Augustine's black eyes met mine, and the corners of his mouth twitched upward.

'I have seen enough,' said the Queen.

Quentin didn't miss a beat. He notched his bow, aimed at the shadow creatures, and let one arrow fly, then another. Each passed effortlessly through the narrow chinks in the fence. The diamond tips struck home. The grotesques howled in hatred and fury. A second later, their bodies shimmered dully and turned to granite in front of me.

One moment, they'd been alive.

The next, nothing more than hideous statues.

I felt hollow.

Marksmen entered the cage, spears at the ready as they approached me. But I stood quietly, folded my wings against my back, and held out my hands for the manacles. I was too hungry to think, too exhausted to care anymore.

'Well,' said Augustine to Quentin. 'Would you be so kind as to inquire about my audience with the Queen once more?'

'Tomorrow,' she said, her expression smoother than stone. 'I will send word concerning the time and place, when I am ready.' The Queen brushed widely past him, holding her skirt to the side as though he was contagious. 'Donani, escort this man out of the Court of Shadows immediately. He knows how foolish it would be to try and enter here again.'

Donani and another Marksman flanked Augustine. I watched through the bars as he dipped his head in respect, but his face went so taut that the scar along his cheek turned pink. He disappeared out the chamber without another word.

*

'Why is Augustine so desperate so talk to the Queen?'

Quentin's answer to my question was to shove me along the narrow corridor. He'd been given the job of getting the gargoyle back to his cell, and I'd never seen the Marksman look so pleased.

Just as we reached the door, I tripped over an uneven gap in the floor and pitched forward, landing on one knee. Fighting the grotesques had used up whatever remained of my reserves, and left me running on empty. Quentin waited while I regained my feet. He tapped the edge of his knife impatiently against his thigh.

His expression was enough to kindle the fire inside me, but I pushed it down and made my face smile back. 'Oh, come on, surely you know the reason? Unless he doesn't share important things like that with you.'

Quentin secured the lock on the cell door and looked down his nose at me, as though I were a piece of dirt he was preparing to flick off his shirt. 'Your trial is scheduled first thing Monday morning, which means you'll be spending the next two days in this cell. You may as well get comfortable.'

Chatting with Quentin Marks was the last thing I wanted to do, but he was also the only source of information I had right now. I pressed against the bars. 'This is totally illegal, you know.'

Quentin seemed surprised, and then he laughed. 'What, do you think your family would actually file a missing persons report on you, a shadow creature, and get the *gadje* authorities involved? Even a dumb beast like you knows better than that.'

'Why not kill me now? It sounds like it'd be a whole lot easier.'

'Oh believe me, it's tempting, but Augustine was right. Once you're convicted, we'll be able to rid the Roma world of all shadowen, beginning with you.' Quentin sheathed his knife. 'I can wait a few days more.'

I leaned against the wall. My joints were beginning to feel stiff, and it hurt to move my fingers. 'I'm flattered you're going to so much trouble.'

'There are other perks,' he replied with a shrug.

The cold in my chest spread to my skin. 'What perks?'

'You mean, besides the satisfaction of seeing you get what you deserve?' Quentin's smile widened. 'Well, that should be obvious, demon. Once you're gone and Josephine and I are married, it's only a matter of time before the Romany clan becomes mine.' He took the lantern from its hook on the wall and called back over his shoulder as he walked out. 'Have a good night, Sebastian.'

Tears threatened again, but I closed my eyes and forced them away.

7. Josephine

Hugo ushered us into the *Dandelion Inn*, which was richly decorated with antique furniture, lace curtains in the windows, and doilies covering every surface. Two women met us in the cozy parlor of the Corsis' bed and breakfast. Both were middle-aged, short in stature, and beaming brightly despite the earliness of the hour.

'Hugo,' said the first one, who appeared to be the older of the two. I watched, amused, as she hugged him fondly and planted a kiss on his cheek. 'It's been far too long.'

The second woman took his hand, patting it affectionately. 'Your ride down was pleasant, I take it?'

'Not unless you call a grotie attack pleasant,' he replied, 'but we took care of it.' His features relaxed a bit as he turned to us. 'These are my cousins, Paizi and her sister Ferka. They own this bed and breakfast.'

'And keep things running smoothly around here,' added Paizi.

'That too,' Hugo agreed. He gestured to me. 'This is

Josephine Romany, of the Romany clan, and her friend Katie, a *diddikoi*.'

'Please accept our thanks for allowing us to stay with you,' I said, shifting into a more formal interaction, one I was used to using as daughter of a *bandoleer*. 'God's blessings on this place.'

'Hugo told us about your guardian and the trial when he called,' said Paizi solemnly.

Ferka nodded. 'You know how Gypsy news usually travels, but this was the first we've heard of it. I had no idea there were any guardians left in our *kumpania*. Present company excepted, of course.' She smiled at Ezzie, who nodded in return. 'Surely, he is innocent.'

'He is,' I replied, without hesitation.

'We'll hear more later,' said Paizi gently, picking up my bag. 'First, you must rest. We'll show you to your rooms. Breakfast is served at seven. That should give you time to settle in.'

'Thank you,' I replied, grateful not to have to relive the *kris* yet again.

The sisters ushered us up the stairs and down a long hallway. The hardwood floors creaked underneath the rugs as we walked. We were quickly assigned rooms; Katie and I were given the one near the communal bathroom. Just as I was closing the door, I heard Hugo's voice from the top of the stairs.

'This is my business, Ezzie.'

'No more than it is mine,' she answered. 'I will return before dawn.'

Hugo's heavy sigh echoed down the hall. 'Alright. It's not like I can stop you, anyway. But you need to watch yourself.

I've had a really bad feeling since we got here, and you're not exactly inconspicuous. Not here.'

'I appreciate your concern,' Ezzie answered.

'Just be careful, okay?'

'It is not I who must be careful, Gypsy.'

I shut the door to our room before Hugo reached the top of the stairs. I turned and nearly tripped over Katie's suitcase. She'd unpacked – or rather, she'd dumped most of her things onto the floor.

I reached the bed and fell back into the mound of pillows as Katie explored the room. She touched every piece of furniture and peered out of the windows multiple times.

Katie bounced on the bed next to me. 'Oh my gosh! We totally need to come here for a real girls' trip. After we spring Sebastian from Gypsy jail, or whatever, I mean. This place is amazing. I mean, do you see that dresser in the corner? It's got to be a hundred years old.'

'Probably,' I replied, kicking off my shoes.

'And this chandelier is to die for. I need one for my room, like right now.' Katie pulled her phone out and snapped a few pictures as she continued to prattle away about the room décor.

She was still a little unnerved, and I couldn't blame her, but at least Katie was talking more like herself again. It was nice to have something else to focus on besides my own worry. I pulled my hair into a ponytail and unzipped my bag, only half-listening to Katie's chatter as I unpacked. I took off my jewelry, hesitating as I held the dandelion pendant in my hand.

I became suddenly aware that it had gotten quiet. I turned around. Katie had taken my place on the bed, propped up against the pillows. She looked from me to my necklace, and her brows rose expectantly.

'Sorry. What were you saying?'

She motioned me over. 'I asked how you felt about Sebastian.'

'What?'

Katie took the pendant out of my hands. She turned it over in her palm and held it up to the soft light of the chandelier. 'You've told me a bunch of crazy stuff that doesn't make sense, but one thing's pretty obvious, and it's the one thing you've totally left out.'

'He's my guardian.' I watched the way the light refracted off the glass, illuminating the yellow dandelion petals inside the pendant. 'He's my friend.'

'And?'

I kept my eyes on the necklace. 'And ... I don't know.'

'Come on, Josie. After everything you've done to get down here – sneaking around your dad, missing your performances, not to mention dealing with those freaking nightmares from hell at the gas station. I mean, you're taking a pretty big risk here, aren't you?'

I nodded. 'Yeah.'

'So, why is it so hard to tell me how you feel about Sebastian?'

I took the pendant and set it on the nightstand. The flower darkened and seemed to lose its life. I touched it with my finger. Even the glass had grown cold. A deep, aching loss curled through me.

'I grew up hearing tales of guardians and their charges from our legends,' I said. 'But they were just stories before I met him. I didn't know it was going to be like this.'

Katie leaned forward. 'What do you mean?'

I pulled my legs up to my chest and rested my chin on my knee. 'In a way, it feels like I've known Sebastian forever. I guess that scared me at first. It was like he could see past the image I'd created of myself, in a way no one had before. Maybe that's why I avoided him in the beginning. And then, afterwards, I didn't know what to do with everything that had happened.'

'You mean the ... gargoyle thing?'

I closed my eyes, so I wouldn't have to look at Katie's half-believing, questioning expression. Immediately, my mind conjured up an image of Sebastian – the firelight glinting off his fierce teeth as he spoke, his silver eyes gleaming. 'Yes and no.'

'So it's really that bad.' I heard the doubt in Katie's voice.

'No, that's not what I meant. It wasn't his change I couldn't deal with. It was my guilt. Maybe it wasn't directly my fault, but I was convinced I'd ruined his life by somehow making it happen.' I pressed the heel of my hand against my chest, trying to ease the hurt. 'I still feel like that, some-times. But I'm learning to deal with it.'

'Go on,' Katie pressed. Not demanding, but insistent.

'The bond we have doesn't scare me anymore. That stopped the moment he came to live at the Circe. It's the only thing that feels right, honestly. I can sense his emotions. I understand the way he thinks. I know when he's near.' My gaze drifted back to the pendant. 'He's become closer to me than anyone else in the world. We're connected in a way I can't really put into words.'

'Well, whatever you want to call it, it's obvious Sebastian loves you,' said Katie. A slow smile spread over Katie's features, lighting up her eyes. 'And now you feel the same way about him, don't you?'

I stood up quickly. The action made my head pound. I crossed the room and opened the closet door. Inside were several stacks of plush bath towels. I grabbed a pastel yellow one from the top of the pile.

'Look Katie, I can't think about that, okay? You know the seriousness of my relationship with Quentin. This guardian and charge thing has put a giant strain on us, and I can't mess that up.'

'Yeah, why not?' she asked.

My eyes widened. 'Excuse me?'

Katie held her hands up defensively. 'Hey, you know I've been totally supportive of you and Quentin, and yeah, pretty much jealous, too. I mean, *hello* … the guy's basically perfection on a platter.'

'Aren't you dating Mitchell?'

'We aren't exclusive, and nothing says I can't enjoy the scenery, right?' Katie shrugged. 'Anyway, that's beside the point. We're talking about you right now. So the question boils down to this: hotness and charm factor aside, is Quentin really the guy you want?'

'It's complicated.'

'I swear, Josie, I'm going to jump out of this window right now. It's not complicated, it's simple facts. Do you love Quentin?'

'Yes,' I said slowly. 'Or, at least, some part of me does. Quentin and I are … I don't know what we are right now. It's been so difficult lately. He's been part of my life for so long, and he loves me. It's always been understood we'd get married. It's something I accepted a long time ago.' I twisted my fingers in my lap and looked away from her. 'It's our way, Katie. I'm not going to try and explain that to you, I just hope you understand.'

'I do,' she said. 'But don't you—'

'Look, I know I owe Quentin the truth. I just don't know what that is, yet.'

Katie frowned. 'Okay, maybe it is a little complicated.'

'None of that matters now,' I said. 'What matters is getting Sebastian out of this trial, one way or another.'

Katie nodded with a yawn. 'Alright, fair enough. Lucky for you, I'm too tired to think straight anymore.' She curled up with one of the oversized pillows. 'I've gotta take a power nap, or I won't survive tomorrow.'

'Then I'll leave you to it,' I said with a smile, glad to be done with the conversation, at least for now. I plugged in my phone and set an alarm. 'I'm going to take a shower.'

*

Katie was sprawled sideways on the bed when I returned, snoring loudly. I tiptoed across the groaning floorboards as best I could. As I placed my old clothes in my bag, my fingers brushed against the small book I'd hidden inside.

I retrieved it and quietly stepped outside. There was a tiny nook at the end of the narrow hallway arranged as a reading area. All the bedroom doors were closed, and the predawn silence permeated the upstairs. I settled into the chair, gathered my legs underneath me, and opened Markus Corsi's book.

The pages crackled as I picked a place, somewhere in the middle. I stared hard at the flowing, handwritten script. Ezzie had said that only Gypsies could read these kinds of books. Some words I could make out, but most were in a Roma dialect I'd never seen before. How could this book be useful if I couldn't even read a full sentence? I narrowed my eyes, desperately willing the words to make sense.

'Josephine.'

I jumped so hard I nearly toppled my seat.

'Ms Lucian!'

She stood a few paces away, leaning against the wall. She wore a long jacket, despite the warm summer night, and her hair fell loose around her face. It was impossible to tell how old she was. At least Hugo's age, definitely, but something about her seemed older – her eyes, and the way fine lines appeared around her forehead and mouth when she frowned – like she was doing at that very moment.

'Josephine, why are you not sleeping?'

I set my feet on the floor. 'I could ask you the same thing.'

A hint of a smirk danced across her lips. Her gaze traveled to the book in my hands. Emotion flickered briefly behind her hazel eyes – a sort of calloused pain. She'd said little of her past when she brought Sebastian and I to her home under the bridge, and I didn't know her well enough to pry. Not too much, anyway.

'I have been out,' she finally replied.

'Where?'

'That is my business, for now.' She drew her jacket tighter. 'It will be time for breakfast soon. You should think about getting some rest.'

'You're an original guardian,' I said quickly. Esmeralda paused at my words, and I ploughed ahead before she could leave. 'There were so many bedtime stories I heard as a child, so many legends passed down through our clan, about how the guardians fought against the Old Clans and helped us break free.'

'Who I once was no longer matters, Josephine Romany.'

Her entire body tensed, and her face turned dark. 'This is who I am now.'

I closed the book. 'Do you … miss it?'

The fire in her eyes dwindled. Her hand drifted to her neck, to the small, faded tattoo. 'With all that I am.'

8. Josephine

Breakfast was served in the parlor, precisely at seven, as promised. Paizi and Ferka made the rounds with cups and saucers as the Corsis gathered in the room. I sipped my tea, fighting exhaustion and a growing sense of apprehension. Beside me, Katie nibbled on a pastry.

'Are you okay?' I asked over the rim of my cup.

'Am I supposed to be here?' she whispered. 'I mean, I feel like they're about to go over some top-secret files or something, and I'm literally the only person in the room who isn't a Gypsy. It's seriously uncomfortable.'

I hid my smile. Katie was her old self again, freak-out and all. I felt selfish for thinking it, but I was glad to have her back. The Corsis may have been Roma, but they weren't my clan.

'If it makes you feel any better,' I said, 'I feel out of place, too.'

'It does a tiny bit, yeah.'

Sunlight filtered through the lace curtains, illuminating tiny particles of dust in the air. James propped himself against the doorframe, as though he didn't trust the structural integrity of the antique furniture. Kris and Vincent sat in two parlor chairs near the kitchen, heads bowed as they talked in low voices. Esmeralda had found a chair in a shadowy corner of the room. I wondered if gravitating towards dim-lit spaces was a habit left over from her days as a gargoyle.

Sebastian had a knack for it as well. During evening hours, it was sometimes almost impossible to spot him, unless he blinked. Or, on those rare occasions, when he gave me one of his full, unhindered grins that brightened his entire face. But even when I couldn't see him, I always knew he was there.

The constant, heavy knot in my chest would never go away. Not until he was safe and near me again. I'd avoided dealing with my frustration and worry, but now that we were in Savannah, fear took root inside me. Real fear. Not only did I feel responsible for Sebastian's acquittal, but now I also had Katie to think about. I stole a quick glance in her direction.

She was licking the frosting off a cinnamon roll and trying hard not to stare at everyone around her. Katie was more than capable of taking care of herself, but my world was way more complex than she knew.

My phone buzzed in my pocket. It was a text from Quentin.

How was opening night?

Everyone was still busy eating and having their own conversations. I tapped out a quick reply.

Good crowd. Everything went fine.

I held my phone in my hand, debating. Then I added another text.

Spending the weekend at Katie's.

Be back on Sunday. See you then?

I felt Katie's shoulder press into mine. She looked at me with her brows raised questioningly. I tilted my phone so she could see, just as another text from Quentin came through.

I'm staying in Savannah.

Your father wants me here to represent the clan.

Just until he arrives for Gathering on Monday.

The remnants of breakfast turned sour on my tongue. Quentin was staying in Savannah. I hadn't even considered this. I'd just assumed he would discharge his duty to escort Sebastian and Augustine to the city and then come back home.

I hurried to type out my next question.

How was the trip? Augustine?

Quentin's response came in waves.

Uneventful.

He wasn't allowed inside. He left pissed.

I'm staying in the Court of Shadows.

I glanced up at Katie. She was reading along, her brow furrowed deep in thought. I swallowed hard, and typed again.

Is Sebastian okay?

I stared nervously at the blank screen. Quentin had to know I'd ask. Sebastian had been my guardian for weeks, and Quentin had dealt with it, even if he was only doing so because of my father.

Haven't seen him.

I blinked at his reply, unsure of what to believe. Quentin was a Marksman, which meant he'd have access to Sebastian, as well as the upcoming trial. He was convinced Sebastian was a killer. Would he really let him out of his sight?

As if reading my mind, Katie said, 'Hey, you told me he's totally not a fan of Sebastian's. If I were Quentin, the last thing I'd want to do is hang around anywhere near him. Besides, don't they have lots of Marksmen protecting this Court of Shadows place?'

I nodded. 'Yes.'

'It sounds to me like the only reason Quentin's still there is because he's following orders from your dad.'

'Yeah,' I said, pocketing my phone. 'Maybe you're right.'

I didn't have a chance to think anymore about it. Just as I picked up a blueberry muffin, Hugo Corsi entered the parlor room, wearing the same jeans and t-shirt he'd had on when we arrived. It didn't look as though he'd slept either. He poured himself a mug of coffee. We waited expectantly. Even Paizi and Ferka ceased their bustling over platters and saucers.

'I went to the Court of Shadows this morning,' Hugo said after several sips. 'Our suspicions were correct. They're keeping a real tight lid on the trial. No one I talked to knew anything about it. Until I ran into Donani Marks.'

'The head of the Queen's Marksmen guard,' I said.

Hugo nodded and wiped his mouth against his sleeve. 'Yeah, that's him. After going 'round with him for a bit, he finally admitted the trial would happen first thing on Monday, before the monthly High Council meeting. Only Marksmen and Council members will be admitted.'

'That's ridiculous,' growled James. 'If the Council is holding a *Kris Romani*, then we can be there. High Court trials are open to any Gypsy who wants to attend. It's the law.'

'In Roma matters, perhaps,' said Esmeralda from her shadowy corner. 'But Sebastian is not Roma, and therefore those laws do not apply.'

'That's exactly what Donani said.' Hugo scowled into his coffee. 'But I wasn't about to let it go at that. Shadow creature or not, Sebastian is my brother and I'm also his *bandoleer*. And as leader, it's my right to see him.'

James rubbed his knuckles like he was ready for a fight. 'And what did he say to that?'

'That I'm allowed one visitation before the trial,' Hugo replied. 'So I'm going to see Sebastian today.'

At the mention of seeing him, my heart sped up. 'I'm going with you.'

'I thought you wished to keep your presence here a secret,' said Esmeralda from the corner. Heads swiveled in her direction. 'A public appearance in the Court of Shadows wouldn't be prudent in that regard.'

'I have to see my aunt. She needs to hear the truth.'

'According to Donani, the Queen isn't even here,' said Hugo. 'He said she's been out of town for a few days but expects to return tomorrow evening, in preparation for the Summer Gathering.'

It was as though someone had set a heavy weight on my chest. I'd been counting on getting to the Queen, on putting an end to this whole thing before it even began. I'd convinced myself that I'd be able to rescue Sebastian. And now—

My phone vibrated again with another text. I peered at it quickly, and the weight in my chest doubled.

Love you Josie

I stared at the three words Quentin had said to me countless times before. They blurred in front of me. I heard Hugo say my name, but it sounded faint and far away.

'Josephine.'

Quentin took my hands in his. His fingers were long and

slender, scarred with years of Marksmen work. They were just about the only thing that wasn't perfect about him, physically. He rubbed my knuckles gently as he spoke. 'I'm sorry you had to go through this. I know you had a connection with the creature that you couldn't control.'

'He has a name,' I replied.

Quentin nodded. 'Of course he does. But that doesn't make him human. I know you wanted him to be. So did your father. But shadowen will never be anything other than what they were created.'

I looked past Quentin to the gates of the Fairgrounds. Augustine stood outside the truck and trailer, waiting for him. I felt sick to my stomach.

'Sebastian is innocent,' I said.

'I know what you believe,' he replied, his voice smooth and gentle. 'But the facts can't be ignored. Karl's death must be answered for. The gargoyle's fate is out of our hands, Josie. It's out of your hands. You have to accept that.'

'And what if I can't?'

'My duty is to your father and this clan. I will ensure that the gargoyle arrives safely in Savannah and that he is given his chance for a fair trial with the High Council. You have a duty to this clan as well. Everyone looks to your family. The Romanys must present a unified front. Whatever your personal feelings for this gargoyle, are they really more important than the welfare of the entire clan?'

Quentin shouldered his bag and leaned down, pressing his lips to mine. I felt myself tense before I could stop the reaction. Quentin's lips immediately tightened, and he pulled back, searching my face.

'I'll be back soon, Josephine.'

*

Katie nudged me in the side. Hugo was looking at me with an expectant expression on his face, waiting, for my answer. I ran over my options in my head. Going to the Court of Shadows meant I would risk running into Quentin. If he discovered I was here, then so would my father. And, if I was being honest, I wasn't ready to face Quentin.

I'd find an opportunity to speak to the Queen when she returned. I could be patient. I could wait. And, if for some reason she refused to hear me out, then I would make absolutely sure that I was there at the *Kris Romani* to testify on Sebastian's behalf.

No matter what.

'You're right,' I said. 'I don't want to jeopardize anything right now.'

'Good,' said Hugo, setting his mug aside and sweeping his gaze around the parlor. 'In the meantime, the rest of you are free to head into the city while I'm gone, but I want everyone back to the inn before sunset.'

'You gotta be kidding me,' growled James. He peeled himself from the wall. 'We've got a curfew now?'

'In case you've forgotten, we had two groties on our tail last night. If they were willing to risk being out in the open, then who's to say it won't happen again? Plus, the more Outcasts there are, the more groties come out to play.'

I nodded in agreement. Summer and Autumn Gatherings always brought more shadowen around, since those were the only times large numbers of our *kumpánia* assembled together in one place. Then, a realization suddenly hit me. 'Your clan has no Marksmen.'

'Never needed them,' said Kris.

Vincent huffed. 'We can take care of ourselves.'

'In the past, maybe,' said Hugo. But I'm not so sure

anymore. So don't do anything stupid while I'm gone, understood?'

The others mumbled their agreement.

*

'We're in Savannah,' said Katie, pressing her face against the bay window overlooking the street. 'And this city is gorgeous. Why do you want to stick around here?'

I swept aside the lace curtain and joined her in admiring the view. Rows of historic homes of varying designs and levels nestled neatly along the thick hardwoods on either side of the quiet road. Several people sat outside a cute little coffee shop the next block down. 'I don't feel like going anywhere right now. Not with Sebastian—'

Katie grabbed my hand and pulled us away from the window. 'Hey, you heard Hugo. There's literally nothing you can do for him right now. Hugo's going to take care of him. I mean, Sebastian's his brother.'

'I know.' It hadn't taken much to convince Katie, but I wasn't so sure. 'But anyway, I also don't want to risk anyone recognizing me, since I'm not supposed to be here.'

'It's a really big city, Josie. Are you telling me you're that much of a celebrity in your world that you can't leave this house?'

'Definitely not a celebrity. It's just—'

'Just what? I mean, come on, you're over eighteen. You can make your own decisions. Besides, it's not like they could force you to go home or anything.'

Katie's question sent a rush of heat to my face. Clan honor and family loyalty wasn't something I could explain to her in a few sentences. Traditions and stringent expectations were the backbone of everything we were, but they were our customs, not those of the *gadje*.

Katie was trying hard to understand, and I could've hugged her for it. I felt the corner of my mouth lifting in a smile. 'You know, it's been a few years since I've been here on Outcast business. I guess as long as I stay away from the Court of Shadows ...'

'That's more like it.' Katie walked past me to the stairs and swung around on the bannister. 'I'm mean, after all, you're doing no one any good just moping around here.'

'Okay, then,' I said. 'What do you want to do?'

'Shopping and lunch,' she replied. 'Be right back.'

Katie bounded off to take a shower, which meant she'd be a while. I did my best to stay out of the path of the sisters. Ferka and Paizi were buzzing like frantic bees, getting everything in order. In two days, hundreds of Outcast Gypsies would descend on our primary Haven for the Summer Gathering, a two-week reunion of clans in our *kumpania* – which meant the bed and breakfast would soon be crawling with Corsis.

I explored the house while I waited on Katie, finally ending up in the kitchen, where a large pot of soup simmered on the stove, filling the room with the scent of meat and onions. I opened the door to the cellar. I expected cool, musty air, but instead, I smelled and felt the warmth of a fire. Curious, I made my way down the groaning steps into a decently sized room with a low ceiling. Part of the room had been furnished, with a sitting area and a couple of twin beds.

Esmeralda sat in a chair with her nose in a book. Other than the light bulb above the stairs, the only illumination came from a low fire in a small fireplace in the corner.

'Does the sun bother you, like it does Sebastian?'

Esmeralda turned a page. 'Not anymore,' she replied. 'I just prefer evening hours and dark spaces. Old habits, I suppose.'

'Ezzie?'

She lifted her eyes from the book she was reading. Their color was hazel, soft and unthreatening, not the silver glint they often took on when she was irritated. I took that as a good sign.

'Well?' she said.

'Can I talk to you?'

The muscles in her neck tightened against her dark hair, but she nodded and set the book aside. She leaned against the back of the antique chair. 'Yes, of course. I was actually wondering how long it would take you to come find me.'

I settled into the chair opposite her. Embers crackled in a small fireplace, producing enough heat to suck the chill from the underground cellar and make the room comfortable to sit in. I watched their pulsing glow for a few breaths.

'Ezzie, what happened to you, exactly?'

One of her arched brows lifted. 'Could you be more specific?'

'After Markus,' I said carefully.

Creases formed along her forehead and the sides of her mouth. 'After Markus died, I was brought before the *Sobrasi* in their Court in Paris. I thought they would kill me, which would've been a sweet release. But instead, they did something much worse. I don't know how it happened. All I remember is waking up in one of their dungeons ... as you see me now.'

'But how did you end up here?'

'It is a long story through many years,' she replied.

'That's code for more secrets, I take it.'

She almost smiled. 'I am not the only one with secrets, *Kralitsa*.'

My breath caught. The traditional title was reserved only for our rulers. I'd never been called it, but again, no one knew I was the future queen. I lowered my voice. 'How did you know?'

'I know many things,' she said simply. The wrinkles eased around her eyes, smoothing her skin once more. 'After all, I *have* been around quite a while.'

'But how—'

'You have said it yourself. I am an original guardian. I came into existence as a result of your ancestor himself, Keveco Romany, during the seventh century. The year six hundred and ninety-nine, to be exact.'

My mouth dropped open.

'But you must remember,' she continued. 'I was not awake during all this time. In fact, I slept for hundreds of years.'

I studied her features, this time more carefully. 'Do you age?'

Ezzie's lip quirked. 'We age, the same as all of God's creation, unless we sleep. During that time, our life is suspended – frozen in stone. The moment we awaken, we become a part of this world, subject to the effects of time once more.' She tilted her head, seeing the question in my eyes. 'Why have I not died of old age by now? When the Outcasts fled Europe, I was taken with the Corsi clan, who had found a way to allow me to sleep, even in my human form.'

'You've been alive for hundreds of years,' I mused. 'Which means you could be alive for hundreds more, if you slept, I mean. You're basically immortal.'

She laughed, but I heard pain underneath it. 'To begin with, I am not nearly as young as I would wish for such a life. But we are not made to live out eternity here, neither shadowen nor humans. Our immortality lies in the hands of God.' Esmeralda paused, and her fingers touched her neck, gently prodding her faded tattoo. I couldn't make out the design. 'I was awakened fifteen years ago,' she continued. 'By Zindelo and Nadya Corsi.'

I sat upright in the chair. 'Hugo's parents.'

'They gave me some semblance of life, human though it is. I may no longer be a guardian or have a charge, but I still feel the pull of loyalty and duty to the head of the Corsi clan.'

So that's why she was always so intent on looking after Hugo and the guys. It wasn't just because Markus had been a Corsi. I clutched my hands together in my lap as I worked through my thoughts.

'You once told us that love between a gargoyle and charge was forbidden, because of you and Markus. You didn't want to talk about it then.' I glanced up at her. 'What about now?'

Esmeralda uncurled herself from the chair and rose. I thought for a moment she was going to leave the room, but she paused at the bottom of the stairs. She ran her hand over the wooden railing.

'Markus was not my first charge,' she said, turning her gaze to the fire. 'During the first several hundred years of our existence, gargoyles remained statues far longer than they were alive, only awakened when there was a threat, sealed to Roma as needed. But as clans began fighting amongst themselves, gargoyles were used as weapons, rather than guardians. The *Sobrasi* were formed to regulate the shadow world, but eventually, they came to care more for the power and wealth that control brought them.'

'But Markus was not one of those,' I said.

'No.' Esmeralda turned her attention to the fire. 'There were still noble *Sobrasi* back then. When awakened, gargoyles were given time to acclimate to their surroundings before being sealed to a Gypsy. Markus was the *Sobrasi* tasked with assimilating them. I was under his care.'

I frowned. 'So you weren't his guardian?'

'Not at first. At that time, every member of the *Sobrasi* had their own guardian, and I had been selected for someone else. But Markus and I ... there was something between us. Something I'd never experienced.' Ezzie's eyes glazed over in memory. 'He went against the head of the *Sobrasi* and chose me instead.' She looked back at me. 'It did not win him much favor among them.'

'How did you ... I mean, how did you fall in love?'

The expression on her face shifted. 'Even before we were sealed, I felt connected to him. He wasn't like my past charges. With those, the bond had been strong, but it was born out of a protective duty, a deep and compelling calling. But with Markus ...' Esmeralda hesitated, and I saw the corner of her eye twitch, the only evidence of whatever emotions she was dealing with. She sighed. 'I don't know why it happened to us. Why we were the ones to be cursed.'

'How could your relationship be a curse?'

'Because it got him killed.'

'Ezzie.'

'Please,' she said, holding up her hand. 'I don't wish to continue speaking about me. I've spent many years trying to move forward.' She moved to her chair and sat in front of me. 'But you haven't asked me the real question yet. The one that concerns you most.'

Ezzie waited patiently.

I fumbled with my pendant. 'How was it possible? Shadowen are …'

Creatures.

I didn't want to say the word aloud. But Ezzie seemed to know it, anyway. She perched on the edge of her chair, reminding me of a cat about to pounce. Her eyes locked onto mine with a fierce intensity.

'When shadowen were first created, they were indeed, creatures of stone, brought to life. The grotesques were once noble beasts, charged with protecting holy places and innocent Roma. Until the blood feuds ripped the Old Clans apart and mutilated the shadow world in the process. Then chimeras were crafted to be even more brutal. You must remember, gargoyles were fashioned by the Roma to fight those evils.'

'I know, but—'

'Gargoyles are closely connected to your people, integrally linked in a way no other shadowen has ever been. You have only to look at Sebastian to see that our kind have far more in common with you than with our primal cousins.'

I felt the sting of chastisement. For all the wings and teeth and claws, Sebastian wasn't that much different from the human boy I first met in school. Not really. Wasn't that what I told him when he first came to the Circe? Isn't that what I confessed to Katie just last night?

'Yes,' I replied softly.

'We may begin as stone, brought to life by *prah*. But also,' Ezzie leaned closer to me, 'also by Roma blood. It flows in the veins of every gargoyle, setting them apart from all other shadowen. So no matter what protests we may give, no matter what laws are handed down by your people, one thing remains true. Our stone hearts beat with human blood. And because they do—'

'You're capable of love,' I finished.

'In every aspect of the word,' Ezzie replied, fixing her eyes pointedly on me. 'Sebastian has love for the clan he serves. Love for his friends and his family. But also, love for another who he believes is far more than simply his charge. Yes, Josephine, we can love in every way humans are able.'

Shame burned my cheeks. Sebastian wasn't monstrous, like he thought he was. I'd firmly believed it from the start. Yet, somehow, internally, I'd contradicted what I felt about him by voicing my questions. I raised my eyes to see Ezzie, regarding me. There was no judgment in her countenance.

I wrapped my fingers around the dandelion pendant. Its glass surface burned hot against my skin, but it made me shiver, as though someone had thrown open a door in the dead of winter. I breathed deeply through the ache inside me. 'Ezzie, do you think he's okay?'

She tilted her head to the side. 'Why do you ask?'

'I can't really explain it,' I replied, tucked the pendant under my shirt. 'Just a bad feeling. I didn't say anything to Katie. I don't want to worry her, not after she's finally coming to grips with our world, and I didn't want to say anything to Hugo, either, not when it's just a feeling.'

'You're right to trust your feelings, Josephine, even if you do not understand them fully. Sebastian is your guardian, regardless, and you've experienced how strongly that bond links you together. I also have an unsettled feeling, about many matters. I am anxious to hear what Zindelo has to say.'

My eyes widened. 'You've talked to Hugo's father?'

She smirked, but there wasn't any life in her eyes. 'I have the means of contacting them, when needed.'

'But Hugo—'

'Doesn't know,' she replied.

'Even though Hugo is technically the *bandoleer* right now?'

Esmeralda's shoulders rose for a moment, and then sunk lower. A shadow crept across her countenance, and the cold, confident air that usually radiated around her seemed to fizzle. 'I must admit, it has been difficult. I do not enjoy keeping things from Hugo Corsi.'

My phone buzzed and I glanced at the screen.

Where r u? Ready?

Katie. I'd forgotten all about going out. I hadn't been too keen on it to begin with anyway. Now, after hearing all this, I definitely didn't want to go anywhere. What if Hugo came back while we were gone? I needed to know how Sebastian was, to make sure he was okay.

'Josephine.'

Ezzie had retrieved her book and settled back into her chair. She was studying me, but her eyes were kinder than before. As if reading my thoughts, she said, 'You should go with Katie. Sitting here worrying about things you cannot change is pointless. I can, however, tell you this: I believe, come tonight, we will have the answers.'

9. *Josephine*

'You have to try this,' said Katie.

I made a face. 'It's okra.'

'Yeah,' she said, thrusting her fork in my direction. 'Try it.'

The chunky vegetable clinging to the utensil looked unappealing in every way. I'd let Katie choose the restaurant – something completely *gadje* and away from our connections in the city. She'd gone with a place called Auntie Mae's, where everything on the menu was either fried or drowning in butter.

'Keep that on your side of the table.'

'Your loss.' Katie crammed the fork into her mouth.

Our window seat afforded a great view of the square. Tourists gathered around the water fountain in the center. Kids played in grassy spots underneath the canopy of trees. Two older gentlemen wearing straw hats sat on opposite ends of a park bench, both reading papers.

I'd forgotten how much I loved the feel of the city, with its bustling coastal charm. If I became Queen of the Outcast

Clans one day, this would be my home and my life at the Circe would be over. The weight of responsibility settled over me again. I never could get rid of it for long.

Katie reached for the last piece of cornbread. 'Are you going to eat that?'

'*Are you going to eat that?*'

Sebastian glanced sideways at me. The apples of his cheeks and the tips of his pointed ears darkened slightly, which I'd come to realize was the equivalent of a blush on his gray skin.

I shook my head. 'All yours.'

'Thanks.'

He picked up the uneaten half of my sandwich and set it on his paper plate, contemplating it only a moment before proceeding to pull it apart with his formidable claws and retrieve the thick slabs of ham inside. He gnawed on one, and I watched as his eyelids drooped contentedly.

I considered commenting on the meat thing, but he'd only just gotten comfortable eating with me during my lunch breaks. I didn't want to spoil the few quiet minutes we had before Andre called me back to rehearse another balancing act. I crumpled the plastic wrapper and tossed it into the trash bin beside the bleachers, keeping my attention on Claire and the other trapeze artists as they worked high in the tent's canopy. Finally, I broke the silence between us.

'Do you ever think about your future, Sebastian?'

He brushed his hands off on the sides of his jeans, and his dark lips parted as he took in a breath. 'Well, it seems my future is pretty obvious, don't you think?'

I heard the catch in his voice, but it didn't sound bitter, or even sad, really. In my heart, I sensed another emotion, which layered his words, even as he tried to hide it with a close-lipped smirk.

Fear.

He was afraid.

Not only could I feel it, but I could read it in the occasional shudder of his wings and the haunted look in his uniquely colored eyes. I didn't know what to say. I wanted to tell him so much, but not here – not with Marksmen everywhere and the unrelenting schedule leading up to opening night. I placed my hand over his. I felt him flinch, but he didn't move away. A picnic, I decided. We'd get away from the Circe, and then I'd be able to tell Sebastian my secrets.

And maybe he'd tell me his.

'More sweet tea, honey?'

I blinked away the memory and nodded to the rosy-faced server as she filled my glass and bustled away. Katie wiped her chin with the linen napkin and sighed happily.

'I'm totally stuffed. We're going to need to do some serious walking to work this off. Ready for some shopping?'

We were in Katie's element now. I knew she wanted to take my mind off things, so I consented. We paid the bill and stepped outside. The air clung to my face sticky and hot.

'Got any preferences?' I asked.

Katie's light brows scrunched together. 'Gosh, I don't know. You know this place better than me.'

'Well.' I checked the street signs. 'Let's go down to the waterfront. It's really pretty by the river. There aren't many Outcast-owned businesses there – that I remember anyway. It's been a while since I've stayed here.'

My phone buzzed. I took a breath before checking the text. Two different messages had come through, one an hour ago, and the other right then. The earlier text was from Francis, asking how things were going. It was easy to tap out a quick reply to my brother. But the more recent one was from Quentin, and my stomach tightened uncomfortably as I read it.

Josie text me back.

Why aren't you replying?

'What are you going to tell him?' said Katie, looking over my arm at the messages. 'Are you going to keep him thinking you're at my house, even though you're here *and* he's here?'

'It's a big city,' I replied. 'He doesn't have to know.'

'I get that Quentin doesn't like Sebastian,' said Katie, 'and I know you're worried he would tell your dad you were here. But Josie, you're his girlfriend. He could help you, right? Get you in to see the Queen?'

'He wouldn't,' I replied, starting off towards the river and choosing not to meet Katie's look. 'No matter what our relationship might be, Quentin wouldn't interfere with these proceedings. He wanted Sebastian to stand before the *Kris Romani*. That's why he refused to cast a vote back at the Circe. Quentin sees Sebastian exactly the same way as he sees any other shadowen, as an evil curse from our past that only wants to destroy us.'

'Wow,' said Katie slowly. 'You really are in deep.'

We stared at each other for several seconds. Katie was right. My jumbled feelings for Quentin and my family's expectations about marriage and my place in the clan had swirled into one painful lump. I tried to swallow, but it was as though I had a tennis ball wedged in my throat. I had to get a hold of myself. And I also had to be careful with whatever I said back to Quentin. Too much would look bad, but so would not enough. I took a breath and punched in my reply.

Sorry. Been shopping all day with Katie. Will be out late.
Then I added,
Call you tomorrow. Love you.
The last bit gave me an unsettled feeling. It wasn't like I hadn't written that I loved him in a thousand texts, but this time, it didn't fill me with anything positive. The words were heavy now, full of things I wasn't ready to confront.

I hit send.

'You think that's enough?' Katie asked, as we started towards the river.

'I hope so. But I'm going to have to talk to him tomorrow. I don't want him to get suspicious.'

'Don't worry,' she said, as we started towards the river. 'We'll come up with something before then.'

The walk was longer than I remembered, and the sun sweltering. I wrapped my light jacket around my waist and maneuvered us through the shady squares, cobblestone and ballast streets. Katie took at least a hundred pictures on her phone, squealing excitedly and grabbing my arm whenever she saw something that looked more than twenty years old.

I kept on the lookout for shops bearing any kind of *patrin* indicating that Roma ran the business. At one point, I completely stopped walking altogether, and Katie had gone ahead a considerable distance before she realized she was talking to air.

'Hey, what's up?' she asked as she jogged back.

I moved to the edge of the sidewalk, away from the door of a Georgian-style building with a bright white exterior. A man in a dark suit and tie had just opened the door and stepped outside. I waited until he'd gone in the opposite direction before answering her question.

'I'm looking for *patrins*,' I said. 'They're like little sign-posts. My people used to leave them beside the roads a long time ago, to communicate with other Roma. Outcasts use them to tag Gypsy establishments in the Havens we travel to. But in this city, *patrins* signal entrances to the Court of Shadows.'

Katie stared at the building, squinting hard against the glare. 'What do one of these things look like?'

'The dandelion is our most used *patrin*, but sometimes, it might be a design that's colored in purple and silver.'

I pointed to a set of narrow, lattice-covered windows above the front door. 'Look at the one on the right. See in the corner, there?'

'No,' said Katie, shielding her eyes with her hand. 'I have no clue what – oh, wait! Are you talking about that little decal?' She took a step closer. 'Oh, yeah, it's a dandelion! Just the top, though, no leaves.'

'Which means this law firm,' I replied, observing the brass sign beside the door, 'is run by Outcast Gypsies.'

'Do you know which clan?'

I shook my head. 'I can't tell, based on the names. Sometimes, Roma use *gadje* names, especially when they want to keep a low profile. I do know that lots of people from the Joles, Mustow, and Heron clans live here.'

'And no one's caught on to the secret code thing?'

I glanced around before changing direction and guiding us down a smaller, side street. 'People only see what they want to see.'

The riverfront was busy. A street market, lined with white tents, ran parallel to the water. Katie hovered excitedly over tables stacked full of artwork, pottery, and homemade beauty products, chatting at me non-stop. The tension eased between my shoulders as we strolled beside the river, but guilt held on with stubborn fingers.

I was used to living a regulated life. There was security in it that Katie probably wouldn't understand. But my heart felt divided, caught between respect for my customs and the fierce urge to throw everything aside. I wanted to use my position to get Sebastian released, even if meant betraying my father, but more importantly, the Queen herself.

'Josie, what's going on in your head?' Katie asked, stopping to brush the remains of her sampling of peanut brittle into a trash receptacle. 'You look like you want to murder somebody.'

I toyed idly with the straw of my smoothie cup. 'Nothing.'

'Look, I told you, Hugo's gonna take care of Sebastian.'

'It's not that,' I replied. 'It's just a feeling I can't shake.'

A streetcar approached, its little bell dinging a warning as it neared the pedestrian crossing. We made our way across the brick street, away from the riverfront.

'Feeling?' Katie pressed. 'You mean, like a bad feeling?'

My conversation with Esmeralda Lucian flittered through my head. She seemed so sure we'd have more answers to our questions tonight. I only prayed she was right. 'It's nothing,' I replied. 'Just nerves, I guess.'

Katie gave me a swift hug. When she pulled back, her eyes were deeply serious. 'Hey, I get it. My uncle had to go to trial a few years ago. He was accused of a hit-and-run, but it totally wasn't his fault. But it was really scary at first.'

'What happened to your uncle?' I asked, hesitantly.

'They got the whole thing cleared up. A witness came forward who'd seen what actually happened. Turns out, the guy was trying to get money.' Katie held onto my arms with a firm grip. 'My point is, Sebastian didn't do anything wrong. And he's got all the Corsis, and you and me, and we're all on his side. I don't care what this Gypsy court throws at him, it's going to be okay.'

And then what, I asked myself as I looked back at her. Would they just let Sebastian return to the Circe, like nothing had happened? To resume his guardian duties with me? Would my troupe ever accept him again?

'Yeah, he's going to be fine.' I swallowed hard and forced a smile. 'Now, come on. I'll buy you an ice cream.'

As we crossed through one of the historic district's numerous squares on the way back to the *Dandelion Inn*, I glanced nervously at the time. Sunset had turned the sky into a mixture of pink and orange, and cast long shadows underneath the trees. It was definitely later than I'd planned to be out – and almost later than Hugo wanted us back.

'Did you enter us in a race or something?' Katie clutched the strap of her purse as she walked briskly beside me. 'What's the rush?'

'I wasn't paying attention to how far we walked today,' I said, checking the map on my phone to get my bearings. I picked up my pace again. 'We should've headed back after the ice cream instead of shopping.'

'But that antique shop was so cute.'

'We were there almost an hour,' I said, irritated with myself. 'That was way too long. I knew it was a bad idea, but I did it anyway. We can't take as many chances in big cities.'

Katie sighed, but her pace increased to meet mine. 'What's the big deal, Josie? It's not even time for dinner yet.'

I glanced at her. 'Sunset, remember?'

'Oh, right,' she said, looking up. 'The bad things come out at night.'

'Most of the time. They don't like the sun.'

'Sebastian hated the sun,' said Katie, her face lighting up with revelation. 'He always complained when we went out on my dad's boat in the summer. And to think, it's all because he's a … gargoyle.' Katie said the word as though she still didn't buy it. 'Is he allergic to other stuff?'

'He's vulnerable to diamond weapons,' I said. 'Diamond is the only substance that can pierce shadowen skin.' I led us past the square's enormous fountain, feeling the spray on my face as the wind filtered through the trees. 'Oh, and he can't eat anything except meat.'

'Why?' asked Katie, still struggling to keep pace.

A horse-drawn carriage lumbered past. The harness bells jingled faintly underneath the sound of clopping hooves. I moved to the sidewalk, walking even faster. Why hadn't I paid more attention to the time?

'It's a shadow creature thing,' I said over my shoulder. 'Now, hurry up.'

Katie finally drew even with me as I sidestepped an open gate. 'So,' she said breathlessly. 'Do these shadowen go after any old Gypsy they meet on the street, or are you guys, like special?'

'I don't know.'

'What do you mean you don't know?'

I hesitated at one corner, getting my bearings. 'I mean, yes, they'll attack any Outcast Gypsy. But it's never been like this before, at least, not in Sixes, anyway. That's why Hugo and Ezzie are so on edge. Something's definitely changed over the last few months. But I honestly don't know if it's the Corsis who are being targeted ... or if it's me.'

I didn't want to think about it, but what if it was true?

A long row of homes spread out before us, with fences and stone walls separating them from the street. The inn was only two blocks away. Hugo had to be back from the Court of Shadows by now. My heart stumbled over a beat inside my chest. He'd seen Sebastian.

A breeze whipped through the overhanging branches. I pulled on my jacket, too concerned with getting back to really think about the rapidly cooling temperature until I heard the flapping of heavy wings in the distance. I put out my arm, halting Katie in her tracks.

'Off the sidewalk,' I whispered.

We darted through a narrow opening in the fence and ducked behind it. I peered between the slats, scouring the street in both directions while slowly pulling out my knife from my cross-body bag. Katie's eyes grew twice their normal size.

'Guns don't work on shadowen,' I said, keeping my voice low.

'How do you people live like this?'

'This,' I replied, 'isn't normal.'

I put a finger to my lips to keep Katie from asking anything else. The air went suddenly still. Nerves prickled up my back. I gripped the knife so tightly my knuckles stung. On the opposite side of the street, I saw it.

Something dark moved across the rooftops.

10. Sebastian

A glint of morning sun caught my wings as I stretched.

It was one of my favorite places – the roof of my trailer at the Circe de Romany, as I waited for the Gypsy troupe to start their day. Francis Romany was usually one of the first faces I glimpsed, checking and rechecking equipment. More often than not, Phoebe Marks went with him.

Marksmen changed guards, reducing the numbers during the daytime hours. Warmth from the dawn helped offset the chill they produced in my insides when they patrolled too close. I took a deep breath and let it out. It was beginning to feel more like home here. I missed Hugo and the guys, without a doubt, but the sense of purpose within me grew the longer I stayed.

My senses alerted me to Josephine, awake and stirring inside the Romany family trailer. I still wasn't quite sure how I knew, but I'd given up trying to figure it out. It was just something I could do, whether I actually tried or not. I pressed my wings against my back and leapt from the roof.

I landed on all fours, clawed fingers splayed wide and feet cushioning the impact. Even folded in, my wings trailed the ground behind me. I glanced over my shoulder at the massive things, and they shuddered in response – an action I didn't have mastery of – begging to fly.

A shadow crossed my face, and I looked to the sky. Clouds were rolling in, puffy and tinged with gray. The sun glared angrily behind them, but I breathed a sigh of relief. It would be nice to walk around without the headache and the sluggish sleepiness. Overcast days were definitely easier on me.

I stood and made my way around the trailer, casting a sideways glance in the window as I passed. The sight of my new horns sprouting through my hair made me jolt. I slowed, studying my reflection. It felt like an eternity since I'd stood in front of the bathroom mirror in Hugo's apartment, gawking at a single patch of gray hair and wondering what was wrong with me.

I turned stubbornly away and hurried to the pavilion. The more like a gargoyle I looked, the easier it was to accept my role – to truly see my relationship with Josephine for what it was. To admit I wasn't human.

No matter how hard I kept pretending.

A bucket of cold water splashed me in the face.

'Time to clean up.'

I shoved my dripping hair out of my eyes to see Donani opening the cage door. Two Marksmen lumbered inside as I struggled to my feet. The first Marksman examined my shoulders and arms, noting the fading lines from the teeth and claw marks I'd received from the two grotesques.

'Healed,' commented the Marksman. 'Just dried blood.'

'Let's see the manacles,' said Donani.

The Marksman unlocked the cuffs at my wrist. I hissed as he pried the short diamond spikes from my skin. Drops of fresh blood instantly welled up, oozing across my red, inflamed tattoo. The Marksman handed the cuffs to Donani.

Then he took a towel and scoured the remains of caked, purple-black crust from my shoulder blades and the edges of my bound wings – all the while looking as though he'd rather be cleaning the latrine.

'What's going on?' I croaked. My throat ached.

The second Marksman hurled a fresh towel at me. 'Dry off.'

I picked it up and scrubbed my hair and face. The second Marksman produced the same heavy cloak I'd arrived in. He threw it over my shoulders and secured the hood low over my face. They ushered me out of the cage. I grit my teeth in pain as Donani replaced my cuffs with a firm click of the metal lock, and he wiped his hand off against his leg.

The Marksmen remained silent as we ascended the dungeon stairs – Donani leading the way – and through a wider corridor. Anytime I attempted to look down one of the many halls, I was hurried along with excessive force. The stone ceilings and walls gradually grew lighter and the passageway became warmly lit with hanging lights. Smells turned from dank and musky to more appealing odors – scented candles, oil lanterns, and the richness of cedar wood.

My blood felt increasingly hot in my veins, and it filtered through my brain like steam, causing everything around me to go blurry – just like when Augustine had me shot with an arrow coated with *prah*. It had to be my body rebelling against the lack of food, though I hadn't actually felt hungry in several hours.

I shook myself off as we entered a spacious room that appeared to be some kind of library. Plush couches and inviting-looking chairs filled the middle of the space, along with a few wooden tables. Floor-to-ceiling shelves encompassed every wall, filled not only with books, but also a variety of exotic decorations – similar to ones in Josephine's living room.

My lungs constricted when I thought about her.

'Sit,' Donani commanded. I moved to the closest couch, but he kicked me in the shin and jutted his chin in the direction of a simple, backless wooden chair. 'Over there, demon.'

I growled low in my throat. The truth was, I was too exhausted to waste my words on him. My arms had taken up the permanent shakes, and it felt like my body weighed the equivalent of a small car. And my head was on fire. I slid into the seat, grateful for something solid underneath me.

A small boy appeared in the doorway, a silver tray in his hands. He crossed the room to me and set the tray on a table. My lip curled instinctively at the sight and smell of fresh steak. The boy – who was dressed all in black and seemed to be some sort of Marksman-in-training – refused to meet my eyes as he hastily poured a cup of water from a glass pitcher. Then he backed away as fast as he could.

Donani scowled at him disapprovingly and dismissed him with a wave of his hand. 'Eat,' said Donani, turning the same expression towards me. 'Compliments of the Queen.'

I eyed the steak as it taunted me on the plate – all medium rare and dripping with fat. I waited for my body to go into crazy appetite overload, but nothing happened. My stomach had ceased rumbling a while back. My mouth no longer watered, and my gums had gone numb.

Perhaps, I'd finally conquered my insane appetite, but I couldn't really appreciate any of it, because I was left feeling sick and … cold. The unexplained, fiery heat abandoned me, and I was suddenly colder than I ever remembered being in my life.

'I'm not eating,' I said through bared teeth.

'Suit yourself.' The Marksman motioned for the guards to leave, and he sauntered to the door, adjusting the glittering knife at his belt. 'Oh, I almost forgot,' he continued in a bored tone. 'You're going to have a visitor.'

'Who is it this time?' I snarled.

'Hugo Corsi,' he replied.

My careening senses jolted to attention. I stared Donani down, trying to read his expression. 'My brother doesn't know I'm here.'

Donani's scowl returned, deeper than before, and then, unexpectedly, he broke into a sharp laugh. 'Brother? And just where did you get such a ridiculous idea as that?'

The cavernous cold within me began to melt. It swirled and simmered, like water coming to a boil. I dug my claws into my palms. 'He doesn't know I'm here,' I repeated, with slow determination.

'I'm bound by law to allow this one visitation, but don't expect this will change anything for you.' Donani placed his hand on the door handle. 'I do promise you this, gargoyle, nothing you say or do will be kept private, so I'd remember that, if I were you.'

The wooden door closed with a heavy thud, leaving me alone. I let out a breath into the silence. It rattled in my throat like a growl. I willed myself from the chair, forcing one foot in front of the other as I paced the room.

Was Hugo really coming here?

I'd refused to entertain the thought, not since they'd thrown me in the dungeon. Now, anticipation rippled through me. I hadn't seen my brother since I'd left for the Circe. So much had happened since then – so many things I wanted to tell him. But, would he believe me?

The chill in my bones was completely gone now, but in its place, a blistering heat. My head lit up again, and I felt feverish. The inexplicable return of heat loosened my stiff limbs and scorched my veins. I pinched my nose between my clawed fingers and tried to take a deep breath. What was going on? My chest heaved, like I'd just sprinted down the hall. I concentrated on the bookshelves, endeavoring to ignore the unbidden anger rising up my throat.

The door lock clicked, and I bolted from the chair, dropping into a crouch. Two Marksmen shoved a person inside. He hit the edge of the couch with a grunt. The door slammed shut again as the Marksmen left without a word. The bolts and lock of the door echoed hollowly in the room.

'Hugo!'

I started forward, but instantly froze. Red tendrils wafted around the edges of my vision, and I felt the stirrings of adrenaline and instinct move up my spine. I scooted back to the bookshelf on the farthest side of the space.

My brother brushed off his tattooed arms. 'Those guys get really testy when you start talking about their moms,' he remarked, a hint of a smirk playing over his face. He looked me up and down, noting the cloak. 'I know it's not the best of circumstances, but I figured you'd at least be a little happy to see me.' When I didn't reply, his thick brow lowered, turning his eyes to shadows. 'Sebastian, are you okay?'

He moved closer, and my lip curled. 'No, don't come any closer.'

119

Hugo's humor flashed to immediate seriousness. 'Sebastian ...'

I choked down a growl and pressed my back hard against the bookcase until my wings burned. Blood pounded in my ears. 'Please, Hugo. I don't feel totally in control of myself right now.'

'What are you talking about?' Hugo started forward again.

I shoved off the heavy, stifling hood, taking shallow breaths. Through the crimson film across my eyes, I saw my brother stop dead, staring at my face in surprise. My horns, I realized. He hadn't seen me since they'd been added to my transformation.

Hugo hesitated, scrutinizing me with more attention now. Then he nodded, and took a step back, keeping his distance from me. His acute gaze swept over the room until it landed on the untouched slice of meat, still steaming on the plate. Understanding flickered in his eyes. 'You're refusing to eat.'

'Part of my master plan.' I attempted a grin, but my lips wouldn't obey. I pressed my fingers into my temples. 'Quentin says he wants me coherent for the trial. I think a gargoyle who's too weak and sick to stand isn't going to look like much of a threat.'

'So how's this plan working out for you?'

My teeth sliced into my lips. 'Terribly.'

'Sebastian, you have to eat. You won't make it two more days.'

The pounding in my head grew worse as my temper teetered dangerously. My vision tunneled on Hugo. 'I don't know what else to do. I tried to reason with the Queen, but she looked at me like I was a piece of garbage. I'm not going to be able to talk my way out of this. Karl is dead, and everyone thinks I'm the killer.'

'Not everyone.'

'Doesn't matter,' I growled. My voice had thickened. The haze was like a film over my eyes I couldn't blink away. 'They're going to kill me, anyway. Or lock me up until I die, so what's the difference?'

Hugo took a step forward. My back hunched automatically. 'No, you don't get it, Sebastian,' he said. 'If you don't eat, you'll turn to stone.'

I stared hard through the red. 'What?'

'Only two things can kill you, diamond weapons and other shadowen. Turning you to stone, though? That's easy enough. If you get too much sun ... or not enough meat.'

My gaze flicked to the plate. 'Stone ...'

'Yeah,' he said, looking me up and down. 'You know, like a statue.'

I curled my stiff fingers. 'Why didn't Karl tell me this before?'

'Because he didn't think you'd be stupid enough to starve yourself.'

In another life, I would've laughed. But the anger inside me had churned into a white-hot rage, and I could only reply with a rippling hiss. My body shook, my muscles flexed taut along my back, my wings straining against the metal bindings. Hugo held his ground, but I smelled his fear.

'You knew this, too?' I snarled.

'Not until Karl called me a few days ago. He told me a lot of what he'd found, things he said he was going to tell you, but he also wanted to meet with me. Said he'd found something important in his grandfather's books.'

I worked to regulate my breathing, but the air broiled in my lungs. 'He told me he wanted to talk ... and then he was murdered.' My head buzzed, and I ground the heels of my hands into my temples. 'I didn't know … not eating … would do this to me.'

'Do what?'

I clenched my fists. 'Everything's going red.'

'Lack of meat shouldn't affect you that way,' said Hugo, now watching me like I was a bomb about to explode. 'Not eating enough means you weaken to the point of turning to stone.'

'Then what—'

'Sebastian, is that *prah*?'

Hugo's eyes fixated on the metal cuffs at my wrists. Something in the shock of his question subdued enough of the fiery emotions inside me that I was able to hold them up to the light and look.

From underneath the metal bands, my inhumanly colored blood trickled where I'd strained against them, but there was something more. The thick fluid seeping from my arms shimmered with flecks of silver and purple.

My heart screeched to a halt. That's why Donani had been so concerned about my healed wounds. That's why he'd taken my manacles. He'd coated the diamond spikes in *prah* – and now, the substance was running its course through my blood.

'Hugo,' I panted. 'You have to get out of here.'

He kept the same distance he'd established between us as I began to circle the room, moving against my will, trapped by an instinct I couldn't control. The same way I'd felt at the Circe when Augustine—

'Why?' Hugo demanded. His face was a mix of concern and resolution. 'Sebastian, what's going on with you?'

I gritted my teeth, forcing out the words. 'Augustine

experimented on his gargoyles ... turned them into chimeras ... said he was going to use *prah* to ... to burn the humanity out of me.' I took a shallow breath through my nose and out of my mouth. 'And ... I think it's working.'

'No, Sebastian. You've got to fight it.'

It was the moment from the Circe repeated. I was vaguely aware of my actions, but just as when Augustine ground the *prah* into my open wound, a terrible fury engulfed me, propelling me forward.

Hugo retreated with slow steps. 'Hey, just calm down.'

A deep, vicious roar burst from my lungs.

'Crap,' said Hugo.

I tensed and sprang, but managed to twist my body out of the way at the last second, barely missing him as I collided with the bookshelf, spewing its contents. I whirled around, teeth fully exposed. 'You don't ... understand. I ... can't stop it.' Underneath my cloak, my wings convulsed against their metal bindings, snapping one band free. 'They want me ... to hurt you.'

Hugo dove for a wooden chair near the door. He slammed it against the floor, shattering it. He brandished a chair leg in front of me. 'Well, that's not going to happen, so tell me what I can do. How can I help you beat this?'

'Just go,' I snarled. 'I'll be fine ... it will wear off.'

Hugo braced himself. 'But we haven't talked. And the trial—'

I cried out as a violent, gut-wrenching shock tore through me. My limbs crumpled. I caught myself before hitting the ground. My gargoyle radar fired off like cannons in my brain.

'Josephine!'

I clutched my head.

Josephine's in danger! Help her!

Protective instinct streaked through the *prah*'s red fury, yanking me back from the edge long enough for me to meet my brother's eyes. Understanding clicked in his expression. He didn't argue, didn't try to talk me out of anything. He simply tossed the chair leg aside and moved to the door.

'I'm on it,' he said.

That was the last thing I remembered.

11. Josephine

I stared, transfixed, at the dark figure on the rooftop. Options scrolled frantically through my head. *The Dandelion Inn* was at least thirty yards away. We'd never be able to run fast enough to reach it. If it really was a shadow creature, it could surely smell me by now.

The dark figure moved on all fours, gliding with inhuman grace over the length of the rooftop across the street. My stomach clenched. I could handle myself well enough, but not against a shadowen, with its beastly strength and ferocity. We only had one diamond weapon between us. The chance of she and I both getting out alive weren't too good.

'Stay here,' I said.

I tried to stand, but Katie yanked me back down, her eyes even wider than before, if that was even possible.

'Josie, whatever you're thinking about doing—'

'As soon as I have its attention, run for the inn.' My blood pounded so loudly in my ears I barely heard myself. 'Get help from the Corsis.'

Katie hesitated, conflicted. Then, she nodded. 'Okay.'

My phone buzzed in my back pocket. It had to be Quentin, trying to get hold of me. He'd have to wait. Instead, I gripped my necklace, finding strength in the sudden warmth of the glass. I watched Katie until she disappeared through some hedges out of view, and then I stepped out into the street.

The creature instantly halted, raised its head, and sniffed the air. Then it leapt from the roof, spreading its bat-like wings as it landed ten feet in front of me. My stomach plummeted.

The shadowen rose menacingly on two legs, shoulders thrown back. Its masculine face was a foul mixture of human and animal, contorted with deep black fissures that ran through its skin like cracks in a sidewalk. Its lips pulled back, exposing rows of teeth sharp as needles. They glinted in the glow of the street lamps. The creature's purely silver eyes glared back at me, its expression so full of malice that it burned in my chest.

'Gypsy,' it said, drawing the word in a hiss.

This was no grotie. The shadowen's ability to speak, combined with its decidedly male, humanlike form could only mean one thing: Chimera. But this didn't look like the chimeras Sebastian and I had faced in Sixes. Its long jagged face and oozing skin was easily ten times more disgusting.

No time to plan or think. I turned the knife over in my hand, wielding it like a stake. I sprinted straight at the creature, full speed. The action caught the chimera by surprise. It reared back, then sprang forward onto all fours, heading right for me. Just as it rose off the ground to dive at my throat, I fell to the pavement, sliding feet first across the asphalt.

The chimera's massive wings were directly over my head. I ripped my knife through the one leathery flap. The diamonds sliced through as though it were made of hot butter. The creature howled, stumbling over its feet and careening into a metal trash bin on the sidewalk.

A sizzling burn shot up my leg where I'd skidded. My jeans had ripped and my leg was scraped and bleeding. I blinked back tears and rolled to my knees, but before I got to my feet, the chimera recovered. In the space of a single breath, it loomed over me – quicker than I could react. I stared in terror as it sniffed the air hungrily, like a beast readying for the kill.

'Back away, shadow creature!'

The chimera's head snapped up at the sound of the voice. Esmeralda Lucian appeared in the center of the narrow street, with Katie right behind her, holding a trash lid like a shield. Ezzie's eyes flickered silver in the twilight. She planted her feet wide and let out a snarling sound.

The chimera roared back at her, claws flexed and wings extended. I took the opportunity to scurry out of its way. I dragged myself to the curb, wincing as my bloody leg grazed the concrete. Katie ran to my side as the chimera turned its attention from me and faced off with Esmeralda.

'Leave now,' she commanded. 'And I let you live.'

The chimera tilted its hideous head to one side and back to the other, inhaling deeply. Black liquid oozed from the corner of its mouth as it choked out her name. 'Esmeralda.'

'You know who I am,' she answered calmly. 'So you know you better run.'

Its nostrils flared, then it hacked out a low, grating laugh. 'Human now.'

I watched as Ezzie's face turned dark with a barely controlled fury. She widened her stance, shoulders thrown back. 'Test me and see.'

The chimera inched forward, quivering with bloodlust and rage. Then, it hesitated. Its silver-orbed eyes darted skittishly between us. Suddenly, the creature screeched – loud and defiant – spread its wings and took to the air, vanishing into the violet sky.

Ezzie scanned the buildings and shadowy street in both directions for several moments before pulling her phone from her back pocket, pressing the call button, and putting it to her ear. I heard it ring only once. 'I have her,' she said as someone picked up. 'She is safe. We'll be there shortly.'

Ezzie put away her phone and approached. Katie offered me her hand.

'Thanks,' I said as she pulled me up.

Ezzie glanced at my knife, her expression holding an air of appreciation. 'You are proving yourself to be quite resourceful with Marksman weaponry. Now, come on. We need to get inside.'

I nodded and we followed her to the opposite sidewalk. The three of us walked hurriedly down the block, nearing the white picket fence that surrounded the *Dandelion Inn*'s front lawn.

'So, Katie told you about the chimera,' I said.

'I didn't have to,' answered Katie. 'Ms Lucian was already coming to find you.'

'I've told you, call me Ezzie.'

Katie grimaced at her. 'Right, sorry.'

'But, I don't understand,' I said, as I fell into step beside our former teacher. 'You were already on your way? Why were you looking for me?'

'Hugo called me, after he'd tried unsuccessfully to reach you.'

I fumbled for my phone. It hadn't been Quentin at all.

'It was on silent.'

'He'd just left the Court of Shadows and said I had to find you immediately.' Ezzie paused, her hand on the gate leading into the yard. 'But that wasn't actually how I knew you were in trouble.'

My skin tingled strangely. 'How did you know?'

Esmeralda gestured for us to go through the gate ahead of her. She closed it, taking one last survey of the street and sky before answering. 'It was Sebastian,' she replied. 'I heard him in my head.'

'You mean the telepathy thing,' I said, remembering what had happened between them in Ezzie's home underneath the Sutallee Bridge.

She nodded stiffly. 'Gargoyles can communicate this way, but only when we are near each other – a useful ability when fighting other shadowen in close quarters.' Her arched brows knotted low over her eyes. 'What Sebastian just accomplished defies anything I've ever experienced.'

I swallowed past the lump in my throat. 'What did he say?'

'It was a short, strained burst, but very powerful. He said you were in trouble and needed help. Well, I should say he screamed it in my head, to be perfectly accurate. I tracked you down as fast as I could.'

However Sebastian had done it, I was beyond grateful. But the dull ache inside my chest grew more pronounced. My ribs felt suddenly too tight. Despite being held in the Court of Shadows awaiting trial, Sebastian was still managing to look after my safety.

'Thanks again,' I said.

'We should be getting inside,' she replied. 'My reputation alone kept that chimera from attacking, but it will only be a matter of time before it realizes I am not as powerful as I once was and decides to return.'

'You don't have to tell me twice,' said Katie, scurrying up the steps.

Ezzie put a finger to her lips as we reached the top. Katie and I stared curiously at her as she fished a key from her jeans pocket, turned the lock, and then quietly pushed open the door.

Inside the parlor, Paizi and Ferka were in the process of serving coffee, their arms loaded down with trays. James stood in the same place as he'd been earlier that morning, looking like he was trying to hold up the wall. Kris and Vincent were near the hearth, their faces grim.

Hugo sat – with his phone still in his hands – facing two strangers who were perched stiffly on the couch. The unfamiliar man and woman looked up sharply as we entered the room, their eyes marking each one of us, but lingering the most on Katie.

Esmeralda stepped aside, moving with silent steps until she stood behind the guests. Katie inched closer to me as Hugo rose from his seat and offered the two of us a tense, carefully placed smile.

'Are you guys okay?' he asked in an even tone.

'Yes,' I answered.

He nodded, and I saw relief flicker behind his dark eyes before his countenance warped into something impassive – a calm lake on a windless night. He cleared his throat and turned back to the strangers.

'Allow me to introduce my parents,' he said. 'Zindelo and Nadya Corsi.'

12. *Josephine*

The family resemblance between father and son was unmistakable. Zindelo shared Hugo's same rough features, thick torso, and piercing brown eyes. In contrast, Nadya was tall and slim with a commanding chin. Her black hair was neatly braided in a traditional style and fell long over her shoulder.

All eyes in the room shifted to us. No one spoke. Even the inn owners froze in the middle of serving. At last, Zindelo set aside his cup, ran a napkin over his dark moustache, and moved to the front of the room. He surveyed us both, pausing for an extra few seconds on Katie. When he glanced back at me, his thick brows pinched together.

'A *gadje* and a Romany.'

Hugo answered before I could. 'A *diddikoi* and Sebastian's charge.'

'So you've informed me,' Zindelo replied, keeping his eyes on me. 'Greetings, Nicolas' daughter. We have been made aware of all that has passed between you and the gargoyle we entrusted to Hugo's care.'

Katie made a weird sound in the back of her throat.

'Sebastian is my guardian,' I said, keeping my voice steady. 'I'm here to assist the Corsis in getting him back.'

Zindelo frowned. 'And the *gadje*?'

'I'm her friend,' Katie blurted out. 'And Sebastian's. And if he's in trouble—'

'You've said enough,' Zindelo said, cutting her off.

Katie huffed and opened her mouth, but I yanked on the back of her shirt. *Diddikoi* or not, Katie's involvement in all this was fragile. At any moment, the Corsis could kick her out of the meeting.

'Pardon my interruption, *Rom Baro*,' said James, using the term of respect. 'But how did you arrive so quickly from Europe? We only learned about the trial yesterday evening.'

Zindelo scratched his chin, his eyes narrowing. Then he returned to the couch. I breathed an inward sigh of relief and gently nudged Katie over to two parlor chairs near the stairs.

'Nadya and I came to the States three weeks ago,' he said.

Hugo, who'd been closing the curtains of the bay window, turned suddenly at this. His face took on an expression I couldn't totally read.

Zindelo continued. 'We'd heard rumors regarding the disappearances and deaths of head family members across our *kumpania*. We decided to first visit several clans to see if these rumors were true. Our last visit took us to the Boswell clan in North Carolina. While we were there, Peter Boswell returned from Sixes with a Romany Marksmen escort.'

I jolted in my seat. Peter Boswell, the crazed man who'd arrived at the Circe, claiming he was being hunted down by shadowen and who my father sent back with Quentin

132

to investigate the claim. Everything had happened so fast after Karl's murder that there was no time to question either Quentin or my father about the events.

'We know the rumors,' said Kris.

'Yeah,' agreed Vincent, snatching a cake from Paizi's tray. 'It's no secret Peter wanted the *bandoleer* position after his father Fennix died, but it went to some black sheep half-brother instead. Some people think there was foul play involved. There's been dissension and back-stabbing going on in that clan for years.'

I jumped into the conversation. 'Peter came to our camp looking for protection. He said his brother was killed by shadowen and the creatures were after him, too.'

'Indeed.' Zindelo flicked his narrowed gaze to his son. 'Had you heard this?'

Hugo turned back to the window. 'No.'

'Why would we?' said James. 'It's not our business.'

'Clans prefer to leave other clans alone,' said Zindelo. His gaze moved like a steady searchlight over the members of the Corsis. 'So it isn't surprising that some things might go unnoticed.'

'Like what?' questioned Vincent.

'Peter never had a brother,' said Zindelo. 'The unknown man who Fennix named as his successor shortly before his death wasn't a Boswell.' Zindelo fixed his stern gaze on me. 'There was an attack by shadowen a few weeks ago. Three of the head family were found dead, but we don't believe the *bandoleer* was one of the victims.'

I gripped my chair, fighting off the sense of foreboding that swirled in my stomach. 'But Peter was scared out of his mind. He told us he'd seen the whole thing, that he'd watched his brother die and barely escaped with his own

133

life. And a shadow creature did follow him into our camp. Our Marksmen killed it.'

Zindelo nodded. 'Peter told us the same thing, and I have no reason to believe he's lying. The imposter fooled him as well.'

'How do you know the *bandoleer* wasn't murdered?' I asked.

'Because the man posing as Peter's brother was Augustine.'

Hugo spun from the window, fire in his eyes. 'What?'

Zindelo gestured for more coffee, and Ferka hastily poured. I noticed the dark circles under his eyes and the exhaustion written in the lines of his face. He rose with a stiff movement from the couch and joined his son at the window.

'I don't have definitive proof,' said Zindelo. 'But I am of the conviction that it was Augustine, using this infiltration of the Boswell family, who is second in influence and power only to the Romany family, to stir up distrust among the northern clans these last months.'

Vincent sat his mug down with a bang. 'So, you think Augustine's using the Boswell clan to start an internal conflict?'

'For what reason?' asked James. 'What does that get him?'

'A distraction,' answered Zindelo. 'To hide his true purpose.'

Hugo stared hard at his father. 'And what purpose is that?'

'The shadowen attacks,' Zindelo replied. 'It's no coincidence that Augustine has resurfaced amidst them. Which brings us back to why we are here now. The gargoyle.'

'Sebastian,' I answered automatically.

'Yes,' said Zindelo in a strange voice. 'Sebastian.'

Unlike the Marksmen around the Circe, he didn't appear to resent or dismiss my correction. If anything, he looked pained.

'We expected to find him in your care, so you can imagine our distress when we found out all that has transpired since we left you in charge.' On the last word of his statement, he turned to his son.

The muscles bulged in Hugo's neck. 'You have no idea wha—'

'I do,' snapped Zindelo, cutting him off crisply.

Silence hit the parlor hard. Katie squirmed in her seat. My fingers found their way to my dandelion pendant. The warmth seeped into my fingers, bringing images of Sebastian to the forefront of my thoughts.

Zindelo walked with slow, deliberate steps, making his way behind the couch, where Ezzie stood, unmoving. 'I'm not here to blame anyone,' said the Corsi *bandoleer*. 'Esmeralda made it perfectly clear to us not only what had happened with Sebastian, but why. There were too many circumstances out of your control.'

'Esmeralda?' asked Hugo.

'Yes. We've been in contact with her since we returned.'

If it had been silent before, it was nothing compared to the blanket of quiet that now smothered the room. I glanced over at Ezzie, carefully poised with her hands behind her back and her face solidly blank. Hugo openly gaped at her, but she stared ahead at a fixed place on the wall.

'We asked her to keep our communications private,' said Zindelo. 'There were too many eyes on our clan, Hugo. More than you could possibly know. We couldn't risk someone finding out where we were, not after our failed quest in Europe. We had larger secrets than even that to guard.'

Hugo's jaw clenched. Devotion to clan often meant putting personal feelings aside, but that didn't mean it didn't hurt. 'I'm sorry,' said Hugo. He wasn't looking at his father. Instead, his gaze rested on Ezzie. 'I'm sorry you had to shoulder that responsibility alone.'

Esmeralda's eyes met his, and her arched brows lifted just enough to reveal her surprise. Her lip then turned upward at one corner, showing her gratitude. She dipped her head. 'Your clan will always have my loyalty.'

Hugo's gaze lingered on her a few seconds longer, and his dark look was gone. When he turned back to Zindelo, whatever emotions he been wrestling with had been checked, and he was all business.

'The last letter I received from you said you'd had no luck in finding the urn of Keveco, but you never bothered telling me why you were so desperate to find it, or even exactly what this thing was. All I know is it has something to do with Sebastian.'

'It does,' said Zindelo. 'But I'm afraid it's going to be a very long story.'

Ferka stepped into the center of the room, the tray of coffee still in her hands. 'Then I must insist you tell it in the kitchen, *Rom Baro*. You look half dead on your feet, pardon my saying so. You need something more than coffee.'

The Corsi leader nodded. 'Very well.'

The two ladies led us through into the kitchen. The wooden farm table had already been set for us, minus our two new guests, but Paizi was quick to remedy that. We found places and settled in. Zindelo pulled out a chair for his wife.

Though she hadn't said a word in the parlor, Nadya Corsi's presence radiated through the room. She sat with her back so straight it made me hurt to look. Sensing my attention, she glanced down her nose at me in a way that wasn't condescending, but not really friendly either.

Paizi ladled out bowls of stew. We ate without speaking, a weird kind of quiet before a storm. The sisters fussed over us, keeping glasses full and adding cornbread to plates. I ate impatiently, and nothing sat well in my stomach.

Tea and cookies were brought out after the meal. Tension set in around the table. As I folded my napkin across my knee I felt Katie's hand reach for mine under the table. She squeezed tightly. I wasn't sure if it was for my benefit or hers.

'Okay,' said Hugo, who was in the chair directly across from me. His elbows rested on the white tablecloth, making his tattoos stand out in stark detail. 'Let's get this over with. I'm tired of waiting for answers.'

'Agreed,' said Zindelo. 'But to do that, we have to start at the beginning of our story, for it's the reason for everything that has happened since, and what we fear may happen soon.' He leaned back in the chair and gestured to me. 'Josephine, what do you know of your ancestor Keveco Romany and the monster *La Gargouille*?'

All eyes turned in my direction.

'When I was a kid, my mother used to tell me stories before bed about the shadow world,' I said. A cold, slithering sensation worked its way through me. '*La Gargouille* was a terrible creature that terrorized villages in France during the Dark Ages.'

Zindelo laced his fingers together. 'Go on.'

I called on memories, grasping for my mother's words.

'It lived in a cave beside the river and no one could get near enough to kill it. But a brave priest decided to challenge the monster. He took with him a Roma convict named Keveco who had been wrongly accused of robbery. Together, they fought *La Gargouille* and defeated it. The priest granted Keveco his freedom in return for his help.'

'Yes, but what of *La Gargouille*?'

'The monster was taken back to the town. The villagers burned the body at the stake. But the priest took its head and mounted it on the roof of the village church as a reminder of the power of God.'

Katie balked. 'That was your *bedtime story*?'

'What you were told is not a story, but truth,' said Zindelo. 'But that is not the end of the tale. The priest was sympathetic to your ancestor's plight and to the suffering all of our people have endured through the years. So he ground the body of *La Gargouille* into ash and presented it to Keveco as a gift.'

'*Prah*,' said Hugo from across the table.

Zindelo's dark eyes met his son's. '*Prah* is what remains of *La Gargouille*. Blessed by the priest and given power from God to form shadowen – protection, not only for those of the Romany line, but also for all Roma connected to the *Arniko Natsia*.

'The Old Clans,' I said, for Katie's benefit.

'The *prah* was kept in an urn,' continued Zindelo, 'and small portions were allotted to each clan. When feuding broke out among the *natsia*, this supply was quickly depleted as each clan sought to gain the upper hand. Vicious shadowen were created in large numbers. Our people lost control over them. It was at this point in our history that the *Sobrasi* were formed.'

The atmosphere of the room instantly changed. This was new territory for the Corsis, I realized, just as it had been for me the first time Ezzie had mentioned them to me.

Zindelo glanced around the table, carefully regarding each of us. 'The *Sobrasi* were a group of powerful Roma. They were established by the High Council of the Old Clans to oversee the shadow world.'

Kris looked skeptical. 'Why have we never heard of them?'

'Their existence has always been shrouded in secrecy,' Zindelo replied. 'It was feared that if knowledge of shadowen lore became available to all clans, it could be detrimental to the entire *Arniko Natsia*.'

'But that's exactly what happened,' said Kris.

'Unfortunately, many *Sobrasi* became corrupted. They allowed themselves and their services to be bought by powerful *bandoleers*. But there were some that remained true. After the Sundering, when the Outcasts broke away and severed ties with the Old Clans, those *Sobrasi* took the remains of the *prah*, along with their books, and hid them to prevent anyone from finding the urn.'

Hugo grunted. 'Not hidden anymore, I take it.'

'Nadya and I have spent two decades searching for this urn. Four years ago, we had a breakthrough. We traveled throughout Eastern and Central Europe, and then finally to Paris, to the original sanctuary of the *Sobrasi*. There, we found a collection of books that gave us clues as to the urn's location. Unfortunately, we also realized we were not the only ones on this quest.'

'We tracked the urn to the ruins of an old church outside the city, but we were too late. By the time we arrived, not only was the urn gone, but also the books that were hidden with it.'

'Augustine,' growled James, pounding his fist on the table.

Hugo pushed his chair from the table. 'So not only does he have the urn, but you're telling us that he's now got the formula to create as many shadowen as he wants?'

'It requires more than just the *prah* to create and awaken a shadow creature,' said Zindelo. 'But I believe he is well on his way, gleaning everything he can about the contents of the urn and how to use it.'

I looked from Hugo to Zindelo, and suddenly, a horrible feeling hit me. 'Augustine turned his gargoyles into chimeras,' I said. Zindelo gave me a surprised look. 'A chimera attacked our camp, but Sebastian killed it.' I paused. I knew Sebastian tortured himself over what happened, even though he'd only acted in order to protect us. 'Sebastian said the chimera used to be Thaddeus, one of Augustine's gargoyles, and that something had happened to him. His other gargoyles changed, too.'

I had tried to push those images out of my head – the pure and malicious evil in their faces, and the way Sebastian had seemed to go void of himself during the battle, like a container emptied of its contents.

Zindelo spread his hands over the table, his knuckles turning white. 'Then it appears Augustine is much farther along with his learning than we first thought. If he has discovered how to manipulate the shadowen form, then it will not be long before he gains a control over the shadow world that has not been possible since the Sundering.' Zindelo sighed heavily. 'But that, I'm afraid, is not the worst of it.'

The Corsi *bandoleer* looked over to his wife, who'd been staring downcast throughout much of the conversation. Slowly, Nadya raised her eyes. An eerie calm aura surrounded her, combined with a quiet authority that now held every one of us in check.

'No,' she said, her tone deep and crisp. She blinked slowly, and her eyes glittered as they caught the light. 'The worst of it is, Augustine has been allowed contact with Sebastian Grey.'

13. Sebastian

'Josephine!'

I rolled into a crouch, frantic. Where was she? Where was I?

What was going on?

My heart banged out an irregular pattern in my chest. I sucked in several ragged breaths, feeling off-balanced, until I realized one of the metal binding bands had snapped across my chest, leaving my left wing trailing the ground. My vision faded from red to gray, and then snapped back to normal.

I was in the library. Books littered the floor, their pages loose and shredded. Shards from broken vases shone jutted out of the thick carpet. And claw marks – *my* claw marks – marred the thick wooden door in deep, crisscrossed patterns.

I'd torn the room apart.

'Hugo?'

My throat was drier than dead leaves, and I tasted blood on my lower lip. I shoved my hair out of my eyes. Hugo was gone. But how? They'd locked the door after he'd arrived. I studied the claw-marked door, half-expecting to find it torn off its hinges. But it remained intact. Which meant the Marksmen had let Hugo out.

My legs went limp with relief. If they hadn't come before I totally lost it …

I shuddered. The dark thing and the wild rage had gutted me out. It had taken everything in my being to hold myself together as long as I did, but the *prah* eventually won – as the room clearly displayed.

Had Hugo gotten to Josephine in time?

I didn't feel the threat of danger anymore, and my gargoyle radar had switched off completely. It was all I had to go on, but I was just going to have to trust in that, and in my brother.

I looked back to the door, expecting the Marksmen to appear, since my visitor was no longer here. However, it remained silent on the other side of the door. I rolled onto my side with a groan. The dark emotions inside me felt dormant once again, but Augustine's voice echoed through my memory.

When the prah *enters your veins, it runs through like poison, eating away the human blood you have within you. I've found a small amount produces a temporary reaction …*

I slid my thumb under one cuff, gingerly touching the diamond spikes. Was it true, what Augustine claimed? It wasn't like he'd ever given me reason to believe anything coming out of his mouth. Still, I couldn't deny the effect the *prah* had on me. And if that much was true—

'No,' I snarled aloud.

My head wafted in and out of cloudy haze. Just a few feet away, the table lay on its side, the water glass shattered and the plate of steak overturned on the floor. I tentatively sniffed the air, expecting the pain of hunger to double me over. But nothing happened. I didn't feel hungry at all, just cold. But Hugo's revelation on my eventual fate shocked me back to my senses.

If you don't eat, you'll turn to stone.

I flexed my fingers. Without the wild rush of adrenaline coursing through me, I realized how taut every muscle felt and how stiff my joints were when I moved. My veins were more pronounced – black in color and running in spidery patterns along the backs of my hands and the undersides of my arms, making my gray skin look eerily like ... marble.

If you don't eat, you'll turn to stone.

I scrutinized the overturned plate. It came down to this: I had two choices. Neither one was appealing. A ripple of a snarl traveled across my upper lip. I was so sick of being controlled, but it was time to face facts. I couldn't escape it. I was either going to be controlled by Augustine and his paid-off Marksmen, or I was going to be controlled by this strange, inhuman thing that I had become.

If I didn't eat, I'd be the one in charge of my fate. I rubbed my arm tentatively. But if I turned to stone, it would mean leaving the Corsis, my brother ... and Josephine.

My heart drummed painfully against my ribs – each thump reminding me of why I was what I was. I was a protector. A guardian. A gargoyle. As long as I was still flesh and bones, I had to act like one.

I scrambled across the floor, flinging the plate aside, and took the steak in my claws. The smell hit me full force, rich and full. And this time, the hunger I'd beaten into non-existence suddenly returned and took hold of me with a terrible, vengeful grip. I ripped the meat apart with my sharp teeth; juices dribbling down my chin as I took a massive bite.

I ate greedily, snarling like an animal as I devoured every morsel. When I finished, I collapsed back to the rug floor. Gradually, the coldness inside me diminished. The stiffness left my fingers, and I raised my arms for inspection. My skin had lost some of its marbled sheen, and the veins had shrunk considerably, though still visible underneath the gray.

My gums ached now, and I pressed my hand against my jaw. My body wanted more food. The piece of meat appeared to have kept the threat of turning to stone at bay, and it had taken the edge off my renewed hunger, but the single helping of food was far from satisfying. Still, it cleared my head, and I felt more myself than I had since leaving the Circe.

Without the heavy haze in my brain, I was able to concentrate again. I propped myself against the flipped-over table and focused my energy on Josephine Romany. While the warning shocks I'd felt earlier had ceased, I knew I hadn't imagined the sensation of Josephine being in danger. For that brief moment, I'd felt the connection between us again.

She was here. She was in Savannah.

Somehow, despite everything that had happened the night of the *kris*, I wasn't surprised. I could still feel the reassuring touch of her hand on my face as she'd promised to find a way to help me – as I'd stared back at her with my own hands chained to the Circe's massive tent pole.

I knew Josephine had meant every word. It was that stubborn streak in her I'd gotten to know during our weeks spent together. I closed my eyes, feeling my lip curl into a half-smile.

'Are you ready to go?' Josephine asked.

I looked up from her kitchen table, where I'd just polished off the large helping of bacon she'd prepared. 'Go where?'

'To the rehearsal tent,' she replied. 'I've got practice.'

My brow furrowed. 'But your knee—'

'Is fine,' Josephine finished, in a tone that didn't allow for arguing. 'Andre and I are behind on our routines, and if we want to be ready by opening night, I can't miss a rehearsal.' She caught my look. 'Don't worry, I won't endanger myself this time.'

I pushed away from the table, feeling like the proverbial bull in the china shop as I awkwardly straddled the Romany family's chair in a backwards position to accommodate my massive wings in their small kitchen. I stood and brushed my clawed fingers off on the legs of my jeans. 'I go where you go.'

We exited the RV and stepped into the bright summer day. I squinted my eyes against the sun, fending off a headache and trailing behind Josephine as she walked briskly to the rehearsal tent.

All around me, Gypsies moved about in their everyday routines, and the effect of my unexpected, gargoyle-y appearance around a corner never failed to produce a reaction. Some veered quickly in another direction, and others refused to meet my eye. But, there were more than a few who smiled and even said hello.

I was gaining their trust, as Nicolas promised I would.

Josephine glanced over her shoulder at me, as if to make sure I was still there. She was doing an impressive job of hiding her slight limp as she walked – the result of straining her knee the night before during an extra long rehearsal – but I sensed her pain wafting through the strange connection between us. Josephine didn't seem to know I could feel it, and I didn't say anything. But I knew it was there.

She spoke briefly to everyone she met – the ones I hadn't

scared off by my proximity, anyway – and her bright smile made it easier to believe that I'd eventually fit in here.

When we reached the rehearsal tent, I hesitated. This was Josephine's territory and the part of her life that was completely new to me. As if reading my thoughts, Josephine pulled back the flap – wide enough to allow me and my bulkily-bound wings through the opening.

'Let's go,' she said, still beaming that smile. 'I don't like being late.'

Suddenly, I grinned with fully parted lips before I could stop myself. There was something about that simple admonition that set me at ease more than anything else since I'd arrived at the Circe. I stepped inside the tent and, at that same exact moment, into my new life as Josephine Romany's official guardian.

The sound of the door opening snatched me from my memories. Donani took three steps inside the room and glanced at the surroundings before ending his visual circuit on me. Behind him, Quentin and two other Marksmen stood with weapons drawn. None of them looked in the least surprised by the demolished room around me.

'Let me guess.' I rose on steady feet and wiped my chin. 'We're going on a field trip, right?'

As thanks for my attempt at humor, Donani handcuffed me, using metal links to connect my wrist manacles across my pinned wings. It was a technique I'd gotten used to, even as my shoulders lit up with fire. The wing dragging the ground hurt more now, but I grit my teeth and pushed the pain aside. After the manacles were secured, a fresh cloak was draped over my shoulders and head, and the Marksmen herded me out of the library.

Instead of going back the way we'd come, Donani took us down another corridor. I was thankful for my clearer head; even it came with a price. At least I had a better sense of my surroundings. We definitely weren't going back to the dungeon, that I could tell from the smell of the air and the incline of the passageway through which we walked.

The underground labyrinth of the Outcast Gypsies was larger than I ever would've thought possible. I knew vague details about Savannah's mysterious tunnels that dated back to the city's founding, but this was definitely not in any history book I'd read in school. The enigmatic tunnels referred to in my textbooks were closed off and caved in, with no access or clue as to what they'd been used for in the past.

These tunnels, however, were very much in use. The floors and walls were clean, though uneven and jagged. Old pipe-lines ran parallel to the ceilings, and from them hung a mixture of lanterns and lights, some of them electrical and others oil based. Every room, every passage was bathed in a soft, golden glow.

From every direction, sounds filtered into my gargoyle ears – women talking, music playing, food being prepared and eaten, a television broadcasting some pre-season football game, men playing cards. I focused my attention on the back of the Marksman in front of me in an attempt to sort it all out in my head.

The Court of Shadows was more than just a location for trials and Council meetings. It was a hidden refuge for the Outcasts, a place where they could gather in one collective community, on their own terms and set apart from the *gadje*. Here, Gypsies could be themselves, complete and free.

I wondered, had circumstances been different, if I would've

148

had the same opportunity. Unfortunately, I was a prisoner in this underground sanctuary, at least, until my trial. And after that …

Beside me, Quentin kept a casual pace, one hand gripping my arm, and the other making sure his knife got nice and cozy with my ribcage. What bothered me the most was the smug look on his well-manicured face. I had gotten way too familiar with most of his expressions during our stint together at the Circe de Romany, but this time, there was also something jovially malicious in his smile.

He couldn't wait to see me dead.

I felt the beginnings of a snarl, and I turned away before it came out, beating my emotions down automatically. But why? The question rattled in my brain. I studied the Marksmen as we walked. There were only four of them. Armed and trained, sure, but still just four. Suddenly, I knew – I couldn't put a finger on exactly how I knew – but I was certain I could overpower them, if I really wanted to.

Die now or die later, did it really matter?

Already, heat churned inside me. The dark thing was tapping on the back of my skull, demanding to be let in, urging me to take action. If I just let the dark thing have its way, it would be over quickly, for all of us.

My pace slowed as my body responded to the urge. I hesitated. There were still mysteries I wanted answered about Augustine and his business here. And what about Josephine? My heart welled with emotion, but the sensation came too late. I'd messed up. I'd let my guard down for a split second. I'd opened the door to that part of me I'd been straining so hard to keep shut.

Now, it wouldn't close.

I pushed off sideways with all my weight, slamming my

body into Quentin. He hit the stone wall with a grunt. I felt his blade pierce my side, but I didn't stop. Continuing the movement, I whipped around, taking out the Marksman to my left with my mass of bound wings.

I charged Donani, who had already turned, spear drawn. He jabbed, and I ducked, barreling into him with my right shoulder, lifting him into the air and flipping him over me. The last Marksman leapt on my back, his arm around my throat in a chokehold.

A violent tremor shot across my shoulder blades, so strong I nearly pitched forward. There was a loud pop of metal bands snapping. The links connecting my arms broke apart. My wings exploded from their confines, taking the Marksman with them. He hit the wall and ricocheted off it with a sickening thud.

The cloak lay in tatters at my feet. My wings took up the entire corridor, blocking the light on either side. I panted wildly, adrenaline surging through my veins. Through my red-tinted vision, I saw Quentin scramble up, a second blade drawn and ready.

I met him head on, knocking both weapons aside and pinning him against the wall. My lips pulled back, and I bared my teeth. I felt the hot flash of heat in my eye sockets. I yanked my arm back, fingers splayed and claws extended. For a split second, there was something resembling fear in the Marksman's face. Then, it was gone. Dark fury glinted in his eyes.

'Go on!' Quentin spat. 'Let's see what you've got!'

I let out a furious snarl and swung.

14. *Josephine*

Nadya Corsi peered across the kitchen table at me.

'Yes, Augustine had contact with Sebastian,' I said, unable to break eye contract with her. 'But only to transport him to Savannah on my father's orders. Our head Marksmen accompanied him as well.' My cheeks burned with anger, but I didn't know where to direct my feelings. 'Why is that the worst of it? Augustine is *marimé*. He's not allowed into the Court of Shadows, much less participate in Sebastian's trial.'

'You don't understand,' Nadya said fiercely. 'None of you do. This is not about the trial.'

'Then tell us what it *is* about,' snapped Hugo, his face twisting darkly for a moment. He then seemed to rein himself in. 'With all due respect, of course.'

The sarcasm in his voice was palatable. His mother ignored it.

'Since Sebastian's awakening,' Nadya began, 'there has been an increase in shadowen activity – not just here, but throughout the Southeast. Chimeras appearing in greater

151

numbers, grotesques lured from their lairs and attacking with boldness we haven't seen in decades. It's a disturbing trend, and it's also happening in Europe.'

James let out a huff. 'You just told us that Augustine's got this urn, so obviously he's controlling the creatures. We need to take this information straight to the Court. They'll deal with him.'

The Corsis voiced their agreement loudly, except for Hugo. In my head, scraps of information were trying to piece themselves together, to connect the dots of so many questions.

Zindelo raised his hand sharply, putting an end to the discussion. 'Augustine may have figured out how to manipulate existing shadowen and even control them individually, but to do so, he would need to be in direct contact with the shadowen, using the *prah* to bend it to his will.'

My breath caught hard in my throat. The night Sebastian tried to attack me, when he'd been so vicious and his eyes so blank – Augustine had been right there! He must've had *prah* from the urn with him and somehow used it on Sebastian.

'Could he could do that on a larger scale?' questioned Kris.

'It's impossible,' Zindelo replied. 'No Roma has that ability, not even the *Sobrasi*. What is happening here has proven that our speculations were well founded. The source of these occurrences is based in the shadow world, not the Roma.'

Nadya's frown deepened. 'From the moment we placed Sebastian in your care, we had concerns. Zindelo and I hoped that everything we'd done for him would negate his circumstances. I fear we may be wrong.'

'What are you saying?' I asked, feeling suddenly cold.

'All shadowen are brought to life with *prah*,' said Zindelo. 'Which is the essence of what remained when the body of *La Gargouille* was ground into dust by the priest and given to your ancestor, Keveco Romany. But the dust must be infused with human blood to fashion shadowen into guardians. Humanity forms the shadow souls of the gargoyles. It sets them apart from other shadowen, and it's for that very reason that gargoyles are the protectors of the Roma.'

'That is the history of the urn,' said Nadya. 'But there is more.'

'Oh, fantastic,' said Vincent.

Kris elbowed him hard in the ribs.

'The head of *La Gargouille* remained intact,' continued Nadya, giving no attention to the interruptions. 'Mounted on the roof of the town's cathedral, for many, many years. When our people started using shadowen to do battle for them in clan skirmishes, the dwindling *prah* became a valuable commodity. As we have said, the *Sobrasi* who remained faithful to Keveco Romany's wishes hid the urn. It wasn't long, however, before attention turned to the head of the monster itself. The *Sobrasi* feared that the head would be stolen and used in the same way, so they hid it as well.' At this, a ghost of a smile flickered across her lips. 'Though we may have failed to retrieve the urn, we were successful in this quest.'

Ezzie sat up straight. 'You found the head of *La Gargouille*?' Her fingers clutched the edge of the tablecloth, wringing the fabric into knots. I'd never see her so emotional. 'Where is it?'

Zindelo and Nadya exchanged glances.

'Close,' said the *bandoleer*. 'Very close. But there is something you must know first before we can proceed.'

'We are *Sobrasi*,' said Nadya.

'As were our parents and our parent's parents,' added Zindelo. 'The position is inherited, along with the knowledge and abilities to awaken shadowen. This requires years of training to master.'

It was obvious this was as much news to Hugo as it was to the rest of us. He leaned against the chair back slowly.

Nadya directed her next words towards her son. 'It was not our choice to keep these secrets from you, Hugo. The *Sobrasi* remain a corrupt and power hungry group. There are only a few of us, like those who hid the urn, that remain true. We fled to a monastery in Germany, but our whereabouts were discovered. Rather than allow the head to be taken by the corrupted *Sobrasi*, we turned it to ash.'

'We could not risk leaving so much as a single particle of dust, lest it fall into the hands of those who wanted it for evil purposes.' Nadya's gaze drifted to an indistinct point across the room. 'There was a statue in the monastery,' she said, resuming her account. 'Fashioned in the likeness of the one for whom the monastery was named. What we decided to do was unorthodox, but we were desperate and out of options. We performed the ceremony for awakening – mixing the ash with our blood – and infused every last bit of the *prah* into the statue.'

'What statue did you use?' said Hugo lowly.

Zindelo met his gaze. 'Saint Sebastian.'

I sank down into my chair. The room felt as though it were spinning around me. There was a strange ringing in my ears.

Hugo turned away. 'That's why he looked like he did when you brought him to us.'

Nadya nodded. 'Yes.'

'Never had a shadow creature been created in this way,' said Zindelo. 'Our order requires all shadowen to be carved into specific designs by gifted Roma masons and then prepared for new life by the *Sobrasi*. What we'd done was against every rule. In fact, it should not have worked at all.'

'But it did,' said Hugo, his face an unreadable mask.

'Something about this *prah* was different,' agreed Zindelo, rubbing his creased forehead. 'The statue awoke. It maintained its human appearance, but remained lethargic and unable to speak. The three of us were able to hide with the assistance of a Roma monk, and he showed us a secret passage out of the monastery once the *Sobrasi* had searched the place and left.'

Nadya placed her hand on Zindelo's arm. 'It was a difficult journey back to the States, but we had to hurry. We weren't sure how long it would be before shadowen physiology would begin to merge with the human form Sebastian had taken from the statue. That's why we wanted him to stay hidden within our clan and sealed to us at the first sign of his gargoyle nature awakening.'

'We planted memories inside him,' said Zindelo. 'Things to help with his transition; to insure he would feel a familial bond towards us. But also because we were afraid of what the *prah* might do.'

My stomach curled inside me, like a snake. 'What do you mean?'

Zindelo rose and moved away from the table. Everyone watched in silence as the *bandoleer* leaned hard on the counter and looked out the small window above the sink. He spoke, keeping his back to us. 'As the head controls the body, so it is with this. We believe whoever possesses the head has the power to control the entire shadow world.'

Esmeralda stood, her glittering silver eyes round and wide. 'Zindelo, if what you are saying is true …'

'It is,' said Zindelo, turning around. 'Sebastian is *La Gargouille*.'

The Corsis stared at one another in shock, and I put my head in my hands. No one needed to voice what came next. Everyone felt the power of Zindelo's words like a low, rumbling earthquake in the room.

The power to control the entire shadow world.

15. Josephine

The horrible reality of everything Zindelo and Nadya just shared worked its way through my body, as though it were a heavy anchor, thrown overboard and sinking bit by bit until it hit bottom.

Sebastian was *La Gargouille* – the monster from our legends, the very origin of our connection with the shadow world itself. I clutched the dandelion pendant at my neck. How could this be possible? How could they have let this happen?

The anger that had been swelling inside me channeled itself towards Hugo's parents, even though I knew, deep down, it wasn't really their fault. What they'd done had been for the safety of our people. They had sacrificed everything – including their relationship with their own son.

Suddenly, Katie's voice resounded in the room.

'Okay, just hang on a second. Are you telling us that Sebastian's actually a monster? Like a for real, evil monster that went around killing people in medieval times and had his head cut off by a priest?'

Zindelo's eyebrows nearly obscured his eyes. 'Roughly speaking.'

'But, Sebastian's so … sweet,' said Katie, dumbfounded. 'I mean, he's a social disaster, sure, and I honestly don't know how he made it through high school, 'cause sometimes he just gets so weird, but he was always nice, you know, not a jerk like some people, and he's totally not a monster, especially not this thing you're talking about.'

Nadya joined her husband. 'I don't doubt it,' she said. 'In fact, it is probably that sweet nature, as you put it, that has most likely held back *La Gargouille* for so long.'

'You messed with his mind,' I heard myself say, but the words were muffled, like I was underwater. 'You planted stuff inside his head.'

Nadya's face softened somewhat as she met my eyes. 'We only gave him memories, Josephine. That was the extent of it. Who Sebastian is … his demeanor and personality … those are his own. The human component – given to him when he was created – is unique to him, in the same way children are unique from their parents.'

'But the fact remains,' said Zindelo. 'He is the head of the beast.'

Another thick and stifling silence fell over the group. Hugo hadn't taken his eyes off his parents. After a few excruciatingly tense seconds, he stood up as well, moving past Esmeralda, his steel-toed boots heavy on the tile floor.

'All this time,' he said, biting off each word. 'All this time, he was under our roof and you knew what he was. Yet you left me in the dark about everything. Everything! Sebastian was part of our family!'

'And, God willing, he would've stayed as such,' said Nadya in a gently earnest tone. 'Those were our plans for him. He was born a shadow creature, but our blood made him a guardian. He would be the gargoyle of the Corsi clan, the first our family has had since we arrived in this country after the Sundering, and the head of *La Gargouille* would be out of the *Sobrasi*'s reach forever.'

Hugo tugged at his goatee, struggling to maintain his composure. The rest of the clan watched the interaction warily. To my surprise, it was Esmeralda who spoke next.

'Hugo, your fight isn't here. We must be united on this.'

He looked at her, long and intently. As her unblinking eyes connected with his, I felt something pass between them – something that reminded me of the connection I shared with Sebastian – though I couldn't quite explain it. Before I could contemplate it, though, Hugo let out a loud, heaving sigh, carrying with it either resignation or acceptance, I couldn't be sure.

'What's done is done,' he said, turning his steely gaze back to Zindelo. 'So we'll leave it there. It's more important that we deal with what's happening now, and what we're going to do about it.'

'Agreed,' Zindelo replied.

Hugo pressed his back against the counter and folded his arms over his chest. He looked us all over. I sensed more than ever, there was something deeply important at work, but until I knew what it was, I wasn't going to speculate.

Hugo cleared his throat. 'I hate to say this, but my parents' account does explain a great deal of what has been going on the last six months. I can confirm at least part of their story, based on what I saw today.'

In all the insanity of the last hour, I'd completely forgotten that Hugo had been to see Sebastian. His parents must've arrived at the *Dandelion Inn* before he was able to relay the events to the clan. I sat up straighter in my chair.

'He wasn't himself,' continued Hugo, his jaw clenching.

'Understatement of the year,' muttered Kris under his breath.

Hugo kept speaking. 'They had him waiting for me in the Court library, all cloaked up and hooded like some medieval monk. He wouldn't let me near him when I came in. He said he didn't feel in control.' Hugo's eyes narrowed in a strange way. 'He hadn't been eating, for who knows how long, and it showed.'

Ezzie drew in a sharp breath. 'Stone.'

'Yeah,' said Hugo. 'He was well on his way, completely oblivious to what he was doing, too. Karl hadn't told him about the whole turning to stone if he doesn't eat bit.'

'Trying to starve himself?' said James. 'Why would he do that?'

'He wasn't planning on going that far, at least from what I could tell. There was a plate of meat on a table in the room, so he's been given food, obviously. He just thought he'd have a better chance in front of the High Council if he seemed as weak and unthreatening as possible.'

My heart stung, as though a needle had pricked it. It was so typically Sebastian: taking the sacrificial way, always looking for the best option that didn't involve acknowledging the shadow creature he'd become – *had always been*, I corrected myself. It was a gargoyle's nature, I'd come to understand, but it was more than that.

It was also *his* nature.

'He's changed since I saw him last,' said Hugo. 'He's sporting some wicked-looking horns, but it's more than that. He's just … I can't really describe it. Just different.' He shook his head, as though he were trying to clear away the bad memories, but without success. 'Anyway, the longer we talked, the worse he seemed to get. I'd never seen him fighting against himself like that before, like he was doing everything he could to hold himself together.'

I shuddered, remembering when I'd seen him that way, like he was holding on for dear life, refusing to let whatever it was inside him free. Now, I realized with a cold chill, I understood a little more what he was fighting. But Sebastian didn't know ... he had no idea. A sour taste filled my mouth.

'That's how he was the last time I saw him,' I interjected quickly, swallowing it down. 'I've seen Sebastian struggle before, but this was different. Augustine was there when it happened. He used *prah* from the urn, I'm sure of it now. Sebastian would never act like that on his own.'

Hugo registered this piece of information for a breath or two before nodding back at me. 'Sebastian said the same thing, though I only got bits and pieces of it through all the growling and snarling at me. Augustine experimented on his own gargoyles by using the *prah* to burn away the human blood and changing them into chimeras.'

'Now he's attempting the same with Sebastian,' finished Ezzie.

'But what is one chimera?' demanded Vincent. 'Yeah, they're bloodthirsty and nasty hard to kill, but what difference does it make to Augustine if he has one more for his collection? I don't see the worth in that. It's hardly an army.'

As soon as the words were out of Vincent's mouth, everyone in the room seemed to have the same thought at once. It was Zindelo who vocalized it.

'Not an army, no. But a shadowen to lead one, perhaps.'

Hugo turned to Esmeralda. 'What happened to Augustine's other gargoyles?'

Ezzie made a hissing sound. 'I do not know. Anya and Matthias fought with the Romany Marksmen in the woods on the night of the *kris*, providing adequate distraction while Augustine entered the camp. I thought at first they had been killed, but now I'm not so sure.'

I looked at Hugo's parents. The question of how Augustine had acquired the three gargoyles in the first place had never been addressed. I had an awful feeling that the answer to that lay with my own family, not the Corsis.

'Three chimeras would be formidable, but nothing the Marksmen don't handle on a regular basis around here,' said James. 'Still doesn't explain all the attention on Sebastian.'

'Unless Augustine knows about Sebastian,' said Hugo. 'What he is.'

Zindelo shook his head. 'Augustine had no way of discovering the truth of Sebastian's origins. Not even our friend in the monastery was aware of what we had done.'

'Augustine sees in Sebastian some potential he did not see with his own shadowen,' said Nadya. 'But there is far more danger in what Augustine intends to do than he is aware.'

'What do you mean?' demanded Hugo.

Nadya answered. 'Augustine is using the *prah* from the urn to manipulate the shadow creatures he comes into contact with. It's only a matter of time before he does, in fact, have something of an army at his disposal.' Nadya turned her gaze from her son to focus on me. 'But the danger lies in this: We don't know what might happen to Sebastian, when the *prah* of both the head and the body of *La Gargouille* join together within him.'

16. Sebastian

Sharp pain lanced through my arm, bringing me to my senses.

Through my crimson sight, I saw my hand – plunged deep into the wall, claws and fingers completely embedded – just centimeters from Quentin's temple. The stone had cracked in multiple places, like it had been jackhammered. The Marksman's face was contorted, as though still waiting for the blow.

But I hadn't.

Somehow, I'd won, even if for just an instant. The dark thing didn't succeed – even if a part of me wanted it to – in going through with the deadly strike. I wouldn't kill. I refused to kill.

I pressed my face in close to Quentin's, pulling back my lips and flashing all my sharp, jagged teeth. Then, with a huge effort, I yanked myself back, releasing my claws from the stone. I collapsed my wings tight against my back, spun on my heel, and ran.

Without any idea where I was going, I ploughed ahead

in the direction we'd been going. The corridor was widening out and the light growing brighter. At points, I felt I was running on all fours, and other times, on two legs – I was no longer sure of my actions.

Then, abruptly, I screeched to a halt. The corridor had emptied into a giant circular room. It was void of furniture, except for a series of sprawling candelabras lining the wall. Multiple doors led into the room from various hallways. A painted design of entwining dandelion leaves and flowers covered the entire floor.

Above me, a jagged ceiling disappeared into shadows I wouldn't have been able to see through, had it not been for my gargoyle night vision. Below the ceiling, a railed balcony ran around the entire circular space, a perfect platform for looking down into the room. Several thick wooden columns, carved with intricate designs, supported the structure. I had seen this place before, when I'd first arrived, though I'd been hastily pushed through it then.

This was the Court of Shadows.

Only this time, it wasn't empty.

I smelled them before I saw them – four hooded figures stood along the balcony in the shadows, at the farthest point away from me, looking down over the railing. The dark emotions inside me retreated back, like water ebbing from the shore. I sniffed the air once more, as if to convince myself of what I already knew.

Gargoyles.

The middle figure in the group took one step closer to the railing, then slowly lowered its hood. I found myself looking straight into the eyes of someone like me. Not since those early days when I first encountered Anya and her gang – in their original forms – had I seen another gargoyle.

However, this one looking back at me was nothing like them.

He looked older, maybe a few years past Hugo's age, though I knew now that meant nothing, really. The dark lips, shadowy features, and the eerie silver eyes that stared back at me were like looking in a mirror. The gargoyle wore his hair tied back at the base of his neck, and long pointed ears jutted through the pewter color.

It was his face that set him apart from Anya and the others – maybe it was the lack of a sneer or the way he glanced down his nose at me without distain, the way Augustine's gargoyles had – as though I was a disgrace. He reminded me more of Esmeralda, and I suddenly had a glimpse into what she might've been like, before she'd been turned human.

Black mist suddenly engulfed the balcony where the figures stood, and before I could take another breath, the figures disappeared within the smoky haze. The doors to the room shut with thuds and clicks of locks, while as the exact same instant, the figures reappeared on the ground floor, encircling me. Each stood a good eight feet apart from each other, and from me, making me a strange center point of sorts.

One by one, the other figures also lowered their hoods. Four gargoyles gazed on me, and I could do nothing but simply look back. It was a weird sensation, to see them. To see others of …

My kind.

I'd hated that phrase for so long, but now, it fit in a way that it hadn't before. It didn't link me to grotesques and chimeras anymore. It linked me to the four shadowen around me.

One male and three females. Unlike the other types of shadow creatures, who were repulsive mixtures of all kinds of beasts and animals – the gargoyles each held their own unique human-like appearance. They shared the same coloring, canted ears, clawed hands, silver eyes, and probably the sharp jagged teeth, even though I couldn't see them.

They were dressed in outfits that seemed weirdly out of time. Each was fitted with a hood, and the design of their shirts allowed their wings to hang freely. The fabric was a dull, shimmery sort of gray that nearly blended with their skin. It gave the impression that it was all the same – like they'd literally just sprung to life from their cathedral perches and swooped down into the room.

A thought, however, lurked on the edge of my consciousness – one I'd been trying to ignore because I didn't like the way it felt. Grudgingly, I acknowledged its reality: none of the gargoyles had horns like mine. Their marbled gray skin appeared smooth, not traced with weird veins the way mine was – though the blackish color had faded a little since I'd eaten.

I was reminded of my only partially satiated hunger. I swallowed hard as my stomach growled unceremoniously, but I couldn't break eye contact with the head gargoyle. At least, I assumed he was somehow in charge, based on the way the others mimicked his movements.

His sharp silver gaze finally left mine and traveled over my face, noting the same differences between us that I had. The gargoyle's expression changed, molding into one of wary suspicion. The momentary connection I'd experienced with these shadowen faded away.

My head buzzed like a swarm of bees.

By what name are you called?

It was the head gargoyle who'd spoken telepathically. I heard the voice as clearly as if he'd spoken out loud. The tone was low and steady, like those huge bells in cathedral towers.

Sebastian Grey.

At my answer, a hint of a frown turned his dark lip downward.

That name means nothing to us.

I blinked at him, not really sure what to say. It's not like I was some famous guardian from Outcast legends, like Ezzie. Or even an established guardian. I'd been a gargoyle eight months, and almost seven of those had been spent in the confines of Hugo's apartment and the *Gypsy Ink* – where I spent most of my days pretending that none of this existed and that I wasn't what everyone said I was.

I'm a guardian.

I inwardly cringed at my reply. I was stating the obvious, but I wasn't sure what was safe. Should I mention the Corsis? I was clueless about my past or where I'd even come from. I didn't want to unwittingly drag Hugo and the others into something bad. If I claimed Josephine as my charge – not that I was in any way worthy of being her guardian anymore – would that be even worse?

The head gargoyle tilted his head to one side.

You are different.

It wasn't a compliment or an insult, not that I could tell, anyway. I shook it off and formulated my next thought.

Who are you?

No reply to my question buzzed in my brain. Instead, the head gargoyle tilted his head to the side, as if hearing something far off. He raised his hood once more, obscuring his face from view. The other gargoyles did the same.

Without warning, they shadowed again, returning to their original positions above me.

The black mist dissipated as rapidly as it had appeared. The gargoyles took four steps backwards in tandem, retreating from the railing until their winged backs touched the jagged wall. After that, none of them moved or spoke. They seemed, instead, to be waiting on something.

As I stood in the deafening silence of the room, I sensed in these gargoyles the nobility that Esmeralda had often spoken of in the first weeks after my transformation – during those evenings we spent together going over my work when I could no longer attend school.

My vision clouded over in memory.

'This is torture.'

Ezzie glanced up at me from where she'd been reading over my final two assignments of my senior year. 'It's not that bad. However, your grammar leaves something to be desired, not to mention the penmanship ...'

I huffed. 'Try writing with claws, Ezzie.'

Her look held absolutely no sympathy at all. I kicked myself mentally for the hundredth time. It was so easy to forget she'd once been like I was now. If I was being honest with myself, I was actually glad she didn't pity me.

It wasn't something I could take.

'Anyway,' I continued, moving to the window of my room in Hugo's apartment. 'That's not what I meant.'

'I know,' she answered simply, returning to her work.

I peeled back the curtain, and I felt my upper lip curl in disgust as I looked at my gray hands and the long, curved, and sharply tipped claws that used to be my fingernails, so dark a gray they were nearly black against the fabric of the curtain. I saw Josephine's terrified expression flash before me again, as it had over and over since we'd parted ways.

The ever-present ache underneath my ribs sharpened, rubbing me raw from the inside out. I'd lost her, just like I'd lost myself, trapped in this new body that I couldn't understand.

'How could you want this life back?' I asked, turning from the window. 'It's a curse.'

Like she'd been hit with a hot coal, Ezzie leapt up from my desk chair. Her eyes sparkled with a silver tint, and her face was suddenly fierce. 'Never speak that way to me again,' she said, her voice nearly a snarl.

I leaned back, instant regret pouring through me. 'I didn't mean—'

'The life of a gargoyle is a gift, Sebastian Grey.' She bore down on me, her arched brows low over her narrowed eyes. 'It is an honor bestowed upon us by God, and a solemn duty to serve a greater good. You may not see your new calling in this way yet, but you will. Until then, I suggest you step away from yourself long enough to see you are not the only one whose life has taken a turn they did not desire.'

We stood in silence, inches apart, eyes locked on each other. Regret molded into shame inside me. I couldn't find my voice, but it made no difference. Emotions passed between us wordlessly. Finally, Esmeralda turned, seating herself at my desk. She picked up my work and continued on, as if nothing had happened at all.

I shifted my attention back to the window, which looked out into the twilight, the trees, and the edge of the alley. My irritated outburst was gone, but I was left with a hollow, empty sensation of grief. I didn't want this, but the reasons went far deeper than my hatred of my appearance. I closed my eyes and admitted the truth to myself.

I wasn't worthy of it.

A narrow door on the balcony level creaked opened. Several grueling seconds passed, and then I had my answer as to what the gargoyles were waiting for. Through that opening, seven more figures entered the room. These weren't shadow creatures. These were Gypsies, but not like any Outcasts I'd encountered. Even their scents were strange – like different kinds of coppery metals, turned old from the elements and giving off unpleasant smells.

My heart drummed in an uneven pattern against my sternum.

Four were men – some middle-aged and others older. The rest were women, who were roughly the same age. Each wore identical cloaks, made out of some thick silken material, with holes for the arms and held in place at the neck and chest with heavy metal clasps.

Their cloaks were deep purple; so dark they seemed nearly black – like the shade of midnight seen through city lights. Along the edges of the collars, hems, and fronts were letters, embroidered in silver – spelling out words from a language I didn't understand.

The newcomers spanned out across the balcony. The gargoyles had blended perfectly into the shadows, as though they didn't exist at all. I took several steps back as a strange sensation of awed respect wafted through me, as powerful as the individual scents still heavy in my nose. It was as though something in my blood knew who these Gypsies were, but I couldn't place it – like something that had faded away long ago.

The door behind me also opened. Quentin, Donani, and the rest of the Marksmen I'd escaped set foot inside the massive room. Each held similar expressions of thinly masked fury, directed at me, but as soon as their eyes fell on the crowd above, their faces went stoically blank.

I wasn't sure if they'd been waiting for that precise moment to join us, or if they'd been prevented by the locked doors. Either way, between the cold chills provided to my stomach by the Marksmen and the new scents infiltrating my senses, my head spun uncomfortably, and I felt the prick of my claws as my hands turned into fists at my sides.

A woman, standing exactly where the head gargoyle had stood earlier, raised her hands, as if she were quieting down a crowd, though no one had said anything. She was short in stature, but I felt her influence like a heavy blanket over the room. 'Is the assembly ready to begin?'

Assembly? I frantically counted over days in my head. It was Saturday, but I didn't really know what time it was. I had another day left until my trial. Unless I'd mixed up my days while in my strange, hazy state. No, that couldn't be right. No one was here from my clan. And the Queen ...

'Please,' I called up, straining to conquer the gravelly quality of my voice. The animalistic loss of control I'd suffered with the Marksmen wouldn't work for me here – not that it had done me any good, since it seemed I was being escorted here in the first place. 'I don't understand. I'm not supposed to see the High Council until Monday.'

I could hear the shallow breathing of the Marksmen behind me, and the stares of the purple-robed Gypsies pressed down on me, but I kept my focus on the woman. Her thin lips jutted downward as her hands came to rest along the wooden railing.

'We are not the High Council,' she replied.

Then, like a key inside a lock, snapping into place, my brain produced the word I'd been searching for, the faded memory of somewhere else and something else came back to me. I suddenly knew and understood.

The Sobrasi.

17. *Josephine*

A round of black coffee later, the Corsis had moved back into the parlor to continue the discussion. I'd followed with Katie, both of us sinking into a small, antique settee.

I desperately wanted a few minutes to myself, to clear my thoughts and put rational meaning to all this new and terrible information. I glanced dully around the room, only half-listening to the conversations that continued to whir around me like angry yellow jackets.

My sympathy for Hugo and his clan had blossomed over the last twenty-four hours, not to mention my respect for Katie for sticking with me the way she had, with no more proof to hang on than her brief glimpse of the shadowen we'd come up against so far. She hadn't even seen Sebastian.

I pressed the heel of my hand against my chest. *Sebastian.* This couldn't be real. Not after he'd overcome so many things to finally accept who he was. For me, I'd only just begun to put words to my feelings for him – but they were still fragile. I'd been afraid they might crumble before I could really examine them.

And now, this.

I felt the spark of anger. I wasn't going to sit here, curling up into a useless ball while everyone around me argued over what to do. Maybe I hadn't come into my own yet, by Outcasts standards, but I was *me* – and that version of myself had nothing to do with titles or expectations.

But I needed to find out more before I could act. I pushed my feelings to the side and I brought my focus back to the room.

I wasn't the only one in the parlor who'd gotten control of themselves and the situation. Hugo stood in front of the window, his expression smoother than glass. As if responding to some unspoken cue, the rest of the Corsis ceased their talking and turned attentive eyes on him – including his parents.

'Okay,' said Hugo, steady voiced. 'We need to figure out our next move.'

'I think it's obvious,' said Kris. 'We've gotta get Sebastian out of there.'

'Yeah, and how are we going to do that?' demanded James. 'They don't set bail for shadow creatures. And there's no way the High Council is just going to release him to us before the trial, especially not with this crack-pot story.'

'We're not telling the High Council anything,' said Hugo. 'Not yet.'

Zindelo nodded affirmatively. 'A wise choice, I think. If the Marksmen of the Court were to hear any of this, they might take it upon themselves to kill Sebastian straight away, to protect the Court.'

I thought about Quentin, staying somewhere in our underground Haven. In all the time Sebastian had lived with us at the Circe, I'd never believed Quentin would ever do anything to truly hurt him, even if only for my sake. But what if I was wrong?

Kris glared at Hugo. 'So, what, we just let the trial happen?'

Hugo scratched his chin. 'That might be the best thing. Right now, we know Sebastian's protected by Outcast law until a verdict is given. We know the Council has already been summoned, so the trial's definitely going to happen.'

'But aren't we forgetting about Augustine?' asked Vincent. 'The longer Sebastian's down there, the easier it's going to be for that *marimé* scum to do whatever mumbo jumbo crap he's gotten up his sleeve.'

'As you've said, he's *marimé*,' said Zindelo. 'That status is his disadvantage here. Apart from whatever meeting he managed to arrange with the Queen, we can rest assured he won't be allowed to stay. My thought is, he waits for the trial as well, expecting the Council to find him guilty.'

Hugo pondered this for several seconds. 'The trial is a day and a half away. There's still a chance they'll find Sebastian innocent. In that case, he'll be released back to us.' He glanced briefly at me.

'And if they rule him guilty?' asked James.

'His sentence will be the *kokkero*,' said Zindelo.

I saw Esmeralda visibly flinch from across the room. 'The worst of all punishments for a guardian.'

'The return to stone,' explained Zindelo. 'Never to awaken again.'

'Death,' said Esmeralda.

Nadya raised her hand. 'Performing the *kokkero* is a skill that hasn't been used in many years. Only those of *Sobrasi* learning may do it. If he's found guilty, the High Council would be required to bring in someone of our order to carry out the sentence.'

A ghost of a smile flickered across Hugo's countenance. 'Let me guess. You've already made the offer.'

Nadya returned her son's smile – guarded but sincere. 'As soon as Esmeralda told us of Karl's murder and the *kris*, we contacted the Council and made them aware of our presence. Though we had few details, we knew we had to prevent any other *Sobrasi* from having access to *La Gargouille*.'

'Sebastian,' corrected Hugo, before I could speak.

We exchanged a swift look. I felt the connected unity we shared.

James shifted in his chair, looking dubious. 'You're telling us the High Council doesn't keep people like you around to do that sort of thing? Seems like it'd be common sense, when you've got a whole world of shadow creatures you're constantly dealing with.'

'How many gargoyles have you seen in your lifetime?' snapped Ezzie in such a curt tone that James' eyebrows lifted nearly to his hairline. 'Only a fraction of our number came to this country after the Sundering.'

'The *Sobrasi* and their knowledge remains in Europe, with the Old Clans,' said Nadya. 'With the success of the Marks clan in training shadowen killers, the High Council decided there was no need for people like us.'

Zindelo sighed heavily. 'There were very few gargoyles here, as Esmeralda said. Unfortunately, as the decades passed, gargoyles came to be feared at much as the creatures they fought. Over time, as the role of the Marksmen grew in importance, the noble past of the guardian was largely dismissed as nothing but fairy tales and legends.'

'Which led to growing animosity towards the ones who should have our respect,' said Nadya. She shifted her gaze to Esmeralda and dipped her head slightly. 'The true guardians of the Roma.'

Ezzie sat back into the shadows in the corner of the parlor. 'Many of my kind were forced to abandon their calling and flee for their lives, lest they be hunted down like grotesques.' Her silvery eyes faded to hazel, as though the life had been sucked out. 'A few turned on the Roma, their fear changing to hatred. They became traitors to their purpose. The fates of some of these gargoyles, I know. Others, I do not.'

I noticed Hugo's stare had not left Esmeralda since she'd first spoken. There was a definitely a strange kind of formality between them most of the time, but every once in a while—

'Which brings us back to Sebastian's trial,' Zindelo was saying, pulling me back. 'There have been no documented cases of gargoyles sent before the High Council since the Sundering. We can only assume they would not conduct this as a normal *Kris Romani*.'

'Which means it would be kept secret from the general population of the Court,' said Nadya, continuing her husband's thoughts, 'as is only done for the most serious of crimes. But this works in our favor. If he is deemed guilty, then Zindelo and I would be asked to prepare the *kokkero*, which is a lengthy process …'

'Which would buy us some time,' said Hugo.

'And the way to rescue him,' I said.

I was startled by the sound of my own voice, ringing out in the room. I hadn't meant to speak, but the words came before I could stop them. The others turned to me, and I met all their stares, one by one.

'Exactly,' replied Hugo, with a satisfied nod.

'But what about Sebastian?' Vincent asked. 'I mean, what about the way you said he was when you saw him today? If he's that bad off right now, how do we know he'll even last until the trial? What if he flips out and the Marksmen decide to end it?'

Hugo walked through the middle of the room; his pace like a somber march. He tugged at his goatee again, and I knew he was replaying his visit to the Court of Shadows in his mind. 'Sebastian said the *prah* would wear off. I don't know how many times Augustine's used it on him, but he seemed to know. I think he's going to start eating from here on out, which will help. He'll pull himself together.'

'How can you know for sure?' asked Kris.

Hugo turned on his heel and faced me directly. 'Because no matter what happens, Sebastian is still a guardian,' he said. I felt a weird fluttering in my stomach as he approached and put a hand on my shoulder. 'And he knows his charge is right here.'

18. *Josephine*

I sat alone at the kitchen table.

The discussion had come to a halt after it was decided that we would let the trial unfold. It seemed as much of a win-win situation as we were going to get. I didn't believe anyone actually thought Sebastian would be found innocent – especially after all the things that had been happening up north and the rumors flying around the *kumpania*.

Attention would be given more to how we were going to get Sebastian out of the Court of Shadows. Zindelo and Nadya were convinced that they'd be able to put Sebastian into a sleeping state – one that would make him appear like he was a statue. It wasn't permanent. Unfortunately, it didn't answer the question of how we'd be able to leave the Court with him.

Or how we could fix Sebastian after he woke up.

I rested my elbows wearily on the table. The last time I looked at the wall clock it was almost four in the morning. Now that things had settled down, I was feeling it. My head was so heavy I could barely keep it upright.

The dandelion pendant had worked its way from underneath my scoop-necked shirt and hung freely. It caught the light from the overhead chandelier and sparked to life, like golden fire. I studied its depths until I felt myself sinking drowsily into a moment from the past.

I caressed the dandelion pendant between my thumb and forefinger as Sebastian knelt beside the couch in my RV's small living room. The ice pack he'd brought from the kitchen was uncomfortably cold against my strained knee, but the rest of me felt oddly warm. I reached behind me to adjust one of the pillows, and the ice slipped. Sebastian caught it, guiding the pack back into place.

I glanced up to find him looking at me with an expression that made me hurt somewhere deep inside. His eyes, which I'd found so foreign at first, were such a bright silver that, at certain times, they took on a glow – not like a reflection, but more as if they were lit from the inside. The pupils were smaller than normal and not entirely circular, which made the surrounding silver stand out and turned his eyes even more inhuman.

Impulsively, I placed my hand over his and squeezed gently. His dark eyebrows lifted for the quickest of seconds; like he was surprised I'd touched him. Then his face went still again, unreadable.

'So, what else can you do?' I asked. 'Besides saving stubborn girls who don't listen to their doctors, I mean. I remember that day in the cave under the bridge; you could see in the dark.'

My free hand searched out my necklace automatically as I remembered how he'd asked to be my guardian and our dandelions had touched – my pendant, his tattoo. And then, only minutes later, facing down the shadowy figures on the bridge, Sebastian had changed forever.

'Yeah, I can,' he said after a few moments. He offered me a shrug and a trace of a smile. Then he proceeded to tell me how his night vision worked.

'That's gotta be cool,' I said.

'Well, it keeps me from stubbing my toe on the way to the bathroom,' he replied.

His humor, always his humor.

I laughed as my heart warmed underneath my shirt. As long as he was willing to make light of things, I felt as though I could continue, which I did. I asked about his hearing – trying hard not to stare at his ears – then about his other senses. He answered my questions politely, though I saw the darkened tinge in his cheeks as he ran his hands through his pewter hair.

I also felt his discomfort keenly, in that undefined place inside where we shared our strange kind of connection. So I kept my questions confined to his abilities, rather than anything about his appearance.

I'd told Sebastian once that he was still the same person, and I'd meant it. The shape of his face, the curve of his smile, even the way he'd crinkle up his nose before making a funny comment. All of it was the same boy from school.

But he had *changed, and I couldn't pretend it was just what was obvious on the outside. I heard it in his voice. I saw it behind his eyes. The months we'd spent apart after the Circe left town had changed me, too – not in the same way, but I knew I looked at life differently. I'd only just gotten to know Sebastian before he became my guardian. Now, I was getting to know him again, but slowly this time, and with more deliberate steps.*

I bit my lip. There was so much I wanted to ask him – a thousand questions about this new person he'd turned into. Out of curiosity, sure, but more than that. Out of wanting to understand, of wanting, somehow, to comfort him, to let him know ...

But I didn't dare tread into that territory. It was way too fragile for him. I knew because I'd catch him – when he thought I wasn't looking – staring at his hands, turning them over, palms down, to examine his claws – all the time with such a look of self-loathing that I felt it like a slap. I'd seen the way his gaze drifted to the edges of his wings as he walked, again with that same haunted and awful look. But never, ever when he knew he was being observed.

He took their stares – the others in the camp that made me ashamed of my troupe. Sebastian took everything with a firmly controlled grace that I hoped I would one day be capable of myself. Only the Marksmen seemed to affect him. And, I was forced to admit, Quentin, most of all.

I realized I was still squeezing Sebastian's hand, and I quickly let it go.

'Hey,' said Katie, leaning over me. 'You're going to break that.'

I shook myself awake and I glanced down at the dandelion pendant in my hand. I wasn't aware I'd taken it off, yet here it was, clenched so tightly between my fingers that when I opened my hand, I could see the indentions the edges of the glass left in my skin.

Katie yawned loudly. She pulled out a chair; its legs scraped gratingly against the tile floor. She plopped down next to me. 'Josie, talk to me.'

'There's nothing to say, really. You heard everything.'

'That's not what I mean.'

I smoothed my hair across the back of my neck and replaced the necklace, tucking it under my collar. I stretched my legs underneath the table. They felt stiff and sore. I touched my right leg, feeling the large rip in my jeans I'd gotten from sliding across the road. I hadn't given it a thought since we'd returned, but now, I became aware of a dull throbbing in my shin.

'Josie.'

Katie's voice was less soft. More demanding. Her emotions were always on display, turning feelings turned into words as fast as she felt them. I felt a prick of jealousy towards her open nature, immediately followed by a stab of guilt. Hadn't I confessed to Sebastian just days ago that I didn't really have any real friends? But, that wasn't true.

'I'm sorry,' I said, not as a cop-out this time. 'Katie, I'm really, really sorry. You've been ... I mean, I couldn't ask for a better friend. And I know I've said that before, but I'm going to prove it to you this time, I promise.'

Katie shrugged. 'Hey, you don't have to prove anything to me.'

'Yeah,' I replied. 'I do.'

She kept a casual expression on her face, but she couldn't hide the hint of smug triumph. 'Look, I know you think I don't get all of this. And, well, maybe you're right. A little. But I get the stuff that counts, I really do. And what counts the most is being here for you, okay? I'm sorry if I'm pushy. Well, no, I take that back. I'm not sorry.' A grin brightened her features. 'People like you need it sometimes. Otherwise, I'd never get any details. Just like some other people I know.' Katie rolled her eyes. 'I swear, you and Sebastian really were made for each other.'

Made for each other.

The words turned me hot and cold, all at once. Sebastian and I were bonded, no doubt. Guardian and charge. I knew now there was so much more. But there was Quentin. There was my family, my position – and the unclaimed throne, which I had pushed so far away from me that I didn't even want to see the Queen.

The Queen.

I let out a frustrated cry. 'What am I doing?'

Katie looked at me doubtfully. 'You mean, besides sitting here talking to me?'

'I need to go see my aunt.'

'The ... Queen?' asked Katie, using the word hesitantly.

'I told Hugo I'd wait until he got back from the Court of Shadows. Well, he's back, and I need to see her.' I pushed myself away from the table with more force than was required. 'I know we have a plan for what to do if Sebastian's found guilty, but I don't *want* him to be found guilty, Katie. He didn't kill Karl.' I felt a burning in the back of my throat. 'He's never done anything wrong. He doesn't deserve that.'

'But the Queen's out of town, remember?' said Katie. 'That Marksman guy with the D name told Hugo she was gone on business and wouldn't be back until the trial. Right?'

The air deflated out of me like a balloon. 'Right.'

Just like that, I was back to that helpless lump of nothing again. I smoothed my shirt over my stomach, using the movement to calm my fidgeting fingers. There was a time I used to consider myself patient, content to wait for things and trust in the structure of my clan and of our ways.

The floorboard in the hall creaked, and right after that, Esmeralda appeared in the kitchen. She didn't stop at the table, and she didn't even look our way. Instead, she headed straight for the back door, undoing the chain lock with one hand.

'Where are you going?' I asked, standing.

She opened the door. 'Out.'

'No, you don't,' I said, suddenly finding a mass of hot anger that I thought had cooled. 'Not by yourself.'

Ezzie glanced over her shoulder. 'I must. The chimera from earlier has returned. Whether it came because it was tracking Hugo's parents, or because it smelled so much Gypsy flesh in one place, I can't be certain. But since I'm the only protector this clan currently has, I'm going to make sure it does not threaten any under this roof.'

Katie screwed up her face. 'Gypsy *flesh*?'

Esmeralda studied her with the patience of someone contemplating the actions of a small child. 'Yes, Katie Lewis. Shadow creatures need meat. For a chimera – vile abominations that they are – this isn't limited to just partaking of wild animals.'

Katie's eyes went super wide. 'Does that mean that gargoyles … do you … I mean, you don't do that, too … do you?'

The patient expression warped quickly into one of offense. Ezzie straightened to her full height, shoulders back. 'That would be murder,' she replied darkly. 'Punishable by death, as well it should be. Human life is precious, and to take it would be to sin against the Maker himself.'

Katie backed up. 'Sorry, I didn't mean—'

'This world is new to you,' said Ezzie. 'I realize there is much you don't understand and even more that you haven't yet seen.' Her countenance softened. 'You're forgiven.'

Katie smiled for a second, then puckered her lips. 'Okay,

so chimeras are evil, but that doesn't really explain why these things need to ea*t people*.'

To my surprise, Ezzie didn't seem irritated, or even offended, anymore. There was a strange, ghostliness in her eyes.

'It's not a need,' I said, understanding. 'It's a want.'

Ezzie nodded. 'Keveco Romany, in his wisdom, was able to take what was once a force of evil destruction and shape it into something good – defenders of the Roma, pledged to the safety and justice of those who did not have such. But without a human component inside them, shadowen are no different from the terrible monster from whom we are descended.'

'The terrible monster,' I repeated. '*La Gargouille*.'

A conflicted look passed over Ezzie's features like a dark cloud. 'Yes.'

My throat closed up, like I was being choked. I couldn't accept it, the claim that Sebastian encompassed everything that was *La Gargouille*. It felt like a never-ending nightmare, worse than any I'd been subjected to all those months before he came into my life.

No, it wasn't that I couldn't accept it. I *refused* to accept it. Sebastian hadn't become a monster after he transformed from that sweet, shy boy into a living, breathing gargoyle. And he wasn't a monster now.

The assurance of that fact awakened something in me, gave me new life and energy. 'Ezzie, if you're going out there to fight a chimera, you're going to need help. You said yourself it was only your reputation that kept it from attacking before.'

'That's true,' she replied. 'But this time, I am more prepared.'

She turned around fully now, and I saw a weapon at her side. It resembled a medieval mace, but each of the spikes sparkled with a sheer diamond coating. My eyes widened. I knew how rare diamond weapons were, and I'd never seen anyone apart from a Marksman wield one this large.

'Where did you get that?'

She held it up to the light, creating an odd picture. A woman with red-streaked black hair, standing in a farmhouse-style kitchen, dressed in jeans and a t-shirt, with her eyes sparking silver and a glittering mace in her grip.

'Zindelo,' she replied. 'The *Sobrasi* also have access to such defenses.'

She stepped out onto the covered back porch, but Katie and I were on her heels. Ezzie was nearly down the steps when she abruptly stopped, forcing us to do the same before we ploughed into her. Esmeralda was only a couple of inches taller than me, but at that moment, she might as well have been a skyscraper.

'This is not where you need to be, *Kralitsa*.'

I brushed aside the formal title. 'I'm sick of being helpless.'

She paused at that, her forehead creasing, and lines appearing on either side of her mouth, aging her in the way a hard life ages some people. 'I know,' she replied, in an empathetic tone. 'Perhaps you won't be much longer. For now, you and Katie go back inside and wait for me until I return.'

Esmeralda Lucian leapt off the last step, mace raised menacingly. She rounded the back of the house and melted into the oppressive night. I waited a few seconds, listening carefully. Then I eased down the stairs.

Katie grabbed my arm, the question written plainly in

her eyes. I found myself smiling back at her, more than I had all night, more than I probably should have. I pulled my knife from my back pocket and shrugged.

'I don't always do what I'm told.'

19. Josephine

We hid behind the hedges lining the back yard of the *Dandelion Inn*. My tennis shoes were soundless on the thick grass, but Katie's sequined flip-flops made a slapping noise with every step. I wasn't sure how good Esmeralda's hearing and scent were as a former gargoyle, but I didn't want to make things any more obvious than they already were.

'What are we doing, exactly?' Katie whispered harshly in my ear.

'I just want to make sure Ezzie's okay.'

We got as far as the garden gate when I saw Ezzie pull up short in the center of a wide row of tomato plants and look in our direction. I hadn't tried to persuade Katie not to follow me, since I knew she was just as stubborn as me, but she was scared.

Fear wasn't a bad thing. It was a natural part of my balancing acts at the Circe. Not too much of it, though, just enough to sharpen your senses and keep you aware of your surroundings.

The houses on either side of the inn were still dark. It

was early Sunday morning, I realized, which meant no one was stirring yet. The sky had shifted from bluish-black to nearly gray, clinging to the last remnants of night.

I stared hard into the garden, straining to see. Ezzie's attention shifted back to the rows of plants, and she hunched low. The mace glittered faintly, catching some bit of light that filtered through the curtained windows along the back of the house.

The thick branches of the overhanging trees swayed under the stirrings of a breeze. I brushed a strand of hair out of my face. It was slick with sweat. The air around me thickened, humid and sticky, like it did after a rain shower.

Esmeralda glanced to the left, and then she ducked into one of the rows. I moved forward and hurried along the length of a line of potatoes, trying to catch sight of her again. Katie copied me, but her shoulder pressed into mine. An inhuman screech sounded inside the garden.

I shuddered and looked at Katie. She immediately read my thoughts. She shook her head vehemently, and when she spoke, her voice was a harsh, snapping whisper.

'Ezzie told us to stay inside.'

'What if she needs help?'

'She's *one of these things!* I think she knows what she's doing.'

I turned the knife over in my hand for a better grip and started down the row. Katie, for all her protests, fell in right beside me. Up ahead, a clump of tall sunflowers swayed violently in a suddenly chilly breeze. The hair on the back of my neck prickled in warning. The screech rang out again.

'Katie, maybe you should go back,' I said, keeping my eyes on the sunflowers. 'Just in case.'

'I'm not a Gypsy,' she huffed. 'It wants to eat you, not me, remember.'

I jerked to a stop. 'That doesn't make you immune to an attack. I doubt it's going to care who its victims are. I've got a knife and a little more experience.' I flicked my gaze briefly in her direction. 'If something happened to you, I'd never forgive myself. And your parents ... what would it do to them?'

'Oh, so your death is just going to be totally okay with everyone? Seriously, this is stupid. If you really think Ms Lucian is in over her head, then let's go back and get some of the guys. I mean, they're huge and tattoo-ey, surely they'd be more than—'

'Katie.'

It was no longer a request from me, and she knew it. Her pale face turned an ugly shade of red. 'Fine. Have it your way. I'm going back. But I'm telling Hugo you're out here. And I don't care if I just sounded like a five-year-old.'

She whirled around, blonde hair fanning out behind her, and trounced back to the house, like we'd gotten in a disagreement over what movie to watch. I hoped I hadn't done any irreparable damage to our friendship – but as soon as she was gone, I felt a hundred times lighter. I prayed she'd eventually understand.

Clenching the knife tightly, I dropped my body as low as I could and waited. Scenarios played out in my head as the cold breeze bent the sprawling limbs above me. Minutes passed and my legs began to cramp. I shifted to my knees in the dirt. What if Ezzie had already killed the chimera or, at least, frightened it off? But if so, then where was she?

Sebastian told me once how Esmeralda had single-handedly fought off the three gargoyles during my ribbon act at the Circe, saving his life in the process. Whatever she lacked in her former abilities, she definitely had gained in other ways. She could still shadow. I'd seen her do it myself. Katie was right; Ezzie knew what she was doing.

Still, a nagging sensation pulled at me. The breeze continued, frigid now. Something wasn't right. I hesitated, torn between going forward and heading back. I clenched my teeth and stood up quickly.

A dark form loomed in my periphery.

I spun, knife out. The figure ducked out of the way.

'Whoa, hold up!' growled a deep voice.

I clamped a hand over my mouth to keep from screaming. My heart pounded in my ears. Hugo stood in front of me, his eyes dark and glittering in the pre-dawn light.

Before I could say anything, another screech – ear piercing and deadly – pealed out from somewhere to our right, followed by a woman's cry. Hugo charged through the vegetable plants, and I didn't hesitate this time. I ran behind the Corsi leader, letting him barrel through the tall plants and wired cages, clearing out a path.

He had a weapon in his hand as well, similar to Ezzie's. We burst into a clear patch of garden. Esmeralda crouched, surrounded by three shadowen. One sprang at her and she swung her mace with both hands. It connected with a sickening crunch against the creature's temple, and the feline-looking grotesque spun through the air, landing with an equally disgusting thud.

A second grotesque, a lizard thing, screeched with fury and reared its head. Hugo let out a yell of his own and rushed in, aiming for the creature's feathered wings. The diamond spikes in his mace drew blood.

The third shadowen watched the proceedings with a

wicked gleam in its solid silver eyes. It was a chimera, but it wasn't the same one as before. It was female. Black, oozing drool seeped from the corner of the chimera's mouth as it fixed those ungodly eyes on me and sniffed the air. The chimera's gaze shifted down my body, resting on the rip in my jeans. I glanced down and noticed the dried blood.

The chimera's black lips pulled back, revealing wicked teeth. As I stared into that face, a wave of nausea crashed up my throat. I knew that face. Sebastian had called her Anya – one of Augustine's failed experiments. Recognition clicked in the chimera's eyes as well, making it look even hungrier for a piece of me.

I raised my knife. The breeze caught the cold sweat on my neck, lifting it away. My pendant burned uncomfortably hot against my tender skin. A warning? Anya crept towards me on feet and legs that were more animal shaped than human. Her dark, crackled skin moved across muscles in her neck and arms as she spread her bat-like wings.

'Sebastian,' I heard myself say.

A painful shock, like a surge of electricity, went up the back of my neck and skittered across my scalp. Suddenly, in that strange place where we shared that bond, something sparked to life and buzzed through my brain. I squeezed my eyes shut and poured everything I had into it.

Sebastian …

I opened my eyes. Ezzie and Hugo battled the grotesques around me, but Anya continued to advance. I searched frantically for something else to defend myself with, though I knew it was useless. I flipped the knife over in my hand and threw it as hard as I could.

Sebastian …

The name resounded in my head, an internal scream. The

knife found a home deep in the chimera's thigh. Anya roared, her talon-hand going to the wound. Thick black blood poured out as she ripped the knife from her skin. My heart hit the bottom of my stomach.

This was it.

Tears wet my face. A prayer crossed my lips. Then I cried out inside my head once last time.

Sebastian!

A white flash exploded all around me, following by a shattering pain. I felt myself crumpling to the ground, had a vague knowledge than it was a blow to my head from the chimera. But even that thought was gone as quick as it came. The white faded to gray, then black.

Then nothing at all.

*

The wind rushed through my hair, yanking it from the clip I used to hold it out of my eyes. The air was uncomfortably cool on my face, and I shivered, but only for a second. Sebastian, as if sensing I was cold, pulled me a little closer to his chest as he carried me towards Copper Mountain.

I studied his wings as we flew. In the beginning, I thought they looked like giant bat wings, but after watching Sebastian get his wing stitched up by Karl and seeing them close up, I'd changed my mind. His wings were like something you'd see on a dragon, with large, curved talons making up the end of each center point. They were easily a foot taller than his head when they were folded in – unless weighed down and hidden inside his long jacket.

I was glad he was finally done with wearing the last remaining bit of his disguise, even though I knew it was a hard decision for him. He didn't talk about it, but I knew. I watched the light from the overcast sky reflect across the thinner parts of his wings. The leathery-looking skin glistened. It was like staring at an oily patch of water in the road and seeing the refraction of colors inside the darkness.

His clawed hands held me securely, but gently, as his wings pumped several times, increasing our altitude. I glanced at his fingers, wondering if his feet were anything like his hands. I'd never seen him without his beat-up pair of Converse. Sebastian suddenly tilted one wing and angled his body. We veered to the right and picked up speed.

'This is amazing, Sebastian!' I tightened my arms around his neck. 'I feel like I'm dreaming!'

Something jostled me awake.

I opened my eyes, expecting to find Sebastian staring down at me with his silver-moon eyes, but instead, it was Hugo, holding me propped up in his arm. I blinked away the confusion, then blinked until he was in totally in focus.

'What happened?' I demanded, struggling to sit up.

Ezzie knelt nearby, wiping her blood-splattered mace in a clump of grass. 'I could've sworn I told you and Katie to remain inside,' she said, her attention focused on her task. When she finished, she looked at me with narrowed eyes. 'Why should I be surprised you didn't listen?'

'Funny,' said Hugo, shifting his gaze to Ezzie. 'I pretty much said the same thing to you.'

I twisted free from Hugo's grasp and maneuvered into a more upright position. The movement made my vision swim. 'I sent Katie back to the house, but I couldn't leave until I made sure you were okay.'

'And are you?' asked Hugo, still looking at her.

A trace of a smile rested at the corner of Ezzie's mouth. Then she glared back at him, chin raised. 'Of course I'm okay. I told you, even in my current form, I am still better at dealing with shadowen than you are, Gypsy.'

'Not anymore,' he said, patting the second diamond-coated mace, which was lying on the ground beside him. 'Not since we got these babies. Did you see how easy that beast went down?' He nodded smugly at me. 'We killed the groties,' he said, jutting his thumb towards the two stone bodies in the garden clearing. 'But we don't know what happened to the chimera. It just took off.' He snapped his fingers. 'Just like that.'

I tried to stand, but Hugo held me by the shoulder. 'Don't get up. Not until we get you looked at.' His eyes drifted towards my temple. 'You've got a pretty nasty cut.'

My parched throat felt like sandpaper. 'It was Anya.'

'Yes,' said Ezzie, pursing her lips together. 'I had suspected that Augustine's minions had survived your Marksmen's attack outside the Circe. Now we know for sure.'

'So that other chimera—'

'Was Matthias,' she finished. A shadow crossed her face. 'I didn't realize at first. His scent has changed, even his voice. He is nothing of the gargoyle I once knew, traitor though he was, even then.'

I probed the side of my head, feeling stickiness. 'But what happened? She was going to kill me.' I glanced at my blood-stained fingers, wincing as I became conscious of the pulsing at my temple. 'She would've killed me.'

Hugo pulled out his phone and tapped out a quick message, and then he stuffed it in back in his pocket, all the while still holding me firm in the crook of his other arm. 'I was hoping you could answer that.'

'I'm okay,' I said, pushing against him. He reluctantly allowed me to sit up straight. 'I don't have a clue. I mean, I got her in the leg with my knife, which really only made her mad. She was coming for me, and then ...'

'And then,' said Hugo patiently when I didn't continue.

'I called out to Sebastian,' I said, shoving aside the grogginess I felt, forcing my memory to clear. 'I don't know why I did it, but I just knew I was supposed to. I yelled it in my head.'

Ezzie moved quickly forward, grasping my leg. 'How did it feel?'

I frowned. 'Feel?'

'When you spoke to him,' she replied.

'I didn't speak to him. I just said his name in my mind.' I reached up and pressed my hand against the back of my neck. 'No, wait. I did feel something. It was like electricity. A buzzing, right back here.'

The lines and creases reappeared on Ezzie's face. 'And what else?'

'The chimera hit me,' I said slowly, piecing together those last few seconds before I lost consciousness. 'But then, it was like ... like she'd hit a brick wall, or something. She froze. I saw the hatred in her eyes; she wanted to rip me apart. But she couldn't. Something stopped her.' My heart beat faster, and I clasped my dandelion pendant as warmth filled every part of me. 'Ezzie, I think ... I think it was Sebastian.'

20. Josephine

'Have you ever experienced this before?' Ezzie questioned.

I massaged my neck to keep my mind off the pain in my temple, and to distract myself from the weird feeling in my stomach. 'Not like this.' I hesitated. But maybe Ezzie would understand. I licked my dry lips. 'I could read his emotions before, but there were times that I felt, like if I tried really hard, I could do something more. I don't know if that makes sense.'

'You communicated with him tonight,' said Ezzie, 'in a way that goes even beyond the unspoken communication shared between guardians and charges through their bond.' She stood and stared up at the night.

'The gargoyle telepathy,' I said.

She nodded.

'The gargoyle *what*?' said Hugo, looking back and forth between us.

At that moment, Nadya Corsi appeared from around the sunflowers. She held a small bag in her arms. She turned a quick, casual circle around the space, taking everything in.

The three of us watched quietly as she pulled out a glass vial from the bag and popped off the lid.

She approached the bodies of the dead grotesques and sprinkled the contents over them. It was the same stuff Quentin and his men used to dispose of shadowen bodies. Within seconds, the stone corpses crumbled, turned to dust, and floated eerily away on the breeze.

Nadya came to me next, shooing Hugo away like he was a kid. She knelt down and took my chin between her fingers, turning my head to examine me. 'You're lucky I'm here,' she said. 'Shadowen wounds can fester if not treated properly.'

She pulled a smaller pouch, a metal box, and a wooden bowl from her bag, reminding me of a sort of weird Mary Poppins. She poured light gray powder into the bowl and added a sprig of some kind of plant that she'd taken from the box. She crumbled it all between her fingers.

'What's that?' I asked.

'Shadow medicine,' she said, like I should know.

Nadya licked her thumb and stuck it in the mixture. She then placed her thumb directly on my temple. I scrunched up my face, caught between curiosity and total disgust. But the pain immediately stopped. Nadya removed her hand and studied the wound with satisfaction.

'Better,' she said.

She licked her other thumb and used it to wipe away the weird mixture. It was gross, but it worked. My headache disappeared, and I felt worlds better.

'Thanks,' I managed.

Hugo helped me to my feet. The garden was still, and the breeze had ceased, leaving the air cool, but not like it was before.

'Ezzie,' I said, turning to her. 'I don't understand. How

could I talk to Sebastian? I thought only gargoyles could communicate with each other. Do you think it had anything to do with this?' I undid the necklace and held it out.

Nadya stepped forward, tilting her head to the side. 'Is this your *sclav*?'

'Yes.'

'May I?'

I dropped the pendant into her open palm. She rubbed her fingers along the glass, examining it with the same intensity as she had my wound. It felt like a painful eternity since I'd held the same necklace out to Sebastian, allowing his tattoo brand and my Outcast trinket to link us together.

'Who in your clan has the power to initiate a *sclav*?' Nadya questioned, a hint of suspicion in her level tone. 'Only those of Corsi blood or members of the *Sobrasi* have the ability to tattoo brands and awaken bonding objects such as this.'

'Nobody,' I replied, my uneasiness rising.

Nadya tapped the surface. 'It's also a dandelion.'

'It belonged to … to my boyfriend's grandmother.'

As the sentence left my mouth, I flinched. Saying the word out loud didn't feel right. That's what Quentin was. My boyfriend. My intended. A cold tendril curled around my shoulders.

'This belongs to the Marks family?' said Hugo, drawing up like he thought the necklace might bite.

'His grandmother was from the Harven clan originally,' I replied. 'At least, that's what he told me, anyway. He thought I'd like it, you know, because of the dandelion and the Circe logo.'

'Hmm,' said Nadya, handing it back to me. 'Does it change at all?'

I fastened it around my neck, feeling instantly better with it securely in place. 'Well, it gets warm sometimes. Hot, even.' I paused, quickly going back over the last few minutes in my mind, and then going further back, to Matthias' attack out on the street. 'Do you think this has something to do with me being able to communicate with Sebastian?'

Esmeralda looked skeptical. 'I've never heard of such.'

'There were once Harvens in the *Sobrasi*,' said Nadya. 'It's not a stretch to think that perhaps his grandmother's necklace had once been used in some other shadowen manner.' She packed up her bag and held it in her hands. 'But I'm afraid there's no way of knowing.'

My heart raced. Was it possible that I could talk to him the same way he did with Esmeralda? A smile crept across my lips. Even without Sebastian beside me, I sensed a closeness with him that flooded me with an overwhelming sense of peace.

'Sebastian stopped Anya from killing me,' I said.

Hugo rested his mace against his shoulder and shot me a strange look under raised brows. 'You really think he had something to do with it?'

'Yeah, I do,' I said. 'Don't ask me to explain it, because it's just like everything else we're dealing with. It doesn't make any sense, and I don't understand any of it. But I just ... *felt* it.'

Hugo rolled his eyes up towards the trees and shrugged. 'Well, who am I to question anything going on around here? Next you'll be telling me that he can shoot laser beams out of his eyes, and you know what? I'll probably believe you.' He turned his gaze in the direction of the trees beyond the back yard. 'Meanwhile, let's get back inside. I've had about all I can handle tonight.' He grimaced. 'And I think I pulled a muscle.' He rotated his shoulders around and stretched his arm.

Ezzie smiled at him. 'You should start training with the Marksmen.'

He grinned back at her. 'That hurts.'

*

We made our way through the pre-dawn darkness back to the inn. The guys were in the parlor. Kris looked up from his game of solitaire. Vincent continued flipping through television stations. And James let out a really loud snore from the couch. Hugo propped his mace against the stair railing and plopped into the leather armchair by the window. I kept walking, straight through the parlor and up the stairs. I needed a shower. And I wanted to talk to Katie.

She wasn't in our room. I figured I must've missed her in one of the many rooms downstairs. Or maybe she was avoiding me. I closed the bathroom door and turned on the water. Katie didn't usually hold grudges, but I *had* been pretty firm with her. I knew she felt left out of this whole thing, and I didn't know how to change that.

Having her here was harder than I thought it'd be.

I got out of the shower and put on some fresh clothes. Once back in our bedroom, I stood in front of the long, oval wall mirror and studied my reflection. The dark circles under my eyes glared back at me.

I fastened my pendant around my neck and stared at it carefully through the mirror. It had been Quentin's gift to me and yet, it had been the very thing to bring Sebastian into my life. The irony of that occurrence had never truly hit me until that moment.

I pictured Quentin in the Court of Shadows, interacting with people and charming them as only he could do. He'd always had a way with others. Even if his sense of duty prevented him from physically hurting Sebastian, would he go so far as to try and sway Council members against Sebastian before the trial?

I didn't know the answer to anything, anymore. For all his heart-felt assurances, Quentin had never trusted me when it came to Sebastian. The bond he knew Sebastian and I shared was a raw spot with him. I had tried – and found myself *still* trying – to understand where he was coming from. But it was more than just his feelings about my being sealed to Sebastian. Quentin had been trained his whole life to protect us from shadow creatures who hated us. He refused to see beyond that.

He wouldn't accept what I knew was true.

And now, I was beginning to doubt he ever would.

The bed looked inviting as I dumped my old clothes into my bag. I really could use some sleep. But Katie first. I stepped into the hall and the wooden floor creaked in protest. I shut the door behind me. Instead of going down the main staircase, I turned right and took the smaller, secondary flight of stairs down to the lower level. This one opened into the study, which I'd only glimpsed in passing so far.

The room was decorated with rustic-looking rugs and old paintings with gold frames. A tiny desk lamp had been left on, providing enough light to see by. Two wingback chairs faced a large fireplace, their backs to the door. I stepped around the first one and sank into the thick cushion. Everything about the room reminded me of my father.

One day. That was all I had left of the flimsy story I'd given him about spending the weekend with Katie. Then, just like with Quentin, I was going to have to come up with something new – something that would get me through until the trial. After that, I didn't care. Sebastian would be free, and I'd deal with whatever happened next.

I set my phone on the marble end table beside me and took the dandelion pendant between my palms, staring hard into its center. The flower's pedals shimmered with sun-lit gold, even in the dim light of the study. Was I imagining it, or was the glass getting warmer?

I closed my eyes, conjuring up an image of Sebastian – one of the last times we'd been together before he was yanked in front of the *kris*, accused of Karl's murder. I put the necklace to my lips and dove into the memory.

I stood at the opening of the old mineshaft underneath the Sutallee Bridge. Late afternoon had turned to evening while we'd been inside Esmeralda's hidden cave home. The woods held shadows tightly between tree trunks. We needed to get back to the Circe and tell Karl and my father about Augustine's chimeras.

Sebastian leaned wearily against the dirt wall, clutching his stomach. His eyes were shut tight. His teeth were clenched, and I saw their sharp points poking out between his dark lips as he took several deep breaths. I winced at the sight of him, but I didn't say anything.

He'd just learned he could shadow through walls, which was crazy enough, but now he had to deal with the way it made him feel, especially after carrying someone with him, like me. I chewed my nail guiltily. It was my fault he looked like he was about to throw up.

'I'm okay,' he said softly, as though he knew I was staring at him. 'Just give me a minute.'

I wanted to go to him, but something held me back. Maybe it was the guilt.

Slowly, Sebastian opened his eyes. Their silver depths glimmered back at me like a forest animal caught in the light of a campfire. He smiled and straightened himself up, nodding that he was ready to go.

We walked with more distance between us than before the mountain picnic. I sensed Sebastian's guarded emotions, which he held carefully at arm's length. I also felt how hungry he was getting. I bit my lip, wondering if I was that much of an open book to him.

'What went on between you and Esmeralda back there?' I asked, mainly to get out of my own head. 'It's like you guys went in and out of conversation, and then, you'd just stand there, staring at each other.'

Sebastian scratched his head, which looked a little comical, with his pointed ears and curved horns. 'Sorry about that. I didn't realize it was that obvious. We can speak to each other inside our heads. It freaked me out the first time it happened, but I'm getting used to it.'

My breath tripped up my throat. 'You can read minds?'

'No, nothing like that,' he said quickly. 'It's just like talking, only without using your voice. That's all.'

'And you can do this with anyone?'

'Just shadow creatures, as far as I know.'

I was ashamed at the relief that flooded through me at his answer. The thought of another level of contact with him was terrifying, because it meant one more barrier I'd constructed would be torn down. I stole a glance at him as we walked. Why was it so hard to admit that maybe I wanted to cross that barrier?

'Josephine?'

I lifted my head and looked at him fully. 'Yes?'

Sebastian hesitated, and then came to a stop. The way he looked at me made my heart beat quicker. I edged closer to him, determined to hold his gaze. He blinked down at me, and I smiled in surprise. The guarded expression I'd gotten used to seeing from him was gone. Here was the Sebastian I was growing to—

'Do you think ...' he began.

I'd never hear the rest of the question.

Marksmen appeared out of the shadows. Sebastian's face went fierce, his upper lip pulling back to show his top row of gargoyle teeth. He whipped around, instantly stepping in front of me like a giant gray shield. I felt the shudder of those massive wings against my arm.

I yanked free from the memory, but I held onto his face in my mind – tighter than I'd ever held onto anything. The pendant spiked with heat, radiating through my fingers. I froze the image of Sebastian into place in my head, like he was a painting on the wall in front of me. It's just like talking, but without using your voice, he'd said.

Sebastian?

I opened my eyes, waiting for something. The room was as quiet as my head. What was I missing? Right before Anya hit me, there'd be something – a feeling? No, it was a buzz, like electricity going through a wire. I tried again, a longer burst of thought this time.

Sebastian, it's Josephine.

Slowly, a weird ringing echoed in my ears. The pendant throbbed in my hands. The ringing got louder until it became a definite hum. I held my breath and yelled more forcibly inside my mind.

Sebastian, if you can hear me, please listen. I'm here, and I'm going to get you out of there. Just hold on, okay? Hold on for me.

The pendant slipped from my hand. It fell soundlessly, disappearing into the fibers of the rug. The fireplace in front of me went lopsided. I tried to stand, to stop the furniture from spinning like the whirling cars at the Circe. The room swirled like a tornado and the lights went out.

21. *Sebastian*

I wasn't sure if staring down a group of *Sobrasi* was better or worse than facing the High Council. Both were groups I knew practically nothing about. But no matter which way I looked at it, I was on the receiving end of something I probably wasn't going to like.

I'd navigated through my brother's Gypsy revelations. I'd managed my own gargoyle transformation – more or less. I'd dealt with the unfamiliar world of the Circe de Romany. But this, this was a whole new level of the unknown.

'What am I doing here?'

They looked at me like watching an animal from behind the viewing area in a zoo. Spindles of adrenaline wound up my vertebrae, settling at the base of my skull. The cloaked Gypsies didn't move. It would've been better if they'd moved – just the shifting of feet. A head scratch. Even a cough. Anything was better than this.

My breathing increased and grew shallow. I adjusted my stance, distributing my weight more evenly as my back hunched into a crouch. The instinctive dark emotions inside me awakened. Warning signals fired in my brain.

'What am I doing here?' I asked again, my voice changing under the influence of the thing beating on my chest cavity, ready to be released. I choked it down and clenched my hands at my sides. 'You've gone to all this trouble; you could at least let me in on it. Or do you have to wear purple to get any answers around here?'

'Shut up,' barked Donani, kicking me squarely in the back, right between my wings.

I went down on one knee, but I was quick to rise. I growled, deep in the back of my throat. The other Marksmen shifted closer to me, looking more than ready to take me out. And I'd already given them plenty enough reasons. Quentin's hatred was so palatable I could almost taste it.

The woman lowered her chin, obviously unimpressed with my outburst. Her thin lips pinched so tightly together that her entire face seemed stretched, like old parchment. Her hands fluttered from underneath her cloak, and she made a sign in the air with her fingers.

'Bring him in.'

Her voice, heavily accented but clear, rang through the room. She didn't take her eyes off me. A door clanged open from the opposite side of the balcony, and the scent that poured into the room turned everything in me to liquid anger. I spun on my heel, glaring up into the space as a snarl forced itself past my lips.

Augustine ignored me and bowed low to the woman. '*Rani.*'

He'd used that word before with the Queen, and I assumed it was some kind of title. At the moment, I concentrated mainly on preventing myself from flipping out again, as I had in the corridor. I felt dangerously close. I breathed in through my nose and out through my mouth.

'Where's the Council?' I demanded.

Augustine looked at me for the first time. 'Oh, you were never going to stand before the High Council, I'm afraid.'

I took another slow breath. 'Then why am I here?'

'Nicolas Romany was only following Outcast law,' said Augustine. 'You see, if a Gypsy is found guilty during a *Kris Romani*, he loses his Roma blood in the sight of our people. He's handed over to the *gadje* authorities for punishment.' He smiled, and the motion tugged at the white scar on his face. 'But, surely you've realized by now that you aren't Roma. The High Council has no jurisdiction over you. The *Kris Romani* was just a diversion. Something for the Council to focus on while I secretly brought in those who represent a different authority.'

The way he said 'different' sent fiery spikes up my back. I studied the cloaked people staring down from above. The woman shifted her gaze to me. Her face twisted into a scowl.

'I see only a gargoyle,' she said, 'and a fledgling, at that.'

Augustine's smile remained fixed. 'Appearances can be deceiving, Vadoma.'

The woman locked eyes with him. 'I hope, for your sake, that you aren't wasting our time. We have traveled far because you claimed to have what we've sought. But this,' she gestured to me, 'is simply a guardian. We have no need of another guardian. Ours are sufficient.'

I glanced beyond Vadoma to the shadowy wall behind her, using my night vision to peer into the darkness beyond the reach of the lights. So these gargoyles were the *Sobrasi*'s guardians. As far as I could tell, they were also the only gargoyles in the Court of Shadows, besides me. Were they original guardians, like Ezzie? Something strange and foreign thrummed deep inside my chest.

'Trust me,' answered Augustine from the opposite side of the balcony. He placed his hands on the railing and looked at me. 'I won't be wasting anyone's time.'

'I'm not your circus act,' I spat at him. My muscles tightened along my shoulders. 'Release me. Now.'

'Oh believe me,' he said darkly. 'I shall.'

Warning blasts fired in my brain. Instincts burst through my chest. I snapped my wings full with a furious explosion of adrenaline and launched through the air – right at Augustine's throat. I was almost on him. His face drained of color, smile faltering. I thrust out my hands—

Pain blazed through my wing and shoulder. My fingers missed their target. I gasped. My body jerked backwards. Augustine's shocked expression grew farther away as I fell. I hit the floor, and bells clanged in my ears as my skull connected with stone. An arrow jutted through my shoulder, the diamond-coated tip dulled with my blood.

I rolled and turned my eyes on Quentin, blinking through the red haze coating my vision. Another arrow sat notched in his bow, ready to fly. I didn't care. I ran at him full speed. His second arrow sliced through my side, but it was a distant pain, like a faraway memory.

I hit the Marksman so hard his bow wrenched free and clattered across the floor. We slammed into one of the columns. The wood groaned against our weight. Quentin swung at my face, but the blow, like the arrow, felt slight and feathery. He punched again, and I swatted it like a fly. I grabbed his shirt and threw. Quentin's body spun and then crunched into the opposite column. A crack splintered upward in the beam.

The rest of the Marksmen circled me. I sized them up, sighting the smallest of the three. His spear missed me by inches. I grabbed his throat and slammed him to the ground. The terror in his eyes faded as the redness thickened around me, swirling and engulfing. I tried to breathe, but the floodgates opened, and I was drowning. The dark thing was going to take over. I couldn't fight it anymore. The red consumed me. Let it take me.

Sebastian.

I jolted as my name screamed through my head. The red haze shimmered across my vision. The hold weakened. I retreated, backpedaling on unsteady feet, looking wildly around. My head buzzed, like stepping on a live current. A radio signal. Disjointed. Full of static.

Sebastian.

Her voice. It was her voice!

Then, out of the haze, like a vision or a dream, I saw her. Standing in the middle of a garden. Eyes wide. Diamond knife flashing. It left her hand like a rocket, striking its target. A chimera – Anya! Rushing at Josephine. Death in her eyes.

'No!'

My voice rattled the vision like thunder. The chimera screeched at the sound. It threw clawed hands over its ears, face wrenched in fury. Then it bolted into the air, wings beating like a tornado as it fled. Josephine lay across the ground. Hair across her face. But safe. She was safe.

'Josephine!'

The vision shattered like glass.

'Come now, Sebastian!' Augustine called down to me. His fear was gone, replaced with smug laughter in his voice. 'You can't keep fighting like this forever. The sooner you accept your fate, the easier it will be.'

My fate.

The world righted itself. Augustine was wrong. It wasn't about my fate. It was about my duty. Josephine was here. My charge was in the city. That's where I was supposed to be. That's where I'd always be.

I had to get out of this place. *Now.*

My wing wouldn't obey. It hung, half open. The sharp tip of Quentin's arrow mocked me as it protruded through my skin, just above my collarbone. The arrow had pierced both wing and shoulder, pinning my wing to my back.

I heard the twang of a bowstring, and I ducked as another arrow whizzed by, this one from Donani, who stood over Quentin, the Marksman's bow in his hand. Quentin struggled to his feet, holding his arm, limp and broken, at his side. His face contorted with pain and rage.

'You're dead!' Quentin yelled.

A third shot fired. But the column was my shield. The arrow aimed for my chest sank into the wood. I turned my good shoulder into the beam and pushed. It shuttered, already compromised from our fight.

'Don't kill him, idiot!' yelled Augustine as an arrow whizzed by my head. 'We need him!'

I roared and slammed into the beam. It wrenched free from the balcony with a crack. Boards snapped and shattered. I spun around and rammed the next column. It gave way. The balcony on Augustine's side teetered.

The purple figures retreated, but I didn't see anything else. I hit the third beam and then ran through the doorway as the sound of collapsing wood erupted behind me.

I stumbled down the corridor, running the best I could with a half-spread wing. I pinged off walls, gritting my teeth with pain as my wing continually smacked into stone. I wrapped my fingers around the arrow at my shoulder and snapped off the tip. But I couldn't pull it out. I'd bother with it later.

When I was free.

*

I put as much distance between the Marksmen and myself as possible, though I was forced to slow in order to get my bearings. I maneuvered through corridors, allowing my senses to lead me – sniffing for Gypsies and listening for voices. I needed to get to the surface, so I took any hallway with an upward slope or stairs, keeping to the shadows and avoiding anyone I sensed approaching.

The urge to find Josephine roared inside me like a fire that I couldn't extinguish anymore. And I didn't want to. Keeping her safe had been the whole reason I'd ended up here. But she wasn't at the Circe anymore. Things had changed. All my old promises faded away, but in their place, new ones grew, stronger and more resolute.

I coaxed my breathing into a normal pattern. The dark thing had retreated, though not very far. I felt it biting at my heels as I walked. I touched my side, right underneath my ribs. Blood pooled along the waistband of my jeans. The diamond weapon had sliced through my gargoyle skin like it was paper, leaving a nice-sized gash, but the wound wasn't deep. The other injury was definitely the more serious of the two. And it hurt a lot worse.

The network of tunnels wound like a narrow maze, nothing like the broad rooms and wide corridors I'd seen so far, which meant I was at least heading somewhere different. Unfortunately, I had no idea where. My shoulder pulsed insistently, and I winced. I needed a moment to rest before I went farther.

After two more right-turns, I reached a narrow hall with a metal gate at the far end. On the other side, a staircase wound up out of sight. I paused in front of it, taking a tentative sniff. No Gypsies. The gate was locked on the opposite side of the bars. I reached through and wrapped my fingers around the large padlock and squeezed. The metal snapped like a twig. I smiled grimly. Gargoyle strength to the rescue again.

I pushed open the gate, which seemed well oiled and didn't squeak, and closed it quickly behind me. The stairwell was dark. My eyes shifted into night-mode. I counted fourteen steps to the top. I pushed open another door, this one solid, and stepped into a tiny room, piled high with crates, as well as shelves stocked full with boxes and cans of food.

My stomach grumbled, but there wasn't anything in the room I could eat – not without puking it right back up, anyway. My gums prickled, demanding meat, as always. The deep, pounding ache in my shoulder spread through every membrane of my left wing, out to the very tip. I sank to the floor.

My survival instincts lessened once inside the quiet of the room. I wondered how long it would take the Marksmen to get out and hunt me down. I know how much damage I'd actually done to the room. Just a few minutes, I told myself. Then I'd get moving again. My eyes drifted closed.

'Josephine,' I whispered. 'I heard you.'

*

215

'Sir?'

Somewhere, my brain registered that someone was speaking. I groaned, brushing the sound away. Just a few more minutes.

'Sir?'

In an instant, I was in a crouch, teeth bared. A figure fell away with a cry. I snarled again before I managed to yank the dark thing back to its resting place inside me and focus on what I saw.

A boy cringed in front of me.

His dark hair fell across his eyes, which were also dark, but wide and scared. It was the same boy who'd brought me the plate of food in the library. I jumped back, startled. The pain in my body surged to life, and I put my hand over the section of arrow still jutting from my shoulder.

The boy shook all over, but he pushed himself up, keeping a careful distance between us. His gaze went from my face to my wings, and then to the arrow wounds. He licked his lips. 'Are you okay?'

I tried to speak, but my throat constricted. The pain intensified, like a hot brand sizzling into my skin. The wound at my side had scabbed over, but my shoulder continued to ooze purple-black blood. I had to get the arrow shaft out so I could heal. But it wouldn't budge, pulling from the front. I grimaced.

'Need ... to get ... out of ... this place.'

Each phrase took effort to say. I pulled myself up, grabbing hold of the shelves for support. The boy hesitated, then put his hand out to stop me.

'Not like this,' he said. 'Wait here.'

The boy exited through another door on the opposite

216

side of the room I hadn't seen. I sank back to the floor, exhausted. Minutes crept by. Nerves sparked along my arms, growing into dread. What if he'd gotten the Marksmen, told them where I was hiding? I wasn't in any kind of shape to fight them. Finally, the door creaked open and he entered, carrying a bundle in his arms.

I glanced at the items skeptically, and then looked back to the door. I didn't smell anyone else nearby. I didn't feel ice-cold blocks in my stomach. The boy unfolded the bundle. Wrapped inside the fabric was a package of hotdogs. I could make out the scent through the sealed plastic, and it made my mouth water.

'It was all I could get from the kitchen,' said the boy.

I didn't hesitate this time. I needed the food. Ripping open the package with my claws, I greedily stuffed the cold hotdogs into my mouth, growling softly. The boy watched me eat, caught somewhere between curiosity and fear. When I finished, I wiped my arm across my sleeve. My gums ceased throbbing, and my stomach thanked me.

'Wear this.' The boy held out the bundle of fabric, which was actually a black cloak, like I'd seen Quentin and his Marksmen wear when patrolling the Circe. 'You can hide better.'

I took hold of my half-unfurled wing and pulled it into my body. The movement felt like stretching a sore muscle. The boy threw the cloak around my wings and shoulders and fastened the clasp. He skittered back as soon as he was done, putting several feet of floor between us. But he wasn't shaking anymore, and the fear on his face lessened.

'Why … are you … helping me?' I asked.

'Because.' He almost smiled. 'You're a guardian.' The boy

studied me a moment more, then pointed to the door. 'Go through the kitchen. There's a screen door that goes out to our back yard.'

'The ... street level?'

'Yeah.'

I got to my feet again, steadier this time. The food had already worked its way into my system, giving me strength. The arrow wound stung fiercely. I opened my mouth to ask for the boy's help getting the arrow out, but I suddenly changed my mind. He'd done enough, and I couldn't waste anymore time. I pulled the hood over my head.

The boy opened the door. 'It's clear.'

'Thank you.' I stepped past him into a small kitchen with dark cabinets. The only light came from a bulb above the sink and the glow of a streetlamp through the window. I put my hand on the screen door, then stopped and turned around. 'What's your name?'

'Ruslo Marks,' he said. This time, he smiled. 'Donani's my dad.'

22. *Sebastian*

I huddled in the alley, between two garbage bins.

A scrawny calico cat with a chewed-up ear hissed at me from his perch on the fence, yellow eyes flashing. I curled my lip and hissed back. The cat screeched and bee-lined it underneath an old Volkswagen Beetle, probably going for reinforcements.

The fading stars, peeking through the oak tree branches, told me it was early morning, maybe just an hour or two before dawn. I couldn't stay here until daylight, when some unsuspecting person came out to dump their trash and had a heart attack when they saw me. But where to go?

I was out of the Court of Shadows, but totally lost. I snarled irritably. I had no idea where Hugo was staying, and even if I did, I wasn't familiar with the city, and I definitely couldn't take a cab. I clutched my shoulder as a spike of pain radiated through my arm.

And there was the arrow to deal with.

I leaned sideways against the cold metal, weighing my options. Josephine's face flittered across my mind. Had I gotten a glimpse of something that had actually happened? Was she okay? A prickling sensation buzzed across the back of my neck and settled at the base of my skull.

Sebastian ... it's Josephine.

The buzzing increased to a steady hum, vibrated in my head in the same way it did when I talked to Ezzie – but it was different, more intense. It warped into Josephine's voice, and I heard her speak as clearly as if she stood beside me.

Sebastian, if you can hear me, please listen. I'm here, and I'm going to get you out of there. Just hold on, okay? Hold on for me.

The current immediately stopped, like a plug yanked from a socket. But Josephine's presence lingered, even if it was just in my mind. I squeezed my eyes shut and mustered a reply.

Josephine, I'm here.

I waited, but the buzzing didn't return. Was it telepathy or something else entirely? I tried again, my head pounding with the effort, but nothing happened, and my reply went unanswered. Still, it had been more than enough. I knew what I had to do next.

I swallowed hard and pressed the heel of my right hand against the broken arrow tip. If I couldn't get it out by pulling forward, then there was only one other direction it could go. I sucked in air, held my breath, and pushed. White-hot fire detonated inside me. I convulsed as the arrow thrust outward from my wing. I stretched my arms behind me, but I couldn't reach it.

I inhaled through my mouth, waiting for the pain to ease. I got up and tugged the hood lower over my face. The hunger in my stomach pounded on my torso with two fists. I was hurt, and I needed food even more – that much I realized. Maybe it helped my gargoyle body heal faster. I licked my lips as saliva built rapidly inside my mouth.

I switched to breathing out of my nose again, instantly catching every scent of thrown-out food in both garbage bins – soured, old, and pungently rotten. My stomach reacted to the smell of fast-food beef nachos, and I wrapped my arms stubbornly around my body.

'I don't think so.'

I moved quickly away from the trash while I still had control of myself. I exited the alley and emerged between two cars, parallel parked on the street. In both directions of the residential areas, I was met with dark windows and empty sidewalks.

I glanced back at the house. Either Ruslo had gone to bed or he'd returned to the Court of Shadows. Either way, I hoped his father stayed ignorant of what his son had done. Helping a shadow creature probably wasn't on the list of Marksmen do's and don'ts. I wondered if there were other entrances to the Gypsy's underground haven. It made sense. You couldn't have the entire population of Outcasts coming and going through one door.

I made my way along the sidewalk, edging away from streetlights or oncoming headlights from the occasional car. As soon as I turned the corner, I stumbled on exactly what I was looking for.

A restaurant.

The small diner took up very little real estate, with only a few narrow windows lining the street, decorated on the inside with red-and-white checkered curtains. Keeping to the heavy shadows, I inspected the restaurant all the way around until I came to the back door, the one used for deliveries.

As I approached the door, I noticed a small dandelion painted in the upper right corner. The scent of Gypsy permeated the air, but it was faint and hours old. A Roma establishment. If I got caught, I certainly liked my chances better here than anywhere else.

At least they'd know what I was.

'I'm really sorry,' I said to the door.

Then I rammed it with my good shoulder. The frame splinted and gave way, and the door creaked open with no resistance. I scanned the room with my night-vision, searching for any signs of an alarm system. I didn't see anything, though it wouldn't have stopped me anyway. Hunger-need had taken over.

I shuffled between the metal counters, squeezing my winged body around shelves of pots and pans. A large boiler toppled under a sideway graze of my wing, hitting the counter and then clanging loudly against the floor. I cringed and froze, gargoyle ears prickling for any sound.

Satisfied that no one was in the restaurant, I continued my search until I located what I was looking for: the diner's industrial-sized refrigerator. I pried open the door. Drool trickled down my chin, and I wiped it away with the back of my hand. The smell of fresh meatballs, prepped and ready for the next day, hit me right between the eyes. I grabbed a rectangular pan and ripped off the tin foil.

Dozens of meatballs, in all their raw, seasoned glory. I set it on the counter and dug in with both hands, eating so fast I knew I'd probably get sick. But I didn't care. Raw meat or not, it was the best thing I'd tasted in forever. I plunged my head under the gigantic faucet, soaking my head, my hair, and gulping down water like a dog at a fire hydrant.

I rummaged through drawers. I found soap and stacks of thick dishtowels. I stripped off the cloak, and using my new supplies, I took a messy, standing shower – the first real cleaning I'd had in three days. I scrubbed my hair and my face, soaped up my body and wings, and took special attention with my wounds. I dried off and dumped the towels on the soaked floor.

'Sorry again,' I said to the empty space.

I yanked several paper towels from a nearby roll and dabbed my wounded shoulder, so I could see it better. The splintered shaft glittered inside the bloody hole in my shoulder. I wrenched my neck around and lowered my wing as much as I could. The black feathers were wedged firmly into the outside of the leathery membrane, keeping it trapped against my back.

I curled my claws around the wooden shaft and broke off the feathered section. My wing yanked free, and almost instantaneously, it ceased hurting. The ten inches of arrow still buried in my shoulder was another matter, but it was a small victory, at least. I expanded my wing to its full length, careful not to destroy anymore cookware, and then retracted it tight against my back. I ripped the rest of the paper towel into thin strips and packed it into the wound to staunch the bleeding. I regretted not asking Ruslo for help.

Feeling decently clean and completely full, I refastened the cloak around my body and meandered into the dining area. The checkered linoleum floor made me think of the *Gypsy Ink*, and a bout of homesickness gripped me. James' bad cooking on late Saturday mornings, shop talk with the guys, even Hugo's constant drilling questions.

I hopped up on the counter, wincing slightly. My bulky

wings spilled over the back. The silence of the empty room was peaceful, and the smells wafting around me were pleasant and comforting. So much better than the dirty cell in the dungeon of the Court of Shadows. I shifted uneasily. Hugo was here for the trial, obviously, but he had no way of knowing what had just gone down.

The urge to find my brother stirred inside me, only usurped by the insistent need to get to Josephine. Maybe they were in the same place. The idea tightened into a more realistic theory. She'd gone to Hugo after Augustine took me away and told him everything. But she hadn't stopped there. My heat warmed inside my chest. Josephine hadn't given up on me at all. She'd come to Savannah to find me.

I hugged my right arm to my chest as my thoughts drifted.

'Maybe we should think about returning to the Fairgrounds.'

Josephine kept her eyes glued to the scenery beyond us, the acres of forest and fields spanning far below our perch on Copper Mountain. She placed her hands on the guardrail separating the trail from the rocky edge.

'Not yet, Sebastian, please. I'm just not ready to return to real life yet.'

I put my hands on the railing next to her. Josephine's scent mingled with the smells of earth and nature. The truth was, I didn't want to go back either. Just being here alone with her, away from the Circe and from everyone's expectations, was an amazing reprieve that I wanted to go on forever.

I leapt easily over the metal railing, landing sure-footed on the flat granite rock. I turned and offered her my hand. 'Then allow me to take you on the unofficial tour of Lover's

Leap. But we'll just keep this between you and me. Park rangers aren't real keen on this sort of thing.'

'I'll keep that in mind,' she said, sliding her hand comfortably into mine.

I glanced away, pretending I didn't see the overwhelming distinction between her narrow, brown-tinted hand, and my ugly clawed gray one. Josephine swung herself over the railing with a performer's practiced grace. 'Look,' she said, pointing to a groove in the rock. 'That spot's perfect.'

She seated herself first, and waited as I followed her actions, shifting my body different angles until my wings were sufficiently out of the way. The rock encased us both, nearly rendering us invisible from the trail.

Deep in the core of my being, emotions curled in smooth, lazy spirals. But they weren't mine. They belonged to Josephine. Almost as if they were a language I'd learned ages ago, but couldn't fully remember. But maybe, if I tried hard enough ...

'I might even blend in with the scenery,' I said, pushing the thought aside. I slid my hands along the smooth granite. 'You have to admit, there's a certain resemblance.'

My heart did a backwards flip as Josephine hid her laugh with the back of her hand. Her laugh, like her voice, was something I would never get tired of. Ever. I wasn't sure what else to say, though. I concentrated on the view in front of me, the clouds rolling in towards us in giant, grayish puffs.

'So, how do you like living at the Circe?' Josephine asked. 'When you're not fending off groties or narrow-minded carnies, that is.' She leaned forward, wrapping her arms around her knees. 'Do you miss your clan?'

I watched a hawk flying low over the tree line. 'Sometimes. Especially my brother. He's the only family I've known.' I made a sound somewhere between a laugh and a huff. 'But the Corsis aren't really my clan. In some weird way, I wish I did have a clan. A group I belonged to.' I studied my dandelion tattoo. 'And not because I'm some possession; the way your clan views me.'

'I don't think you're a possession, Sebastian.'

'I know.' I glanced at her. Our earlier conversation replayed through my head, mixing with the weird emotional connection we somehow shared. 'Josephine,' I began with some uncertainty, 'what did you mean when you said you understood what it's like to be scared of something you can't control?'

I felt her body stiffen beside me. 'I'm not allowed to say.'

'Hey, I told you about the whole Jekyll and Hyde thing I've got going on.' I'd meant it as a joke, but the deeply serious, conflicted look in Josephine's eyes staunched the humor I'd been going for. 'I'm sorry, Josephine. I didn't mean to pry. Just forget about—'

'I'm next in line,' she said.

'What?'

'To be Queen,' she finished in a strained voice. She crossed her legs and clasped her hands in her lap. 'My aunt is the Queen of the Outcast clans. The Romanys are more than just a head family. We're Gypsy royalty.'

'So that's why I'm your guardian.'

Josephine shrugged. 'That's why Father thinks you were sealed to me, yeah. The Queen bears the responsibility of maintaining order within our kumpania. All bandoleers are under her authority. She's also the only Outcast allowed communication with the Old Clans in Europe. We've maintained a pretty uneasy truce with them, which basically means we stay out of their business, and they stay out of ours.

'Lots of bandoleers and even members of the High Council

are hungry for the throne. No one knows who the Queen intends to name, and many are vying for their chance. My aunt believed keeping her decision secret was the best way to keep me safe. Our next meeting in Savannah is soon, and there are rumors that the Queen is supposed to make a public announcement.'

'Will she?'

'No.' Josephine plucked a strand of moss from one of the cracks in the stone. She picked it apart with her fingers. 'Even through I'm eighteen, I'm not quite an adult by Outcast Gypsy standards yet.' Josephine tossed the greenery aside, irritated. 'There's still one requirement I have to fulfill.'

The emotional flow inside me sharpened suddenly. It ran up and down my nerves like a current. Something in her face gave me a nervous, jittery feeling. I opened my mouth to ask exactly what she meant, but I quickly changed my mind. It was clear by her expression that she wasn't fond of the subject, and I wasn't about to push. One step at a time, I reminded myself. I waited a few moments before cautiously venturing ahead.

'So why are you telling me all this now, especially if your father ordered you to be silent about it?'

'Nicolas wanted to test you,' she replied, 'to see how far you would go to protect me, and to reassure himself of your loyalty to our clan. But I don't feel the same way he does.' Josephine held my gaze with a strength that made the hair on the back of my neck rise. 'I trust you, Sebastian. I always have. I don't need a test for that.'

A key jingled in the lock of the front door.

I jerked back from wherever I'd been. Early morning light illuminated the checkered curtains.

'Mama, come on,' said a man's voice from outside. 'You'll be late for church.'

The door started to open. I flipped backwards over the counter and landed in a crouch behind it, just underneath the cash register. I heard the door squeak and the scents of Gypsies filled my nose.

A woman spoke. 'I'll just be a second. I've got to check the meatballs and make sure they thawed. You know how many we're expecting for lunch.'

'Service starts at 8:00.'

'Two seconds, Yoska,' said the woman.

My stomach plummeted. I held my breath as the two Gypsies walked past the counter and headed straight for the kitchen. I had to get out! I crawled around the counter on all fours, struggling to get my hood up at the same time. Suddenly, the woman's startled shriek filled the room, followed by a long string of words I didn't understand.

I shot through the front door into the sunrise.

23. *Josephine*

My eyes fluttered open.

I was staring at the underneath portion of the wingback chair. The legs were scratched and worn with years, and a thin layer of dust had turned the black fabric spider web gray. Beside me, my necklace lay in a crumpled pile, nearly obscured inside the thick rug. I reached out to grasp the pendant; thankful the glass bauble hadn't hit anything hard.

My temple pulsated with the beating of my heart. I touched the wound Anya had left me. A fresh trickle of blood ran down my hairline. I must've hit my head when I—

What *had* happened? I remembered concentrating on communicating with Sebastian, and then darkness. Had I fainted and then hit my head? I stood carefully to my feet, found a box of tissue on the end table, and dabbed the blood away.

My senses gradually refocused. I stepped to the window of the study and yanked aside the curtain. The sky was deep purple through the thick, moss-laden trees. It was almost dawn.

I rubbed my shoulder muscles, working out the kinks, and then refastened the necklace around my neck. I touched the pendant hesitantly with my fingertips. The glass was cool now. Not like it'd been when I'd …

Had Sebastian heard me?

If he had, then it was definitely a one-way vibe, because I didn't feel anything back. My heart sank a few inches. Maybe Ezzie was wrong. Maybe I'd just imagined the whole thing.

I left the study and made my way up the back stairs. I approached our room, keeping close to the edge of the hallway so the floorboards wouldn't squeak as I walked. I opened the door and stepped in as softly as I could. Katie needed sleep as much as I did.

I tiptoed across the room, concentrating so much on being quiet that it was several seconds before my brain registered that the dresser lamp was still on. A weird prickle went up my spine. I whirled around.

The bed was empty.

I looked to the open bathroom door. The room was unoccupied. Then I studied the bed again. The comforter was pulled up, and the pillows were in the same scattered arrangement they'd been when we'd first gotten here and Katie had taken a nap on top of them while I showered. Nothing had changed.

Katie hadn't come back to the room.

I hurried down the hall, my phone in hand, taking the front stairs a little too fast and almost tripping before I got to the bottom. The parlor was dark and deserted. I dialed Katie's number and waited. It went directly to voice mail. A heavy, ominous feeling began to spread outward through my body. I fired off a text to her as I made my way to the kitchen.

The room was also empty. I opened the cellar door. 'Katie?'

Everything was quiet. I turned and headed back up the stairs to the bedrooms. The bad feeling was rapidly forming into a knot in the center of my chest. I hesitated at the top of the stairs, unsure who was in what room. I took a random guess and knocked on the door next to ours.

'Yes?' answered a female voice.

'Ezzie, it's Josephine.'

The door opened almost immediately. Esmeralda was dressed in jeans and a new top and her bed was neatly made. I wondered if she'd even slept since we'd been here. She ushered me inside the room and shut the door.

'What's wrong?' she asked, seeing my expression. 'Has Sebastian communicated with you?'

'No,' I snapped, feeling a rush of frustrated anger that ricocheted in every direction. I wanted to think about Sebastian – so much of me wanted to think only about him – but not now. Not when the bad feeling thrummed inside me like rain pelting a glass window. 'I'm not here about that. This is about Katie.'

'Go on,' said Ezzie with an odd frown.

'She's missing,' I replied. I paced the length of the plush rug beside the bed. 'I thought maybe she was just ticked at me for making her go back to the inn and not letting her come out to the garden with us. I thought she was avoiding me while she cooled off. I figured she'd just gone to bed. But she's not in our room.'

'It's a big house. Have you checked everywhere?'

I held out my phone. 'She's not answering.'

'Do you think Katie might've left the inn?'

'No,' I said firmly. 'She'd never do that. She's had the

231

crap scared out of her more than I can count since we got here. She's definitely not going out looking for trouble.'

Even as I spoke, I felt a twinge of doubt. It's not like we'd had an earth-shattering fight or anything, nothing serious enough that she'd just take a cab and leave. Plus, she'd left all her stuff in our room. But still ...

I'm not a Gypsy. They don't want to eat me.

Katie's words flashed through my mind. Maybe she wasn't as scared as I thought. She'd seen shadowen go after us three times in less than two days, but they'd never been after her. She just happened to be with us.

'Is everyone asleep?' I asked.

Ezzie sat on the edge of the bed, watching me pace. 'All except Hugo and his parents. They left a few minutes ago to attend the early church service. They believed it would be less populated, and therefore, they would be less conspicuous.'

'Sunday service,' I said quietly, chewing on my nail. During the Gatherings, most Outcasts attended one of the many churches in the city, and then met in the Court of Shadows to kick off our weeklong reunion party, followed by a midnight service.

'Do you think Katie might have gone with them?' said Ezzie. 'Especially if she was seeking to avoid you?'

I pulled up short. 'Have you seen the way Hugo's parents look at her? She's *gadje* who knows about the shadow world, thanks to me. And I think they only tolerate my presence because of my family.'

'Perhaps she spoke with them after she returned to the house.'

There was a beat of silence between us. Then, it was as though the same though struck us both simultaneously. We locked gazes. I hadn't seen Katie after I'd told her to leave.

Ezzie and Hugo had been battling the grotesques. What if Katie never made it back inside?

'The shadowen,' I breathed.

Ezzie bolted from the bed. I ran after her through the inn, our feet pounding across the wooden floors. We burst through the back door and careened around the porch, taking the back stairs to the garden at break-neck speed.

I rushed to the patch of sunflowers where we'd been hiding, and then searched frantically through the tomato plants. No Katie. I searched up and down the fence while Ezzie took a circuit around the house, her eyes flashing bright silver as she searched the ground and the sky. My heart pounded so hard I could barely breathe, and every breath I took hurt.

I stumbled on a rock and went to my knees. As I regained my balance, I realized it wasn't a rock at all. I knelt down. A piece of one of the grotesques' hideous bodies had escaped Nadya Corsi's *Sobrasi* powder – a section of a scaled talon. The groties were dead. They couldn't have done anything to Katie.

But there had been another shadowen here.

'Oh God,' I whispered. 'Please ... no ...'

I threw the talon far away from me and leapt to my feet. My chest lodged with cold. Anya. We hadn't killed Anya! I wanted to retch, but I forced my feet to move. I ran hard through the garden, my worry and panic giving me energy and breath.

Esmeralda stood beside the steps to the inn. Her body was completely still, almost like a statue herself. As I reached her, she turned her face slowly towards me. Her eyes were a cold, dull silver, and her mouth was drawn into a rigid line.

'Ezzie!' I panted. 'I know what happened to Katie!'

Her eyes drifted over my shoulder and upward. 'So do I.'

I turned and followed her gaze. Fifteen feet above our heads, wedged into a thick clump of oak leaves, was a pink, sequined flip-flop.

*

James met us at the kitchen door, bleary-eyed and confused. Ezzie pushed past him into the kitchen, and I did the same. To my surprise, the other Corsis were all gathered there, seated around the kitchen table, each one looking as though they'd just woken up.

'What's all the ruckus about?' asked Kris, rubbing his face.

'Some of us are trying to sleep,' said Vincent.

'The chimera,' I blurted out. 'It's taken Katie!'

'Wait.' James shut the door quickly, looking suddenly alert. 'Are you guys talking about those beasts from last night? I thought they were dead.'

'Anya escaped.'

Kris shoved back in his chair so hard he left a mark on the floor. His face reddened. 'We never should've let that girl come here with us. There's too much stuff happening, and a *gadje* has no place in our business.'

'Katie's *diddikoi*,' I shot back. 'And she was my responsibility.' I put a hand across my mouth, breathing hard through my fingers, until I found the strength to ask. 'Do you think it … killed her?'

Esmeralda put her hand on my arm. 'Chimeras would have no craving for *gadje*. Their sole purpose is revenge on those of Gypsy blood. This wasn't an accident. Anya took Katie for a reason.'

'Took her where?'

'I don't know.' Ezzie rubbed her temples. 'I might be able to track her. My skills are not what they used to be, but I managed to do it before, when Anya and the others first arrived in Sixes.'

'Okay,' said James, 'Let's go.'

'No,' said Ezzie.

He stared at her like she'd just lost her mind. 'What?'

She crossed her arms and looked around the room, in many ways, like the Ms Lucian I used to know as my teacher. 'I can't have a bunch of Corsis getting in my way. You will be too slow and entirely too much to look after.'

Vincent reacted like he'd been slapped. 'Too much to *look after*?'

'I've committed to act as your guardian,' she replied. 'Which means keeping all of you safe. There are more shadow creatures here in the city than you are accustomed to dealing with in Sixes and, in case you haven't noticed, they seem to have no trouble finding you.'

'Maybe,' said Kris. 'But why should that stop us? It's almost daylight now, so I don't think we have much to worry about. Besides, it's not like we're members of a head family or anything.'

'But Hugo is,' she replied, 'whether he wants to admit it or not. Now that his parents are here, it makes your clan a more prominent target.'

'We've had a lot of close calls already,' I added.

Ezzie nodded. 'Kris, you and Vincent need to go to the Court of Shadows and alert Donani. His men need to know what else they're dealing with. Matthias and Anya were formidable enough when they were gargoyles.'

'Donani?' growled James. 'You can't be serious.'

I whirled on him. 'Like it or not, the Marksmen are still the best protection the Outcasts have. This isn't business as usual, and you know it. My best friend's out there, maybe hurt. Definitely scared. If something happens to her ...' I clamped my mouth shut, refusing to complete the thought. After a breath, I continued. 'We need to stop wasting time.'

Ezzie raised an eyebrow at me, and her half-smile returned – it was a pleased, almost smug expression. 'Josephine's correct.'

'Okay,' said Kris. 'Me and Vincent will go to the Court.'

Ezzie looked at James. 'You need to stay here until Hugo and his parents return from the church service. They need to know exactly what's happened and what is being done.'

'I'm not getting benched on this one,' said James defiantly.

Esmeralda glared at him. I stepped between them.

'No one's getting benched,' I said firmly. Then I turned to James and took his large hand in both of mine. He jerked a little in surprise. 'James,' I continued calmly. 'Someone needs to stay here. Someone who can make sure Ferka and Paizi are safe. When Hugo gets back, he's going to want to know every single detail and we need a reliable source to tell him. Can I count on you to take care of all that?'

My words had the effect I was hoping for. James hesitated. His eyes roamed the room, like he was looking for a reason to turn down my request but couldn't find one. He let out a resigned huff.

'Fine. But for the record, Ezzie, I think you need someone with you. You know Hugo won't be happy when he finds out you went alone.'

Ezzie shrugged. 'Hugo is very much used to me by now. As for being alone, I'm not.' She gestured to me. 'Josephine is more capable for this than the rest of you.' The guys stared at me with the same curious expression I was sure I was giving Esmeralda. She glanced at the wall clock and continued speaking. 'Tell Hugo to give us one hour to conduct our search. If you haven't heard from us by then, he will know what to do.'

24. Josephine

I yanked my hair into a ponytail as Ezzie and I left the *Dandelion Inn*. A trickle of sweat slid down the center of my back, even though the sun was just peeking over the horizon. Ezzie walked urgently beside me, adjusting her bag – which contained Zindelo's mace – on her shoulder.

I'd taken my knife with me, along with, for some reason, Markus Corsi's book. I didn't know why I'd brought it, just a weird feeling that I should. Since the book fit neatly in my back pocket, it didn't bother me.

Not wanting to interrupt Ezzie's tracking, I kept several feet between us, watching guardedly as she moved with a steady pace, pausing only to sniff the air or, more often, take a few seconds to close her eyes, twist her face in concentration, and then nod to herself.

But finally, the dread that had wedged itself tightly in the center of my stomach became too much to handle.

'Ezzie,' I began with some trepidation. 'You really think Katie's alive?'

'If Anya wanted to kill Katie, she would've done so right

then. It would've been easy. She was weaponless and alone.'
She glanced sideways at me, seemingly judging my reaction
before proceeding. 'For a chimera to carry off its prey is
highly unusual – but since that prey is a *gadje* – there has
to be a reason for it. In other words, Anya was acting under
orders.'

'From Augustine.'

'I can think of no other,' she replied.

'Then he knows I'm here, too. And that I brought Katie.'

'That was my thought as well.'

I rubbed my arms briskly to tame the goosebumps that
sprang up despite the heat. 'So, maybe taking my best friend
is a warning for me to stay away from the trial.'

'Perhaps.' Ezzie pursed her lips. 'Or he seeks to flush you
out of hiding.'

We stopped at a crosswalk, waiting for the light to change.
I thought back, remembering how we'd left Matthias and
Anya on Copper Mountain – their twisted forms so different
from Sebastian. Failed experiments, Anya had said. And
he'd abandoned them to our Marksmen.

'But I don't understand why Anya would do anything for
him,' I said. 'I mean, Augustine left them to *die*.'

'They were his gargoyles once,' she replied. 'Maybe something still remains.'

'What do you mean?'

The sign's red flashing hand morphed into a flashing
white stick figure. We hurried to the opposite side of the
street, and I let Ezzie take the lead again. I didn't know
where we were going, but it definitely seemed like we were
heading away from the city's center.

'What do you mean,' I repeated. 'What remains?'

'Some piece of their bond,' she replied.

'You think Anya and Matthias are still bonded to Augustine? Is that why they follow his orders?'

'It is the only explanation I have,' she replied. 'The *prah* from the urn might enable him to have control over grotesques, but chimeras are too intelligent to be so easily manipulated. But neither do they have the capacity to bond with a Gypsy charge. Gargoyles were the first of our kind to have that ability, the result of our being created with Roma blood in our veins.'

I nodded, understanding. 'But since Anya and Matthias were gargoyles before Augustine experimented on them ...'

'They may retain part of the bond,' she finished.

'How did Augustine end up with those three gargoyles to begin with?'

Ezzie shook her head. 'That, I'm afraid, is one question I can't answer. I slept for many years, until Zindelo and Nadya awakened me. Whatever happened between the High Council and Augustine, resulting in his *marimé*, and the acquisition of his gargoyles, I'm in the dark as much as you are.'

Ezzie led us away from the crowded streets and into a different part of the city. Only minutes later, we entered the quiet of an enormous park. Giant trees created massive overhangs of branch and moss over the pathways, and rolling fields of thick grass spread out on either side. Underneath the canopy of trees, the sun's increasing rays were stifled, and I felt like I could take a deep breath again.

'So, what *is* our plan?' I asked. 'You weren't really clear on that when we basically told all the guys what they should be doing.'

Esmeralda smiled, a full smile this time that eased the lines on her face and made her instantly younger. 'You handled yourself quite well with the Corsi clan, *Kralitsa*. You have the makings of a worthy Queen. You haven't yet been given the chance to prove yourself.'

While the reality of my future always lingered in a section of my mind, it was way easier to pretend it didn't exist. My aunt was still young, just a few years older than my father. Succeeding her was an event so far away that it never affected me. But what if the rumors around the Court were true. What if she did choose to announce her chosen heir this year?

Would my life change once my secret was out?

'I'm not sure I'm ready for that chance,' I replied. 'Unless it means getting my best friend and my guardian back. Which brings me back to my question. Do we have a plan?'

Esmeralda's smile dropped, and she was all concentration and business again. 'Yes and no. I'm familiar with where grotesques tend to hide during daylight hours in the city. But wherever Anya's taken Katie, I think we can safely assume it would also be a place suitable for Augustine.'

'Right,' I said. 'Because he couldn't stay at the Court, and no Gypsy establishment would house a *marimé*.'

Esmeralda cut through the hedges lining the path we were on, and I followed closely behind. Several yards ahead, a long brick wall blocked off the park from another wide section of land. As we got closer, I noticed the tips of stone monuments peeking over the wall. It was a massive cemetery – one of several located throughout the city.

'What are we doing here?' I asked, as Ezzie stopped beside a large crypt.

She placed her hand on the stone. 'You've heard tales of haunted cemeteries here, I assume?'

I studied the old, crumbling slabs that lay over the ground

around us, along with dozens of taller monuments that sprouted from the earth like giant pieces of an ancient marble chess set.

'Of course,' I said. 'The city has ghost tours and everything.'

Ezzie huffed softly. 'If only the *gadje* knew that what they've seen passing quietly through these places in the dead of night were not spirits at all, but rather, creatures of the shadow world.' She looked reverently around her. 'In fact, there are many statues in these cemeteries who once were living, breathing shadowen, turned to stone by the ones who created them, yet came to fear them.'

'Really?'

Her eyes drifted closed, and she didn't say anything else for a long time. Her shoulders lifted and fell, like she'd fallen asleep. Then, her eyes snapped open again, focusing on me. 'Chimeras have been here. The scent is still fresh.'

My heart began beating faster. 'Can you track them?'

Ezzie looked up, weaving her head in one direction, and then the other. Almost trance-like, she turned and headed in the opposite direction from where we'd entered, moving deftly between ancient-looking grave markers and tall marble obelisks.

'I'm going to take that as a yes,' I said, hurrying to catch up.

Esmeralda paused between two large mausoleums nestled beneath a thickly branched oak tree. The tombs were made of white granite and lined with columns. Looking at them gave me an uneasy feeling. But Ezzie didn't seem fazed. She examined each structure intently. Her expression turned uncertain, as though she couldn't decide between the two. I leaned against a tree, not really to rest, but more to steady myself for whatever was going to happen next. We'd been gone thirty minutes already, and Ezzie had asked for an hour.

'I believe they've been staying here,' she said, turning to me. 'Sepulchers make excellent resting places for shadow creatures. No one, either *gadje* or Roma, wants to disturb a grave – which means both are safe.' She patted one column. 'Plus, it's cool and protected from the sun.'

'Okay, but what about Augustine?' I felt suddenly impatient. 'And where's Katie?'

'One thing at a time, *Kralitsa.*'

Ezzie continued her circuit of the mausoleums. I tried to keep my thoughts positive. Katie had to be terrified. What if Anya had done something horrible to her? Fear and nausea churned in my stomach.

'They've been here,' said Ezzie, her forehead creasing. She approached the smaller of the buildings, one with a triangular shaped overhang framing an iron-gate door. Ezzie tried the door, but it was locked. She pushed her head through the bars. 'And the stench is recent, even strong. But the door is secure, and I see no evidence of anything amiss within.'

I joined her, peering through the struts. The narrow room was framed with metal placard, six on each side, detailing the remains of the people entombed inside. In the center of the structure was a stone crypt, probably the head of the family, whoever it was.

I studied the door handle. It was a ring latch, but it hadn't budged at Ezzie's attempt. I knelt beside the door and brushed away the layer of dried mud from the foundation. A tiny dandelion the size of a half-dollar had been carved into the stone. I glanced up to find Ezzie staring back at me, her brows raised.

'An Outcast tomb,' she said. 'How did you know?'

'I didn't see a family name on the front,' I replied, smiling. 'You know how we like our secrecy.' I reached my hand between the iron shafts and felt around the inside wall, in the same position as the outside dandelion carving. I located another carving, this one raised. I traced the etching, and then pressed it with my fingers.

The turn latch rotated, and we heard it release.

My smile slid into a grin. 'I was always the one who listened to the history lessons my aunt told us about this Haven when she used to visit our clan. My brother always fell asleep.'

Ezzie grasped the bars and shoved. The door creaked open. Cool air brushed my face, flowing in a lazy current between the gate and a small barred window on the opposite side. The room smelled pleasantly old, like a library might. It was rich and earthy, and comforting. I swallowed hard, my thoughts going to Sebastian.

'Okay,' I said, forcing my attention to the present. 'My aunt told us all kinds of stories when we were kids, about the Court of Shadows and the Outcasts who established it. I thought all the tunnel systems were so amazing, like a magical kingdom, all hidden away.' I wrapped the end of my ponytail around my fingers as I talked, like I was coaxing my childhood back to me. 'There's lots of tunnels connecting the Court to street level, but there are plenty of others that had fallen out of use and were blocked off.'

'Ones that even led up to places such as these,' said Ezzie. 'In the early days, when the Outcasts first came to Savannah.'

'Yeah.'

'You're not the only one who has heard such stories,' she replied. She breathed in deeply through her nose. 'And since it's clear that chimeras have been in here, it would mean that Augustine also knows and has used this particular structure to access the tunnels.'

Ezzie tested the slab of granite covering the top of the center crypt. 'As is the way with our world, many things aren't what they seem.' She lifted it an inch. 'Your help, Josephine.'

I hurried over and took the opposite side of the slab. It wasn't heavy at all. We picked it up and set it aside. I braced myself and looked inside the crypt, expecting to see the skeleton of some long-dead Gypsy. Or, even worse than that, a rotting corpse.

The crypt was hollow, with no bottom. An iron ladder had been fixed to the inner side of the rectangular tomb, disappearing into a pitch-black opening descending far below the ground. I switched on my phone's flashlight, but it wasn't powerful enough to illuminate the bottom.

Esmeralda swung herself over the side of the crypt and placed her feet steadily on the ladder rungs. 'I can't see in the dark as well as a guardian, but my eyesight is still better than yours. I'll go first and call up to you when I determine it's safe.'

She didn't wait for me to answer. In a matter of seconds, her form vanished from view. All I could hear were her footsteps on the ladder, which grew more faint and distant. I chewed repeatedly on my thumbnail, nerves standing on end. What was taking so long?

I slipped the diamond knife from my back pocket. 'Ezzie?'

My voice ricocheted off the walls of the tunnel.

But there was no reply.

25. Sebastian

I threw my hand over my face and stumbled backwards.

The morning sun hit me hard. I could only squint, half-blinded, at my surroundings. My heart screeched to a halt. I was above ground, in the city. And it was morning.

My senses went into overdrive. Sights, smells, and sounds. There was a couple, five yards away, staring at a tourist map. A woman walking her dog. A runner checking his time on his watch. A green sedan idling in a parking space. Three customers seated in a coffee shop's outdoor patio.

People. *Gadje.*

Humans.

Adrenaline poured through my veins. My breathing turned shallow and my instincts screamed. My lip curled away from my teeth. *No, not now. Don't freak out now.* I took off, running for all I was worth, holding tight to my hood and keeping it low over my face. I veered from the sidewalk and into the street, searching desperately for cover.

Then, I saw it, a tall brick wall running parallel to the street, easily five feet high. I looked frantically around, checking for onlookers, then, without halting my stride, I leapt over it, landing in a patch of well-trimmed grass.

My shoulder lit up with fire, and I fell back against the wall, gritting my teeth to keep from crying out. The sun's intensity eased as my eyes grew accustomed to the light, and I was able to see clearly where I was: a cemetery. Old tombstones and markers dotted the yard, scattered in various places with no clear pattern around a network of landscaped scrubs and bushes. I knew Savannah had its share of historic cemeteries, but I had no idea which one this was. Not that it would've helped, anyway.

Getting out of the open was my only priority.

That, and getting hold of myself again. My body trembled uncontrollably. I placed a hand across my stomach. I wasn't hungry yet, but I felt strange inside – a familiar kind of strange that made my heart sink. I pulled aside the cloak with shaking fingers and examined the arrow wound again.

Flecks of purple and silver oozed from the opening, mixed with my odd-colored blood – just like it had when the Marksmen had tainted my manacles with *prah*. This was more than the result of an arrow tip being dipped in the Gypsy dust. I jabbed my claws into the wound, grunting with pain, and extracted a piece of the wooden arrow, wiping it clean against my cloak.

Though mostly disintegrated, it was plain to see the arrow was hollow, and it had been packed full of *prah*. I slumped sideways into the grass. No matter what I did, Augustine kept chiseling away at me in his efforts to create ... what? A leader for his army? All the *prah* did was make me a furious, slobbering beast, totally out of control.

I started to pull back my hood and froze at the sight of my arms. The black veins running underneath my grey skin were heavily visible on the underside of my arms and along the backs of my hands.

If Augustine turned me into a chimera, the way he'd done with his gargoyles, why would he think I'd serve him? Anya and the others only seemed to hate him more. In fact, all they seemed capable of was hatred and vengeance, fueled by a primal evil that turned my blood to ice the last time I'd encountered them.

And what army?

My chest tightened. The *Sobrasi*. They'd let Augustine into the Court of Shadows, let him speak freely, didn't negate anything he'd said about me not standing trial. Did they have something to do with whatever army Augustine was so bent on?

Cold shuddered my body, turning my tremors to full-on shakes. Adrenaline continued sparking along my skin, making my scalp crawl. The *prah* hadn't caused me to totally snap, like Augustine's other doses, but I felt it lurking in each beat of my heart.

The arrow's casing must've prevented the *prah* from entering my bloodstream immediately, but as my gargoyle body kept trying to heal, it broke down the parts of the arrow that were wood, rather than diamond. I could only assume Augustine knew this would happen, and that knowledge was nearly as painful as the arrow itself.

I pulled the cloak taut against me and scanned the cemetery for a place to hide. Far in the distance, I spotted a row of domed structures, waist high and lined with dark-red bricks. I slinked between trees and hedges until I reached them.

The cemetery was quiet and deserted here. Oaks with gnarled, twisted branches obscured the sun completely. I breathed in deeply, glad for the reprieve. Long tendrils of Spanish oak clung in thick bunches to every branch, some hanging so low to the ground that I had to maneuver around them.

The thick shade prevented grass from growing. Sprawling roots curled above the topsoil like snakes. I stepped over them as I made my way to the unusual structures. As I approached, I realized they were graves, fashioned above ground to keep them dry, but they looked more like giant beds.

Stacked bricks constructed in rectangular and oval shapes made up the headboard, and shorter stacks of bricks on the opposite end were the footboards. In the center, instead of a mattress, lay a thick granite mound. It was easy to imagine what lay underneath the stone covers of that bed.

Something felt weird about the place. My gargoyle senses were still on edge, so why not put them to the test? I planted my feet and took in a very slow, calculated breath, taking in everything about me. I allowed scents to filter through me – all the normal things first – the earthy scents, plants and flowers, the pungent scent of the moss and decaying bits of trees. I could even smell the city beyond, from individual cars exhausts to foods being cooked for lunch.

Then, finally, my senses focused in on other things, Roma things. The air mingled with the spiced and exotic smells I'd come to associate with Outcast Gypsies. Most were so faint I could barely discern them, but some were more recent. I went deeper into my senses, moving past those to something a lot less pleasant.

Shadowen.

A snarl rippled across my lips. Shadow creatures lived here. Grotesques, hiding from the sun and the light of day.

While there was nothing visible within the confines of the cemetery, I felt their presence, growing inside my head – their primal, inhuman sounds buzzed like static.

For one fleeting instant, I wanted to scream in my head, to order them to show themselves to me. The urge was so wild, so fierce that I took a step back under the weight of it. I felt a twinge of fear, because I had a terrible feeling that if I were to broadcast that thought, they might actually obey.

Another presence filtered through my senses. Chimeras had been here, too. The stench of rotting fish and decaying things lingered. Compelling by my instincts, I moved around the side of the largest grave.

A large rectangular opening had been built into the brick headboard wall, but it was covered over by a newer layer of bricks, sealing it off. I crouched in front of the grave, tilting my head to the side. I felt something stir within me, an emotional current. The air caught in my throat.

Josephine.

I didn't see her, but I *felt* her – kneeling in a similar place, somewhere else in the city, another cemetery, like this one. Our bond, our connection or whatever it was planted the feeling, caused my hand to move, almost on its own, to the corner of the sealed opening. I knew that Josephine was doing the same thing wherever she was, like we were mirror images of each other. I swallowed nervously as my claws scraped against a single brick, narrower than the others. I blinked, unbelieving.

A tiny dandelion was etched into the brick.

I tugged on the slab, and the piece slid out easily, like pulling out a cabinet drawer. My gargoyle ears picked up a grating sound from the other side of the wall, the scraping of stone on stone. And then, the sealed part of the wall came free from the rest of the structure. It opened outward, like a hinged door. Old scents filled my nostrils, but there was another smell. Not Gypsy. Not Shadowen.

The opening was just big enough for me to slide into, if I kept my wings pressed tight against me. I didn't stop to think. I shoved myself in, headfirst. Immediately, the space widened. This wasn't a grave at all. It was an entrance.

Wide stone steps led straight down several feet. I turned, carefully pulling the brick door shut, and allowed my gargoyle vision to snap everything into focus. I hunched my back to avoid the low ceiling created by the top of the structure, and I descended the stairs, one at a time and very carefully. The last step led to a room with a ceiling high enough to stand upright.

It was clean and well kept, with rugs on the floor and fabric over the rock walls. Nothing about it smelled musty or stale, so there had to be air flowing from somewhere. A desk and chair nestled in one corner, surrounded by mounds of books, and sleeping cot took up the opposite corner.

Augustine's scent permeated the room, enacting my gag reflex. So this is where he'd been staying. I reached down and took one of the books in my clawed hands. I opened the cover to find nothing but blank pages gaping back at me. But I knew better. These were *Sobrasi* books. Since I wasn't a Gypsy, whatever was written in them was totally invisible to me.

I replaced the book on the stack. Three passages led out of the room, going in different directions I took the center one, led instinctively by the new scent I'd smelled at the entrance. It was one that I somehow knew, not from my days as a gargoyle, but from a time before that.

The tremors wracking my body spread downward to my legs. The effects of the *prah* seemed to be increasing at a slow, steady pace, rather than an instant rush, like before. I clutched my wrist in my other hand. Under my skin, the black veins carried the tainted blood, traveling into my fingers. Maybe I was just imagining things, but it seemed as though my claws had lengthened.

Then, I heard something.

A sniffling sound. A shifting of a body and the creak of a chair. I halted in the passage, listening carefully with my sensitive hearing. It felt as though a heavy weight dropped from my chest to the soles of my feet. I continued, reaching the end of the passage. Another room, roughly twice the size as the other, but furnished only by a single table, six chairs, and two oil lanterns.

Seated at the table, with her back to me was a girl. Her long blonde hair spilled down her back. The girl picked at a plate of food, a peanut-butter sandwich by the smell of it. I caught a whiff of perfume, potent, flowery stuff, and I realized what the strange scent had been all along. And why I knew it.

My heart wedged itself like a knife in my throat.

Katie.

No, this wasn't possible. The *prah* was making me hallucinate. That had to be it. She couldn't be here. There was no way she could be here. I stumbled backwards into the passage. A half-gasping noise escaped my mouth.

The girl spun around with wide eyes.

There was no doubt now. Katie Lewis, my best friend since sophomore year, the girl who loved shopping and blasting music from the *Putrid Melons* while driving, was sitting across the room from me, in the middle of Augustine's hideout, deep underneath a fake grave in the middle of the city cemetery.

She brushed a strand of hair out of her face. 'Who's there?'

I retreated further into the darkness of the passage, but I couldn't take my eyes off her. Questions fired like a Ping-Pong match in my head, but I couldn't decipher them. The shock of seeing her rattled my already teetering instincts. My head pounded, and my wings quivered.

Katie stood and hugged her arms to her chest. She peered blindly into the passageway. 'I know somebody's there.'

Her voice was remarkably steady, despite the terrified expression creeping over her face. I started forward, but my shaking hands pulled me up short. Heat had begun to seep into my veins, and the memory of what I'd nearly done to Hugo flashed in front of my face like a neon warning sign.

She took a tentative step forward. I cringed. Even my blending abilities wouldn't keep me invisible if she got too close. I dropped to a crouch and dug my claws into the dirt, using them as an anchor. I inhaled deeply and spoke.

'Katie, it's me.'

I managed to keep my tone soft and disarming, but it didn't make a lot of difference. My voice had already changed into the more gravelly version as adrenaline and instincts coursed through me.

I cleared my throat and tried again. 'It's Sebastian.'

Her expression fluctuated across her face, going from doubt to realization, and then suddenly, astonishment. Her brows shot straight up her forehead and her mouth gaped open.

'It's ... it's really you?' she breathed.

'Yes.'

She hesitated, squinting suspiciously. 'You don't sound like you.'

'Katie, it's me,' I said, choking down the tinge of snarl that crept into my voice as I talked. 'I promise.'

Her shoulders sank in relief. 'Oh, thank God!'

She rushed forward, heading straight for the passageway. Primal instincts flared to life, and a growl burst from my lips. 'No, don't!'

Katie turned on the brakes so fast it would've been funny, in another time and place. I watched guardedly as she backed up, hovering in the safety of the light spilling from the oil lamps on the table.

I reined myself in, regulating my breathing. 'I'm sorry, I didn't mean to—'

'Growl at me?' she finished, clutching the table.

I flinched. 'Yeah.'

'Don't worry about it.' Katie inched closer, just shy of where the darkness began. She took a breath, like she was making up her mind, and took one step towards the shadows.

'Please,' I said, 'don't come any closer.'

'You growled at me once, at my party, remember? I thought you were just having some freaky mental breakdown or something. But I know what you are now,' she said steadily. 'Josie told me everything, so you don't have to worry about hiding from me or anything. I know all about the Outcasts and the shadow world, and you. So, it's okay. I know everything.'

I wasn't sure if that made me feel better. Or worse.

'Just stay right there, okay?' I ground my claws deeper into the dirt until my fingertips ached. 'It's kind of hard to explain, but I'd just feel better if you did. For now.'

Her face took on the look she used to give me before

doling out a lecture over something ridiculous I'd done. But, after a few seconds, she nodded in a sort of resigned agreement. 'Okay.'

'Katie, are you alright?'

She rubbed her arms more briskly. 'Yeah, I think so. I mean, I'm not hurt or anything, just really, really glad you're here.' Her eyes seemed to widen even farther. 'What *are* you doing here?'

'You first,' I replied.

'Are those your eyes?' she asked, taking another step.

I quickly averted my gaze, so I wouldn't catch the reflection from the light. Even if Katie knew what I was, it felt too new, too raw for me to just swoop out of the dark like this, after all the months of secrecy and lies. Especially not now, when I felt like I was barely keeping my balance on the line between instinct and control. When I didn't answer, she continued.

'Okay, fine, me first,' said Katie, pressing forward when I didn't answer. 'After Josie told me everything, I decided to come to Savannah with her. She tried to talk me out of it, but I didn't give her a chance.'

'I'm not surprised,' I replied, trying to smile in the darkness. I needed her to keep talking, so I could focus on her words. It seemed to keep the instincts at bay. 'You came with my brother, right?'

'Yeah, we're staying with some of Hugo's clan. There's been a lot of shadow creatures hovering around. Ezzie went out to take care of one of those chimera things—'

'Wait, Ezzie's here, too?'

'Yeah, and I'm still trying to figure that whole thing out.' Katie shook herself off with a dramatic flair. 'I mean, she used to be *our teacher*. She was scary enough before all this.

Anyway, Josie told me to stay in the house while she went after her, but I didn't listen because, you know me, I don't ever do that, and then this thing just came at me and grabbed me, and we were up in the air like freaking birds or something. And then it brought me here and just left me.' Katie reached down and yanked off her only flip-flop, holding it in front of her for a moment before tossing it aside. 'This was my favorite pair, too.'

I felt myself attempting a smile again, even through the *prah* haze. 'Katie, does anyone know where you are?'

'No, my phone died, right after dinner. I mean, I was gonna plug it in, but then all that stuff went down and Josephine was being all Josephine and saying she had to go help Ezzie, so I just went after her.'

Josephine.

A rush suddenly went up the back of my neck, like a crisp breeze, and a scent wafted over me – exotic flowers and spices. *Her scent.* I flung my hand out towards the passageway's brick wall to steady myself. Was I imagining things?

'Sebastian?' said Katie, uncertain.

I rose to my feet and was moving forward against my will before I caught myself. I kept hold of the wall. 'Once I get you out, can you find your way back to this place?'

'Yeah, it's the *Dandelion Inn*. But I guess we'll have to, like, use a real map or something because I don't know my way around the city at all.' Her eyes pooled up with tears. 'And I'm so ready to get out of here.' She wiped her face with angry strokes. 'Why didn't you tell me all this stuff, Sebastian? Why didn't you tell me about *you*? We're supposed to be friends.'

'I'm ... sorry.' My stomach churned with ice. My nose

wrinkled. I clutched my shoulder, and tried to blink away the warning haze that kept shifting closer along the edges of my vision. 'I didn't know how.'

Without warning, she reached into the shadows. Instinctively, my hand shot out and grabbed her wrist. 'Katie, no.'

Her attention fell on my hand, and she gasped. I let go of her wrist, resisting the urge to recoil. She stared, gawking, taking in the gray skin stretched over the black veins. Her gaze rested longest on my claws. After a moment, I pulled my arm back and anchored myself in the passageway again. 'I've been told the way I look takes some getting used to,' I said, hearing bitterness creep into my gravelly voice. I swallowed it down. 'Why don't we just take it a little at a time?'

Her head bobbed like a cork. 'Okay.'

'Okay,' I said. 'So what can you tell me ab—'

A mass slammed into me from behind. My body launched into the room. Stars scattered across my vision as my head hit the floor.

26. Josephine

I called to Ezzie in a tense whisper, clutching my knife in a stranglehold. The tunnel below the crypt remained dark and noiseless. I ground my teeth, frustrated. I was getting sick of people disappearing around me.

I checked the gated door of the mausoleum, making sure it had locked behind us. Then I returned to the crypt and propelled myself over the side. I eased down the ladder, pressing the inside of my arms against the rails so that I could keep my phone and knife ready in my hands. The phone's white light bathed the tunnel in a spectral flow.

The tunnel opened into a wider passageway, but there was light at the far end – not a flashlight, but a warm, golden glow that had to come from a torch or lantern. The air smelled decently fresh, almost as good a quality as the Court of Shadows. Wishing that I had some special abilities of my own, I made my way cautiously, doing my best to listen to my limited human senses.

'Josephine.'

I jumped so high I was convinced I hit the ceiling. Ezzie solidified out of the darkness like a ghost.

'Please don't do that again,' I said.

'I think I've found a promising intersection,' she replied, beckoning me with her hand. She'd also pulled out her phone for light. 'The air moves freely, and—'

'What about there?' I questioned, pointing towards the warm glow.

Ezzie stared down the passage. Her back straightened into a rigid posture, and her upper lip twitched. 'I didn't see that one.'

I kept my mouth shut, allowing her to take the lead, which she quickly did with an indignant walk. Either Esmeralda Lucian wasn't as intimidating as I used to think, or I was getting bolder. Either way, a mutual feeling of respect had developed between us over the last couple of days, and I felt we stood on equal footing.

We made slow progress, taking turns with our phones to try and conserve our batteries. The thick silence permeating the tunnel seemed to make the ceiling and walls close in around us. I had to take my mind off the shrinking feeling that I couldn't shake.

'Ezzie,' I said quietly.

She glanced back at me. 'Yes?'

'Do you trust Hugo's parents?'

I hadn't intended to make her stop, but Ezzie immediately pulled up in the middle of the passage and turned over her shoulder to look fully at me. 'Why do you ask?'

'They're *Sobrasi*. How do you know they aren't bad, just like the rest of them? What if they did that to Sebastian on purpose? How do we know they don't want him for the same reason as the people they were hiding the head from in the first place?'

'I may not understand, or even agree, with all that Zindelo and Nadya have done,' Ezzie replied, 'but I trust that their motivations are pure. They want what is best for the Outcast clans, and they know the only way to ensure your safety and protection is to restore order to the shadow world.' Ezzie paused, and her eyes took on a faraway gleam. 'Hugo's parents awakened me. If it hadn't been for Zindelo and Nadya, I would still be trapped in stone. All they ever asked in return was that I offer whatever help I could to their clan.'

I frowned. 'But you aren't bound to them.'

'No.'

'Yet you've stayed near them all this time.'

Her arched brows lifted. 'Have you *met* the Corsi clan? They need all the help they can get.'

'Fair enough,' I said, smirking a little in return. I ran my hand along the jagged wall of the passage. 'There's something I still don't understand, though. If Hugo's parents are so powerful, and they were able to awaken you, why are you still human? I mean, couldn't they make you a gargoyle again?'

Ezzie's expression turned serious, and the shadows of the passage seemed to grow long across her face. 'They didn't know how. Too many decades have passed since my punishment was enacted.' She sighed heavily. 'Sebastian thinks I'm fortunate. I can understand his feelings. Being human was all he knew from the moment he awakened in the home of the Corsis. Even now, despite his best efforts, Sebastian clings to the idea that he's still human.'

'Why is that such a bad thing? I asked.

She studied me with silvery eyes. 'I never said it was.'

We continued down the passage, now walking side by side. The silence engulfed us again. I wanted to call out Katie's name, but I knew better. I turned the knife in my hand, watching how the flashlight caught every diamond particle. They twinkled like deadly stars. I'd put Quentin's weapon to use more than I ever imagined I would.

As we walked, I slowly became aware of a tiny flitter in my stomach. Emotions swirled like a slow-moving river through my head. Beside me, Ezzie decreased her pace and raised her chin curiously.

'Can you sense anything?' I whispered.

'I believe shadowen are close,' she answered. Then she looked at me strangely. 'Do you sense something?'

My heart began skittering underneath my ribs, and a warm-cold feeling settled over me – a sensation that caused tears to prick at the edges of my eyes. I *knew* that feeling.

'Maybe,' I said. 'I'm not sure yet.'

As we approached the light on the far end of the long passageway, noises filtered faintly towards us. I glanced at Ezzie. Her face had grown hard and cold, like the walls around us. My insides fluttered like a caged bird. Ezzie motioned me against the wall. She took the opposite side. We eased steadily along the tunnel, keeping our backs firmly against the stone.

'We're supposed to be friends,' said a familiar voice.

Though I couldn't see anything yet, I exchanged a relieved look with Ezzie. Katie was alive! But who was she talking to? I quickened my pace, holding my knife ready, unsure of what we'd find when we reached the end.

'I'm sorry,' said another voice. 'I didn't know how.'

I stopped dead. It was him! I hadn't imagined the feeling.

261

It *was* Sebastian! However, his usually mellow voice had changed into that strange growling tone. It sent a cold prickle down my spine. I clutched Ezzie's arm from across the tunnel. Sebastian was fighting that other part of him.

'Katie, no,' he said harshly.

She gasped loudly. There was a painful pause.

'I've been told the way I look takes some getting used to,' said Sebastian finally. The hurt was plainly evident in his reply. I heard him take a long, steadying breath. 'Why don't we just take it a little at a time?'

A loud scream split the air.

27. Sebastian

Katie's scream rocketed through the room. I snarled and kicked at the mass on top of me. I twisted my body around. My lip curled in disgust as the smell hit me. Anya. She was more revolting than the last time we met.

The gargoyle-turned-chimera stood on legs inverted from the shin down, bent like an animal's, with talon-toed feet. Hair grew in matted gray patches through deep cracks in the skull. The mouth warped misshapen around rows of long fangs. Primal eyes, solid silver, gleamed with hatred so odious I tasted it. Black saliva leaked from between her bottom teeth. I felt a nauseous heave.

My ... kill ...

The thought bursting inside my head was a curdling shock. Each telepathic word seemed a colossal effort to produce, as though Anya's language had deteriorated, existing only a fraction above the grotesques and their inhuman, screeching communication.

Her head whipped up, solid silver eyes rotating around, and fixated on Katie. She licked her black lips hungrily, then snapped her attention to me, each movement like the cracking of a whip. Her teeth glimmered in a wicked grin.

You ... first ...

She tackled me. Her body pressed against my chest with her full weight. Wings spread above me and filling the space to the ceiling. My own wings cramped under the strain, trapped inside my cloak and pinned under my body. The adrenaline coursing through me hit capacity. I bared my teeth. Every molecule of my being burned with scorching fire.

I sank my claws into the chimera's sides and threw her off me. Anya landed like a cat, a guttural laugh splitting her black lips. I scrambled up. My wings burst free, destroying the cloak as they unfurled to the ceiling. I faced off with the chimera, back hunched and claws spread wide.

I was no longer shaking. My shoulder didn't hurt. All I felt was heat and fury. I glanced over my shoulder, peering through the thickening red haze. Katie was pressed against the wall. Her eyes shifted from the chimera to me. She stared at us with the same level of horror.

'Katie,' I growled. 'Take the steps and get out of here!'

She didn't move. She mouthed my name, but no sound came out. The color drained from her face as her knees wobbled and she sank to the floor.

Anya reacted like she'd spotted a wounded animal. She turned with the force of a tiger about to pounce. I countered, just in time. I knocked the chimera sideways, throwing her off course, but the impact sent me reeling. We both rolled over the dirt-packed floor and came up again, like boxers in a ring, ready for the second round.

Katie wedged herself in the corner, her eyes only on me. I felt disbelief and terror radiating off her in a waves. The part of me I was still desperately clinging to withered under her stare. Whatever she'd been told about me hadn't been enough. She gaped at me like I was a monster.

I turned away, concentrating on the chimera.

Another rotting stench permeated the room. Matthias streaked through the opening where I'd entered, trailing oily black smoke. He thrashed his wings, smashing the oil lanterns on the table. Katie screamed again as the room plunged instantly into darkness.

Both chimeras were on me at once, a savage ruthless attack. My night vision was useless against the assault. Talons lashed my chest. Skin split with excruciating pain. Katie's cries pierced my ears. I was slipping too fast to hold on. The dark thing leapt to the surface. My blood boiled with *prah* and primal instinct. A grisly sound erupted from my throat, and the gates of my control crashed down.

I let the dark thing take me.

It came easier this time, the giving up of myself to the primal force. It surged through my blood and moved within me, enveloping me in a field of red fury. I fought the chimeras as they fought me – like vicious animals.

I heard my name in the air. Someone pleading.

But I couldn't come back. Not anymore.

Blood ran from claws. Teeth. Mine or theirs.

Wings beat. Ripped.

Falling.

Darkness. Alone.

28. Josephine

Another scream from Katie reached us.

I broke into a run, Ezzie beside me. I heard chimera shrieks and the sound of flapping wings. They grew louder as the tunnel turned wider. There was an inhuman roar, which I recognized as Sebastian's. My chest throbbed at the sound.

The passage suddenly gave way to an enormous room. In the middle of it, Sebastian and Anya grappled with each other like wild animals in a vicious fight. Katie crouched a few feet away, her face glued solid in fright. I gripped my knife and hurried forward. Then, another chimera was in the room.

The lights went out.

Glass shattered on the floor, followed by the smell of oil. My feeble phone light did nothing to help. The room was full of shadowen battle. I fumbled through the room, keeping to the outer edge, trying to find Katie. Ezzie called out, and I whirled on my heel.

She had Katie under the arms, dragging her back towards

the passage. I scrambled on my hands and knees after them, avoiding the slash of giant wings overhead. My heart wrenched so tight I could hardly breathe. Here and there, in the pale light, gray forms blurred by. Table and chairs were smashed and pieces strewn across the floor. Blood splatted the dirt.

I made it to the passage and grabbed Katie by the shoulders. 'Katie!'

Her eyes were like a blind person's, unfocused and wild. She whimpered softly, curling her arms over her head protectively. Ezzie moved, like she was going back into the room.

'No,' I cried. 'You'll get killed.'

'I can see well enough,' she snapped.

'Stay here,' I ordered Katie, pointlessly. She hadn't moved.

Ezzie and I went in together, and holding our phones high, striving to get as much light in the room as possible. What I saw made my stomach turn. The stone body of Matthias lay crumpled on the floor, his wings bent back in awful directions, and his neck broken. Anya hovered over Sebastian; her talons plunged deep into his left shoulder. He swayed unsteadily, looking dead on his feet.

Anger tore through me. 'Get away from him!'

I ran with no thought for anything but him. Ezzie matched me, stride for stride. She swung her mace in a giant arc with one hand. The contact was solid. Anya's wing snapped like a twig. The chimera wailed and lashed out, crushing Ezzie's phone. The loss of light made it difficult to see. Ezzie yelled and took aim, but the chimera was faster this time. Her talons struck Ezzie in the stomach.

I drove my knife into Anya's ribs. The chimera's body convulsed. She snarled and fixed her silver eyes on me. She knocked the phone from my hand, and it flipped and clattered away from me, landing face up. The light shone weakly at the ceiling, but it was enough to see my fate.

Anya descended on me. Her nasty, taloned hands clutched my arm, pulling me towards her. Her grip was like steel, and I couldn't wrench free. She leaned forward, ooze dribbling from her mouth, dripping on my neck. Her wicked teeth were inches from my face.

'Gypsy ... flesh ...'

Then, I was free.

Sebastian was somehow in my place, his body shielding me from Anya. She lunged, but he was faster. His claws sliced straight through her mid-section. Anya screeched. She stared at him with a face twisted by hate and pain. Her skin began to harden into stone. In one swift, powerful move, Sebastian hurled the chimera clean across the room and into the wall. Her body cracked and shattered – a hideous statue, broken forever.

Sebastian snarled at the dead chimeras. Then he threw his head back and roared. The triumphant sound pinged around the room. Then, suddenly, he clutched at his shoulder, and everything about him seemed to change. It was like he was bursting through the surface of a lake. His chest heaved, like he was struggling for air.

Sebastian!

I wasn't sure if I said his name aloud or in my head, but he turned. For the briefest of moments, our eyes met. His wings slumped. I saw pain behind the soft, tortured look on his face. He opened his mouth to speak. Then, he fell hard to his knees and pitched forward into the bloody dirt. In the faint light, his body seemed almost like a dark shadow, barely there at all.

'No!' I yelled.

I scrambled frantically for my phone, and then knelt in front of him, holding the light closer. His face was mostly hidden in the dirt, and also by his matted hair, which seemed longer than I remembered it – though it had only been three days. I tried turning him on his side, but his enormous splayed wings made it impossible, and he was so heavy. My heart felt like it was going to stop beating. I touched the side of his face – the little that I could see of it – stroking the skin with my fingers, waiting for his eyes to open. But they didn't.

He was completely still.

'Sebastian, it's Josephine,' I said, choking back a sob. 'I'm here.'

A moment passed. Then another. Suddenly, his back expanded in a breath. He wasn't dead. I lifted my eyes to the ceiling, thanking God. I pressed my hand to the center of his back, in the space between where his wings grew out, just beneath his shoulder blades. I felt his breathing growing steadier, each inhale moving his back more regularly. My fingers drifted towards his left wing. I'd never had the opportunity to observe them from this angle, and so close.

I noticed the evidence of a recent wound in his wing. The hole had closed over with fresh leathery skin, like what made up the rest of his wing. I took the top section tentatively in my hand. The bone that made up the framework was thicker than my arm. I lifted it away from his back, and my stomach turned.

Several inches of a Marksman's arrow protruded from the back of his shoulder. The feathered end had been snapped off, leaving a crumbling, hollow shaft. Blood still trickled, but it glittered weirdly in the white light, a mixture of purple-black, but with silver specks. Around the wound, black veins sprouted like branches of a tree, just underneath his gray skin.

Ezzie groaned from the corner. I took my phone, leaving Sebastian in darkness, and went to her. She pushed herself up into a seated position and hissed through her teeth.

'Vile creature,' she said, spitting into the dirt.

I looked her over. 'You're hurt.'

Ezzie pressed her hand against her abdomen. Her fingers came away smeared with red blood. She grimaced. 'It looks worse than it is. Help me up.'

I didn't argue. I got her to her feet and she leaned against the wall. Her eyes were on Sebastian – or rather, the shadowed lump in the middle of the floor, which was all I could see of him.

'Is he ...?' she began.

'No, he's breathing. But he's unconscious.'

Ezzie shook her head in disbelief. 'How did he get here?'

'Josie?'

Katie's voice startled me so much I almost dropped the phone. I'd forgotten she was there. She stepped warily into the room. Tears streaked her face, which was ghostly white in the dimness. I hurried over to her and wrapped my arms around my best friend.

'Katie, I'm so sorry.'

She clung to me, little sniffles escaping every few breaths. Everything about this was a total mess. A dangerous and terrible mess. I squeezed my eyes shut, wishing it all away. It was Katie who pulled back first.

'I'm okay,' she said. 'They didn't hurt me. He ...' she almost looked at Sebastian's body, but her eyes never quite made it there. 'He didn't hurt me.'

'Katie, I don't—'

'What *happened* to him, Josie? God, this is so not what I was picturing at all. I mean, I don't know what I was thinking. You said he wasn't like them, but I thought he'd still be ...' She shuddered. 'Josie, the way he went after them, what he did, and he's got these giant bat wings, he has freaking *wings*, and I just don't ... how could he keep this from me?'

I let her ramble until she finally went quiet. I held her hand. 'You've seen him now, Katie. You know he couldn't tell you.' I let her go and walked back towards Sebastian. 'He couldn't tell anyone.'

I shone the light around the room. A black piece of fabric was scrunched up among a pile of broken chairs. I picked it up and shook it out. A Marksman cloak. I got on my knees and carefully eased one wing in towards Sebastian's body. The bony framework bent stiffly at the joints, but without too much resistance. Then I repeated the action with the other wing. I draped the cloak across Sebastian's body and stood.

'We need light,' I said. 'My battery's almost dead.'

I explored the room quickly. The two lanterns were smashed beyond use, and there was nothing else in the large, empty space. I studied the three passageways leading out. One, we already knew, led back to the ladder and the crypt. I shone the light inside the far right tunnel. The passage was bricked over – which left only the center one.

'Stay here.' I glanced at Katie. 'And don't move. It's going to get dark.'

'Then you better be fast,' she replied with an edge to her voice.

I took our only light and entered the passageway, which was short and emptied into another room. The space was smaller, but furnished, with books scattered in every corner. I located a small lantern and a box of matches, sitting on the desk. I returned to the other room.

'Hold this,' I said to Katie, handing her my phone.

I struck a match, lifted the glass, and lit the lantern. A warm glow instantly bathed the room in a soft, golden light. Katie switched off my phone light and handed it back to me. We stood quietly, waiting while our eyes adjusted.

Ezzie clutched her side and she moved away from the wall. 'We need help, Josephine. Sebastian's obviously in no condition to shadow anywhere, and we won't be able to carry him to the ladder, much less up it.'

I looked at Sebastian, and I made up my mind. 'Ezzie, you're wounded. But Katie can help you out. You guys get back to the inn and get Hugo's parents. Nadya has medicine. I'm going to stay here with him until you return.'

Katie bristled. 'No way. We aren't leaving you.'

'You have to,' I said firmly.

Ezzie took a few steps forward, inhaling sharply. Blood trickled between her fingertips, and I saw the deep talon slashes beneath a ripped section of her t-shirt. Katie watched her, too, and I saw her resolve falter.

'The quicker you go, the sooner you get back,' I said.

Katie pursed her lips together. She glanced sideways at Sebastian's form, but only for the briefest of seconds. Like she didn't trust me being left with him. And I couldn't really blame her, after what she'd just witnessed. But she only knew the Sebastian from before. I knew him now.

'Okay, fine,' Katie huffed, brushing off her face. She hugged me so tight it cut off my air supply. 'Just, I don't know, be careful.' She released me and looked at Ezzie. 'And that weapon thing of yours stays here, with her.'

'Very well,' said Ezzie, her eyes half-closed.

I walked to the stone corpse of Matthias and picked up the discarded mace Ezzie had lost in the battle. I sat cross-legged beside Sebastian and laid the weapon across my legs. 'I'll be fine. *We'll* be fine. Just hurry.'

Esmeralda wrapped her arm around Katie's shoulder. 'We'll return as soon as we can.'

I nodded and watched as they disappeared into the dark.

29. *Josephine*

As soon as they were gone, I turned my full attention on Sebastian, still unconscious on the floor, with the cloak hiding his upper body and a large portion of his wings.

His jeans were frayed at the bottoms, his Converse muddy and ripped in several places. I set the diamond-studded mace aside and slid my hand along a section of his wing not covered with the cloak. The texture of the leathery membrane was thicker than I remembered. Maybe it was a trick of the light, but they looked duller, too.

He took a sudden harsh breath, and I tore my hand away. The exhaling sounded more like a low growl, but he definitely wasn't awake. The neck muscles underneath his pewter hair were so tight that they bulged like iron cords under his skin. Even unconscious, there was nothing about Sebastian that seemed relaxed.

I wanted to turn his head, to get a better look at his face. But it was like an unseen hand held me back. There was something was different about Sebastian – I sensed it, more than anything. The weird kind of undercurrent that always seemed to flow between us when we were together seemed altered, if that was even possible, leaving a mysterious force I didn't recognize.

'Sebastian,' I whispered.

Why was he *here*, of all places? He couldn't have known about Katie. He was supposed to be in the Court of Shadows, awaiting his trial. Hugo had just seen him yesterday.

So why?

I thought about the arrow wound on his shoulder. He'd escaped. That was the only possible explanation. Had he given up on any chance of being acquitted? Tiny hope rippled inside me, like the effect of a pebble tossed into water. Was he trying to get back to me?

I rubbed my eyes as exhaustion set in, making me feel heavy from head to toe. The way he'd fought Anya and Matthias, it was like watching him that night at the Circe, when Augustine let him out of the cage. He'd lost himself. I glanced warily at his motionless form. Was he still lost?

'You asked me to forgive you,' I said softly. 'But there's nothing to forgive, Sebastian. Nothing, unless you give up. Please don't give up. I need you. Not as my guardian. I need you as my friend.' My throat constricted. 'And ... as more. Sebastian, you're so much more.'

I felt something shift behind me.

'Well, that's quite touching.'

Augustine stepped into the room from the center passage. I stumbled over Sebastian's body in my haste to retrieve the mace from the floor. I spun around, holding it straight.

'Get out,' I demanded.

His brow lifted, and the white scar on his cheek reacted to the motion, like a snake on skin. 'That's a bit rude, don't you think? After all, this is my home, not yours.'

'*Marimé*,' I said, spitting out the word like the curse it was.

'Yes, yes,' he said, sauntering further in. 'I've heard the term before.' His eyes quickly took in the room, noting the stone remains of Anya and Matthias. His expression was casual enough, but I sensed the irritation behind it. 'So what brings you to my humble abode? You'll have to forgive my lack of reception, but I was under the impression you were still at the Corsi inn.'

'Your chimera took Katie. I came after her.'

'I see the girl is no longer with us,' he replied. 'Freed her, did you?' When I didn't respond, he continued. 'Kidnapping your friend wasn't my intention. I sent the shadowen after you.' Augustine paused in front of the stone corpse of Matthias. He knelt, shaking his head, as though he were looking at a glass of milk spilt by a misbehaving child, and not the dead body of one of his shadow creatures. 'Unfortunately, Anya and Matthias have proven to be unreliable since I transformed them into chimeras.' He rose and kicked a chunk of stone, sending it into the wall. It disintegrated to dust.

'Why were those shadowen following me?' I demanded.

Augustine chuckled lightly. 'Because you left Sixes, my dear. Of course, I should've expected as much. In fact, I'd have been quite disappointed if my niece hadn't shown some of that stubborn Romany spirit.'

He stepped closer, and I moved as he moved, planting myself firmly between Sebastian's unconscious body and the man who used to be my uncle. 'What do you want from me?'

Augustine crossed his arms and changed directions, circling around again. 'Honestly, nothing, had you remained at the Circe. But since you insisted on coming to Savannah, it became imperative that I kept you away from the Court until the Gathering Celebration. Telling Hugo Corsi that the Queen was out of town, sending chimeras to keep you all occupied. Those tactics worked well enough.'

The mace grew heavier in my hand, but I refused to let it drop. 'Why go to so much trouble?'

Augustine rubbed his chin. His gaze shifted to Sebastian. 'It appears our young gargoyle here is having a difficult time transitioning. He clings to your bond. He keeps calling out your name, fighting my efforts to free him from his miserable state. It's not been enough simply to remove him from your presence.'

It was a terrible time for my heart to soar in my chest, but the sensation lightened my body and added to my resolve. Sebastian and I hadn't come this far, only to have Augustine destroy it all.

He frowned in mock chastisement. 'Of course, Sebastian Grey nearly cost me everything I've been working towards with his futile stunt. He had to know he'd be found eventually.' Augustine took a visual circuit of the room. 'I was baffled as to why he would come here.' He narrowed his eyes pointedly at me. 'Now I understand.'

I blinked, careful to hide my emotions. 'So he did escape.'

'I prefer to call it a brief detour,' he replied.

'Sounds like you're in over your head,' I said curtly. 'Sebastian's stronger than the others. And when the High Council discovers what you've tried to do to him, you're going to be the one on trial.'

Augustine laughed then, full and deep. The sound of it made little spiders of fear crawl up my back. 'Dearest niece, I apologize for how much you've been kept in the dark. Sebastian was never going to have a trial. The Queen has seen him for herself, and she was satisfied.'

I went cold all over. 'Satisfied with what?'

'That such a volatile gargoyle should be given over to those with more skills in dealing with his kind.'

'You're not getting him,' I snapped.

Augustine chuckled, amused. 'I'm afraid that's not up for debate. This gargoyle has already been awarded to me. He is my initiation payment into the ranks of the *Sobrasi*.' He studied me a moment. 'Ah, I see from your expression that you know precisely who I'm referring to. It seems you've been speaking to someone with intimate knowledge of our clandestine little group.'

I clutched the mace until my fingers burned and narrowed my eyes. I refused to give anything away to him with a rash reply. I worked his words through my head again before speaking.

'The *Sobrasi* let you join? They obviously don't have any standards.'

I smiled grimly. It was a retort Sebastian would've given, were he awake – wry and sarcastic. The thought gave me strength. Augustine's own casual smile stayed fixed across his face, but it didn't reach his eyes.

'I possess something they cannot refuse.'

Dread pressed in on me from all sides. Did Augustine know the truth about Sebastian and about the head of *La Gargouille*? Zindelo had been convinced that no one knew except them. They'd been the only ones there, when the statue of Saint Sebastian and the head of the monster were brought to life, combined into the form of the boy – of the *gargoyle* – who'd turned my life upside down. I breathed out slowly, my face a mask. No emotions, only facts. I needed to know what Augustine knew.

'I don't get it,' I said, 'Why do you keep trying? Sebastian's not a chimera, and he never will be. If you want more shadowen to replace your others, why don't you ask your *Sobrasi* friends? Can't they just create them? Why do you need Sebastian?'

Augustine tilted his head slightly. 'He has qualities the *Sobrasi* believe will be useful to eradicate the shadowen scourge that has plagued our people since the Middle Ages. And isn't that enough to bring us all into some agreement? Isn't that what we all want as Outcasts? To live our lives, free of the constant skirmishes? To allow our children to play without fear outside the walls and tunnels of our Havens?'

I kept pressing. 'What qualities?'

'As much as I would love to spend more time with my lovely niece, I must return Sebastian to his holding cell and then clean up the mess he left.' Augustine smiled brightly at me. 'But don't worry, I am leaving you in the best of company.'

I frowned. 'Company?'

Footsteps crunched in the dirt floor behind me. I turned.

Quentin walked into the room, dressed in full Marksman gear. His jaw was purpled over in a deep bruise, and there was a small cut above his eye. His left arm was in a sling. As he met my eyes, his lips curled into a smile.

'Hi, Josie,' he said. 'I'm still waiting on that phone call, by the way.'

My tongue sealed itself to the roof of my mouth. All the pieces of my world collided in front of me, and I suddenly knew the awful truth: Quentin hadn't stayed in Savannah to represent my father. He was here *with* Augustine. He'd been going along with him the whole time. The room tilted around me. I started forward, but he held out his other arm, preventing me. I found my voice. 'Quentin, wh—'

'Let's just keep this business,' he said.

He whistled sharply. Several Marksmen filed in through the passage. They surrounded Sebastian and lifted him up. His arms fell limp at his sides; his wings dragged the floor.

Augustine approached. He produced a syringe from inside his coat. Before I could even protest, he plunged the needle into Sebastian's neck; one quick motion, in and out. Sebastian's body twitched.

'There,' said Augustine, putting the syringe away. 'That should keep him nice and quiet, should he decide to wake up before we reach the dungeon.' He dipped his head slightly. 'I thank you for your assistance, Quentin. I will see you shortly.'

Quentin nodded in return. The Marksmen carrying Sebastian shuffled out of the room, with Sebastian in tow. Augustine leaned down, brushing Anya's stone remains off his boot, and then he followed them out. Two Marksmen remained, taking up positions near the passageway entrance.

I hoisted my mace, but the gesture felt weak and pointless against the heavily armed men. I turned my anger on Quentin. 'You can't possibly be helping him,' I said, jutting my chin in the direction Augustine had gone. 'Quentin, you know what he is. And you're a Marksman. You're sworn to protect and serve the—'

'Don't talk to me about duties,' he said coldly. 'Your entire family is a disgrace. And you.' He glared down his nose at me. 'You have a lot to change before you become Queen.'

My mouth fell open. 'How did—'

'Your family's secrets have always been mine. Your father trusted me. Still does, in fact.'

I recoiled from Quentin like he was toxic. 'What is it you think I've done?'

'Defying your *bandoleer*. Bringing a *gadje* into our affairs. Siding with a shadowen who murdered a Roma.' A smile twisted his chiseled face. 'And you never called me back.'

Hot tears threatened behind my eyes. He'd never thrown accusations at me before. 'And you just accept all of it? Just like that. You don't even bother to hear my side before making your own conclusions. How is that love?'

I regretted the words as soon as they flew from my mouth.

He drew back. '*Love?*'

The tears retreated far back inside me. 'I loved you, Quentin.'

'When you were thirteen, Josie. When your father made the match and we became tangled together in traditions that were bigger than us and out of our control. But years pass, and duty and love have a way of getting mixed up sometimes.'

I dropped the mace limply at my side. All the questions I hadn't been ready to face were being answered, right in front of me. This was Quentin Marks. This was who he truly was.

'Maybe you're right,' I replied. 'I haven't been honest with you, and I'm not going to try and justify that. I've avoided you lately because I didn't know what to say, and I'm sorry.'

'Sorry for what, exactly?'

I looked at him steadily.

'That I didn't put an end to this months ago.'

Quentin toyed with the handle of the Marksman sword sheathed at his hip. He looked back at me. I couldn't read his expression at all. He ran a hand through his black hair and then pinched his lips together.

'It doesn't have to end, Josephine.'

I blinked. 'What?'

He leaned forward, looking once more like the man I'd convinced myself I knew. 'We've been together a long time,' he said. 'Maybe what you felt for me then was a childish love. Maybe it grew into something else, maybe it didn't. But it doesn't matter anymore.' He smiled, and it was warm this time. 'You could learn to love me differently. We're Roma, Josephine. Our duty, our traditions, they are what hold us together. You've always known this. You've always accepted it.' His hand found mine, his skin warm as his smile. 'If you have the faintest desire to be Queen one day, you're going to need someone by your side who understands this, too. Who understands what it's like.'

I stared at him, frozen in disbelief. There was no amusement in his eyes, no snide quirk of his lip. His expression was sincerity. Had his sharp replies been jealous anger? I shook my head to keep the emotions at bay.

'You can't be serious,' I replied.

'Why not?' he questioned. 'Josephine, what has that gargoyle brought you that was any good? What has he done that was beneficial to the Circe, to your family? Guardian or whatever he claims to be, he's done no more than our Marksmen have done. Everywhere he goes, chaos seems to follow, and behind that, even more trouble.' He squeezed my hand, his voice gentle. 'Maybe it's not even his fault. He didn't choose to be what he is. I don't blame him for that. But he doesn't have power over it, either, and that makes him dangerous. To everyone.'

I slid my hand out of his and stepped away. My gaze fell on the chimeras' stone debris. No, it wasn't Sebastian's fault, what he was. He never asked for it. But I refused to believe he was powerless against it – as long as he didn't have to face things alone. It wasn't Quentin I wanted by my side.

'No,' I said out loud.

Quentin acted as though he hadn't heard me. 'Augustine has already given his word, Josie. Whatever aspirations he has within the *Sobrasi* have nothing to do with us. The throne will be yours, the shadowen will be destroyed, and you and I can start over. Our *kumpania* can be stronger than ever before.'

I looked at Quentin for a long time. Once, his smooth words or fiery kisses were all it took to make things right between us. But that time was done. He was right about one thing: I wasn't a child. I hadn't been for a long time. I'd been content to hide behind my duties instead of embracing them.

'You really believe that,' I said.

He nodded. 'I have no doubt in my mind.'

I hesitated, turning the mace over in my hands, struggling to conquer the surge of disgust and betrayal that threatened to drown me. I forced myself to look straight into Quentin's eyes, and I saw clearly that darkness within them that I'd refused to acknowledge for so long.

I had to push aside my feelings and focus on what was important. Sebastian. I took a deep, steadying breath. If I rejected Quentin right now, I'd lose any chance of finding Sebastian, wherever they took him. But after what had just happened, if I accepted too easily, then Quentin would know I was just playing along.

'So what happens now?' I asked warily.

Quentin narrowed his eyes, probably trying to decipher my thoughts. At last, he shrugged. 'We bring the gargoyle to the *Sobrasi*. Augustine gets what he wants, which means, ultimately, so do I.'

'But what will they do to him?'

'I guess you'll find out,' he replied. He gestured to the Marksmen. 'Take her.'

'What?' I struggled against their hands on my arms. One wrenched the mace from my grasp. 'Quentin, what are you doing?'

'We've lost a lot of trust between us,' Quentin replied, smiling. 'It will take some time to build that back up. In the meantime, I suggest you come quietly. Your actions from this point on will determine your future.'

30. *Josephine*

The tunnel system was nothing I'd ever seen or heard anyone tell about. It was unkempt, encased in dirt and cobwebs, scarcely lit by cloudy lanterns. The air felt thick and unused. I was completely lost, with no sense of direction, but Quentin seemed to know the way like he'd walked it in his sleep. The two Marksmen guards kept me firmly between them as Quentin forged on ahead.

I studied his tall frame and steady gait. Any guilt I'd felt over how I'd treated him had grown cold, and my feelings shriveled to nothing. My anger turned inward, biting at me with sharp teeth. Had I been *that* blind all the years we'd been together? I clenched my teeth. No, he *had* changed. But I'd missed it, somehow, while I was wrapped up in fantasies and well-paved futures.

Some part of Quentin still loved me. I saw that glimmer along with the darkness of his gaze. But whatever part of him I'd been in love with wasn't there. Maybe it had been once, and I just never saw it go. I felt like an idiot, but I couldn't wallow over questions rooted in the long-dead past.

Christi J. Whitney

I had to concern myself with the present.

The Marksmen carrying Sebastian were too far ahead of us for me to see. The connection I always sensed between us felt distant, and I prayed it was only because he was unconscious. Seeing his lifeless body made me scared in a way I hadn't been before.

We were heading in the direction of the Court of Shadows, based on the widening of the tunnel and the light provided by a mixture of lanterns and electric bulbs.

The Marksmen had lied to Hugo about my aunt being gone, which meant the Queen was somewhere inside the Court. If I could get away, if I could find her, then maybe everything wasn't lost. Augustine might have some deal with the *Sobrasi*, but he wasn't above Outcast law. My fingers itched to get to my phone, which I'd stuffed in my back pocket. Even a quick text to the Corsis could bring help. But there was no way. The two men had my arms pinned firmly to my side. But the thought of my phone made me think of something else.

'You know,' I called out to Quentin. 'You're not the only one I haven't called. My father thinks I've been at Katie's all weekend. I'm expected back at the Circe tonight, and you know how my father gets when he doesn't know where I am.'

Quentin slowed. 'Yes, I do. Which is why I've already taken care of that for you.' He nodded his head, almost like a bow. 'No need to thank me.' He waited for my reaction, which I wasn't great at concealing. 'All it took was a few texts, explaining the situation to him – leaving out certain details, obviously. He knows you're with me, and everything's fine.'

'Perfect,' I said.

286

'I thought so,' he replied.

My gaze drifted to his sling. 'What happened to you, by the way?'

His fixed smile faltered a bit. 'Keep moving.'

He turned and put distance between us, continuing up the tunnel. But I'd seen the expression on his face, and I knew, Sebastian had been the cause. I'd never seen anyone else rattle Quentin that way. Once, I would've felt bad for him. Now, I only felt a smug satisfaction.

*

A good while later – I couldn't be sure of the time in the constant golden glow of the underground – we stopped in front of an arched doorway. Quentin stepped aside, allowing my guards and I to go first.

At first, it seemed like a giant wine cellar, but as I scanned the stone columns and arched ceilings, I dismissed that idea. There were several long pews with faded cushions pushed up against walls. In the corner sat a small round table with matching stools. A rectangular table surrounded dominated the center of the room. An old communion table, I realized, seeing the etchings along the front.

The Marksmen who'd been carrying Sebastian placed his body on the table, lying him face down. If I hadn't seen his back continuing to expand and contract, I would've sworn he was dead. Augustine sat on one of the pews, smiling with a look of disgusting contentment.

'What is this place?' I demanded.

He glanced around, like he was seeing it for this first time. 'Well, I believe some churches call them catacombs. Others, cellars or basements.'

'This isn't part of the Court of Shadows.'

'Definitely not,' he replied. 'These are a collection of tunnels once used to transport the dead to the cemetery during one of the early Yellow Fever outbreaks.' He smiled. 'Or perhaps, simply places to bury the bodies when there was no more room. Either way, these tunnels, as you can image, are shunned by the Outcast population, which means there are no patrols here. I've found it to be a nice little way to get around the city without being seen.'

I shivered, but not from cold. To lounge around tunnels and rooms used for the dead only added to Augustine's *marimé* status. I moved away from the walls as much as possible. He saw my actions, and his smile only grew. I chose to speak to Quentin instead.

'Why would you worry about patrols, anyway?' I asked. 'It looks like you've got the Marksmen working for you.'

'Not all,' said Quentin. 'But enough for what we need.'

I started towards the table. One Marksman reached out to hold me back, but Augustine put up his hand. The guard backed away. As I approached Sebastian's comatose form, my throat ached. I wanted to reach out and hold his hand, to brush the hair way from his face so I could see him better.

'What's wrong with him?' I asked instead.

'Ah,' said Augustine, rising from the cushions and coming to the opposite end of the table. 'I believe this is probably the culprit.' He pulled back the cloak and started to lift Sebastian's left wing.

'Don't touch him.'

Augustine paused, then nodded. 'Be my guest.'

I gently moved aside the upper portion of his wing, exposing the bloody mess that was his shoulder. The blackish-purple blood oozing from the wound gleamed with

silvery speckles that shone with an eerie, otherworldly bright-
ness. I'd never been squeamish, not even when I broke my
wrist so badly during a Circe stunt that my bone went
through the skin. But this was a different kind of wound.
It made my stomach turn.

'A nasty little present from Quentin,' said Augustine,
observing the shattered arrow shaft that remained firmly
planted inside Sebastian's shoulder. 'It refuses to heal, you
see.'

I shot a look at Quentin, who only stared back nonchalantly. Then I studied the injury to Sebastian's wing. Unlike
his shoulder, it had mended cleanly. The hole I'd seen earlier
had nearly disappeared altogether. Only a faint outline of
the wound remained.

'And you know why, I take it.'

'It's his own fault, I'm afraid. If he'd listened to me, we
wouldn't be in this situation. I was merely going for a
demonstration in front of the *Sobrasi* – something to really
showcase my skills in shadowen control. It was a speedy
method. Each of Quentin's arrows were hollowed out, and
filled with—'

'*Prah* from the urn of Keveco Romany,' I said, cutting
him off. 'I heard you had it.'

He looked surprised. 'From whom, might I ask?'

I paused, afraid I'd given away information about Zindelo
and Nadya. I had to come up with something else. 'Karl
Corsi.'

'Really?' Augustine placed his hands casually in his
pockets and rocked back on his heels. 'I didn't give that old
man enough credit. He put more together than I thought.
It's a good thing he's no longer with us.'

Outrage rose inside me. 'Because of you.'

'You're correct, though,' continued Augustine, as though I hadn't spoken at all. 'It's the *prah* from the urn, very special and very rare. But I suppose I don't need to bore you with all those details.' He stared down at Sebastian. 'I've been chipping away at this gargoyle, bit by bit. Small doses, here and there. Starting with the night I took him from the Circe.'

'I knew that wasn't him,' I replied. 'Sebastian would never act that way.'

Quentin's face went dark. 'That's been your problem all along, Josephine. You refuse to see the truth. In fact, you run away from it completely. You've got a naive ideal of good-hearted nobility, but it doesn't exist! *Prah* or not, this creature is what he is.'

'If Sebastian's already so terrible, then why do you need the *prah*? You're trying to force him to be something he's not.'

Quentin scowled. 'He was a monster before this, Josephine. He needed no help when he tore that chimera apart in our camp.'

I shoved my finger in Quentin's chest; so mad I could taste the bitterness on my tongue. 'How does that make him different from you, Quentin? You took an oath to protect the Outcast world from shadow creatures. You've killed more than you can count. Are you saying that's not noble? If that's the case, then the Marksmen are nothing but a pack of murderers.'

Anger slipped through Quentin's dark mask. His hand clenched around his sword hilt, as though it were keeping him anchored in place. He opened his mouth, but Augustine didn't give him a chance.

'We've wasted enough time,' he said. 'It's time to pay a

visit to the Corsis' inn. I'm ready for Hugo's services now.' Augustine glanced at me. 'And we need to make sure the rest of their clan stays right where they are. We don't want anything getting in the way of the first night of the Gathering Celebration.'

Frigid fingers curled around my neck. 'What do you mean?'

Quentin stepped around me. 'I'll send Donani.'

'No,' said Augustine. 'His absence would be missed at the Court. I'm sure you have someone just as loyal among your ranks you could place in charge of this task, don't you?'

Quentin's eyes narrowed dangerously as they looked at each other. He gestured to one of the Marksmen who'd escorted me. The man stepped forward. He looked several years older than Quentin, with a deeply lined forehead and scraggly brown hair.

'Kennick,' said Quentin. 'Go to Donani and ask for six men. He'll know who to send with you. Be discreet. If anyone asks, you're doing your patrols. I suggest you split up and meet at the Corsi establishment.'

'Consider it done,' said the man.

'And Kennick,' Quentin said lowly. 'Hugo Corsi is your responsibility.'

The Marksman dipped his head and exited out the way we'd come in, followed by the remaining guards, leaving only Quentin and Augustine. I took careful, even breaths. Augustine knew Hugo and the guys were at the inn, but he hadn't mentioned anyone else. I prayed I had enough battery left to send him a text – if I could find a way.

'What an intense expression, dearest niece,' Augustine remarked, looking me over. 'Tell me, are you wondering

291

how you can get the word out to your Corsi friends? I do apologize, but I can't allow that.' He held out his hand over Sebastian's immobile body. I yanked my phone from my pocket and handed it over. 'Good girl,' he said, pocketing the device. 'Now, Sebastian and I have some work to do. I'd let you watch, but honestly, I think you'd be too much of a distraction right now, so we'll chat in a bit.'

'No, I won't—' I began.

Something hit me hard from behind, and the room went black.

31. Sebastian

Murky cold.

Formless. Underwater.

Forever lost.

I would never wake. But I didn't mind. It felt peaceful here; deep inside the other place where the dark thing always lurked. We had switched places, the two of us. The dark thing wore my skin, and I huddled where it used to hide, way down in the marrow of my bones. I would remain here.

And it would live in my place.

But something prevented me. There was a presence, and I sensed it, like a thick cord, wrapped around my chest. It refused to release me; it dragged me upward through the muddy waters. I struggled. Let me go.

Just let me stay.

I felt emotions that weren't my own, churning into other things in my head. There were words, strung together nonsensically. Bits and pieces. I knew the voice behind them.

It belonged to Josephine.

She was the rope, yanking me from this place. I clung to it frantically, desperate for escape. My body rose higher. There were lights, images I couldn't make out. But I was nearing the top.

The dark thing battled. It tasted freedom, and it screamed for more. But I held tight to the rope, focusing only on Josephine and the scent of exotic flowers and spices. I passed the dark thing by. It lashed at me. But it was too late. I was out of its reach.

I surfaced.

'She'll be fine, Quentin,' said a voice. 'She's a resilient girl.'

My body felt frigid, but not from the inside. I was lying on something cold and smooth. Not the floor of the room where I'd found … Katie. I remembered Katie, wide-eyed and staring at me in complete horror. And there was Matthias. And Anya. I fought them both.

I remembered it all, but vaguely, like snatches of a memory where people look like fuzzy blobs and the events are muddled. I felt the effects of Vitamin D coursing through my blood, keeping my body immobilized. I worked at prying my eyes open. They only budged a slit, but it was enough for me to get a hazy view of the scene in front of me.

Two men stood over something I couldn't see. One man wore black. His angular face and tall form I knew at once. Quentin Marks. The other man's white scar was clearly visible in the golden glow of the room. My lip twitched as my warning senses awakened and Augustine's stench filled my nostrils.

Quentin sighed. 'Resilient or not, I don't think knocking out my fiancé is a healthy way to begin this new stage in our relationship.' He ran his fingers through his hair and shrugged. 'I'm not sure she'll forgive me for that one.'

I hadn't imagined Josephine's scent. She was here in the room, on the floor in front of me! I strained to move, but my muscles refused to respond.

'You still think Josephine is going to consider you?' questioned Augustine, his voice laced with sarcasm. 'I don't mean to pry, of course, but it didn't sound like you two were getting along very well.'

A soundless growl formed in my throat.

'She'll come around,' Quentin replied. 'Josephine might be stubborn, but she's smart. She'll do what's best for the clan.'

'The future Queen,' said Augustine, musingly. 'Thalia made an interesting choice, picking my niece. Had you not told me, I wouldn't have believed it. But, my sister was never one for convention.' He laughed, a short, snide burst. 'That wretched cow. And to think, she promised me the throne, when the time came for her to step down.'

'You?' Quentin sounded baffled. 'That's not possible.'

Augustine's head snapped up, his eyes dangerous. 'Because I'm *marimé*? A punishment handed down by the Council, at the Queen's command.' His face contorted, stretching the scar. 'The throne should've been mine to begin with. I am the eldest. When our father grew too old to manage the *kumpania*, he appointed Thalia.'

'Why?' questioned the Marksman.

I took slow, clarifying breaths – curiosity the only thing keeping my protective instincts in check. I kept my slit eyes fixed on Augustine while he rolled his own eyes towards the ceiling, seemingly more annoyed than anything.

'Because I'm only half Romany,' he replied, his tone sharp as cut glass. 'My mother was from the Old Clans. It was a short-lived first marriage for my father, but I'm sure you can understand the complications I represented. Our people severed all ties with the Old Clans long ago. Keeping with that tradition, our father didn't think having someone of shared blood sitting on the Outcast throne would be beneficial for our *kumpania*.'

'Then Nicolas is the only full-blooded male heir.'

'Your intelligence astounds me,' Augustine replied.

I saw Quentin's fist clench at his side. 'Why didn't he challenge Thalia?'

'Nicolas didn't want to give up his precious Circe and the freedom it has provided the Romany clan over the years. But your observation is correct. Since he is a son, and the throne passes first to sons before daughters, Nicolas had to formally renounce the throne and any possible claim to it in the future. Which he did in a private ceremony.'

The pieces of Josephine's deep secret suddenly locked into place. She was the heir to prevent Augustine from getting his chance at the throne. I watched with growing anger as Augustine brushed off the sleeves of his dark shirt in the leisurely manner of one who knows he's superior.

'The Queen is sick,' said Augustine. He nodded at Quentin's surprised look. 'She's been battling her illness for almost five years, unknown to the majority of the *kumpania*. And, poor thing, she had no husband and no children – no one to follow after her. You can see her dilemma. If she died, the throne would pass out of Romany hands for the first time since the Sundering. Her pride could not allow that to happen. I saw her illness as my opportunity. I returned from my exile in Europe and proposed a solution to her: when the time came that she could no longer perform her duties, Thalia would lift my *marimé* status and announce me as her choice.'

'So she'd rather a traitor take the throne than an outsider,' said Quentin.

'Blood ties run thick,' he replied. 'She looked at the matter in the long term. She weighed the odds. I'm not a young man. My years as king would be numbered. But I promised her I would take a wife and ensure that a Romany would always be on the throne.'

Quentin's brow furrowed. 'What about your father?'

'Oh, he never knew,' said Augustine. 'He passed away quite suddenly.'

I could tell the look on his face meant that there was more to that part of the story than he was telling. Quentin obviously thought the same thing. He pursed his lips together, choosing not to delve farther.

'I was content to wait at first,' continued Augustine. 'I knew this would not be something that would happen immediately. During that time, I was able to go abroad and continue my research and study of shadowen lore. But when I began to hear rumors that the Queen might publically announce her successor, I returned at once.'

'But she hasn't named anyone.'

'How observant,' said Augustine suddenly, bitterness ripening in his voice; his expression no longer amused. 'Five years I waited, believing that at any time, my darling sister would call me back from my exile in Europe. What I didn't know was that she had betrayed me – chosen my niece instead.' Augustine's lip curled up into his scar. 'I have you to thank for that piece of information.'

'It wasn't the easiest secret to acquire,' Quentin replied.

Fury reddened Augustine's face as he spun away from my view. 'I hadn't even considered it,' he uttered, almost to himself. 'With Nicolas abdicating the throne, I assumed that would extend to his children as well. I did not know the law as much as I thought.'

'Guess not,' said Quentin, sounding pleased.

When Augustine crossed my line of sight again, the anger had melted from him countenance. His imperious manner was back. 'Our law is vast, but it is also resolute. You are aware that only adult Outcasts are eligible for the throne.'

'Yes,' said Quentin, eyeing him with barely contained hostility.

'According to Roma custom, Josephine needs a husband to be considered an adult,' Augustine commented. 'And I do believe my niece is well beyond the age for acceptable marriage proposals.'

'She's been … difficult,' said Quentin, darkening. 'She wanted to put off any official engagement until she'd turned eighteen. I thought we'd come to an agreement, but afterwards, she insisted we wait until after graduation from her *gadje* schooling institutions. And then, after she met that gargoyle, she wouldn't even talk about it. Especially after …'

'After they were bonded?'

My heart skittered between my ribs.

Quentin's whole body went rigid. 'She said it had nothing to do with us, but I knew, the moment he set foot in our camp. The way she looked at that abomination, that demon spawn. It makes me sick.'

'Well, those problems will no longer be an issue for you, Quentin. Your service to me has been appreciated, and your reward is the Outcast throne, through Josephine. And I give you my blessings. Once, being king was my desire as well, but I have different aspirations now. The Outcast throne is a small thing, compared with my goals.'

'I'm quite content with these small goals.'

Augustine chuckled. 'Yes, Quentin. With you as Josephine's husband, I'm sure the *kumpania* will be in excellent hands.'

'And the sooner we're rid of this gargoyle, the better.'

Augustine walked out of my limited sightline. 'Oh no, I disagree. He's everything to my plans at the moment. But, as I told you before, you needn't worry yourself with Sebastian Grey once we've met with the *Sobrasi*.'

Quentin gave a huffing laugh. 'Are you sure you didn't just nail your coffin shut with them? After what this demon did—'

'Yes, he did put a kink in things with his behavior in front of the *Sobrasi*, not to mention making a mess of the Court. If you'd been able to get two more shots in, as I hoped, then we would most likely not be here right now. But, all is well. We weren't quite ready for that. Things have worked out.'

'Meaning?'

Augustine moved back to Quentin and clasped his shoulder. 'Don't worry about that. Just make sure your man – Kennick, wasn't it? – is back in time, and that he has Corsi with him.'

Augustine had to be talking about Hugo. I pushed with all my strength to move. My wings quivered slightly.

'He will,' said Quentin in a sharp, cutting tone.

Augustine looked down. 'Now, why don't you take your unwilling fiancée and find her some suitable accommodations? And some aspirin. I think she'll have quite the headache when she awakes.'

I tried one last time, willing strength into my arms.

'Josephine …'

I pushed myself up on my elbows. They both whirled

around with shocked expressions. I clutched the edge of what I saw now was a table in the middle of an arched room. The edges of my vision darkened. I bared my teeth in one long hiss. My arms gave way and I collapsed. My body refused to move again.

'There was enough Vitamin D in that syringe to turn three groties to stone,' remarked Augustine, sounding impressed. 'Yes, I'd say it's definitely time.'

Quentin growled. 'He just won't give up.'

'Indeed,' Augustine replied. 'A quality I'm looking forward to exploiting.' He stepped back. 'Now, if you'll just take Josephine ... oh, I suppose you can't, can you? Not with the broken shoulder and all.'

'He'll pay for that,' snapped Quentin.

'Looks to me as though it's the gargoyle who has done the paying back,' said Augustine with a snide laugh. 'But not to worry.' He bent down, disappearing momentarily from my view. When he rose, he had Josephine in his arms. My heart petrified at the sight of her, not even two yards away from me. Her hair had mostly fallen from her pony-tail, and dirt stained one cheek. Her eyes were closed, her lips parted slightly.

It was like a terrible dance – she and I revolving around each other, so near, yet miles apart. I felt tendrils of our bond, weak but holding. Instincts flared inside me, to protect her, to throw myself between her and Quentin. I forced my eyes open to their full extent. They burned hot in their sockets.

Quentin seemed to sense my unblinking stare. He turned and met my gaze. I studied him, feeling the blood boil in my veins, and I allowed every fierce emotion I had to pour freely through my glare. There was an instant shift in his expression, a colossal effort to remain stoically cold.

'Come Quentin,' said Augustine.

'Are you sure the beast is immobile?' asked the Marksmen, his voice carefully constructed to match his expression.

'For now,' said Augustine, shifting Josephine's weight in his arms. 'But we shouldn't waste time. After you, Quentin.' The banished Gypsy nodded in the direction of the door. Quentin tore his gaze from mine and left without another word. Augustine passed in front of me, making absolutely sure I could see Josephine in his grasp. 'Make yourself comfortable, Sebastian. I won't be long.'

*

I wasn't sure how many minutes I lay frozen in the unfamiliar room, but finally, I felt the loosening of muscles, starting at my neck and continuing down my back, out to the edges of my wings. Still, I didn't make any attempt to move. I took in a breath through my nose, filtering smells.

Quentin and Josephine's scents had grown cold, along with most of the other Marksmen who'd been in their company. But Augustine's pungent odor went straight to my core, along with the icy chill and scorched scent brought on by Marksmen – but only two this time, not the larger number from before. The sounds of shoes on stone reached my gargoyle hearing, mingled with the hum of oil lanterns burning around me.

I pushed myself up and the black cloak, which had been thrown over me, tangled up in my wings. I tossed it aside and threw my legs over the slab of wood at the same time. I'd been lying on a large rectangular communion table. I clutched my shoulder. It burned like acid.

I placed my feet on the floor, but before I could go any

farther, the two Marksmen I'd smelled appeared in the doorway. They aimed small crossbows at me, half the size of Quentin's bow, but the arrows cocked and ready to fly were just as intimidating. Augustine came in next, and he smiled brightly as he saw me.

'Good morning,' said Augustine. 'Or, I should say, evening.' He gaze roamed over me, scrutinizing every detail. 'How are we feeling?'

'I think you can see for yourself.'

My head felt decently clear, but my voice still carried the growling twinge that accompanied my surges of adrenaline and instinct. Augustine noted it as well; his smile turned thin.

'All of this would've been over by now, had you not made such a foolish attempt to escape,' he said evenly. 'The *Sobrasi* did, at least, receive a taste of what you're capable of, which worked favorably for me, even if I was forced to postpone the remainder of our demonstration. No matter. This will work just as well.'

I rose on shaking legs and grasped the corner of the table for support. My wings expanded, helping regain my balance. I took a step towards him, but the Marksmen were on me at once, their crossbows bringing me up short.

'Where's Josephine?' I growled.

'She's fine,' he replied. 'She's with Quentin.'

A snarl welled inside my throat. The Marksmen tensed and held their crossbows even closer. But Augustine wasn't fazed. He sauntered with a slow, arrogant pace to the far corner of the room, past a long pew lined with a faded red cushion. He stopped at a small table, pulled out one of the stools and sat down, propping his elbows in front of him.

It was then that I noticed the variety of items on the table: Vials of tattoo ink. A cordless gun. A bottle of rubbing

302

alcohol and a box of wipes. I jerked my head up, meeting Augustine's smug gaze.

'I've already got a brand,' I said through clenched teeth. I pressed my hand to my manacled wrist. 'Don't need any more, thanks.'

'Oh, this isn't for you.'

Augustine rolled up one of his sleeves, and then the other. Dozens of tattoos covered his arms in intricate detail. I studied them with a sinking sensation in my chest. The tattoos were of shadow creatures, each black-and-gray design forming unique shapes in various degrees of hideousness.

'Haven't you wondered how I controlled my chimeras, Sebastian?' he said as he turned his arms towards the glow of the lantern light, showing them off. 'I worked for many years, studying how best to master the grotesques. Because they aren't guardians, they don't have charges. But I've found a way, a rather ingenious reverse order of things. I use the urn's *prah* in these tattoos. When a grotesque is injected with the same batch of *prah*, it creates a type of bond between us. Nothing like the beautiful bond between guardian and charge.' He spoke with such sarcasm that it twisted his face. 'But rather like a dog and its master.'

'An arrow shot from a safe distance is usually all it requires to subjugate a grotesque. Chimeras require a much more involved process, which I've not completely mastered. But I've had success enough for what was required.'

I touched the arrow wound on my shoulder. He watched me steadily as he continued.

'I knew I must begin by burning the humanity out of you, small portions at a time. I was too eager with my own gargoyles and experimented too quickly, yielding unfavorable results. I've used modest amounts, monitoring you

303

as I've done so.' He frowned disappointedly. 'You didn't change, at least, not in the way Anya and the others did. So I realized I needed a larger dose, one that would release slowly and more effectively.'

'You hollowed out the Marksmen arrows.'

'Figured that out, did you?' Augustine chuckled. 'Yes, Quentin was more than willing to give up his weapons to my cause. I did not anticipate you would break free so easily. We had two more arrows lined up for you, but you didn't give that poor boy a chance, breaking his arm and all that. Quite a pity.'

'Two more arrows,' I snarled. 'You think that's all it's going to take?'

'I hope so,' he replied, chuckling again. 'It's all the *prah* I have left.'

I couldn't hide my surprise. Augustine had used the entire contents of Keveco's urn? I glanced at his arms again. If each tattoo represented a shadow creature he'd done this to, then he really did have the makings of an army. But how was this possible?

'The *Sobrasi* have been giving you the tattoos,' I said. 'That's why they're here. Did you strike some deal with them too, like you did with the High Council? Is this just another way to save your pathetic neck?'

'The *Sobrasi* are not the only ones skilled in branding shadowen. Any descendant of a member carries the ability, and can utilize it, if properly taught.' He picked up the tattoo gun, probing the surface with his thumb. 'But you've had first-hand experience with that yourself, haven't you, Sebastian? In fact, I had a change of plans after you briefly left us, and I feel this is a much better solution. It gives us a chance to really make sure the process works.'

Augustine's continuous talking made my head pound. Tendrils of black fury slithered up my esophagus. But I couldn't let the dark thing free again. I almost didn't come back the last time. I ground my teeth, speaking with difficulty around their sharp points. 'What are you talking about? What process?'

'Shooting you full of *prah* was to showcase to the *Sobrasi* exactly what your shadowen capacities were, but that was only intended to be part of my demonstration.' He grinned maliciously. 'The second part has to do with what I can do to you.'

Augustine clapped his hands once. 'Bring in our guest.'

A new scent hit my nose and I turned so fast I knocked over the chairs on either side of the table. Donani passed through the arched entryway, his dark eyes narrowing on me. And after him came Hugo.

Augustine didn't have to say anything else. It was obvious why my brother was here. The Corsi clan could tattoo brands for guardians. Hugo had tattooed the dandelion that sealed me to Josephine.

Hugo shoved past Donani and got within several feet of me before the Marksmen prevented him with their weapons. He glared at them with the same look he used to give rowdy drunks who came into the *Gypsy Ink* – right before he tossed them out. Hugo turned back to me.

'You've lost your shirt again.'

Hugo smirked, but I saw the worry in his eyes.

'Yeah,' I replied, my voice like gravel. 'Bad habit.'

'I'm sorry, Sebastian,' he said, the smile vacating his features. 'They didn't give me a choice. After Katie came back, Donani's boys arrived. They've got everyone under lock-and-key back at the inn. My cousins and the rest of the guys.'

'And bad things were going to happen to them if you didn't agree to come here and tattoo him,' I replied, flicking my gaze to Augustine.

Hugo studied my face carefully. 'Yeah.'

'Then you need to get to it.' I said levelly. 'Don't waste any time.'

My brother looked as though he wanted to say something else, but thought the better of it. His lips drew into a rigid line. Hugo squared his shoulders and walked heavily to the small table where Augustine sat, looking like he'd just won the lottery. Hugo pulled out the stool and started prepping the equipment.

Suddenly, I knew what Hugo desperately wanted to say. Keeping my face blank, I said, 'I get it, Hugo, and I don't blame you.' I chose my next words carefully. 'You said they had everybody from the inn?'

Hugo turned over his shoulder. 'Yeah.'

I nodded and turned around, folding in my wings and slumping to the floor – but only so Augustine wouldn't see my face. I needed a second to think. Hugo hadn't mentioned Ezzie. But more importantly, Augustine hadn't mentioned her, either.

Katie had been underground with me when I fought Anya and Matthias. When I'd *killed* them, I reminded myself. I squeezed my eyes shut. Memories fluttered like bats through my head. I knew, deep down, what I'd done, even if I didn't remember exactly how. A nasty taste filled my mouth.

No. Focus on the now.

If Katie was at the *Dandelion Inn*, then she'd told them what happened. I forced my memories to release. It hadn't just been Katie in the room with us. I remembered their smells – Ezzie and Josephine. They'd been there, too.

Josephine was still here, but Esmeralda must have helped Katie get away.

The buzzing of Hugo's tattoo needle jerked me around. Augustine rested his right arm across the table, exposing a blank section of skin on the underside of his arm, just above the wrist ... uncomfortably similar in placement to my own tattoo. My brother was already beginning to outline the design, working completely by hand with no drawing or stencil. He'd done the same with my dandelion.

I stared, transfixed, as Hugo's art came to life across Augustine's skin. The shape of a body materialized first – human, with two arms and legs. But the bottom half of the legs were misshapen, like the chimeras. The wings came next, taking up the entire area of empty skin. And then finally, the head, with its fierce, sharp-toothed expression, wild hair, and ... spiraling horns.

It was *me*.

32. *Josephine*

I woke up on a plush bed. For an instant, I thought I was back at the *Dandelion Inn*. I stared at the thick wooden posters and tried to get my bearings. The room was decorated with mahogany furniture. Bold green wallpaper lined the walls, and a scarlet rug covered the floor.

I sat up, and the back of my head wailed at me. I touched my scalp, feeling a knot beneath my hair. I rubbed my eyes, trying to sort out the last thing I remembered. On the nightstand next to me sat a tall glass of water, along with a bottle of headache medicine. I popped the lid and took two pills, choosing not to give a thought to whether they were actually aspirin or not.

A knock came from the other side of the door. Whoever was outside must've been waiting for me to wake up. I wiped my mouth and threw off the ornately patterned bed covers.

'Come in.'

The door opened soundlessly and Quentin appeared. He walked across the thick rug, placing his good hand on the hilt of his sword, which hung in a sheath at his hip. He settled himself into the armchair opposite the bed, pulled out the sword, and set it across his lap.

'How's your head?' he asked, smiling gently.

I didn't answer.

'You slipped,' he continued. 'These old tunnels can be pretty dangerous.'

Whether I believed his explanation or not didn't matter. It was clear that he was sticking with his story. I got out of bed quicker than I should have. The room tipped sideways in my vision. I kept my hand on the edge of the mattress, determined not to fall.

'Where's Sebastian?'

Quentin's lips tightened as he leaned back in the chair and rubbed his bandaged arm, adjusting the sling across his shoulder. 'Seriously, Josie, that's the first thing you're going to say to me? Don't we have a little more history between us than that?'

'What do you want me to say, Quentin?' I shot back. 'You're working with Augustine. He's a traitor to our people. He tried to kill Sebastian. You always had standards. I don't get this at all.'

'Josephine.' He held my gaze. 'It's not what you think.'

'Oh, it's not? Then please, explain it to me.' I glanced at the diamond weapon, gleaming in the soft light. 'Obviously I'm not going anywhere for a while.'

'Augustine is a means to an end, Josie.'

'And what end is that?'

Quentin ran a practiced hand along the sword blade, testing its sharpness, as I'd seen him do many times before. 'You have to understand, I don't care what he's got planned with the *Sobrasi*. That's his deal. My only concern is our *kumpania.*' He sighed heavily. 'I'm a Marksman. I come from a clan dedicated to protecting the Outcasts. That's my first priority.' His eyes shifted around the room, his lip curling in resentment. 'But our leadership has grown weak. We've allowed shadowen to overrun us, and the High Council has done nothing. Head families are bickering for power, and all eyes turn to the throne. But your aunt has lost her capacity to rule. She doesn't have the strength to bring unity to our people anymore.'

I guided myself around the bed. There were no windows in the room, which made me feel unsettled and trapped. Paintings of exteriors had been fashioned with curtains on either side to represent windows, but it wasn't the same.

'How long have you known I was heir to the throne?'

'Almost as long as you have,' he replied.

'I was fourteen,' I said, reaching out to touch one of the paintings, an autumn landscape. 'My father brought me to Savannah and the ceremony was performed in secret. The head of the High Council was there, along with two priests and two witnesses. After that, I was never allowed to return to the city. No one else knew, except my family.'

'That was the moment it became official,' Quentin replied. 'But Nicolas and Thalia had been discussing the possibility long before that. Why do you think your father was so insistent that you and I were promised to each other?'

'My father would never force me to marry.'

'That's true,' he said, his voice soft and silky. 'Although he would've been within his rights, according to our laws. But I don't believe Nicolas ever thought he'd have to go as far as that. We're a good match, don't you think? At least, you thought so for a while.'

I turned from the counterfeit window. 'Quentin, I loved

you. You know that's the truth. We've grown up with the Circe. I watched you climb the ranks and become the head of the Marksmen. You always knew exactly who you were and what you were supposed to do.' I paused, biting my lip. 'I'd been told my whole life what I was meant to be. But I didn't know who I was, Quentin. I didn't know what I wanted.'

His face turned to marble. 'And you do now, is that it?'

'I'm learning,' I replied evenly. 'And it begins with fixing everything. Our *kumpania* is important. But so are the people who are in it. Sebastian's never done anything to deserve this. He needs to be returned to the Circe so he can do what he's called to do. Augustine is a traitor to our people, and he has to be stopped. There's too much to do first before I can think about what I want.'

'What if what needs to be done is right in front of you?'

I stepped back warily. 'Meaning?'

'You said it yourself, Josephine. Our *kumpania* needs help, and it won't happen on its own. The Outcast clans require strong leadership and unity. You need to take the throne.'

'You know I can't do that, even if I wanted to.'

Quentin set the diamond sword aside and rose from the chair. He moved to the opposite side of the room. His smile was smooth – the calm, reassuring one he used to give me before my Circe performances. 'We both know the law. We don't have a say in our community until we reach adulthood, and only an adult Roma may enter into leadership. You aren't yet an adult in the eyes of our people.' His smile softened. 'But you can be, Josephine. It's very simple.'

'I can't believe you're actually saying this.'

Quentin shrugged. 'You could eventually find some other

Roma to marry. But what will happen in the meantime – to the Queen, to Augustine … and to Sebastian? You are your own person, Josie. You always have been. So look at it this way. What I'm talking about is a business arrangement, that's all. Take it as you will. Our marriage would allow you to legally take the throne. You can deal with Augustine from a position of power. You can get everything you want.'

I stared back at him, frozen to the core. 'So it's love or duty, is that it?'

'Why can't it be both, Josie? You loved me once. You can love me again. We can start this whole thing over.' He moved closer, but I countered. He actually looked hurt. 'You know how I feel about you. We had something. Are you ready just to throw away those five years together?'

'What if those five years were a lie?'

He paused, letting his gaze drift around the room. 'They weren't all a lie, Josephine.'

My hand went to my throat, searching for the dandelion pendant. The instant my fingers were around it, my world cleared. I wasn't the girl Quentin knew from before. I'd changed, and I owed so much of it to Sebastian. He never shied away from sacrifice. But he'd also shown me what it was like to fight against everyone's expectations and judgments; to stand against the power of traditions that had no life; those cold, dead things with no purpose.

'Let me out of here, Quentin.'

His expression morphed. The smooth, handsome smile was replaced with thin-lipped frustration. 'I suggest you reconsider.'

'Or what?' I shot back. Anger licked at me. 'You'll call my father? Tell him why I'm really here and then have him drag me back to the Circe? Trust me, after what I've been through, I can deal with Nicolas Romany and his disappointment.'

Quentin looked down his nose at me. 'Can you deal with everything, I wonder.'

'What's that supposed to mean?'

Quentin returned to the chair and took his sword. He walked to the door, holding it open as he spoke. 'Just think about it.'

'You can't keep me here, Quentin. It's called kidnapping.'

Quentin laughed. 'It's not kidnapping, Josie. You're here at the Queen's invitation, and you are free to leave after your meeting.'

The world suddenly careened to a stop. 'What?'

'Queen Thalia requests your presence,' he said formally. He held the door open wider and stepped away, gesturing with his sword for me to exit the room. 'If you'll follow me, I'll show you the way.'

33. *Sebastian*

I stared at the image inked onto Augustine's arm – my mirror reflection in gruesome detail. My body turned suddenly cold, as though I'd jumped into a freezing lake. Nausea rolled in my stomach again. Hugo's face had taken on his characteristic, unreadable glare as he worked, hunched over the table with his gun and the vials of ink. When the last line was finished, he sat back.

'Outline's done.'

Augustine twisted his arm, surveying the black ink. 'Good. Now do the rest.'

Hugo blinked once, slowly. I knew that look. He was reeling in his emotions guardedly. He began the process of shading the artwork – the bizarre gargoyle portrait of myself. Everything in me wanted to turn away, but I couldn't.

I'd watched Hugo ink dozens of people. He'd always been meticulous, always careful and detailed. I'd never seen him work this slowly. It occurred to me that he was trying to buy us some time. Somehow, Ezzie had flown under the Marksmen's radar. I didn't understand why Anya or Matthias hadn't mentioned her presence to Augustine, but at the moment, I didn't care.

Hope flickered, like a light bulb sputtering to life.

I stayed where I was, observing Hugo's progress with a stoic look. My shoulder burned and throbbed to the beat of my heart. I rose suddenly and started to walk around the table. The Marksmen were at my sides instantly, but I ignored them, keeping my gaze fixed on Augustine.

'I have a question for you,' I said.

'Looking for something to pass the time?' He shot me a pompous smile.

'Well, I figured it was worth a shot, since you obviously love to hear yourself talk.'

He chuckled appreciatively and waved the Marksmen away. They stepped back, but kept their crossbows carefully trained on me. 'What is your question, gargoyle?'

I crossed my arms, ignoring the blazing pain in my shoulder. 'How exactly did you become *marimé*?'

The muscles in Hugo's neck bulged, but he continued to work in silence, his head bent low. Augustine monitored the small, circular motion of the tattoo gun, wincing only slightly as Hugo shaded in a larger section.

'You want the truth,' said Augustine, looking up at me. 'Believe me, you're not the first.' He shifted on the stool, keeping his arm still as he looked me over. 'I don't know how well you understand our customs, but to steal from another Roma is a terrible offense, usually requiring the banishment of the thief from Gypsy society for a time.'

'For thirteen years? Must've been something pretty important.'

'Oh, it was. My father, the former king, owned a very special dagger. It had been passed down in the Romany family for many generations. I needed it much more than he did. So I took it.' Augustine's smile faded. 'My father was old, but he was a fighter. In fact, he gave me this.' He pointed to the long white scar on his face. 'But in the end, I won.'

'You killed him,' I said.

'No,' he answered simply. 'But attacking the King of the Outcast Gypsies was no small matter. A *Kris Romani* was called. I was sentenced to permanent exile and told never to return. I left, but not before my father passed away very suddenly.' He shook his head. 'Very unexpectedly.'

'Unexpectedly,' I repeated.

'Quite the tragedy,' he continued in a solemn tone. 'He was murdered by gargoyles. The very three gargoyles that had pledged to serve the King of the Gypsies as his guardians. What my sister Thalia didn't know was that the dagger was, in fact, the *sclav* that bound them to service.'

I looked away. Three gargoyles.

Anya, Matthias, and Thaddeus.

'The *sclav* was a powerful one,' said Augustine proudly. 'It was capable of sealing multiple guardians to one charge, which is why it was held in such high regard by our family. These gargoyles had served not only my father, but generations before him as well. Never were they allowed to rest in stone. Always serving. By the time they were passed on to my father, they were already weary. And my father was a cruel man, fierce in his kingship. It was not difficult to persuade the gargoyles to assist me.'

My wings felt heavy and dragged my shoulders down. Guardians were meant to protect their charges until death. Only then was the bond broken. For Anya and the others to have helped Augustine went against everything they'd been created for.

'What did you promise them?' I asked.

He nodded with a knowing smirk. 'A promise of freedom given to those in servitude is a strong motivator. Unfortunately, I could never set them free. They were far too valuable to me. I needed their protection. And later, as you've witnessed first-hand, I needed their services in other ways.'

'The Queen,' said Hugo, abruptly looking up from his work. 'Why didn't she just take the guardians from you?'

Augustine's forehead lifted as he shifted his gaze to my brother. 'Thalia didn't know how to use the *sclav*, therefore, she had no control over them. There were many who suspected I was involved in the king's death, though no accusations were ever made. Because of this, I needed a certain level of protection. Since I was no longer Roma, I couldn't depend upon the Marksmen. I agreed to go quietly into my *marimé*, but only if Thalia ordered the Council to hand the gargoyles over to me.'

Hugo grunted. 'Which she obviously did.'

'She didn't have a choice, really. The *sclav* was guarded by my shadowen, and she had no hope of getting either it or the guardians back. I allowed her to save face by publically announcing that she'd given me the gargoyles as a means of protection from those in our *kumpania* who saw me as a murderer. After all, a dead Gypsy cannot be *marimé*, but to live with the loss of one's Roma blood is a punishment worse than death.'

I shook my head, barely able to contain what he'd said. Anya, Thaddeus, and Matthias were once guardians for the king. They'd killed the very person they'd sworn to protect and then gone to serve the traitor responsible for it. No wonder the Outcasts were so wary of gargoyles.

I finally had the answers I'd been seeking, but it definitely made me feel worse. This was so much bigger than me, or my status as Josephine's guardian. Augustine's plans had been years in the making – worked out in intricate detail long before I even had memories of life.

I rubbed at the manacle on my wrist, feeling the sting of the diamond spikes as they pricked my skin in the same place as my dandelion brand. 'You were able to gain control of your father's gargoyles, but it's not going to work on me. You've already tried. I'm seal—'

'Yes yes,' he said impatiently, waving his hand in the air like I was a fly, buzzing around his head. 'You're sealed to my niece, and you'll fight me until your last dying breath, and so on. We've been over this. It's old news. And, quite frankly, entirely irrelevant.'

Hugo sat back on his stool and let out a big puff of air. 'It's finished.'

We all stared at the tattoo. As always, my brother had done a professional job. The shading, the lines, everything was perfect. But even though it shared my appearance, the ink portrait looked like a stranger to me.

Hugo cleaned up the space, like he was back at the shop on a regular workday. He continued to move slowly. I'd lost track of time completely, but I'd never seen him finish an intensive black-and-grey tattoo like that in less than two hours. Was that enough time for Ezzie to figure out what to do? I didn't doubt she could handle several Marksmen on her own.

I glanced quickly around the room, discreetly sniffing the air. I didn't smell anyone besides from Augustine, Hugo, and the two crossbow guys. It seemed weird that he didn't have more Marksmen with him. And Quentin was gone, too – somewhere with Josephine. My chest instantly ached.

'Okay,' said Hugo, pushing away from the table. 'I did what you asked. Don't guess you probably care about band-aging it up or anything.' He suddenly lunged across the table and grabbed Augustine by the shirt. 'Now call Donani and get his lackeys to back off my clan. Now!'

The Marksman on my left whipped his crossbow around, pointed at Hugo's head. But Augustine only tilted his head to the side, looking mildly amused.

'Careful, Hugo,' he said. 'The artwork's quite tender.'

'Call them off.'

'Of course,' said Augustine. Hugo released him, glaring as Augustine admired his arm for several moments before pulling a phone from his jacket. 'Even *marimé* like myself can be honorable. I gave you my word, and I intend to keep it.' He set the phone in front of him. 'Just as soon as I've finished.'

'Finished what?' Hugo demanded.

Augustine nodded at the Marksmen.

The next instant happened in slow motion. I saw the crossbows, and I jolted back, wings parachuting out. I heard the triggers click, the whoosh of the arrows as they released. Pain exploded in my other shoulder. I dove over the table as my leg gave way in a bolt of white fire. I hit the floor and spun around in a crouch, readying myself to spring.

But then, my entire body revolted.

I fell backwards as scorching lava poured over and through me. Vaguely, I noticed the two arrows, one in my arm, and the other embedded deep in my thigh. My body convulsed, wings beating out of my control. Hugo was yelling, fighting with one of the Marksmen, vying for the crossbow in his hand. The other Marksman guarded Augustine, his diamond sword drawn and glittering in the lamplight.

I gasped for air, clawing at my chest. The lava rose higher inside me. I was drowning in it. I rolled over, onto my hands and knees, battling to bring my wings to my back and stand. I locked eyes with Augustine. He clutched his arm, his face contorted into a grimace, his teeth clenched. The tattoo turned viciously red and inflamed.

Invisible spiders scurried up and down my spine, and then moved outwards from my chest, into my arms and legs. I raised my arms in horror. Black veins sprouted like miniature lighting bolts underneath my skin, all over my body. My eye sockets burned like they'd been stabbed with torches. I threw my hands protectively over my head and huddled in the floor, unable to move; to do anything but let the fire consume me.

'Sebastian!'

Hugo's voice, yelling at me. But it was distant. I was caught in the current, and the shore faded away. The current was brutal, unrelenting, pulling me towards something. I was trapped, like a boat going over a waterfall. My body and my mind split. I rose above myself, watching helplessly as the current took me to—

Augustine.

I felt it, just as I had with Josephine – the sealing of a guardian's will to its charge. The fire cooled, hardening the lava around my heart. I saw myself rise to my feet, but not completely upright. I'd changed. It was done. My mind floated higher, farther away from the room. My body

approached Augustine and stood resolutely beside him. Hugo
thrashed wildly between the Marksmen. But I didn't move.
Didn't try to help him.

The room dimmed. And my mind evaporated to mist.

34. *Josephine*

As soon as Quentin escorted me out of the elaborate bedroom and through a set of double doors, I knew we were in the heart of the Court of Shadows. The tunnels were wider here, clean and polished. Electric lanterns hung from the ceilings, connected by metal fixtures and murals of intricate painted artwork lined both walls, depicting caravans and colorful scenes from our past.

'What time is it?' I asked, as we turned walked down several stone steps.

'Late afternoon,' he answered pleasantly, like nothing had happened between us. 'You must've been pretty tired. You hadn't even moved both times I came to check on you.'

I chewed on my fingernail. A year ago, the idea that Quentin had been so attentive would've made me smile. But now, I felt like a stranger had been looking in on me. He wasn't a stranger, though – not really. He'd always been motivated by his job, always dogmatic in his beliefs as a Marksman.

I'd never questioned it because I'd never been presented

with anything else. But the moment Sebastian appeared in my life, my world expanded like a helium balloon. The shadow world changed from being something I feared, to something that held inside it a long-forgotten promise – a hope that made my heart swell in my chest.

Shadowen weren't the curse. It was our refusal to believe they could be anything else besides the curse. We'd been convinced that we could handle things ourselves. We wouldn't accept that salvation was possible outside our own walls. Quentin couldn't change because he'd never see past that. But I had. I'd discovered gargoyles weren't just our guardians. They were living breathing souls. They were good.

And Sebastian represented the best of our legends.

Watching him suffer such horrible things and still endure … it made me want to do better. To *be* better.

The tunnel brightened suddenly, and I looked up as we passed through an opening and into a spacious dining hall. Even though it had been five years since I'd been in our Outcast Haven, I recognized the place immediately: The Gathering Chamber.

Six long tables ran parallel the length of the room, sandwiched between long wooden benches. Chandeliers gleamed from the ceiling rafters. The walls were covered with paintings, fashioned to look like massive windows to the outside world, just like the bedroom where I'd awoken earlier.

The window to my right displayed a wide field underneath a night sky full of stars. The one on my left was a forest meadow with a Gypsy caravan around a bonfire. The painted window in front of me captured my attention – a hauntingly beautiful cathedral with spires and Gothic architecture. Nestled along the parapets were statues of creatures of all shapes and forms. The statues peered solemnly over the rooftops. In the center of the painting was a single gargoyle, crouched, with head bowed and eyes closed, frozen in a prayer-like state.

The painting was almost a replica of the one that hung in the living room of our RV at the Circe. A dull, growing ache seeped through my skin. I remembered Sebastian looking at the painting. He saw himself in the images, I knew. And I watched him, this strange mix of boy and living statue, standing in the middle of my living room. The boy, with his jeans and Converse, t-shirt and slightly messy hair, with that lopsided, somewhat embarrassed smile. And the creature – wings angled over his head, wings so large they skimmed the floor, even when folded to his back. Gray skin, sharp-tipped ears slicing through his pewter hair, and teeth and claws he couldn't hide, no matter how hard he tried.

I took a sharp breath to hold my emotions in check. That's when I noticed there were other people in the Gathering Chamber. Four guards – two men and two women – stood at attention beside a raised platform that ran the entire width of the hall. It held another table lined with chairs, which were the seats of honor for the Queen, the High Council members, and visiting *bandoleers*.

A woman sat alone at the center of the table.

'Go on,' said Quentin giving me room to pass. 'She's expecting us.'

'I thought you said just me.'

'I did,' he replied. 'But I can't let you see her alone. I have to make sure you don't say anything to damage my stellar reputation. The Queen doesn't know about my connection with Augustine. She only knows I've accompanied him here on Nicolas' orders, to ensure he doesn't cause any trouble.'

'Like the dutiful Marksman you are.'

Quentin looked mildly offended. 'I've never done anything that wasn't in the best interest of the clans. As I said, Augustine is a means to an end for me. Someone has to be willing to get his hands dirty to repair what's broken. The world isn't black and white, Josie.'

'No,' I said, studying him. 'It's gray.'

Quentin's jaw clenched, but he didn't reply. He led me down the center aisle formed by the tables. The sound of his boots on the stone floor caused the woman to glance up.

The woman rose and glided around the table. She wore a long, ruffled dress in a patchwork of rich colors, adorned with several heavy pieces of traditional jewelry. Her hair was hidden by a turquoise scarf, which wound tightly around her head and flowed down her back.

'Aunt Thalia,' I said.

Her lips quirked downward. 'Although we're related, my dear, I ask that you address me with proper respect inside the Court.'

I dipped my head in our show of respect. '*Kralitsa*.'

My aunt motioned us forward and stepped down to the floor. Instantly, the four Marksmen guards began to move in tandem, following her closely. One was tall with a buzz cut. He looked at me with particular interest as the Queen paused, scrutinizing every detail.

'I was told you were here in the Court of Shadows,' she said. 'You know your presence here is forbidden until the proper time.'

'I didn't have a choice, *Kralitsa*. My guardian was taken from me.'

'The gargoyle,' she replied, 'is a murderer.'

The words sent a burst of heat through my chest. 'I don't know what lies Augustine has told you—'

'You will not mention the *marimé* here, even by that name.'

She raised her chin, as though the matter was finished. But I'd come too far to be shut down like that. She may have been the Queen, but I was her successor, and that had to mean something.

'May I speak with you in private?'

She folded her arms across her chest, tilting her head in thought. I felt Quentin tense beside me.

His eyes shifted to the Queen. 'With all due respect, *Kralitsa* ...'

'You're dismissed,' she said, nodding at him.

His face darkened, but he managed to hold his perfect smile in place. He bowed low, and when he lifted his head, he looked once more like the smooth, confident man I'd grown up with. I realized then how much of a mask he'd worn around me.

'Of course, *Rani*.' He regarded me with careful eyes. 'I'll be waiting for you outside, Josephine.'

He sauntered out of the room with a casual gait, but I knew him too well. He was completely furious. I felt I'd regained a fraction of control, and I wasn't about to stop there. I glanced at the four Marksmen surrounding us.

'I'd like to speak in complete privacy,' I said. 'If you don't mind.'

Then Queen's harsh lips turned upward. 'Very well, Josephine Romany.'

She clapped her hands once, and the guards left the room, exiting through another door opposite from the one we'd entered. The Queen turned with an air full of absolute authority and walked back to the table. The hem of her dress slid across the floor. After seating herself, she lifted her hand, indicating for me to approach.

'You may speak freely now.'

'Aunt Thalia,' I said, ignoring her previous request, now that we were the only ones in the room. 'I'm here on the behalf of my guardian. It's my fault for not coming to you earlier, but I had no idea what they were doing to him.' I pressed a hand over my chest to squelch the ache. 'Sebastian Grey needs to be released immediately.'

'The gargoyle.' Her gaze was steady. 'I'm afraid that's not possible.'

'Since you're not giving Sebastian a trial, you're at least going to sit there and hear me out,' I said. The Queen raised her hand, but I kept going. 'You tell me I can't even say Augustine's name, but you've allowed him entrance to the Court of Shadows. You listened to his lies. Sebastian is innocent, but you haven't given him so much as a chance to even prove himself.'

'Enough.' The Queen's expression remained firmly composed. 'I will forgive your discourteous outburst, as I can see you're quite emotionally invested in this creature's fate, but I'm afraid you've made the journey to Savannah for nothing. The *marimé* has already shown the gargoyle to me. I've seen his ability to fight, and I've also seen his volatile, unstable nature. It's all the proof I need.'

'So you're just going to let Augustine hand him over to the *Sobrasi*?'

The Queen raised her thin brows and peered down at me, surprised. 'You have knowledge of the *Sobrasi*. That's good. Those with important futures should be aware of all things in their world, whether on the surface, or hiding below.'

I stared at her, exasperated. 'How could you possibly trust him?'

The Queen's composure dropped enough for me to see the venomous fire behind her eyes. She adjusted the sleeves of her dress with deliberate care before answering. 'I've never trusted him.' Her eyes met mine. 'I allowed him into the Court to deliver the creature, but also so that I could see my former brother for myself. It's been many years since he was exiled. He wanted an audience with me, but I had already suspected as much, and I granted it to him.'

The knot on the back of my head throbbed, and I rubbed my neck. 'Why would you do that? It violates the terms of *marimé*.'

'I know the terms,' she replied coldly. 'I needed to know if my suspicions were correct. They were. He had discovered my secret, that I had named you successor. I had betrayed him.' The Queen rose and walked slowly from one end of the table to the other. 'I made a promise to him, just before he was sentenced to exile. I told him that when I could no longer hold the throne, I would pass it to him. I would renounce his *marimé* status and name him my successor.' She paused and stared out over the empty hall. 'In return, he agreed to leave quietly.'

I thought for a moment. 'But that doesn't make any sense. The High Council sentenced him. He would be forced to leave, no matter what. There's more to it than that.'

The Queen rested her hands on the back of one of the chairs and peered down at me. 'Smart and discerning.' She gave me a wry smile. 'It runs in the family.' She drummed her fingers on the wood. 'Yes, there is more. But first, you must know, I never had any intention of giving the throne to my brother. I only made the promise so he would leave the *kumpania*. You were always my choice.'

A ringing started in my ears. I vaguely recognized it as my frustration, welling inside me. I threw my head back, shutting my eyes. 'But why me, Aunt Thalia? I never understood why you picked me. I mean, you could've convinced my father to change his mind, or even my brother. They both have more claim than me. ' I opened my eyes and stared at the floor. 'Why me?'

Her reply came with a more gentle voice. 'Josephine, you know as well as I do that the hearts of the Romany men have always been with the Circe and the clan, and they always will be. I don't fault them for it. I needed someone who would be willing to look at the larger picture, someone willing to give up what they wanted for the good of the *kumpania*. You were my choice, Josephine, because you're not like the rest of our family. You have the ability to bring unity back to our people.'

'No,' I snapped back. My head felt like a beating drum. 'I don't. I'm selfish and I'm blind. If I was smart and discerning, like you say, then I would've seen that Quentin was working with Augustine the whole time, right behind my back, and I wouldn't have been so stupidly naive.' I waited for my aunt's reaction but, to my surprise, she barely even blinked. I sank onto one of the benches and clasped my hands in my lap. 'You knew.'

'Of course,' she replied. 'You are wise for your years, Josephine, but you're still young and learning. I've been Queen for a long while. You'll find that being in such a position teaches you to read people. Quentin is a man of ambition, which is not a bad thing. However, he is also not as clever as he presumes. He needs to be guided, of course. But he can make a worthy husband for you.'

My head spun so fast I pressed my fingers to my temples. This time, it wasn't because of my tender skull. I felt like I was being pricked by thousands of tiny needles. I'd ignored everything about my secret for so long that now, I was being buried alive in it.

'Tell me why you really made that promise to Augustine.'

The Queen lifted the edge of her dress and descended the stairs. 'I know you came here to plead your guardian's case. But there is something you must understand.' She seated herself across from me, holding me firm in her gaze. 'Gargoyles are traitors, Josephine. They are demons, both on the outside, and within. They've been allowed to infiltrate our clans under the guise of protectors. But they care nothing for us.'

I looked up at the massive painting of the cathedral, letting my eyes take in each and every statue. This was our legacy, written so clearly in front of me. I shook my head adamantly. 'Where is this coming from? All our legends, our stories ... how can you not believe them?'

Her eyes hardened. 'Those legends killed my father.'

I felt as though dark fingers curled around my throat. 'What?'

'The King or Queen of the Gypsies has always possessed three guardians. It has been this way since the Sundering. They were bound to protect my father, as they had my grandfather before.'

'Anya, Matthias, and Thaddeus.' The names were painful to say.

'I covered up the murder,' she continued. She placed her hands on the table, as though holding herself in place.

'Augustine had already stolen my father's *sclav*, and he controlled the gargoyles. He gave me no choice.'

'It was really Augustine that did it.'

'The creatures made their choice,' she said, her words like acid. 'The gargoyles may have been acting under his orders, but they willingly murdered a Roma. The protectors of the throne took the life of the one who held it. After my father's death, I swore I'd never allow another gargoyle to be sealed to anyone within the Court. The creatures can't be trusted, no matter how honorable they appear.'

'You should know,' I said, working to keep my voice level. 'Those gargoyles aren't a threat to anyone, anymore. My guardian made sure of that.' I blinked away the image of Sebastian standing over Matthias' stone corpse. 'He's a protector, and he'll whatever it takes to make sure our clan is safe from evil like that.'

The Queen tucked one edge of her scarf neatly behind her ear. Then she sighed, a firm sound of resolve. 'I cannot set this gargoyle free. Shadowen are simply too dangerous, and I refuse to have Outcast blood on my hands. Augustine presented me with a solution I could not refuse. He brought the *Sobrasi*. And they are capable of dealing, not just with this gargoyle, but with all shadowen that continue to plague our realm.'

'We have Marksmen,' I said.

'We do,' she agreed. 'They've kept us safe for decades, but the scourge remains, threatening us every day, and their numbers seem to increase every year. It's time to bring an end to it all. The *Sobrasi* can provide that end. They have the power to turn these demons to stone.'

My heart kicked up a notch. 'And you mean *all* shadowen.'

'Yes, Josephine,' she replied. 'All shadowen.'

It was exactly what Quentin wanted as well. They were on the same side, both using Augustine to get precisely what they wanted – the end of the shadow world, both the evil and the good.

'Sebastian isn't your enemy.'

She reached across the table and clasped my hand so fiercely my fingers stung. 'Your gargoyle is no different, Josephine. I know you've seen what he can do. Threaten him, and he will strike back. What if it's Roma blood that he spills next?'

'Never,' I replied bitingly. 'I know him better than anyone else.'

'He is but one shadow creature, Josephine. I have to look to the safety and welfare of our entire community. This is the critical lesson, and it is the one you must master, if you are to one day take my place.'

'And where does this leave Augustine?'

'He wants this gargoyle for the *Sobrasi*'s purposes. He can have him. Letting the *marimé* go is a small price to pay for the reward they offer. The grotesques will be exterminated, the *Sobrasi* will return to Europe, and our *kumpania* will finally have peace. Is that such a terrible thing to desire?'

I wrenched my hand from her grasp. 'If the *Sobrasi* can turn all the shadowen to stone that easily, don't you think they would've done it a long time ago?'

The Queen placed her hands in her lap. 'There was one thing the *Sobrasi* have always lacked in order to complete this task. There was an urn, given to our ancestor that—'

'I know all about it.'

'I see,' she replied, eyeing me with a suspicious glance.

'If that's true, then you know why I must allow him to take this gargoyle.'

'You can't do this.'

'There are many things I've done as Queen that I'm not proud of,' she said, sliding off the bench and walking back to the platform. 'There are times when I had no choice. This is one of those times. But this is also how I will make things right. I will make sure the shadowen are vanished forever. It will be my legacy, and it will also be yours.'

I jumped up from the table. I felt on the verge of exploding. 'You don't understand. What he wants to do with Sebastian isn't what you think. And your Marksmen aren't all loyal to you. I've seen them with Augustine, following his orders. And Quentin's.' I clenched my teeth. 'Don't you see? You can't trust Augustine with any of this.'

The Queen continued to stare at me. There was absolutely nothing readable in her expression. After several moments of harsh silence, she turned away and stared at the painting over the table.

'If there is any disloyalty within my Court,' she said, with her back still to me, 'you can be assured that I will deal with it most severely. But it does not change my mind about the shadowen. They are the most dangerous threat, and this issue must be resolved first.'

I stood there while my brain clicked like a short-circuited machine, unable to fully comprehend the information I was getting. My faith felt rattled to the core.

'Pardon the interruption, *Kralitsa*.'

We both turned to see one of the Marksmen guards standing inside the door – the same one who'd been studying me earlier. He dipped his head slightly and then approached. When he reached the Queen, he leaned and whispered something in her ear. Then he turned and exited as swiftly as he'd appeared.

'Your gargoyle is here,' she said.

It felt as though someone knocked the air out of me. 'What?'

'Your gargoyle,' she repeated, 'managed to escape our Marksmen a few hours ago, but Augustine saw to his capture and brought him back to the Court. The creature was violent and will be confined to our dungeons until I deem it safe to release him to my traitorous brother.'

I struggled to take a breath as panic grabbed my throat. 'Augustine did something to Sebastian, don't you understand? He's done something to make him that way! Sebastian isn't a grotesque, he's not wild!'

'It is too late for him,' said the Queen. Her voice was soft, her tone smooth and even. 'However, I understand your attachment to the gargoyle. Therefore, I will allow you to see him one last time, if you so choose, and you can make your peace with this before he's gone. I can offer you that much.' She reached out and touched my shoulder gently. 'And then, Josephine, you must put this behind you.'

35. *Josephine*

The Marksmen with the buzz cut – the Queen called him Donani – led the way. The other three guards followed behind. My aunt, Quentin, and I made up the middle of the group as we all descended into a lower section of the Court. We turned a corner, and I looked up as a cold draft brushed against my face.

The tunnel wasn't like the others. I rubbed my arms briskly. Even though it had been five years since I'd seen the Court, I knew this didn't lead to any of the other public areas where Outcast Gypsies congregated for business or to just hang out. I highly doubted it led to any of the Council's private rooms, based what I could see ahead of me. The smaller tunnel became a passage, similar to what Ezzie and I had discovered beneath the cemetery.

An icy sensation of fear crackled around me. 'What is this place?'

'I'm sorry,' said Quentin. 'I don't guess you've ever been here before. It's part of the old dungeon. In the past it was used for criminals. But it also houses a good number of grotesques the Marksmen use in their training exercises.'

'This is where you're keeping him?'

Donani looked over his shoulder. 'It's the only suitable containment.'

Containment?

The ache between my ribs returned in full force, making me wince. Donani pulled open a narrow door, but he went in first, rather than letting us go on ahead. I looked questioningly at the Queen. She only stared mutely ahead, her chin lifted slightly.

Donani's face reappeared in the doorway. '*Kralitsa.*'

The Queen nodded, and then turned to me. 'You may go inside. We will give you a few minutes.'

Donani caught my arm as I started past him. 'The groties are sedated, but I wouldn't recommend getting too close to their cages. You know how nasty they can get.'

I shrugged him off and stepped into the room. Donani closed the door behind me with a heavy, ominous thud. I gathered myself together before looking around me. Numerous dark archways were carved into every wall of the narrow space. Dim, orange-tinted light filtered through the room, as if someone had placed candles in all the corners, but I couldn't see the source.

A sensation flooded my head. I froze in the center of the room, listening. I could hear him breathing. I knew it was him. I felt his presence inside my stomach like a trapped butterfly. But the sound ... the sound wasn't human. Not even close. The intake of air was rapid and shallow, a mixture of hissing and gasps. It scared me. And broke my heart, all at once.

'Sebastian?'

The breaths cut off sharply. Silence permeated the room for so long I thought he'd somehow vanished. Then I heard him draw in a long stretch of air. I tensed, waiting to hear him speak, to call my name the way he'd done some many times in that unassuming, mellow voice – sometimes joking, sometimes serious, but always gentle and sincere.

Instead, he growled, but it wasn't something I'd ever heard come from him before. The sound was low, raw, and threatening. The force of it rattled my teeth inside my mouth and sent ice cubes down my back.

I tried to swallow, but nothing made it past my tongue. I forced my feet forward, one step at a time, peering into the heavy shadows. I realized the dark arches were actually alcoves. Instead of doors, thick iron bars ran vertically from edge to edge. Dungeon cells, like something out of an old history book.

I paused at the first one, mustering the courage to look inside. Donani had spoken the truth. A reptilian grotesque was curled up on the floor, unconscious. The next four cells contained similar creatures, all thankfully oblivious to the one Gypsy in the dungeon. I reached the last arched enclosure at the end of the room.

Just beyond the barred entrance, through the darkness, I could make out the details of a cobblestone wall, dirt floor, and a feeding trough and a cracked wooden bowl filled with water. And, huddled in the corner, a dark shape. I felt relief and dread, all at once.

'Sebastian …'

The shape shuddered violently and another fierce growl echoed within the alcove. He didn't turn towards me. He didn't speak. I inched closer, conflicting emotions stirring inside me. I felt his presence, like always, but I also felt a deep thrumming warning. It flittered through my lungs, and it hurt, like breathing in winter air.

'Please,' I said softly. 'Talk to me.'

The light filtering into the cell from behind me only extended two feet inside the bars, and it was too dark to see further in. The form shifted in the dirt. I heard a grating sound, like metal scraping against stone. A hand appeared from the unlit corner, moving slowly into the dim light.

On the gray wrist was a metal cuff – part of the diamond-spiked manacles he'd been wearing since the Marksmen chained him up at the Circe. I cringed at the dried black blood along the edges of the metal, and my eyes stung as I remembered that underneath, hidden by the band, was his dandelion tattoo.

I'd fixated on the metal cuff so intensely that I barely noticed the hand, until the fingers splayed wide and anchored in the dirt. It was Sebastian's hand, but very different from the last time I'd seen him in Augustine's hideout. Black veins bulged beneath the gray skin. They ran along the back of his hand and continued up his arm. The claws, which looked even longer and sharper, dug deep grooves into the dirt as Sebastian pulled himself from the shadowy corner.

The cold spikes in my lungs urged me to stop, but I kept moving until I was directly in front of the prison cell. I knelt in the dirt and clung so tightly to the bars that my knuckles burned with the pressure. Sebastian's other hand came into view, riddled with the same patchwork of black veins that spidered under his wrist cuff and along his arms.

The silhouette of his body was visible now, and I could see he was curled into a tight crouch. The shadow of his wings expanded across the entire space of the cell. Their talon tips scraped the edges of the walls as the wings flapped eerily back and forth. The noise grated in my ears. I stared into the shadows at his mostly hidden form.

If I could only reach out and touch him. I was sick of being so close, but constantly separated by the unending forces that had been thrown against him. Everything about this made nausea burn at the back of my throat.

'Hey, I'm right here,' I said, forcing the words from my mouth. 'Sebastian, let me see you.' I leaned my cheek against the cold iron. A flash of memory – the first time I'd seen him after he transformed. I'd asked him the same thing, and he'd come hesitantly forward out of the shadows of the forest. I slipped my hand through the bars. 'I'm right here.'

At first, it was as though he hadn't heard me. His body remained motionless; still nothing more than a black form against the dingy cell wall. Then, all at once, he crawled into the dull spillage of light. Black veins had sprouted along his neck and streaked down his chest. His head was bowed. But I knew, even before he raised his chin and our eyes met, that something was horribly wrong.

Sebastian's eyes had turned completely silver, like someone had melted down the metal and poured it straight into his sockets. No separation of iris and pupil, just two solid orbs. He surveyed me, unblinking, and my heart plummeted as the rest of his features materialized from the shadows.

His damp, plastered hair highlighted his pointed ears, but jutting through his bangs, the spiraled horns above his temples had grown and thickened, angling outward and back. Smaller black veins ran like tiny lightning bolts from the base of his horns along his brow line and the edges of his temples.

His teeth were clearly visible over his dark, cracked lips, and they gleamed like rows of sharpened knives – those teeth he used to try and hide from me in the way he would speak or smile, always keeping his lips close together. Like he was ashamed.

Now, Sebastian's mouth gaped wide, showing them off as he drew in ragged breaths. His gray skin looked marbleized in the orange light of the room as his wings began moving methodically back and forth, slow and ominous, stirring up dust inside the small cell. Purple-black blood oozed from new arrow wounds on his opposite shoulder and also his thigh.

'Oh God,' I breathed a prayer, not knowing what else to do. I reached my hand further through the bars, desperate to touch him, to bring him back from wherever he was. But he moved so much faster than I expected. In one breath, he was crouched in front of me. The next, he slammed into the bars. I yanked my hand back just before he hit.

The bars rattled, tiny rocks shook loose from the ceiling. I stifled a scream and scrambled away from the prison as Sebastian hit the bars again and again, each time with an inhuman cry that ripped the air from my lungs. I watched, fighting back tears until, at last, he seemed to exhaust himself. He collapsed onto his side, his wings curling around him like a giant gray coat.

I couldn't see his face anymore, but the image of it burned in my head. There'd been no life in those eyes – nothing that showed he even knew who I was. Every bit of me turned frigid, then numb.

'Come on, Sebastian,' I said hoarsely. I eased closer to the cell. 'You know it's me. I know you're in there somewhere. Whatever Augustine's done to you, you can fight it. Just ... just don't give up.'

The only reply I got was another inhuman growl.

I slumped to the floor and leaned against the wall, staring helplessly into the cell. I couldn't even talk to him, much less find out what happened. Sebastian's wings obscured his body, but I noticed patches of his blood on the floor.

He'd been shot with more *prah*-filled arrows.

The Queen was convinced Sebastian was dangerous. She'd already agreed to give him over to Augustine. She even knew about the *Sobrasi* and their plans for the shadowen. What reason did Augustine have to keep doing this to him?

Nadya Corsi's words came back to me with a jolt.

The danger lies in this: We don't know what might happen to Sebastian, when the prah *of both the head and the body of* La Gargouille *join together within him.*

That's why the *prah* wasn't having the same effect on Sebastian as it had with the others. He was something entirely different. Zindelo and Nadya's fears were taking shape right in front of me, and I had no clue how to stop it.

'Josephine?'

For a millisecond, I thought it was Sebastian, and my heart skidded to a stop. But it wasn't him. I jerked my head up to find Quentin studying me from a few feet away, just inside the opened door.

'Are you okay?'

'Yeah,' I said coldly. I got to my feet and brushed off my jeans. 'Wish I could say the same for Sebastian, but I can't.'

Donani and the Queen entered the room behind Quentin, and her four personal guards followed closely behind. The room suddenly felt cramped and stifling. Thalia approached, raising her hand to settle the Marksmen, who had instantly stepped forward as well.

'You see,' she said. 'It's exactly as I told you.'

'No, it isn't. This isn't him, *Kralitsa.*' I looked over my shoulder. Sebastian lay where he'd collapsed moments earlier, his massive wings like a cocoon. 'You said you saw him when he first arrived. You have to see the difference. He won't talk, he doesn't even acknowledge me.'

She sighed, but it wasn't a sound of sadness or even disapproval. If anything, it was resigned. 'As the old verse says, a leopard cannot change its spots. Neither can a shadow creature.' The Queen looked inside the cell. 'Perhaps this one was just able to hide them from you for a while.'

It was useless. The Queen had made up her mind with the same finality as Quentin. I couldn't talk sense into them, even if I had all the time in the world. 'No, you don't understand,' I said, anyway. 'Augustine did this to him.'

'And what if he did?' she replied with a shrug. 'What difference does it make? His fate will be the same, regardless. He is a shadowen. And that is enough.'

'But he's more,' I shot back.

The Queen's forehead lifted. 'Meaning?'

I gulped down my next words before they left my mouth. If I told her about *La Gargouille* in front of a room full of Marksmen, Sebastian would be dead in seconds. My heart burned seeing him like this. But he was alive. And as long as he was alive, there was hope.

'He's my guardian,' I replied instead.

My aunt sighed. I heard disappointment in the sound. 'I am sorry that your goodbyes were not as you hoped, Josephine. But perhaps it was better this way. A clean break is sometimes the easiest.'

'So, that's it. I'm just to go back to the Circe now and pretend none of this ever happened.'

'Not yet,' said the Queen. 'The Gathering Celebration

begins in two hours. The Court of Shadows is already growing full of Outcasts from throughout the *kumpania*. And you, Josephine, must represent the Romany clan. Quentin has already spoken to Nicolas and told him of the arrangements.'

'Oh, I'm sure he has,' I said icily.

'I don't have to remind you,' she added. 'It's your duty.' She placed her hand on my shoulder. 'I intend to make an announcement to all the *bandoleers*, which will quell their fears and restore their hope. If all goes well, they will return to their clans with the assurance that they will never be threatened by the shadow world again.'

I turned my attention to Sebastian. His wings shook in tiny tremors, and I wondered if he even understood anything going on around him.

'Are the Corsis going to be there?' I asked suddenly.

'Pardon me?'

'Sebastian's family. The Corsi clan from Sixes. Are they going to be present at the Gathering? I mean, I would assume they would be, since every clan is represented.'

Quentin stepped forward. 'The Corsis are being detained at the moment, *Kralitsa*. We believe they had plans to try and rescue this gargoyle. It was a preventative measure, to keep them from breaking any laws they might regret. They are safely in their home and being looked after.'

I kept my eyes on my aunt. 'Their absence would be noticed.'

'Donani,' she said, sweeping her long dress aside as she moved. 'Please see to it than the Corsis are in attendance this evening. All Outcasts should be present.'

He and Quentin exchanged looks.

'Of course,' Donani replied, bowing his head.

The Marksman left the dungeon. Quentin narrowed his eyes at me.

'Now,' said the Queen, walking to the door. 'If you'll be so kind as to escort my niece back to the bedroom I assigned her. I'll have the proper attire sent along.' She looked me up and down. 'Then you will join me for tea, Josephine. We have much to discuss.'

I watched her walk out, followed by two of the guards. Inside the cell, Sebastian made harsh, grating sounds with his claws. I approached the bars and tried to communicate once last time. I touched the pendant at my neck and put all my efforts into speaking inside my head.

Sebastian, say something. Let me know you're still there. Please.

This time, he moved. I held my breath as he propped himself onto his elbow and twisted his neck just enough to focus his solid eyes on me. Then he flashed his teeth in a vicious snarl.

'Let's go, Josie.'

Quentin reached out and took my arm. Sebastian suddenly launched at the doorway. His clawed hands burst between the iron bars, nearly catching Quentin. The force of his wild spring shook the framework of the door. I heard the creak of bending metal and popping bolts. Quentin pulled me back, his eyes betraying his trepidation.

The two remaining guards rushed up beside us, their spears jabbing into the cage until Sebastian retreated into the corner, his body disappearing into the dark shadows. It was the last I saw of him.

We left the dungeon and walked back through the tunnels. Quentin kept his arm on me, his touch firm enough to remind me he was there. As we neared the bedroom, he suddenly leaned into me and pressed his lips into my hair.

'What do you think you're going to accomplish,' he whispered harshly, 'bringing the Corsis to the Gathering? They're not going to be able to help you. Or the demon.'

'Maybe not,' I said, pulling away from him. 'But they deserve to know what's going on.'

Quentin opened the door and stepped aside, waiting for me. I pushed past him into the room. 'I'll see you shortly,' he said. He snapped his fingers and the two Marksmen took up their places on either side of the door.

'Posting guards,' I said. 'Really.'

He bowed low, his face twisting into a sweet smile. 'For your protection,' he replied. 'I wouldn't want anything to happen to you.'

Quentin closed the door, and I heard it lock behind him.

36. Josephine

I studied my reflection in the mirror.

The traditional clothes Aunt Thalia had sent to the room were a perfect fit, I had to admit, even if I hated having them on. I was getting ready for a party, while Sebastian was lying cold and alone in a nasty dungeon cell. The idea that he might not know what was going on wasn't much consolation.

I adjusted the long skirt. The burgundy and orange fabric was covered in tiny yellow dandelion print, and it swished over the tops of my boots as I reached up to finish off my hair. I tied the red ribbons that I'd woven into my braids. They hung low across my blouse, which had a scooped neck and flowing sleeves.

I may not have been a prisoner exactly, but I certainly wasn't free either. For the first time in my life, I couldn't see a clear option ahead of me. I fiddled with the dandelion pendant at my neck, drawing strength from the *sclav* that had joined me to Sebastian, even though the glass casing felt cold as ice.

The door lock turned. Quentin appeared in the doorway. He'd changed clothes in the time he'd been gone. Even though he still wore black from head to toe, it was nicer than his usual uniform. His hair was slicked and styled, his face recently shaved. My stomach hurt like I'd eaten something bad.

'You look beautiful,' he said suddenly.

'That's comforting.'

Quentin studied me carefully. 'The Queen requests your presence in her private chambers.'

I glanced over his shoulder at the two Marksmen guards standing silently in the passageway. There was nothing remotely resembling a request in this. I looked back at Quentin.

'Well, I guess you win,' I said.

He almost looked surprised. 'Oh, yes?'

'I can't go against the Queen's wishes, and you've got my father wrapped around your every word. It doesn't leave me a lot of choice. I'll attend the Gathering. I'll represent my family like the honorable *bandoleer*'s daughter.' I stepped closer. 'But don't think for one second I'm going to forget any of this.'

A glint appeared in his dark eyes. 'Of course, *Rani*.'

His words dripped with every bit of the sarcasm that mine had.

'Then let's go,' I said, smoothing out my skirt and starting forward. 'I know my aunt would be highly disappointed if I was late.'

We turned left at the end of the hall. The corridor was lined with tapestries on either side. Quentin knocked on a thick wooden door.

'Come in,' my aunt said.

He opened the door for me. The Queen's private rooms reminded me of something out of an old-timey Hollywood movie. There was a receiving room and her bedroom lay behind a thick curtained door. The Queen sat on one end of a couch. On the coffee table in front of her was a tray with tea and cookies, along with a glass of water and a bottle of prescription pills. She motioned me inside. Quentin started to move, but I stepped in front of him.

'I can take it from here,' I said crisply.

Quentin's eyes narrowed, but he flashed his perfect teeth at me in an overly pleasant smile and bowed. 'Of course,' he said, stepping out of the way. 'But I'll be close by, should you need me.' He shut the door behind him.

'Have a seat,' said the Queen.

I sank into the cushions of the couch. She leaned over and poured a cup of tea for me, adding a lump of sugar and some milk before handing it over. I took it dutifully and stirred the contents with a fancy teaspoon.

'I trust you're pleased with the clothing,' said the Queen as she placed a few cookies on a plate. 'It suits you.'

'Yes, thank you *Kralitsa*.' Everything inside me felt like it was screaming. I wanted to be out there, back in the dungeon with Sebastian, not stuck in layers of billowy clothes, having tea with my aunt like it was an ordinary day. I raised my teacup to my lips.

'Quentin Marks cleans up quite nicely, doesn't he?' she said, nodding towards the door as she offered me the plate. 'He's quite respected among the Marksmen as well, Donani tells me.'

'I don't doubt it,' I replied.

The Queen shot me a knowing look as she took a sip of her tea. 'Give it time, Josephine. I know you're angry with him, but he's only doing what I would expect from any Marksman who had pledged to look out for the interests of the Outcasts. You would be wise to consider him in your future plans.'

'Aunt Thalia,' I said, brushing off her comments. 'I ask you once last time, please don't let Augustine have Sebastian. If you do, I'll lose him forever. I can't let that happen.'

'Josephine,' she replied levelly, her voice slightly clipped. 'I allowed you to see the gargoyle in the hopes that you would realize what is painfully obvious. He isn't a guardian. Nor is he even a gargoyle.'

'What's happened to him is Augustine's fault. He's not like that. Sebastian is good and kind. If you would just let him go back to the Corsi clan, they could find a way to fix him. I know they could.'

'What's done is done,' she replied. 'You have other things to attend to.'

I sat back, working to control my face. 'What do you mean?'

The Queen set her teacup aside. 'As we speak, the Gathering Celebration is underway. *Bandoleers* from every clan are in attendance. Representatives from all the head families and Outcasts from the city have come.'

'Yes,' I said warily, trying to figure out the switch in conversation. 'That's why you sent me these clothes. I'm attending the Celebration.'

The corners of her eyes tightened. 'No, I'm afraid you aren't. You need to take that time to prepare.'

'For what?'

'The midnight service,' she replied. 'I'm announcing you as my successor at its conclusion.'

I almost knocked over my tea. 'I don't understand.'

The Queen touched the edge of her headscarf, pulling it back just enough for me to see the baldness underneath. 'Josephine, I have been battling for many years, but my health has decided that it no longer wishes to join me. I don't know how much time remains for me, but in this one thing, I still have control.'

'But I'm not an adult yet,' I said. 'I'm not married.'

'You will in time.' She smiled. 'Don't worry, I have no intentions of dying immediately.' She smiled. 'The throne will remain mine. But you need a push in the next direction. Naming you publically will usher in this next chapter of your life. What you decide to do with it, however, is up to you.' She sat back in her chair, and for the first time, I noticed the weariness in the lines of her face. 'As soon as the Gathering meal is finished, everyone will make their way to the Cathedral of Saints for the service. Quentin Marks will accompany you there.'

I stood and walked to the other side of the room, feeling like a zombie. I knew this was coming. I'd tried to put it off, to avoid my inheritance at all costs. But now, it was staring me in the face. I couldn't run anymore.

I adjusted my jewelry and the ribbons of my braids. I refused to marry simply for titles and status, though the practice still existed within some of the Old Clans. But the expectation remained, and with me, it had always carried so much more weight.

'Josephine?'

The Queen looked steadily at me, waiting for my answer. When I didn't respond, she rose to join me. 'My niece,' she said, cupping my chin with her hand. 'I know the burden you carry.' Her green eyes softened. 'If anything, I wish I could take that from you. But neither of us can escape what we were born to do.'

I nodded slowly. 'Yes, Aunt Thalia.'

'Good,' she replied, smiling. 'You may return to your room for the time being. I have an important meeting I must attend first, but I will see you at the cathedral tonight.' The Queen took my hands within her own. 'You are doing a great honor to this *kumpania*. When I step down from throne, I am confident you will do what's required of you.'

*

I sat on the edge of my bed, picking at the tray of food my aunt had sent to me. I glanced at the nightstand clock. It was less than two hours before the midnight service would start, and I'd accomplished nothing apart from bending to the Queen's inevitable wishes.

I studied the locked door in front of me. The man and woman Quentin had posted were still outside, guarding me. Not only were they heavily armed, but they were also trained Marksmen. I'd never be able to overpower them, but maybe, if I could catch them by surprise …

I frantically searched my discarded jeans before remembering I didn't have my knife. My fingers brushed over the small book in my other pocket, and I pulled it out, stuffing it into the leg of my boot. Then I rushed to the desk and took the lamp. I yanked off the shade and ripped the cord out of the wall. I took a large glass vase from the dresser in my other hand and tested its thickness. If I threw it hard enough against the dresser, it would shatter. I just hoped it was enough to bring them running.

Sebastian was in that dungeon. I had to get back to him. We were bonded. If I could just keep talking to him, he'd snap out of it. I'd help him break out of there, and whatever happened after that, I didn't care.

I took up a position beside the door on the opposite side from where I was aiming the vase. Holding the lamp in my other hand like a baseball bat, I took a big breath and got ready to throw the glass. Just then, two loud thuds, followed by a muffled grunt, sounded from outside. The door opened.

I swung the lamp with all my force. A large figure turned just in time to save his head. I struck again, hitting him square in the back, and then I aimed the heavy vase at him. A hand grabbed the glass just before I made contact.

'Stop!'

The whispered command came from a familiar voice, and I stumbled back, nearly dropping the lamp.

'Ezzie?'

She tossed the vase onto the bed. Beside her, the man groaned and reached up to rub his shoulder where I'd hit him. I noted his dark hair, goatee, and tattooed arms and neck.

Hugo Corsi.

'Thanks,' he said, looking at Ezzie. 'She almost took my head off.'

Ezzie smiled. 'I almost let her.'

I set the lamp aside, feeling my eyes bugging. 'What … *how*?'

Esmeralda put a finger to her lips. She and Hugo retreated into the hallway and came back in, each dragging an unconscious guard behind them. Hugo shut the door and spun around to look at me.

'You weren't wearing that the last time I saw you.'

352

I tugged on one of my braids. 'The Queen's choice for the midnight service, but it doesn't matter right now. Is Katie okay? How did you guys find me?'

Hugo jutted his thumb at Ezzie. 'Ask *her*.'

'Katie's fine,' she replied, kneeling down to check on the female guard. 'I got her back to the inn, but we'd only been there a few minutes when we received a visit from a group of Marksmen. They are keeping the Corsis under house arrest. I was able to sneak out the back door, as they didn't seem to know I was staying there. I retraced our steps to the cemetery entrance, and I tracked you from there.'

'Ezzie found me first,' said Hugo. He pressed his ear to the door for a few seconds. When he was satisfied, he continued. 'Augustine left me in some church basement with a couple of guards. Don't know where he got off to.'

'Wait, what do you mean, *left you*?'

Hugo joined Ezzie, looking over the male guard. He retrieved a pair of wickedly long knives from the Marksman's belt. 'I got a nice, friendly escort from the inn to Augustine's little hiding place. He needed me to tattoo him.' Hugo looked up at me. 'That's how he's been controlling shadowen. He came up with some special mixture using the contents of the urn. I guess he'd figured it out using all those books he's stolen. Anyway, he made me tattoo an image of Sebastian on his arm, and then they shot my brother with the last of the *prah*.'

I remembered Sebastian's new arrow wounds. 'All of it?'

'Yeah.' Hugo stood, depositing the knives on the bed. 'Sebastian started screaming and clawing at the stuff like it was acid or something.' He clenched his hands into fists. 'By the time I fought my way to him, it was too late. His eyes were … well, it wasn't him anymore. Augustine was on the floor, grabbing at his own arm like it was burning up. Then, it just stopped. Sebastian went so still I thought … I thought he was dead.' Hugo jaw tightened. 'But then, he just stood up, all blank-faced. I yelled at him, but he didn't even look my way. Augustine told him to go with Donani and wait for instructions. They walked out, just like that. I don't know where they took him.'

'The dungeons,' I replied. 'I just saw him.'

Ezzie rose quickly. 'You what?'

I crossed my arms to my chest, as though I could hold the ache inside. 'He's locked up there. Hugo, everything you said about Sebastian, about how he's acting, I saw it for myself. The Queen let me into the dungeon, but Sebastian didn't even recognize me.'

Ezzie frowned. 'The Queen?'

I hastily explained everything my aunt had told me, as well as what had happened with Quentin. As soon as I was finished, Hugo immediately began stripping the long black coat off the male guard's body.

'Well, that answers everything for me.' He shrugged on the coat, and buttoned it up. It was on the small side, but it fit well enough. 'So the first order of business is breaking Sebastian out of there.'

'What about his current condition?' asked Ezzie, as she took the other guard's coat and adjusted the long sleeves. 'It doesn't sound as though he will come willingly.'

'And I don't have any Vitamin D on me,' said Hugo. 'Though I have a pretty bad feeling it wouldn't matter if I did.'

'Hugo,' I said. 'Was the only thing different about Sebastian his eyes?'

'Isn't that enough?'

My stomach turned unpleasantly. 'Your parents were concerned about what might happen if the *prah* from the urn of Keveco and the head of *La Gargouille* were to mix.'

'Yeah,' he replied, his forehead creasing. 'They were.'

'I think it's already happening,' I replied.

'So you're telling me, this isn't the worst of it.'

'You need to see him for yourself.' I took the smallest knife from the bed and tucked it into my boot. It wasn't the most intimidating weapon from the Marksmen's stash, but I felt better, just having a blade within easy reach. 'We've got to get to the dungeon, but we don't have long. They'll be coming to get me soon, and if I'm not here—'

'Got it,' Hugo replied, glancing at the guards. 'But we should probably take care of these guys first.'

I hurried over the dresser and pulled out several thick ribbons from the drawer where I'd taken mine. I tossed some to Ezzie, and we tied up the guards. Ezzie fished a set of keys out of her stolen Marksman coat.

'Okay, let's go,' I said, heading for the door.

Hugo and Esmeralda pulled up the hoods of their cloaks. From a short distance, they looked convincingly enough like Marksmen. We stepped into the hall and locked the door behind us. They took up positions on either side of me, acting like an escort in case we passed anyone.

When we reached the dungeon, I hesitated at the doorway. I didn't want to see him like that again, but we had to help him. We had to figure out a way to fix the damage Augustine had done. My hand trailed to my necklace. I couldn't feel Sebastian's presence anymore. The sensation made me cold all over, like I'd stepped into a freezer.

Hugo raised his brows at us in silent question. I shook myself off and nodded back at him. Ezzie took out the

Marksmen's keys and pressed one to the lock, but the door swung open. We eased cautiously into the rectangular room, Ezzie in the lead. I listened as hard as I could. The room was uncannily quiet.

Ezzie made a tense noise in the back of her throat. 'Shadowen.'

'Yeah,' I whispered, peering into the alcoves. 'Quentin said this is where they hold shadow creatures to use for Marksmen training.' I shuddered. 'They keep them drugged up, apparently.'

As we neared the enclosure where I'd seen Sebastian, I got a sickly, slithering feeling in the pit of my stomach – worse even than when I'd looked at him for the first time. I blinked my eyes, refusing to believe what I saw.

The barred door had been ripped from its hinges.

'This isn't good,' said Hugo.

It felt like something heavy had been dropped on my chest. I rushed inside the empty cell, pushing down a churning feeling of panic. Something caught my eye on the floor, and I bent to pick it up. It was a metal cuff.

'The Marksmen put these on Sebastian at the Circe.'

Ezzie knelt beside me and picked up the matching one. 'I know these,' she said, turning it into the light so we could see the short rows of diamond spikes lining the inside of the cuff. 'They prevent gargoyles and chimeras from shadowing. The constant pressure drains a shadowen's energy, as the diamonds do not allow them to fully heal.' She looked up at Hugo. 'I hadn't realized that the Marksmen still possessed such devices.'

I rotated the cuff in my fingers. The locking mechanism was wrenched, like it had been pried off with a lot of force.

I threw the band across the cell, and it smacked against the wall. 'Sebastian did this.'

Hugo ran his hand along a severed hinge. 'And this door was destroyed from the inside, which means, he broke himself out.'

I dashed outside, the others right on my heels. 'He could be anywhere,' I said over my shoulder we went back through the corridor. 'He's hurt and he's not himself. We have to find him before something terrible happens.'

'Yeah,' said Hugo. 'To somebody else.'

'What?'

'You saw what I saw, Josephine. I don't think we're dealing with Sebastian anymore. I don't know if it's Augustine fault or if it's this *La Gargouille* my parents say he is, but if he's running around loose down here—'

'Just a moment,' said Ezzie.

The urgency in her voice pulled me up short, and I whirled. Hugo and I watched as Ezzie closed her eyes. Her brow furrowed, and her face turned rigid with concentration. I bit my lip, anxious. We couldn't afford to waste any more precious minutes.

'Can you track him?' Hugo asked.

'I can't tell. There's something else.' She took a deep breath through her nose, and Ezzie's eyes suddenly glittered silver under the tunnel lanterns. 'Sebastian isn't the only gargoyle here.'

'Well, that's just great,' said Hugo.

I ignored him. 'Ezzie, can you find them?'

'I think so,' she replied, glancing at Hugo.

'And you're sure they're gargoyles?' I asked. 'Not the other things?'

'I'm sure.'

I stared down the long corridor. Time was ticking away. Soon, the Queen would come to fetch me. If I wasn't there, she'd send her guard to find me. I would not be forced back, not when I was this close. 'We need help,' I said. 'If there are gargoyles here, then that means they're guardians, too. Surely they'll help us.'

'Perhaps.' Ezzie didn't look convinced. 'There's only one way to find out.'

'Okay.' I'd made up my mind. 'Lead the way.'

37. Josephine

We tried keeping to the smaller tunnels, but it grew more difficult the closer we approached the central portions of the Court of Shadows. Hugo and Ezzie fell back, allowing me to take the lead for appearance's sake, even though Ezzie whispered directions to me as we walked.

For the first time, I appreciated the Queen's gift of new clothes. Even if someone were to recognize me, it looked as though I was on my way to the Gathering Celebration, same as anyone else. Hugo and Ezzie, with their long coats and heavy hoods, blended in tolerably, but we made sure to avoid any Marksmen we saw coming in our direction.

We turned into another hall. Pools of warm light spilled out from several wide, arched doorways on the right. Noises and food smells drifted outside the room. It was the Gathering Chamber, but it wasn't empty anymore, like it had been when I'd met with the Queen. Several hundred Gypsies crowded around the long tables and stood in groups along the walls.

I paused at one of the archways. I scanned the room, but

I didn't see any of the Corsis or Katie amongst the crowd. I felt a hand on my shoulder, coaxing me away from the entrance.

'Turn here,' said Ezzie in a low voice.

I quickly complied, passing through an intersection of corridors that led from the Gathering Chamber and down several steps. The air turned cooler, and the noise and pleasant smells of dinner faded. The hallway veered to the left. Two Marksmen appeared, coming our way up the corridor.

'Hey,' said the first man, the taller of the two. 'You're not allowed down here.'

'The Queen sent me to speak with the gargoyles,' I said. He hesitated, caught off-guard by my reply. I took a chance and dove right in. 'I don't have a lot of time. She wants to make sure everything is in order.'

His eyes swept over me, taking in the style and colors of my clothes. At least I looked like I was a high-ranking clan member, even if there was no evidence of anything else. 'Alright,' he finally replied, 'But make it quick.'

I brushed by him and went straight for the first opening I saw – a large wooden door with an arched top. I prayed that I'd made the right choice as I put my hand on the large iron handle.

'Thank you,' I said, turning over my shoulder. 'That will be all.'

The Marksman moved forward. 'I'm sorry, but I can't let—'

A swift blow to the head cut him off. He fell at Ezzie's feet. The other Marksman didn't even have time to grab his weapon. Hugo's massive arm clamped around his throat, and he slumped unconscious to the floor in a matter of seconds.

'That went better than I expected,' I said.

'Nice job,' Hugo replied.

Esmeralda didn't respond. Her eyes had shifted again, from hazel to a silvery sheen, and expression seemed caught between wonder and disgust. I reached out, touching the sleeve of her Marksman disguise. She flicked her gaze towards me and mouthed one word: *gargoyles.*

Hugo slid one of his stolen diamond daggers from inside his coat, but Ezzie stopped him with a fluid wave of her hand. She closed her eyes, and her thin brows drew close together in concentration. A few moments passed, as Ezzie remained in the same motionless posture, eyes shut and head bowed.

'Something isn't right, Badrick,' said a low, female voice from the other side of the door.

'I agree, replied a deep male voice. 'He is not a chimera. You saw that as well as I when he was brought before us. But neither is he like us.'

'You believe it is true, then,' answered the female voice. 'This Augustine has indeed found a way to manipulate our kind even further. This is why they are allowing him to join their ranks.'

'Do you question it, Tamzen?' said the one she'd called Badrick. 'Their quest is the acquisition of power, as it has been since before the Sundering. Perhaps they were once content to leave these Outcast Clans alone, but when word of a new power comes along, they are drawn to it as insects to flame.'

The female began a reply, but abruptly their voices ceased,

and a heavy quiet fell on the other side of the door. Ezzie's head dropped further, and her lips moved slightly.

'You may enter,' said the male in a louder voice. 'There are no Gypsies here.'

Ezzie opened her eyes, and as she looked at me, I realized she'd been speaking with them telepathically. She nodded at Hugo. He tucked the dagger back into his long coat as I pushed open the door.

The room was a large circular space, with a high jagged ceiling held together by thick wooden rafters. A railed balcony ran around half the space, but the rest had been destroyed. The pillars that held up that side of the balcony were cracked, and wood and debris covered the floor. Before my brain had time to formulate any questions about what had happened, I saw them.

Four gargoyles.

They turned to regard us, and I faltered as I took in the sight of them. Apart from Sebastian, I'd only seen Augustine's gargoyles, and I refused to even put them in the same category, long before they'd become anything else. These gargoyles were nothing like that.

A feeling of ancient mystery wafted around them like invisible smoke. Their gray faces looked noble, despite their intimidating appearance. As I studied them warily, I felt a kind of awed fear, like I might feel if I were to encounter a shark in the middle of the ocean. I'd never been afraid of Sebastian when it came to my own safety, but these new shadowen sent a tremor up my spine.

They were dressed in clothing from a different place and time. The style reminded me of Renaissance tunics and breeches, but the fabric was a shimmery gray that blended with their skin, making the gargoyles appear even more like moving statues. They shared characteristics with Sebastian, but they weren't quite the same. None of them had horns, and the wings that jutted from their backs in sharp angles didn't trail the floor, like his often did.

I'd been so wrapped up in my thoughts that I hadn't noticed the intense, silent standoff going on between the gargoyles and Esmeralda. Hugo stood a little at a distance, watching them carefully, his thick brows lowered in confused concern. They were speaking to each other again. The male gargoyle's expression remained frigidly barren.

'Esmeralda,' he said, finally, speaking out loud for our benefit.

'Badrick,' she replied in a civil tone.

He studied her carefully. 'It has been a long time since last we met. Tell me, how have you fared all these many years since the Sundering?'

'Well enough.'

His expression remained passive. 'And you do not sleep.'

'No,' she said. 'I was given a second chance at life.'

'Is that what you call this?' he asked, gesturing at her with a repulsed grimace. 'Living as a human, and not even one of Roma blood, at that. It appears you have been rejected from not one world, but two.' His features molded into a stoic smile. 'But your judgment was fair. You killed your charge, and you betrayed the *Sobrasi*.'

Hugo inched closer, his hand staying to his inside coat pocket and anger building in his eyes. The gargoyles moved closer. Esmeralda, however, didn't move a muscle. With fierce eyes, she continued to stare down the one she'd called Badrick.

'Markus died because I was not there to save him,' said Ezzie, her voice ripe with tension. 'But I did not kill him.'

'And why did you leave him alone, when the Roma were in such dire need of their protectors, when the blood wars were at their highest point and even the *Sobrasi* were turning on each other?'

'It was the only thing I could do,' she replied.

As I watched the tortured look spreading over her face, I understood why. Esmeralda had fallen in love with her charge, and she knew it was forbidden. She tried to leave him.

Hugo put a hand on her arm. 'Hey, you don't own them anything.' His intense gaze bored into Badrick, and there was no fear behind his glare.

'No, I don't,' she said. She seemed to be fighting an inner struggle, but she didn't pull out of Hugo's grasp. Instead, she spoke only to him. 'I thought there might be a way to release Markus from our bond, that perhaps he would no longer feel the same towards me. I went before the *Sobrasi* and told them all, thinking they would help me. Instead, they dragged Markus before their meeting and accused him of betraying his duties. He escaped their clutches, but they sent shadowen after him. And I was not there to protect him.' Esmeralda's silver eyes flashed. 'The *Sobrasi* ceased being a force of good long ago. The Roma that were worthy of those positions were killed or banished, leaving only greedy traitors in their place. The *Sobrasi* have no honor anymore.'

The lead gargoyle approached until he and Ezzie were face to face. 'In this, we do agree.'

Silence fell. I waited as long as I could. 'If you feel that way, then we could really use your help.'

Badrick's eyes slit toward me. 'Esmeralda, who are these Gypsies?'

'Josephine Romany and Hugo Corsi,' she replied.

He took his time, looking us over. I had the unnerving sensation that a whole lot was being said between the gargoyles that Hugo and I would never hear. Esmeralda didn't react, either way. After he'd completed his internal review of us – or whatever Ezzie said about us – he nodded again.

'It is an honor to meet members from such renowned clans,' he said. 'I am called Badrick. This is Tamzen.' He gestured to the female on his right. She was tall and slim, with cropped pewter hair that hung wild around her shoulders. 'And these are Gussalen and Sunniva.'

The other two female gargoyles made a similar greeting, but they didn't speak. I opted to return their formal introductions with a greeting we used when other clan members came to visit the Circe. 'God has sent you.'

Badrick's expression shifted into one of approval, as through he hadn't expected the words. 'It is by God we have been sent.'

'What are you doing here, Badrick?' asked Ezzie. 'The last time we met, you were guardian to the *bandoleer* of the Dunitru clan in France.'

'That,' he replied, 'was over two hundred years ago, Esmeralda. Much has happened since then among the *Arniko Natsia*.' He gestured to the other gargoyles. 'We no longer have charges to protect. Now, we are in the service of the new order of *Sobrasi*, established many years after the Sundering.'

'That doesn't answer the question,' I said.

He peered down at me. 'The *Sobrasi* have come to initiate a new member, and we are here to collect the gargoyle. We will return with him to Europe, and under the guidance of the *Sobrasi*, he will be retrained and made fit for more suitable service.'

Hugo bristled beside me. 'Yeah, that's not going to happen.'

At once, the gargoyles' demeanors changed, like a shift in the wind. Their wings lifted off their backs, and their bodies tensed. I stepped in front of Hugo with my hands in the air. I felt the heat of his emotions like I was standing next to a bonfire. But we couldn't be emotional now. These gargoyles were our best chance at finding Sebastian.

'Look,' I said. 'It doesn't matter at this point what you're supposed to do with him, because he's gone.'

'Gone?' questioned Tamzen, the tall female gargoyle.

'He broke out of the dungeon, and we don't know where he is. Augustine has promised the Queen that he's going to destroy all the shadowen throughout our *kumpania*, and we have to find Sebastian before that happens.'

'We are aware of their agreement,' said Tamzen, her lip curling. 'And we have pledged to assist in any way we can to eradicate the evil creatures.'

'*All* the shadowen,' I said, frowning. 'That includes you.'

'We are under the *Sobrasi*'s protection,' said Badrick. 'We do not fall into the same ranking as those scum.'

'Neither does Sebastian.'

'We cannot help you,' he said. 'We are bound to the wishes of the *Sobrasi*.'

'You aren't servants,' I countered. 'You're guardians.'

Badrick's lip curled, revealing a row of sharp teeth. 'That was a long time ago. Things are different. And when your charges have power to turn you to stone, it becomes difficult to remain on any equal footing.'

'Isn't there some way you can break free?'

Tamzen folded her arms over her chest. 'We cannot break the seal. It binds us until death, and we do not kill Roma. It is against the morals of our very existence and the reason God chose to make the gargoyle the protector of Gypsy kind.'

I looked from one gargoyle to the next. Their faces reminded me so much of Sebastian – quietly resigned. The faces of those who have been beaten down, who've forgotten their own strength. Almost without realizing it, I'd reached out and touched Tamzen's arm gently.

'The *Sobrasi* have turned into something they were never meant to be. They were supposed to oversee the shadow world, but they've used it for their own power. If you help us, I swear I'll do everything I can to change all of this.'

She blinked slowly at me with her strange, inhuman eyes. The others watched her warily. 'Why are you so concerned with this gargoyle?' she asked.

I stared back at her. 'He's my guardian.'

Badrick scoffed. 'If he were, he would've found a way to your side, no matter what obstacles he faced. You tell us that he has escaped, and yet, you are here and he is not. A guardian would be able to track his charge.'

'He's not himself,' I replied. 'He broke out of his cell in the dungeon, and we have no idea how to find him. But I know you have tracking skills. You could locate him before Augustine or the Marksmen.'

Badrick raised his brow, reminding me a little of Ezzie. 'And why would we want to do such a thing?'

Ezzie stepped forward. 'Badrick, listen to me. Whatever you think of me, you must believe Josephine Romany. She is Sebastian's charge. He's not guilty of any crime. He has been wrongly stolen away from his rightful place and endured much suffering at the hands of a *marimé* traitor who only seeks revenge and power. But it is more than that. Sebastian isn't simply a guardian, or even a gargoyle, for that matter. We have reason to believe he is the embodiment of the head of *La Gargouille*.'

Another thick silence engulfed the room. The silver eyes of the gargoyles glimmered in the light, and I read their thoughts in them, even if I wasn't privileged to hear the words in my head.

'Where do you get such an absurd theory?' demanded Tamzen.

Hugo's jaw worked so hard his goatee twitched. 'From my parents. Zindelo and Nadya Corsi.'

'*La Gargouille*,' Badrick repeated, sounding thoughtful. 'I have been around since before the Sundering, and there has never been any mention of that evil monstrosity. The head was destroyed long ago. Your information comes from two renegade *Sobrasi* who cannot be trusted.'

Hugo's face darkened, and he started forward, but I put my hands out to stop him. 'I heard you say it yourself, before we came into the room. You said you'd never sensed anything like him.' I looked at each gargoyle imploringly. 'Please, we have to find Sebastian. He needs our help to fight this. Augustine's been using him like some pawn in this game he's playing. Even if you don't believe us, Sebastian is still one of your kind; you can't deny that. Are you so cold and heartless that you would just let him be destroyed?'

The four shadowen stared at each other, communicating telepathically between them. If Ezzie was in part of their conversation, I couldn't tell from her expression. Hugo watched them suspiciously. His fingers twitched at his sides. My mouth felt like sandpaper, but I bit my lip so that I wouldn't say anything else. Finally, Badrick addressed us again.

'We do not know whether we believe all you have said, but this Sebastian Grey is a gargoyle, and therefore we do owe him our aid. We will help you as much as we can, but our capacity is limited. The *Sobrasi* are in session now with Augustine, but they will shortly return.'

'Can you track him?' I asked.

Badrick lifted his head, sniffing the air. The others mirrored his actions. Ezzie observed from a distance, her eyes dulling to hazel, before she glanced away. Hugo noticed, too. Badrick seemed to confer with the rest of the shadowen before he dipped his head towards me.

'Sebastian Grey is not in the Court of Shadows.'

I couldn't process what he said at first, and then a freezing dread went up my spine. If he wasn't in the Court—

'Where?' Ezzie demanded. 'We need to know where.'

Badrick opened his mouth, then abruptly glanced towards the door. 'We cannot say more. The *Sobrasi* are coming.'

'Then we need to leave now,' I said. A thought hit me, and I turned to Badrick. 'You can shadow out of here, right?'

'Of course,' he replied.

'Wait a sec,' said Hugo, stepping back in alarm. 'Not that smoke thing you guys do?'

Ezzie smiled wryly at him. 'There is no other way.'

Tamzen sniffed the air. 'If we are going, it must be now. They are very close.'

'Crap,' said Hugo, his shoulders slumping. 'Okay, what do I do?'

'Nothing,' said Tamzen, wrapping her arms around him. 'Just don't let go.'

Hugo gave a startled huff as black, oily mist swirled

369

around them, and they vanished. My nerves prickled along my spine. I'd only shadowed twice before, and it wasn't the best feeling. The other two female gargoyles were swallowed up in a mist of their own. Ezzie nodded at me.

'Go with Badrick,' she said. 'I can't take a passenger, but I can follow your shadows.'

'Come,' he said, pulling me to him. 'We will take you to him.'

I held my breath as smoke engulfed us both.

38. *Josephine*

It felt like a giant vacuum sucked all the air from my lungs until they collapsed inside my ribcage. The world spun like a black whirlpool. My fingers and toes went numb. I screamed, but nothing sounded in the void. And then, like a flash of lightning, I had air and feeling again.

I felt Badrick's hands around my shoulders, steadying me against the wave of dizziness. Out of the corner of my eye, another plume of smoke appeared, and Ezzie materialized out of it. Her face was pale, and she looked nauseous. I blinked several times until my blurry vision cleared. Gussalen and Sunniva shook the remains of oily mist from their wings. Tamzen held tight to Hugo as the smoke dissipated into the air.

Hugo's eyes were huge. He looked dangerously ready to punch something. He struggled out of the gargoyle's grasp and stumbled forward, muttering a string of choice words and nearly toppling over.

'Don't ever, *ever* do that to me again,' he panted.

Esmeralda wiped sweat from her temple. 'We didn't have a choice.'

The whirling in my head eased. We were standing in the middle of a vast cemetery. The night air hung thick and humid around us, like a damp curtain. Tombstones and monuments stretched skyward. Thick clumps of Spanish moss hung like curtains from massive oaks lining either side of a wide, graveled road. Behind us, through a clump of narrow palm trees, I saw the spiraling towers of the Cathedral of Saints. The last time I'd seen it, I was barely fourteen, but the centuries-old church was as beautiful as I remembered it.

'Hide,' whispered Ezzie harshly.

We ducked behind a wide tombstone. Hugo joined us, crouching beside Ezzie. The gargoyles only had to step back into the shadows of a large tree, and their bodies disappeared from view. Had I been a stranger walking by, I wouldn't have even noticed them.

Ezzie grasped the sleeve of my blouse and pointed. I carefully peered around the thick headstone. Several yards ahead, inside a circular clearing, surrounded by trees, just visible in the pale moonlight, Augustine stood, with Sebastian at his side.

Pewter hair hung in damp clumps over Sebastian's forehead, and his horns caught the light ominously. His wings were expanded to their full length, taking up a large portion of the clearing. His bare chest was covered with an alarming amount of black veins that branched out from his neck and continued along his arms underneath the surface of his gray skin. His feet were also bare, revealing clawed feet that resembled his hands. Sebastian's solid silver eyes glowed reflectively, like a cat's, but they were lifeless and unfocused. He stared blindly ahead, his body motionless.

Augustine rolled up his sleeve and raised his arm. I saw clearly the massive number of tattoos covering his skin. Hugo made an odd sound in the back of his throat and he clutched the headstone so hard his knuckles bulged. Augustine ran his fingertips along his arm and fixed his gaze on Sebastian.

Sebastian's wings flexed, and the muscles along his shoulders tightened. His head dropped to his chest. Suddenly, Ezzie gave a choking snarl, and rocked back on her heels. I shifted around to look at her. Her eyes shimmered silver as they locked on Sebastian, and she swayed slightly, almost like she was in a trance.

'Ezzie,' I whispered. When she didn't respond, I shook her gently. 'Ezzie, what is it?'

'He's speaking to us,' she said in a weird, faraway voice.

Before I could ask what she meant I felt it, like an icy hand on the back of my neck – the awareness of things tucked within the shadows of the cemetery around me. Oily mist drifted through the grass and gathered low along the graves. There was movement underneath the trees and eyes, faintly glowing; the scraping of claws on stone, the flap of wings and the rustle of leather and feathers.

Shadowen.

They materialized like ghosts, perching on headstones and obelisks, crouched on columns and graves, and nestled and in the thick, low branches of the mossy oaks; at least forty or fifty shadow creatures of all kinds. I recoiled. Every type of animal representation warped or mutated in some way, combinations of terrible things – some with wings, others with multiple legs, long necks or swishing tails, but all armed with razor-sharp fangs and deadly talons.

I counted six chimeras among a multitude of grotesques,

and their human-looking shape was somehow more terrifying than the animal monsters around them. Their teeth gleamed in smiles that seemed permanently set into their features like carvings on stone.

Augustine thrust his arm higher into the air and Sebastian, as though receiving some kind of wordless order, began to speak. But they weren't words of any human language. It was a low, primal sound that rumbled throughout the clearing.

'What's he doing?' I asked.

Esmeralda closed her eyes. The muscle along the side of her neck twitched. She seemed to be fighting something. She dug her fingers into the grass. I waited helplessly, my attention divided between Ezzie and Sebastian. After nearly a minute of silence, she answered.

'Josephine, this is not good.' She looked at me. 'Sebastian speaks in the tongue of the grotesques. I cannot understand him. I can only feel his intentions.'

The creatures around us swayed eerily – as though listening to a tuneless song only they could interpret. Then, Sebastian's head snapped up. The strange noise died abruptly. My breathing hitched as he swept his gaze in our direction. The corner of his lip rose, revealing his rows of teeth. Beside me, Ezzie was like a statue. I copied her, holding my breath and steeling myself.

He knew we were here.

I almost reached out to him with my mind, but some other sense warned me against it. My eyes started to water as my lungs begged for air. Slowly, Sebastian lowered his head again. Whatever he was communicating seemed more important than our presence. He closed his eyes, but his lips didn't move this time. I drew in a cautious breath.

Augustine kept his focus on Sebastian, and a triumphant smirk stretched the white scar on his cheek.

Esmeralda's eyes widened in a stunned look of dismay. 'He has switched now, and he is speaking telepathically. I could not understand the grotesque speech, but I understand this.'

'So what's he saying?'

She turned stone-cold eyes to me. 'Bow before *La Gargouille*.'

Fear knocked into me, and my legs threatened to give away. It was everything I'd dreaded but convinced myself couldn't be true, despite the evidence looming in front of me. I searched desperately for something in Sebastian's face, anything that would give me a glimmer of hope that he was still there. But his face was a mask of absolute emptiness, and it scared me to the core.

A soft flutter from behind us made me jump. The four gargoyles emerged from their shadowy hiding place. They moved forward like one singular unit, their faces turned towards Sebastian. They approached the headstone where we were crouched.

I crept out. 'What are you—'

Hugo's hand clamped over my mouth. I grasped his wrist, starting to wrench him away, but then I saw the look on his face. I followed his stare towards the gargoyles. Their eyes had turned completely silver. The pupils were gone, and the irises spread to encompass the entire socket. My hand dropped, and Hugo released me.

They continued away from us, moving towards Sebastian in the same kind of stone-like trance. The chimeras hissed at their approach, fading back to the edges of the clearing. But the gargoyles didn't even glance at them. They paused in front of Sebastian, and then with slow, graceful movements, each gargoyle went down on one knee and dipped their heads.

Ezzie tried to stand beside me. Hugo pulled her back down, but not without a struggle. 'Oh no,' he muttered fiercely. 'You aren't going anywhere.'

She struggled against him, but not with her full power. I could tell she was fighting the same battle on the inside. She clenched her teeth until whatever it was seemed to pass.

'I've never experienced anything like this,' she whispered, slumping against Hugo's side like she'd just run a marathon. 'Though I'm not shadowen anymore, enough remains inside me to feel the pull of *La Gargouille*.' She shook her head. 'The grotesques, the chimeras ... even the gargoyles ... they have no choice. His control is absolute.'

'And Augustine controls him,' said Hugo, shaking his head. 'He knew about Sebastian the whole time.' His face became a storm cloud of fury. 'This is my fault. I gave that traitor the tattoo. I was an idiot to even think he'd—'

'Stop it,' I snapped. My fear burned through my nerves. 'Augustine would've found another way. He's been working at this for years. If we sit here blaming ourselves, we may as well just give up.' I looked at Ezzie. 'Can you understand anything else Sebastian's saying?'

Ezzie shook herself off and rose upright. 'He's ceased communicating. I think there might be ...'

She sniffed the air, and a scowl twisted her features. She eased her head around the tombstone. We followed her movement. At first, I couldn't see anything different. Sebastian remained where he was, head down. The chimeras and grotesques hissed and snarled in eerie succession, the unsettling noises filtering through the thick air.

Sebastian tucked his wings against his back and retreated, melting into the darkness at the edge of the clearing. The gargoyles rose to their feet and followed. The remaining shadowen silently disappeared into the trees until it seemed as though they'd never been there at all.

Augustine strolled to the center of the clearing and spread his arms wide. 'So glad you could make it,' he said.

Seven people wearing rich violet cloaks stepped into view from one of the graveled pathways. They lowered their hoods and followed a short, older woman into the center of the clearing. I cast a quick glance at Hugo and Ezzie. Their faces revealed what I'd already guessed.

The *Sobrasi*.

The woman halted in front of Augustine. 'What have you done with our guardians?'

Augustine's brows lifted. 'You've misplaced your gargoyles? How very inconvenient for you. I'm sure they'll be along shortly. After all, they've sworn to protect you.'

'This is your last opportunity, Augustine,' said the woman in a low, threatening tone. 'You've proven yourself incapable of harnessing this one shadowen successfully thus far. We are beginning to doubt whether you truly have what you claim.'

'Tell me, Vadoma,' he said, sauntering around the clearing as though he owned it. 'What do you think these Outcasts clans would do if they had the power to control all shadowen?'

'The Queen has made that perfectly clear,' she replied. 'Destroy them all.'

Augustine smiled. 'And what would you do, if you had this same power?'

The men and woman exchanged looks with each other,

but the woman continued to speak for them. 'We believe that order can be established again in our *natsia*. Shadowen represent power, and power can sway the head of even the most unbending neck.'

'Quite true,' Augustine replied, lacing his fingers behind his back. 'So if you had control of the shadow world, you would use it to gain power.'

'Yes.'

'You realize, of course, that such a gift would have a price.'

The woman's harsh features coiled even tighter. 'We've already agreed to bring you into our order and teach you our ways. We will restore your name among the Old Clans. That is more than sufficient payment, if indeed you can produce that which you've promised.'

Augustine smoothed the cuff of his rolled sleeve. 'The Marksmen pride themselves on their knowledge of shadowen weaknesses, while the *Sobrasi* claim to be the only true experts on the shadow world.' He traced the outlines of the tattoos with his fingertips. 'I, however, am master of both.'

Something shifted inside the shadows of the clearing. I couldn't see him, but I knew it was Sebastian. A terrible feeling wrenched my stomach. Hugo slid his knife out of the Marksman coat he still wore. On my other side, Ezzie rose to a crouch, her shoulders tense.

Augustine spat on the ground in front of the head woman. 'You aren't worthy to be called *Sobrasi*. You lost your way long ago, and now ...' His eyes glittered with a dangerous light. 'You are obsolete.'

Grotesques exploded from the trees and shadows.

They descended on the *Sobrasi* like a tidal wave. Terrible shrieks and screams pierced the air. And then, it was over.

The shadowen vanished. I struggled to comprehend what had just happened – until I saw bodies scattered over the clearing, purple cloaks stained with blood. I cowered behind the tombstone as I choked down the sickness in the back of my throat.

Augustine meandered through the dead *Sobrasi*, chuckling to himself. The sound sent an ugly sensation through me, like thousands of tiny spiders running over my skin.

'Such a shame,' he said, speaking to the dead woman sprawled on the ground. 'Had your guardians been here then you would have stood a chance. Oh, but wait.' He glanced back over his shoulder. 'They are here, aren't they?'

From out of the shadows, Badrick and the other gargoyles materialized into the clearing. They moved like gray zombies, with deadened silver eyes and blank faces.

'The learning I have mastered under your tutelage has been valuable, Vadoma,' he continued, smirking at the woman's corpse. 'Now that you are all gone, I suppose I must find a way to carry on, as the sole *Sobrasi*.' Augustine knelt and removed a cloak from one of the fallen. He fastened it around his neck. The front was sprinkled with blood. 'Pity,' he said, examining the stains. 'I'll have to have this cleaned.'

He rose and flung the cloak behind him. He raised his arm, turning it towards the soft moonlight filtering through the trees. The shadows behind him shifted again, and my heart sank as Sebastian stepped into the light. His expressionless face was so void that I barely recognized him. I felt nothing inside – the bond between us was like a faded memory. I clung fiercely, but it was slipping through my fingers faster than I could stop it.

Sebastian growled low. His eyes flicked sharply in our

direction. Augustine's smile dropped, as he seemed to be listening to something I couldn't hear. Telepathy, I realized. Sebastian was communicating with him. Augustine had accomplished what I couldn't. My neck burned hot.

Then, Augustine's expression shifted into a look of genuine surprise.

'We have guests, you say?'

Sebastian kept his eyes planted firmly on our hiding place. He jerked his head. The gargoyles vanished in mist. Before I could take another breath, cold hands were on me, yanking me from behind the tombstone. There wasn't a chance to put up a fight. Our weapons were knocked away. The four gargoyles dragged us out of hiding.

Augustine slipped a phone from the inside of his coat and pressed a button. 'Quentin, I've found what you were looking for. Honestly, you must do a better job of keeping up with your bride-to-be. This is a terrible habit you've developed.' He smiled at me in mock sympathy. 'She's in the cathedral cemetery. Do hurry, would you? I have a tight schedule to keep.'

Augustine hung up and sighed. Then he gestured for us to be brought forward. Tamzen clamped my arms behind my back and pushed me along, her expression as empty as Sebastian's. Badrick took Hugo by the neck, and the other gargoyles flanked Ezzie as we approached.

'Good evening, Josephine,' said Augustine politely. He glanced around the clearing at the dead *Sobrasi*. 'You'll have to pardon the mess. I wasn't expecting you here.'

I ignored him, turning my attention to Sebastian. He'd turned motionless again, like a piece of machinery that had suddenly been switched off. I swallowed hard past the lump in my throat. 'Sebastian ...'

'Oh, he doesn't know you,' said Augustine pleasantly. 'Not anymore.'

'You're lying.'

'I'm not. Your Sebastian doesn't exist anymore. My *prah* has finally incinerated the last of humanity within him. What stands in front of you now is a creature destined to lead. He's the missing link the *Sobrasi* have searched for in vain for centuries.'

My heart crumbled in my chest. Augustine knew the truth. Of course he knew. Sebastian didn't break out of the dungeon because he wanted to escape. The traitor standing in front of me had summoned him here.

As if reading my thoughts, Augustine nodded. 'And now, the fabled *La Gargouille* serves me.'

I stared into Sebastian's face, desperate for any glimmer of recognition in his eyes. But it wasn't there. Nothing was there.

Augustine glanced at Hugo. 'I suppose I must thank you for your part in it. Not that you had much of a choice, of course.' He shook his head sadly. 'Family is such a weakness.'

Ezzie hissed beside me. 'You have shed innocent Gypsy blood.'

Augustine switched his gaze to her. 'Ah, the famous Esmeralda of the Original Guardians. Still trying to earn back your wings, after all these years. Still failing miserably.' His smile returned. 'You chose the wrong side, you know.' She didn't answer. Augustine tapped his chin and studied the bodies around him. 'As to innocent blood, there is none to be found here. The *Sobrasi* needed to be purged, and now, it is done.'

A flicker of light on the tombstones caught my eye. Two

Marksmen had entered the cemetery through an iron gate at the back of the cathedral. They approached with lanterns in their hands. I recognized Quentin's walk before I saw his face.

Sebastian instantly came to life. He whirled to face the Marksmen, snarling threateningly. Quentin dropped his lantern and drew his sword. Augustine quickly held up his hand. Once more, as if hearing a silent command, Sebastian halted, though his teeth still flashed in the moonlight.

'You have to appreciate his enthusiasm,' said Augustine.

Quentin kept his eyes on Sebastian. 'No, I don't.'

Augustine clapped his hands together and addressed us all like he was the host of a party. 'Well, this has been entertaining, but it's time to go to church. The midnight service is already underway, and the Queen will be making an important announcement soon.'

'Come on, Josie,' said Quentin, taking great care to keep his distance from the dead bodies of the murdered *Sobrasi*. The idea that he was trying to hold to some semblance of Gypsy honor disgusted me. 'You're expected inside.'

Augustine frowned at Hugo and Ezzie. 'Not you, however. I believe you'd be too much of a distraction.' His lips pursed together in thought for a moment. 'Ah, don't worry. I have the perfect place for you to watch the entire proceedings. The best seat in the house.'

Sebastian stepped back and flexed his wings. He thrust out his chest and let out an inhuman snarl. Suddenly, Badrick and the other gargoyles took the air, with Hugo and Ezzie in their clutches.

'Let me go!' yelled Hugo from above.

The world around me sharpened into clarity. I craned my neck, watching helplessly as they were taken away from the cemetery, struggling and fighting against their captors. Their dark forms grew smaller as they headed for the looming spires of the cathedral and then disappeared somewhere along the rooftop.

'See you inside, my dear,' said Augustine.

Sebastian placed a clawed hand on his shoulder, and the two disappeared into the oily shadowing mist.

39. Josephine

We walked up the back steps of the Cathedral of Saints and stepped into a small vestibule. Quentin kept his grip on my arm. I felt the tension radiating out of him. Just beyond a set of looming doors was the sanctuary. Every Outcast Gypsy who'd come to Savannah for the Summer Gathering was in there, observing the midnight service.

The final notes of a song drifted through the cracks, echoing off the vestibule's marble floors. I heard the priest speaking and the quiet hush that blanketed the sanctuary inside. Donani turned to Quentin.

'My place is with the Queen,' he said. 'If you'll excuse me.'

Without waiting for an answer, the Marksman slipped inside the doors and closed it silently behind him.

I glared at Quentin, feeling my anger compacting into a fiery ball in the pit of my stomach. 'And where's your place?'

There was no anger in his eyes. 'With you, of course.'

'Let go of me, Quentin.'

He complied, his fingers slowly uncurling from my arm.

He stared straight ahead as the priest's old, raspy voice filtered through the doors. When the prayer began, Quentin leaned in towards me.

'It's time,' he whispered.

He opened the door and gestured for me to go in first. I found myself in the front corner of the room, just to the left of the altar space. Far above the sanctuary, arches and columns rose into the vaulted ceiling. Stained-glass windows and elaborate statues lined the walls. Two rows of wooden pews, covered in bright red cushions, stretched the length of the space from front to back. Every seat was crammed full of Roma.

Bandoleers from all the clans took up the front row closest to me. Members of the High Council took up the opposite row, wearing shades of green in their hats and scarves to show their rank. Two members at the end of the row wore dark green hoods.

Marksmen were positioned along the perimeter of the room, looking solemn in their black uniforms. All were armed with swords, and many of them had quivers of arrows strapped to their backs.

The priest finished his prayer and seated himself on the other side of the altar. Donani stepped into his place, and his deep voice ran out through the cavernous sanctuary.

'The Queen of the Outcast Gypsies speaks!'

My aunt rose smoothly from the front row and ascended the steps to the altar space. Though the sanctuary was already quiet, she waited patiently until she seemed to feel that everyone's attention was completely on her.

'It is with God you have arrived,' she announced.

The assembly answered in one voice 'It is with God we are received.'

'Our *kumpania* is a proud one,' she continued, her eyes roaming the crowd. 'We rose against the Old Clans two centuries ago, against their corruption and lust for power. We left the *Arniko Natsia* and were named Outcasts. It's not a title of shame for us. It is a reminder of the price of our decision. For over two hundred years, we have thrived here. We celebrate our traditions with our Annual Gatherings. We have our own rulers.'

'May you live on in good health,' shouted someone from the crowd.

It was simple, traditional response, but I saw the Queen's expression falter for a split second. She reached up, as if to touch her headscarf, but she seemed to catch herself and stopped. She smiled. 'May you all live on in good health,' she answered back in our customary reply.

Then she continued. 'Unfortunately, we brought with us the plague of our old *natsia* – the curse of the shadow world. Once, we had gargoyle protectors, guardians, but they failed us. We looked to the Marksmen for our safety in the interim. Still, the creatures lurk, and we must always look over our shoulders, waiting for the next attack.'

'May God have mercy,' shouted one *bandoleer*.

'Rid of us *prikaza*,' said someone from the crowd.

'*Prikaza*,' echoed another.

Several spit on the ground in response to our term for bad fortune. Quentin's hand lingered near his sword, and he slit his eyes in my direction.

The Queen raised her hands, silencing the congregation. 'I have come before you tonight, at the conclusion of this midnight service, to tell you that we can be free of our curse forever.'

Several people in the crowd muttered questions under

their breath. I saw expressions of wary bewilderment on the faces of the *bandoleers*.

'We can step forward into a future without shadowen,' the Queen continued, looking over the crowd. 'The creatures can be destroyed, once and for all. However, it will not be without a price. I come before you now, before the High Council and our people, in hopes that you will agree to the terms.'

A gray-haired man sitting among the High Council members stood from the pew and bowed slightly. 'What terms, *Rani*?'

My aunt nodded at Donani. He stepped forward and called to the back of the room.

'Enter and approach the Queen.'

Two Marksmen opened the center set of double doors. All attention in the sanctuary went to the man who entered. He was dressed in a deep purple cloak, with the hood drawn low over his head. Even this far away, I could see the blood sprinkles on the edge of the material. The ball of fury inside me solidified as Augustine made his way to the altar.

People leaned together, speaking in hushed whispers. Those in the front pews swiveled their necks, trying to see who approached. The atmosphere of the sanctuary shifted, like a giant thermostat had been switched on. Augustine reached the steps and turned to the crowd.

The Queen's expression went taut. 'No doubt many of you remember the transgressions of my former brother thirteen years ago and the sentence handed down by the High Council.'

A low rumble circulated through the assembly.

'An agreement has been made,' she said. 'Between myself

and the one known as Augustine. In return for his help in ridding us of the shadowen, his *marimé* status will be lifted and his Gypsy blood restored as Adolár Romany. He will then be allowed to leave our *kumpania* without penalty.'

The *bandoleers* and Council members suddenly erupted in furious accusations. I felt the warmth of bitter satisfaction rush through me. It may have been thirteen years since Augustine had been banished, but the hatred ran deep.

'Silence,' said the Queen in a loud voice. 'It a small price to pay for vanquishing an entire plague. I have given my word, but contingent on his own word that he will annihilate the vermin.'

Augustine lowered his hood.

'Traitor!' shouted someone near the front.

Several *bandoleers* stood with murderous glares. The Queen waited with a patience that I'd seen from her many times. The authority in her stance was like glue, holding the leaders in place. Once more, I found myself awed by the command she carried. I'd almost forgotten about Augustine until my aunt stepped aside and allowed him to take the floor beside her.

'Thank you, *Kralitsa*.' He smoothed the fabric of his cloak as he studied the faces in the crowd. 'I know how you all feel about me, and this is neither the time nor the place to rehash the things of the past. Rather, tonight is about the fate of the shadow world.' He gestured to the Marksmen lining the sanctuary. 'You kill them with your diamond weapons. You capture them for training tools. You use Vitamin D to subdue and even sedate them. But has this rid you of the menace? No, it only allows you to keep the status quo. But they grow in numbers, looking for opportunities to attack. You've trapped yourself in a cage of your own making.'

Augustine suddenly laughed. He spun to face the Queen. 'You know what amuses me most, dearest sister? You believe yourselves to be so righteous.' A sneer twisted his lips. 'You don't see the corruption within your own ranks. You've allowed yourself to be terrorized by the very creatures who could've been your victory. Instead, you chose to run, to leave the Old Clans. It is weakness, it is a stain on the entire *natsia*.'

'You were once an Outcast yourself,' said the Queen.

'True, and it took your redeeming sentence of *marimé* to push me forward to the truth.'

'What truth is that?'

'You were never fit to rule,' he replied.

The Queen's face reddened in fury. 'So it's the throne you want.'

'Of the Outcasts?' Augustine seemed offended. 'Certainly not. That's for my niece. Oh, don't look so shocked, Thalia. I've known for quite a while.' He glanced around the room before returning to the Queen. 'But since we are sharing such an intimate moment, I'd like to confess something to you.' He smiled pleasantly. 'I never intended to kill any shadowen for you.' Augustine leaned in and kissed her on the cheek. 'I'm going to kill everyone else.'

The Queen's mouth gaped open, and her body shuddered violently. Augustine pulled away, a knife in his hand. Blood dripped from the blade and splattered onto the marble floor. The Queen stumbled backwards. Donani caught her in his arms. I bolted for the altar, but Quentin was faster.

'What did you do?' he demanded, drawing his sword.

'I think it's obvious,' said Augustine. 'I just relieved this *kumpania* of its Queen.' He raised his arms and spread them wide before the assembly. 'And now, you will all share the same fate.'

The cathedral suddenly came to life with shadowen. At least a dozen grotesques descended from the ceiling and crawled out of shadows, eyes blazing with wild, animalistic rage. Screams and shouts came from the assembly. The Marksmen notched arrows and brandished weapons, pointing them in every direction. The shadowen took up positions along the walls, perched and ready, keeping the congregation of Gypsies frozen in their places.

I stared in horror as I saw, for the first time, the Corsi clan, in the very last row of the sanctuary. And seated next to James, was Katie. Her wide, terror-filled eyes rocked me to the core. Sickness filled my mouth. Why had I insisted they be released? They'd still be back at the inn, held hostage, but safe. And Hugo and Ezzie? What had the gargoyles done to them?

'Augustine!' Quentin shouted, shaking with anger. 'We had a deal!'

The traitor rotated his arm, exposing the tattoos to the light. 'Sorry, Quentin, but your crippling hatred of the shadow world disappoints me. Shadowen are too valuable to be destroyed. And now that I have this, I have nothing to fear.'

Sebastian materialized in a plume of black smoke, right between them. Quentin yelled in rage and struck out with his weapon. Sebastian batted it away like it was nothing. He snarled and backhanded Quentin. His body flew backwards, crashing into a brass candelabra.

Whatever side-effects of shadowing that Sebastian had

suffered just a few days ago seemed non-existent now. If anything, he looked more stable than I'd ever seen him. He looked back at Augustine, waiting.

Augustine pointed at the Queen. 'Finish her off.'

Sebastian's wings snapped back, and he moved towards her.

'No!' I yelled.

I rushed forward, throwing myself between Sebastian and my aunt. He paused, cocking his head curiously to one side. He sniffed the air as his solid orb eyes rotated around to focus on me. I stared straight back at him. For a moment, he seemed lost, uncertain of what to do. I held my breath and clutched the dandelion pendant at my neck.

Before I could voice a thought in my head, he suddenly threw his head back in a snarl. I saw Donani yank his knife out of Sebastian's back. Sebastian spun around with a terrible grace. His hand clenched around Donani's throat. The Marksman sputtered, clutching at the clawed fingers until Sebastian flung him aside like he was a piece of garbage.

I heard an awful, gurgling sound from behind me. The Queen had rolled onto her side. She'd gone pale, and wild eyes stared dimly back at me. A bloody red flower expanded across the midsection of her dress at an alarming rate.

I rushed to my aunt, dropping to my knees and cradling her head against my shoulder. Her headscarf had come loose, revealing some of her balding head. A trickle of blood ran from the corner of her mouth. She opened her eyes and clutched my arm.

'I'm ... sorry,' she choked out. 'I have left you ... only destruction ...'

'One's last moments always reveal the truth,' said Augustine, shaking his head sadly.

'Aunt Thalia,' I began, smoothing her scarf back into place for dignity's sake, if nothing else. 'You're going to be okay.'

'Yes,' she whispered, her eyes beginning to glaze. 'But not ... in this world.' The Queen gasped for air, and I heard the fluid in her lungs. 'Josephine ... it is your time now.'

I held her to me, rocking her gently. All the anger and frustration I'd felt for her disappeared. I kissed her forehead. 'I won't let this *kumpania* fail,' I whispered in her ear. 'I promise.'

A hint of a smile passed over her features. And then, she was gone.

I lowered her head gently to the marble flood. I stood slowly. I felt tears on my cheeks, and I brushed them away before lifting my eyes to meet Augustine's. He smiled mockingly back at me and dipped his head.

'All hail the new Queen.'

A tidal wave of fury slammed into me. I yanked my knife from my boot and launched at him. He caught my wrist, but not before the edge of the blade sliced a gash across his jaw. His hissed between clenched teeth and squeezed my fingers until my knife clattered uselessly on the floor.

'Let's not do anything hasty, *Kralitsa*.'

'Agreed,' said Quentin out of nowhere. He held his blade firmly pointed at Augustine's chest. Pain twisted his face, and I saw his broken arm hanging from the ripped sling around his shoulder. His sword, however, remained steady. 'Let her go, and call off your creatures. Right now.'

I ripped my hand out of Augustine's loosened grip. He reached into his jacket pocket and pulled out a handkerchief. He dabbed the blood off his face. 'Quentin,' he said lightly. 'I don't know why you're so upset. This is what you wanted, isn't it? Open season on all shadowen.' He gestured around the room at the shadow creatures lurking along the walls and ceilings. 'Be my guest. Though, I must admit, I don't really like your odds.'

'This wasn't our agreement,' spat Quentin, pointing at my aunt's body.

Augustine glanced down. 'Oh, of course. How thoughtless of me. You're referring to your future wife and the throne. I made a promise to you, and I've kept my end of things.' He shifted his gaze to me. 'I just never said how I would go about it.'

Augustine held up his arm and pressed his fingers against the tattoo. Sebastian's body jerked violently, like a marionette under its master's control. He launched into the air. The beat of his wings was a loud, ominous heartbeat. He bowed up his chest, threw his head back, and roared. The sound was a primal blast that rattled the chandeliers.

Shadowen crashed through the stained-glass windows and joined the others, descending on the assembly of people below. Panic engulfed the room. Gypsies dove under pews and ran for the doors. Marksmen launched forward to defend the their clan members as chimeras poured into the room. Diamond blades flashed and arrows flew. Donani had gotten to his feet and was struggling down the steps, shouting orders to his men.

Augustine laughed, with an almost blissful expression, as he watched his own people fighting for their lives. Sebastian dropped behind him in a flurry of wings, landing deftly on the pads of his clawed feet. I looked at his face, which had gone vacant once more, and a deep, penetrating cold seeped into my bones.

'Consider this an engagement gift,' said Augustine as he

stepped back to stand beside Sebastian. He winked at me. 'Do try to enjoy it. These remaining moments as Queen will be your last.'

He put his hand on Sebastian's shoulder.

And they were gone.

Time slowed around me. The shouts and screams died away. I stood in the middle of the altar space. The fighting became a blur. I could no longer see the Corsis or Katie. Maybe they were dead already. Would I be next? I wanted to be next. I couldn't take another breath.

My gaze drifted to the altar table. The pages of the large open Bible. The thick brass candlesticks on either side. I reached out and touched them. I heard Quentin calling my name. It brought me to the surface.

'Josie, let's go,' he said urgently. 'Let's get out of here.'

I didn't turn around. 'We're not getting out.'

'He could've killed us. He didn't. He's letting us go.'

I slowly closed the Bible and rested my hands on it, just inches from one of the candleholders. 'He's going to kill everyone, and he won't stop until it's done.'

'He's weeding out the corruption in our *kumpania*. So we'll let him. We'll be able to start over. It will make our reign that much easier.'

My fingers closed around the brass fixture. 'Our reign.'

'You're the Queen now,' said Quentin smoothly. 'And I'm—'

I grabbed the candleholder and swung it. The metal cracked against his head. Quentin staggered back and fell into a heap on the floor.

I tossed the candle aside and knelt, checking his breathing. The edge of the brass base left a gash in Quentin's forehead, but his chest moved up and down in a steady rhythm. I grabbed his sword and stepped over his unconscious body.

I reached the bottom step, but as soon as a placed my foot on the floor, a grotesque dove at me from the ceiling. I swung the sword with both hands, falling back into a pew as the force of the creature hit me. The shadowen skidded across the floor, its head disconnected from its body. The sword clattered away from me across the floor.

I gasped for breath, gaping at the stone corpse of the grotesque. Someone grabbed me by the arm. I jerked out of the hold and raised my hand to strike. But I stopped short. The green-hooded couple I'd seen earlier on the first row stood in front of me.

One held a small, diamond-coated axe. The other clutched a mace. Both were smeared with black blood. The taller one threw off his hood, and the other followed suit. I stared into the faces of Zindelo and Nadya Corsi.

'This way,' said Zindelo.

They didn't wait for me to follow. The Corsis hurried through the side door, leaving the battle behind us. But we didn't go outside. Instead, Zindelo led us down a narrow hall and through several small prayer rooms.

'Where are we going?' I panted.

Nadya was at my shoulder. 'You tell us.'

I stopped dead. 'What?'

Zindelo turned on his heel. 'We have to get to Augustine before it's too late. You must locate Sebastian.'

My heart wrenched tight in my chest. 'But they shadowed. I don't know where they went.'

'Yes, you do,' said Nadya, peering up at me. 'You need to stop everything else going on in your head and concentrate.' She grasped the pendant at my neck and held it out. 'Use your *sclav*.'

I didn't ask for explanations. Didn't try to reason. I took the glass between my fingers and held it tight. I pictured Sebastian in my head. Every detail I could muster. Every emotion. The pendant went white-hot in my hands. I dropped it in shock. And then, I knew.

'He's on the roof.'

40. *Josephine*

We took the winding staircase to the cathedral belfry. In the quiet of the tower, I could almost believe none of this was happening, that the fighting in the sanctuary wasn't real, that Sebastian was at home at the Circe, waiting on me with his shy smile and a witty comment. As we neared the imposing iron bells, reality set in.

'Can you help Sebastian?'

My words sounded dull and flat in the stairwell.

'We're not certain,' Nadya replied. She searched through her bag as we reached the top. 'You see what is happening. It is exactly as we feared. Sebastian can control the shadowen. If Augustine has truly gained mastery over him, then all may be lost.'

I paused before answering. 'Augustine told me he'd burned the last of the humanity out of Sebastian. But back there, in the sanctuary, when Sebastian looked at me, I thought maybe for a second, that he might snap out of it. He looked confused, like he didn't know what he was doing.'

Nadya glanced sideways at me. 'You think Sebastian is somehow managing to hold back *La Gargouille*?'

'I don't know. But I can feel him fighting.'

'Then there may still be time,' she replied.

Zindelo nodded. 'Augustine may have control of him now, but I fear he doesn't know what he truly possesses.'

'Do we have a plan?' I asked.

Nadya pulled out a thin syringe. She handed it to me. 'There is a large enough dose of Vitamin D in this to turn one gargoyle to stone. While not pleasant, it is certainly preferable to death.'

I took it from her quickly, so she wouldn't see my trembling fingers. Zindelo pushed open a thick wooden door, and we found ourselves on the roof of the Cathedral of Saints.

Illuminated by the light of the moon, the flat space seemed to go on forever. There were thick parapets and wide ledges on either side, lined with statues and tall spires that cut into the night sky. In the center of the roof was a large domed glass window that looked down into the sanctuary below.

I couldn't see Augustine or Sebastian anywhere. We moved forward cautiously, keeping to the right side, feeling our way along the ornately walled ledge that kept us from falling to the ground below. I started to doubt my senses, but as we reached one of the towering spires, I caught a glimpse of movement on the far end of the roof.

Zindelo nodded at me to continue. We moved around several more spires before ducking behind a section of parapet, using it as our vantage point. Badrick and the other gargoyles were perched along the back ledge of the cathedral, their wings tucked against their backs and their expressions still blank and lifeless.

Augustine stood one side of the glass dome. On the other, two figures knelt in front of it, knees pressed into the packed, pebbly gravel of the roof, looking down though the window into the depths of the sanctuary.

Ezzie and Hugo.

Sebastian crouched several feet away on a narrow section of parapet exactly like the one we were hiding behind. His body seemed almost frozen as he stared, unblinking, into the darkness beyond. I prayed that he and the other gargoyles, in their trance-like states, wouldn't sense we were near.

Augustine's voice carried easily to us in the night air. 'This is fitting, is it not? That *La Gargouille* should have for his first kill a member of the Corsi clan and its banished guardian.'

'He doesn't belong to you,' hissed Ezzie.

'Oh, but he does,' Augustine replied, touching his arm. 'And he commands the shadowen on my orders alone. Observe.'

He pressed his hand against his arm and I watched Sebastian jerk to life, like he'd been shocked with paddles. He lifted his head to the heavens. The veins bulged in his neck as he let out a ferocious snarl.

The glass dome shattered. Two chimeras burst through the window. The creatures shot into the air above us, eyes wide and glaring. Black ooze dripped from the deep cracks in their skin as they hovered in the air expectantly, ready for blood. But they didn't attack. They waited, I knew, for Sebastian's permission.

'You know,' said Augustine, his voice thick with triumph. 'I could've killed you both in the cemetery, but I'll find this much more satisfying. Before you die, you will watch my shadowen eradicate every Outcast in the sanctuary below.'

Hugo glared at him. 'You're gonna burn for this.'

'I'll take my chances,' Augustine replied.

Suddenly, his body hit the ground, crushed by the weight of Hugo's running tackle. Hugo punched him hard across the jaw. Sebastian made another noise. The gargoyles surged to life. Ezzie jolted to her feet, but Badrick was there to intercept her. Augustine pulled himself out of the way, clutching his face, as the gargoyles and chimeras attacked.

Zindelo sprang past me, launching his axe as he ran. The blade caught Tamzen in the shoulder. She fell back against a spire, clutching at the diamond weapon. I looked frantically back at Sebastian. His face was turned to the shattered dome, observing the sight below us with cold eyes. I ducked behind a row of statues and dropped to my knees.

'Don't kill the gargoyles,' Ezzie shouted.

'Trust me,' Hugo shouted back, ducking out of the way of Gussalen's claws. 'Not a problem!'

I turned to see Zindelo, pinned against a spire by Sunniva, her claws splayed to strike. Then, somehow, she turned to stone. Zindelo slipped underneath her frozen arms.

Suddenly, the chimeras grabbed Hugo and began dragging him across the roof. I fixed my eyes on Sebastian. I had to get through to him before Augustine used him to kill us all. I squeezed my eyes so tightly my head ached.

Sebastian!

His name sent painful spikes into my head, taking me off balance. I struggled to my feet and tried again.

Sebastian, listen to me.

The whoosh of giant wings filled my ears. I opened my eyes as he landed in front of me and dropped to a crouch. His lips pulled back, showing all his teeth. My heart beat like a stampede beneath my chest, but I ignored the threatening glint in his eyes and concentrated only on my mental voice.

This isn't you.

He tipped his head to the left, like an animal would when it heard a sound. He blinked slowly, and for just a second, I saw a flicker of something behind his solid silver orbs. I pressed forward with my thoughts.

Augustine is controlling you.

Sebastian's face wrenched up in agony. He ground the heels of his hands into his temples. He took one step back on his clawed feet and shook his head with fierce movements, like he was trying to throw something off. I closed my eyes and tried one last time, yelling inside my head as loud as I could.

Sebastian, you have to stop this!

I opened my eyes again to find him staring back at me, eyes wide and wild. But there was recognition – a flash of understanding. I felt it rip through me like fire. Sebastian's lip dropped, though his face contorted. My head buzzed with electrical shocks. I heard a voice. *His* voice. It was faint at first, barely coherent. And then, I caught the words.

I ... can't ...

The tortured pain in those words sliced into my brain. He was battling, fighting a losing fight that had transformed him inside and out, but he was still in there! Sebastian wasn't lost. Not yet. I raised my hands in front of me and held his gaze with every ounce of determination I possessed.

Yes, you can.

His entire body shook, every muscle underneath his gray skin tight and bulging. The internal war tossed him backwards, and his wings shot out to steady him. He roared, and the sound pierced the air around me. Sebastian threw back his shoulders and advanced on me. Out of the corner of my eye, I saw Hugo bent between the chimeras as they took to the air. I shouted out loud.

'Yes, you can!'

Sebastian stopped dead in his tracks as a violent shudder engulfed him. His eyes locked with mine. I held my breath, my arms still extended in front of me, and I braced myself.

Then, I felt a shift within him.

Sebastian spun away from me and took off like a sprinter, arms pumping as he gained speed. His wings snapped out. He collided with the chimeras, knocking Hugo free of their grasp. Hugo's body skittered across the pebbled rooftop. Sebastian and the chimeras spiraled in tight circles through the air, disappearing into the night.

I crawled out of my hiding space, yanking the syringe's protective top off with my teeth. Gussalen had positioned herself like a guard in front of Augustine. His eyes were closed, and he seemed to be concentrating on something. The gargoyle's eyes were on the sky, looking in the direction Sebastian had disappeared. I took my chance and jabbed the syringe into the back of the gargoyle's leg.

Gussalen hissed in surprise and whipped around. She started to lift me off the ground, and then, her arms began to shake and petrify. I scrambled out of her grasp and watched in horror as the stone coating streaked across the rest of her body, and she petrified into statue.

Tamzen suddenly ripped the axe from her shoulder with a wild snarl. She wielded it as Hugo struggled to his feet. The gargoyle rushed straight at him. I didn't have time to scream. The axe struck home.

Someone fell to the ground. But it wasn't Hugo. I blinked,

only half-believing what I saw. Somehow, Ezzie was there in his place. The axe was wedged in her chest. Her body sprawled lifeless.

A mace smashed into the side of the gargoyle's head. Tamzen went down on her knees. Nadya dropped the mace, whipped out a syringe and plunged it into Tamzen's neck. The gargoyle shuddered into a statue, just like the other.

'Enough,' shouted Augustine.

He dragged me to my feet with a grip that was stronger than iron. Badrick swooped in between Zindelo and Nadya. Hugo dropped to the ground and scooped Ezzie into his arms. His face had gone white.

Augustine studied the older Corsis. 'I see that I am not the only *Sobrasi* on this roof. I must admit, I didn't anticipate your arrival this soon.'

Nadya spat. 'Because you cannot see past your own arrogance.'

Zindelo touched his wife's shoulder and then approached slowly. 'You have no idea what you're dealing with, Adolár. The forces you are attempting to awaken in Sebastian are not controllable.'

Augustine only laughed. 'Your attempts to hide the monster from me have failed.'

'He's not a monster,' I said, struggling in his grasp.

Augustine pulled me towards him. The laugher died on his lips. 'You are holding him back.' His cool demeanor was gone now, and I saw the light of insanity flickering behind his eyes. 'Always you, my dear niece. I should have made sure you were dead before I left you.' He snatched my pendant and yanked it from my neck. He flung it against the stone parapet. The glass shattered on impact. 'I've changed my mind. You will be his first Gypsy kill.'

He raised his arm.

There was a loud rush of wings. Sebastian seemed to materialize out of the darkness. He landed in front of us with an inhuman grace, dropping to all fours. There was black blood on his chest and bits of chimera ooze on his arm. I shuddered to think what their battle must've looked like.

Sebastian's body trembled. The spidery veins along his skin spread. He gritted his sharp teeth as Augustine communicated to him, and his silver orbs focused on me. The internal war worked its way across his face. He took a slow step forward.

'Sebastian, don't!'

My voice seemed to catch him off guard. He hesitated, tilting his head to the side. He was still fighting – just like he'd been fighting with himself since the day he woke up in the Corsi clan. Fighting from the moment he'd transformed into a guardian. And now, fighting to hold back the very essence of the monster that had brought the shadow world to life.

'Please,' I said softly.

Augustine shoved me to the ground.

'That's enough,' he spat. 'Kill her!'

Sebastian shook himself off, under Augustine's control once more. He approached me with menacing steps, wings out and teeth bared. Cold fear clutched at me, but I refused to let it end this way. I clambered to my feet to meet him head on. I shouted his name in my head.

Sebastian!

He stumbled back as though he'd been slapped. I didn't waste the chance.

Listen to me.

404

Sebastian growled sharply, but this time I saw the dead look in his eyes fade away. My heart flew up my throat. He heard me! His mouth worked silently, his body shaking all over. And then,

'Josephine ...'

My name was barely a whisper on his lips, but with it came so much raw emotion that I struggled to stand underneath it.

He gasped for breath. 'Can't ... fight ...'

My heart pounded so hard I thought it would come through my chest. As I watched him struggle, a wild thought entered my mind. Sebastian couldn't fight Augustine like this. He didn't have the strength. But there was something inside him that might.

And at that moment, I knew what I had to do. I devoted all my being to the voice in my head and to whatever connection Sebastian and I still shared, wherever it was. And I spoke.

Don't fight anymore, Sebastian. Just let go.

At my telepathic words, his eyes widened, and the expression on his face deteriorated into a mixture of shock and pain. Sebastian turned away, shaking his head frantically. But I kept speaking.

I trust you.

He went completely still, eyes rotating back to fix on me.

I trust you, Sebastian. And it's okay. Just let go.

He hesitated. My gaze fell to his wrist. Underneath the bloody spike wounds, I could still see his dandelion tattoo. I shifted my eyes to meet his, and I smiled.

Trust us, Sebastian.

His eyes cleared. I saw acceptance in those silver orbs. And relief – relief that flooded through the fierce battle inside him. Suddenly, everything around him seemed to still, hushed and uncertain. Waiting. I steadied myself for one last thought.

Sebastian. Let go.

I felt him leave. Something in my heart ripped.

Oily mist appeared and surrounded Sebastian's body, clinging to him like a cloak. He spread his wings, and the mist tightened and swirled into the center of his chest, piercing through him. His body turned black, like char. Fissures of silver crackled over his entire form sprouting out through his horns, obscuring his face from view.

Augustine released me and held his tattooed arm in front of him like a shield. His dark face grew ashen as he stared up at Sebastian with wide eyes. But it wasn't Sebastian at all. The creature looming before us stared down with flaming eyes. He opened his mouth, and sparks of fire lashed between his teeth as he spoke.

'You have awakened *La Gargouille*.'

The voice wasn't Sebastian's anymore than the body.

'Yes,' said Augustine, in a tone unlike I'd ever heard him use.

It was the sound of fear.

The creature sniffed the air with distain. 'I know your blood. I have smelt the stench before. You are of the same stock as that vile Roma, the one who helped to destroy me.'

Augustine tried to smile, but it became a grimace. 'My ancestor, yes. But I have no intentions of repeating his mistake. Rather, I wish to free you from this prison in which you are caged.' He gestured to what remained of Sebastian's form. 'This weak gargoyle isn't enough to hold you.'

La Gargouille hissed irritably. 'No, he is not.'

'Then allow me to free you,' Augustine continued.

'Together, we can return to the Old Clans, and you can have your revenge on the Roma who have profited so long from your demise.'

La Gargouille laughed. The sound of it was fierce and terrible. 'What care I for revenge? I care only for blood. You have meddled in powers that you have no right to bend to your will. I am beyond you, Gypsy. You are dust under my feet.'

The creature grabbed Augustine's arm. Smoke rose from underneath his taloned hand. Augustine cried out in pain as a nasty burn spread over his skin, obliterating every tattoo. *La Gargouille* released him and he fell to his knees, clutching his charred arm.

'Your blood is mine.'

'No,' I said, moving in front of Augustine.

La Gargouille glanced at me, like someone might look at a mosquito before squashing it. 'I require it.'

'No,' I said again, trembling inside. 'Sebastian wouldn't want this.'

'Sebastian.' *La Gargouille* said it slowly. 'I know this name.'

I hesitated, unsure of how to proceed. Augustine gasped for breath on the ground behind me. At any moment, the creature might throw me aside and continue on.

'He's my guardian,' I said, as I'd said so many times before to everyone around me. 'His name is Sebastian Grey, and he's promised to protect me. And I promised the same thing to him.'

'Josephine,' said the creature.

I nodded cautiously. 'Yes.'

La Gargouille turned away. His form created an ominous silhouette against the clear night sky. When he looked back, his face was twisted into a look of strange, bewildered curiosity.

'He cares for you, this part of me that I do not understand. He is not me, yet, I am what he is.'

'Sebastian,' I repeated. 'Yes, he cares for me, and I care for him.'

His eyes blazed with fiery light. 'What do you wish to ask of me, daughter of the Roma?'

I took a breath. 'Please, give him back.'

The creature's expression shifted like a storm cloud. 'No. At last, I am whole again. I will harness this body and use it. I will have the blood of the Roma who ripped me asunder. I will have his blood, or I will not rest.'

'Then take mine,' I said quickly. 'I am Josephine Romany, daughter of Nicolas Romany and descendant of Keveco Romany.'

41. *Josephine*

'Josephine, no!'

I glanced back at Hugo as he held Ezzie in his arms. Her eyes rolled frantically towards me, her face was deathly pale. But I didn't falter. I stared up at *La Gargouille* with my chin high.

'You want payment,' I said, 'I'm offering it to you right now. But then, you must set Sebastian free.'

La Gargouille flapped his wings lazily. I refused to break my stare with him, no matter how sick I felt inside. He looked at Augustine's crumpled body and then looked back at me. Fire sparked from his lips as he smiled.

'Very well. I accept.'

The creature placed his hands on either side of my head. I felt the heat from his palms. I felt the skin on my neck begin to singe. *La Gargouille* opened his mouth, his fangs dripping with lava-like spittle. I closed my eyes.

Please, make it quick, I prayed.

A moment passed. Then another. I held my breath. Another moment. My skin cooled. I opened my eyes. *La*

Gargouille stepped back, and a vicious, animal fury twisted his face.

'No!' he roared. 'She is mine!'

The creature thrashed wildly. His charred body seemed to cave in on itself in torture. The monster and Sebastian were engaged in war within the smoke and flame, and I could only watch in horror, unable to help.

La Gargouille roared again. 'You ... will ... not!'

He clutched his head and screeched like something out of a nightmare. His body flailed back and forth, like prey caught in the mouth of a predator. I felt a stirring in my heart. And then, the creature's flaming eyes melted back into silver orbs. And refocused on me.

'Josephine, I can't let this go on.' The voice wasn't *La Gargouille*, but it wasn't Sebastian either. It was something in between. 'I have to stop it all. Please ... please understand.'

He launched into the air, straight overhead. Fire and smoke brimmed around him, lighting up the rooftop. He thrust out his chest and roared in a way I'd never heard before. The sky was suddenly filled with shadowen. They streaked through the air, flocking to him from inside the cathedral and all around the cemetery, more than I could name or count.

I stared up in horrified awe. So many hideous forms. So much hatred and malice. They swirled around him like a tornado. I covered my ears against their screeching cries. *La Gargouille* spread his arms wide. A bolt of white energy burst from his body like a streak of lightning. It ricocheted through the mass of grotesques and chimeras around him.

The vile creatures convulsed with ghastly screams as the bolt of light ripped through them. Instantly, they turned to stone. Shadowen bodies fell like meteors to the ground below. The statues shattered on impact, sending clouds of dust hurtling over the cathedral. The wind carried the particles away, and everything went suddenly still. Only *La Gargouille* remained.

I didn't see Augustine in my peripheral until it was too late. My feet went out from under me. My head cracked against the stone. There was a snarling in my ears. A plume of smoke. *La Gargouille* and Augustine plummeted over the ledge of the cathedral. I heard a cry and a sickening thud. By the time I pulled myself up, I was staring into the creature's fiery eyes.

'The blood is accounted for,' he said.

I chose not to look over the edge. I knew Augustine was dead.

The sound of Ezzie crying out sent me whirling around. Zindelo and Nadya had joined Hugo on either side. Hugo held Esmeralda in his arms, and tears glistened against his rough face. 'You listen to me,' he said to her, his gruff voice cracking. 'You don't jump in and save my life and then just check out of here. It's not happening.' He shook her gently. 'You're not leaving me.'

Ezzie's eyes lolled towards him. They were clouded and dull. 'I could not save Markus Corsi,' she said hoarsely, 'but I have saved you. That is enough.'

Markus!

The name hit me like slap. I yanked my skirts aside and retrieved the tiny book from the inside of my boot. The green leather was battered and damp with sweat. I rushed forward, falling to my knees in front of her.

'Ezzie, there has to be something in here that could help.'

Zindelo's brows lifted. 'What is this?'

'It belonged to Markus, her charge.'

411

'Of the first *Sobrasi*,' Nadya said reverently.

I opened the book and thumbed frantically through the pages. I didn't even know what I was looking for. The strange letters and script gave me nothing. 'I see the words, but it doesn't make sense. I can't read it.'

Ezzie's eyelids suddenly fluttered open. Her eyes were full of pain, but crystal clear as she focused on me. 'Yes, you can. You are a Romany. A direct descendant of Keveco himself. If anyone has the ability, it would be you.'

I looked into the book and willed everything I had into the words. They blurred and swirled on the page, and then, suddenly, they became words I could understand. Without understanding why, I turned to the very center of the book and read.

'Ezzie,' I breathed. 'Somehow, he must've known what was going to happen to you.'

'How do you know?' asked Hugo.

'Because it tells how to restore a banished gargoyle.'

Ezzie reached out and grasped the edge of Zindelo's coat. 'Please, I beg of you, do this for me. If I'm to die, then let me die as I was born.'

Zindelo nodded. 'You have done more than is required of any guardian. As the last of the *Sobrasi*, we restore your honor to you.' He held out his hand to me, and I gave him the book.

Zindelo began reading the words out loud. The language was familiar and foreign, all at once. We watched him, with Ezzie's gasping breaths the only sound, apart from his voice. When he finished, Zindelo placed his thumb into the center of the book and pressed it lightly to the page.

'Where is the brand?' he asked.

Hugo smoothed Ezzie's hair away from her neck, revealing

412

the faded tattoo. As we watched, it began to darken into a detailed shape. I saw what it was clearly now – a single dandelion petal. Zindelo touched it with the pad of his thumb.

When he removed his hand, the tattoo had disappeared, like an ink imprint lifted off a sheet of paper. Zindelo repeated the same action onto the book, and the tattoo appeared in the middle of the page. He closed the leather cover.

Gray mist spread over her skin. It shifted through her red-tipped dark hair, turning it pewter. Her skin became gray, and her features changed. Hugo shoved himself out of the way as wings sprouted from underneath her body and expanded, ripping out the back of her Marksman jacket. She was a gargoyle again. A soft, painful smile crossed her dark lips.

'Thank you,' she whispered.

Zindelo bowed his head. 'Go in peace.'

Hugo grabbed hold of her again, desperation in his face. He stared down at her gargoyle form. 'Ezzie …'

She looked up at him with a silver gaze. 'I am sorry, Hugo.'

Her eyelids closed.

'No,' said a voice from behind us.

La Gargouille stood, watching the scene before him. The voice had been Sebastian's this time, but it wasn't quite his own. It was tinged with something ancient and powerful. He approached on clawed feet, his black wings expanding in the breeze. His face was silver and fire, his eyes flamed as they looked at Ezzie's dying body.

'It is time to truly live,' he said.

La Gargouille held out his right hand, palm facing the

sky. He closed his wicked talons into a fist. A silvery glow filtered through his fingers. The veins along the inside of his arm pulsed, and his hand shook as the strain of whatever he was doing became evident in his clenched jaw and gritted teeth. Then, he opened his hand. A small mound of purple-black dust rested in his palm. It glimmered with sparks of silver.

'Josephine,' said the creature in the voice that was and wasn't Sebastian's. I took a tentative step towards him. He regarded me with that same expression of strange curiosity. His head tilted slightly, and his eyes sparked. 'He wants you to have this.' As the words left his fiery mouth, he seemed confused, as though he hadn't meant to say them at all. *La Gargouille* deposited the dust into my hands and backed away.

I cradled the purple powder to my chest and hurried quickly back to Ezzie. Nadya studied the contents of the gift.

'We need human blood,' she said.

She pulled a knife from her belt. Hugo placed his hand over his mother's. She looked up at him as he gently took the knife from her hands.

'I've got this,' he said.

He ran the thin blade across the inside of his palm. Blood welled up. Nadya brought out the small bowl she'd used for mixing herbs from her bag. She held it out to both of us. I brushed the *prah* into the bowl. Hugo held his hand over the bowl, and his blood dripped into the purple dust. Nadya mixed them together with her fingers.

Zindelo wrapped his fingers around the handle of the axe buried in Ezzie's chest. He pulled hard. One sharp movement. The blade came free. Ezzie's body convulsed.

With the axe gone, blood poured freely, soaking her shirt. I clutched my stomach, but I refused to look away. Nadya scooped out the mixture and packed it into the gaping wound. She pressed on it with both hands, holding it in place. Blood bubbled up through her fingers.

'Come on,' Hugo begged through clenched teeth. 'Work.'

Nothing seemed to happen at first. Nadya slowly removed her hands and sat back. Hugo's face wrenched, and he turned away. Then, the blood ceased flowing. The *prah* sank into her wound like it was quicksand. The wound closed over and the red stain across her shirt shimmered into dust and crumbled away. I blinked, hardly believing what I was seeing. Ezzie chest heaved in a giant breath. And her eyes opened.

'Hey,' said Hugo, smiling down at her. 'Thought I'd lost you for a minute.'

She stared up at him. 'I believe I have demonstrated on many occasions that I am difficult to get rid of. Now, help me up.'

Hugo stood and offered his hand. She took it and rose unsteadily, planting her feet for balance. She looked at her hands, turning them over and over again. Then she tested her wings. A slow smile spread over her features, which were somehow softer and more pliable than they had been in her human skin. She turned around and faced Hugo.

'Well,' he said, looking her over. 'This is different.'

Zindelo studied them for a moment. 'According to Markus Corsi's book, Esmeralda will need a new brand in order to remain in this form.'

Hugo shrugged his shoulders at Ezzie. 'Don't worry. I know a guy.'

Her eyebrows lifted. 'Is he any good?'

'Yeah,' said Hugo with a grin. 'He's okay.'

I stepped away from them and turned to thank *La Gargouille* for his help.

He was gone.

A terrible, frantic feeling stuck me square in the chest. I searched the sky, listening for the flap of wings. I ran to the other end of the rooftop and ducked around the collection of spires. And then, I saw him.

He was perched on the corner of the parapet with his clawed hands and feet anchoring him into place. His massive wings were curled in and folded. His eyes were turned towards heaven in a tortured, frozen stare.

A terrible sound rang in my ears. Vaguely, I knew it was my own voice, but it felt like it was coming from someone else. I put one foot in front of the other, pushing away the dread that crashed all around me. When I reached him, all my nightmares came true.

He'd turned to stone.

My heart withered inside me. I slowly reached out and placed my hand on his wing. It was no longer soft and leathery, but solid granite. Sebastian was a statue. I doubled over as the air left my lungs. I'd lost him. After all this, I'd still lost him.

'Somehow, he won,' said Zindelo.

I spun around in the pebbled gravel. Zindelo and Nadya approached, followed by Hugo and Ezzie. Their eyes were on Sebastian. Hugo's dark face drained of color.

'How is this winning?' I shot back.

Zindelo peered over the ledge to the ground below. 'Because of him, the battle is over. He turned them all to stone. Every last shadowen here. Including *La Gargouille* himself.'

'The monster is no longer a threat,' said Nadya softly.

My knees went weak. Sebastian had done what he'd said he'd do. He'd stopped it all. But at the price of his own existence. Everything in me felt like it was going to explode. I didn't know what to do with my emotions. I grasped for my pendant, before I remembered Augustine had shattered it against the wall.

'No,' I said, turning my back on them. 'This can't be over. Not like this. I don't believe he was only *La Gargouille*.' I looked up at his statue form. 'Whatever his origins were, whatever that creature did to him when you brought him to life, he is *still* Sebastian. I don't need books or *sclavs* or anyone else to tell me that.' I stepped in front of him. 'He just needs to believe it himself.'

I placed my hands on either side of his marbled face. 'Do you hear me, Sebastian? It's time for you to be the person you want to be.' I touched my forehead to his, feeling the cold against my skin. Without my pendant, I didn't know if communication was even possible anymore. But I had to try.

You are Sebastian Grey. And that is all that has ever mattered to me.

My lips touched his cold cheek.

I love you.

The only response was silence.

Tears slid down my face and tickled my neck. I reached up to wipe my eyes, and then, I realized ... they weren't my tears. I jerked back and stared into his granite face. The corners of his stone eyes were wet.

'Sebastian?'

I heard a cracking sound. I stumbled back as his stone body began to crumble. Then, a rush of wind and debris circled him like a hurricane. The stone blew apart, and Sebastian melted into life.

His legs and arms became fluid. His eyes fluttered closed and he slumped forward. Ezzie was there with gargoyle speed, helping me to catch him as he fell into my embrace. For a horrible second, I thought he was dead. But I felt the lift and fall of his chest under my hands. We lowered him to the ground.

The bulging veins had disappeared, and the silver cracks and fiery face were gone. He looked like Sebastian again – the gargoyle Sebastian as I remembered him. With slightly larger horns and wings, maybe, but it was him.

Hugo let out a heavy sigh. 'I thought for a second he might—'

'Be a boy again?' finished Nadya, glancing at her son. 'As he seemed when we first brought him to you.' She placed her hand on his shoulder. 'You must remember, Hugo, he was never a boy. Only the statue of one.'

I looked at Sebastian's gargoyle features, as he lay lifeless in my arms. 'But it's gone now,' I said carefully. '*La Gargouille*.'

'Gone?' Zindelo shook his head. 'No, I'm afraid he is not. If the monster were completely gone, then Sebastian would cease to exist as well. They are one and the same. But Sebastian is the master now, as you can see for yourself.'

We all looked at him, watching as his breathing grew steadier and a flush of dark-gray color came into his cheeks. I hugged him protectively to me.

'I knew you could do it,' I whispered into his ear.

Suddenly, Sebastian took a gulp of air and bolted upright. He struggled free of my grasp as his silver eyes flew open. He looked around wildly, trying to lock onto something I couldn't see.

'I am ... I was ...'

He struggled for words and faltered.

'Yes, you were,' said Zindelo. Sebastian fixated on him. There was recognition in his expression, but also confusion. 'And someday,' continued Zindelo, 'you may be again. But for this time and space, you are Sebastian Grey. Be content in that.'

'I know you,' said Sebastian. His voice was scratchy and raw, as though a part of him clung to the remnants of *La Gargouille*. But the glaze over his eyes cleared away. 'Zindelo Corsi.'

'Hello, Sebastian,' he replied. 'It has been a while.'

Zindelo stood to his feet and moved to join his wife. Sebastian blinked slowly, looking around the rooftop, and I could see him trying desperately to process where he was and who we were. His gaze fell on me.

'Josephine.'

Hearing my name on his lips burned into my heart. Because it was his voice again, his real voice. Soft and mellow, and full of emotion. The warmth in my chest spread like wildfire.

Then, I saw everything flood back to him in a startling rush of memories. His face wrenched into a painful expression. His silver eyes widened. He scooted back, fumbling over his wings, and stared at me in horror.

'I'm a monster.'

His voice was somewhere between a sob and a snarl.

'No, you're not,' I said, rushing to take his face in my hands as I'd done just moments before. 'I know you've been told that so many times that you believe it. But now, I'm asking you to believe me.'

'But who I am ... what I did ...' His wings snapped to their full extent and his upper lip curled away from his

419

teeth. His silver eyes were pained, but resolute. 'How can you even look at me?'

Slowly, I removed my hands from his face, but only to take his hands in my own. I wrapped my fingers firmly around his, tracing his claws with my thumb. Then I pulled his hand to my check and pressed his palm against my skin. I held his gaze firmly. 'I'm looking at you, Sebastian.'

His bottom lip quivered. Then his lip settled once more over his teeth. He stared back at me. His eyes, which were still so strange, so inhuman, were also the most human thing I'd ever seen in my life. I read straight into them, down to the depths of his heart. And at that moment, there wasn't anything supernatural about Sebastian Grey.

I traced the crease in his brow with my finger. His eyelids fluttered closed and, after a moment, his forehead smoothed. 'Now,' I said. 'Look at me.'

His eyes opened, like a burst of moonlight from behind a cloud.

'What do you see?' I asked.

His gaze roamed my face and then met my look. 'I see us,' he said simply. And then, he smiled – *really* smiled – full and bright, sharp-toothed and all. And it was amazing. Because it was Sebastian. And he was mine.

42. Sebastian

I took Josephine in my arms, like I'd dreamed about so many times. And she wasn't disgusted. She wasn't afraid. She hugged me tight, and her eyes shone with emotion like I'd never seen them before, like liquid emeralds, staring right at me, through me.

'I love you, Josephine.'

Her smile destroyed the shadows, once and for all.

'I love you back.'

43. Josephine

I didn't want to let him go. I pressed my cheek against his chest, feeling the steady beating of his heart. It felt like we'd been apart for years. So much had changed in such a short amount of time. Now that I had him back, now that I'd finally gotten honest about my feelings, I didn't want this moment to end.

Neither do I.

I startled. Sebastian had spoken in my head. I swallowed hard and answered back.

How did you hear me?

I felt him smile.

You're speaking kind of loud.

I didn't know I was speaking at all. How are we doing this?

Sebastian paused before answering.

I have no idea.

I carefully pulled up a mental wall, at least, as much as I could tell. Not that I wanted to block him out. But I didn't want to say more and risk giving away my thoughts. Ezzie said she'd never heard of a guardian and charge who could speak to each other telepathically. But Sebastian was the essence of *La Gargouille*. I supposed that took everything off the table.

At last, he pulled back, releasing me from the embrace. I reached for his hand. He gave it freely to me. No more cringing away. I let my gaze roam his face, taking in every detail. Sebastian's ordeal had left its mark on him, in more ways than the larger spiraled horns that curled back into his pewter hair. There was a haunted look in his eyes that even our happiness didn't totally eradicate.

'Hey.' I squeezed his hand. 'It's okay. It's over.'

He nodded, and the look retreated to some place deep inside him. His silver eyes sparkled back to life. He took a deep breath and looked around, as if seeing everything for the very first time. His mouth slacked open in surprise as he spotted Ezzie.

'You're a gargoyle.' His eyes flicked to Hugo, who was standing close to Ezzie. His brow furrowed curiously at his brother. Hugo only shrugged. Sebastian glanced back at me. 'I've missed a lot, haven't I?'

'Yeah.' My smile dropped. 'Actually, we should get back.'

He tilted his head. 'Where?'

Nadya moved forward. 'To our people.'

Sebastian blinked several times at Hugo's mother. 'I know you, too.'

'Yes, you do,' said Nadya. 'But now is not the time for re-introductions.' She moved to the shattered glass dome and peered into the sanctuary below. 'The rest of you should get down there. Zindelo and I will meet you, as soon as we've reawakened these gargoyles.'

Sebastian's eyes roamed over the rooftop, taking in the

four statues, frozen in their last battle stances. More recognition flickered in his expression. 'I've met them before. These are the *Sobrasi*'s gargoyles.'

'Not anymore,' said Hugo.

I tugged on Sebastian's clawed fingers, bringing his attention back to me. 'What do you remember?'

Sebastian winced. 'Just bits and pieces, really. I remember Augustine's tattoo and then feeling like I was leaving my body. After that, I have glimmers, like fragments of moments.' He kept his eyes on me. 'Of you, mostly. The rest of it's just a blank. Until here, on the rooftop.' His wings quivered. 'When I ... he ... the creature, I mean ... we killed Augustine.'

'And saved Esmeralda,' added Hugo.

Zindelo joined his wife at the window. 'Go and speak to our people, Josephine. They need the reassurance of their Queen.'

Sebastian's shocked look returned as he stared at me. It was an almost child-like confusion and, combined with his impressive gargoyle appearance, made my heart melt with sympathy.

'I'll try and fill in the blanks on the way down,' I said, touching his cheek with the back of my hand. 'After everything that's just happened, I think we'd better take the stairs.'

44. Sebastian

I had to curl my wings around my body to make it down the spiraling staircase that led from the bell tower to the ground floor. Josephine talked at a ninety-mile-an-hour pace, covering everything that had happened since she'd followed me to Savannah, and finishing up with the stuff I'd missed after my brain had taken a back seat to the creature.

The story of how I was created made my brain whirl. The only comfort I found in it was in knowing that the dark thing I'd been battling inside me for months wasn't my own invention. It had a name.

But I couldn't bring myself to say it, not even in my head. I was scared that if I did, he'd find a way to come back. I ground my teeth together. No, he wasn't gone. He *was* me. We were, somehow, the same. I couldn't wrap my mind around it. But I had to accept it. Josephine had told me it was time to be who I wanted to be. That's exactly what I was going to do from this point forward.

The creature didn't control me. I controlled him.

We reached the bottom of the stairs and turned a few

corners. Josephine suddenly paused and turned around to face me. Her hand was still in mine. Neither one of us seemed to be able to let go since the rooftop. I looked down at her, shaking myself free of my thoughts.

'Do you have any questions?' she asked, apology in her tone.

'At least four hundred and fifty, easily.'

She smiled, and my stomach did flips. I'd do anything for that smile.

'So, we're good,' she said.

'Yeah. I think I've got enough to go on right now. Anymore and I might go all crazy again. I heard that's not such a good look for me.'

'Not trying to be picky,' she replied. 'But I prefer you this way.'

The stairs creaked behind us. Hugo and Ezzie had fallen far behind us, having their own conversation, I was sure. Ours wasn't the only relationship that had gone through some changes, in more ways than one.

I looked over Josephine's shoulder at the door leading into the sanctuary. My humor vacated. 'Are you sure you don't want me to go in with you?' I knew her answer before she voiced it.

'Not yet.'

'I know. I'm the creature who made the shadowen all-call.'

'You were under Augustine's control,' she said firmly. 'We all know it. And soon, they will as well.'

'Are you going to be okay?'

Her shoulders slumped. 'I'm Queen because Augustine murdered my aunt. Her body is still in there, along with who knows how many more. I don't know what I'm going to do.'

I reached up and tentatively took one of her braided ribbons between my claws. The fabric was soft, but nothing compared with Josephine's hair. 'You'll know. Just trust yourself.' We leaned towards each other, but we both stopped short. As much as I ached to kiss her, it wasn't the time. I forced a smile instead. 'I'll be right here.'

Hugo and Ezzie appeared from the hall. I did a double take at Ezzie. For the first time, I saw myself through someone else's eyes – the shock of seeing a person a certain way, and then the change to gargoyle after. I suddenly thought about Katie and my stomach clenched. The Corsis would've protected her. She was okay. She had to be okay.

'You ready?' asked Hugo, looking at Josephine.

'It doesn't really matter either way,' she replied.

She smiled at me once last time, then opened the door and slipped through.

Hugo set his large hand on my shoulder. 'It's good to have you back.'

Several retorts scrolled through my brain, but I didn't use any of them. My heart felt like an anchor, weighed down by everything on the other side of that door, everything I couldn't see, but feared. Augustine may have been gone, but the destruction he left behind would leave us scarred forever.

'Thanks,' I said.

He squeezed my shoulder and let go. Hugo's face arranged itself into the emotionless mask I knew so well. 'Okay, I'm going in to find our clan and make sure everybody's okay and find out what I can do.'

'I'll stay here with Sebastian,' said Ezzie.

As soon as my brother was gone, I began to pace the length of the narrow hall – not an easy task with two gargoyles sporting large wings in close quarters. My instincts had cooled after waking up on the roof, but now, with Josephine absent, I felt the protective stirrings, pricking at me and urging me to go to where she was. I moved closer to the door without realizing it.

Ezzie blocked my path. 'I know how you're feeling. But we must wait.'

Looking into her silver eyes was an odd sensation. I clenched my hands at my sides and nodded. I needed a distraction to take my mind off things and to give me a chance to rein in my instincts.

'What will those gargoyles do, now that the *Sobrasi* are dead?' I asked.

'They are bound to serve the order, and they hold to that with the same conviction as any guardian. Since Zindelo and Nadya are the only living *Sobrasi*, I am certain they will go with them.'

'They won't stay here?'

'It's unlikely. There is still much unrest in the Old Clans. I feel their services would be better suited there.'

'Which just leaves us.'

Ezzie's lips pursed together for a moment. 'Correct.'

'I'm happy for you, Ezzie,' I said, after several beats of silence between us. 'I know returning to your shadowen life is what you've hoped for. And, honestly, though it's pretty selfish of me, I have to admit, I'm glad I'm not alone.'

Ezzie dipped her head low. 'Sebastian, you have my loyalty. I was not always able to help you, as I would've liked before, but now, I offer you all the assistance I can give. You only have to ask.'

I grinned back at her. 'Why don't you just keep doing what you've been doing all along? Look after my brother and his clan. They're definitely going to need someone like you to keep them in line. I mean they're pretty much like the Lost Boys.' I shrugged. 'Only older. And with more ink.'

'Lost Boys?'

'I mean the Neverland ones. Not the Eighties movie ones.'

Ezzie shook her head and moved away from the door.

We continued to wait. I closed my eyes and concentrated on the bond I felt with Josephine. Lying in the dungeons of the Court of Shadows, it had felt like clinging to a flimsy piece of twine. Now, it was strong. It flowed through me like a steady current.

Josephine's emotions tumbled across my soul as well. She was scared, but not distraught. I felt a confidence in her that was new and solid. Every so often, a word or phrase would pop into my head – something she was saying that had filtered somehow into our unusual telepathy.

Without warning, the door swung open. We both sprang back, hissing reflexively and baring our teeth. Hugo pulled up short. He threw his hands up defensively. I immediately straightened, and Ezzie did the same.

'Oh, great,' he huffed. 'Now I'm going to have to deal with that from two of you. I don't know if I'm ever going to get used to it.' He closed the door behind him. 'It was a mess in there. Looks like a tornado went through. Lots of stone bodies from the ones they killed before *La Gargouille* took care of the rest.' Hugo glanced cautiously at me. 'The Marksmen are taking care of that now.'

'And the Gypsies?' I asked, trying to keep my voice steady.

Hugo made a sign with his hand. 'Three dead. Two Marksmen and the *bandoleer* from the Joles clan. Lots of injures, but my mother can treat the shadowen wounds.'

'Your clan?' said Ezzie slowly.

Hugo let out a huge breath. 'All fine. Banged up a bit,

but they'll live. Katie's okay, too. Kris took out of couple of groties himself before he let anything get to her.' He smiled. 'I think he's got a bit of a crush.'

'Katie's here?' I said, almost to myself.

'She's fine, Sebastian.' He crossed his arms. 'Can't say the same for Quentin Marks, though.'

My head jerked up at the mention of his name, and a snarl rippled across my lips. 'What do you mean?'

My voice had gone gravelly. Hugo noticed, but he only shrugged.

'You'll have to see for yourself.'

Hugo took us around the outside of the cathedral to enter the sanctuary from the back. As I stepped into the marble vestibule, I became acutely aware of how I looked. Bare feet, no shirt, scabbed-over arrow wounds and dried, purple-black blood. Ezzie didn't fare a lot better. She'd tied her ripped shirt underneath her wings, but the fabric was dirty and stained.

To my relief, Zindelo and Nadya were waiting for us and quickly offered up their dark-green cloaks. A few rips and ties up the backs, and Nadya managed to alter the cloaks enough to allow our wings to hang freely behind us. As I turned to thank her, the four gargoyles shadowed into the vestibule.

The male, who I now knew was called Badrick, bowed low in front of me, and the others copied him. The action made me uncomfortable. I wasn't in charge of anyone, shadowen or otherwise.

'You have our loyalty,' said Badrick.

I cast a sideways look at Esmeralda. Her expression was stoically blank, but her chin lifted slightly. I got the feeling she was proud.

'Thank you,' I replied. 'But you don't owe me anything.'

Badrick expanded his wings once, then pressed them to his back.

'You are *La Gargouille*,' he said.

'I'm just Sebastian.'

'Whatever name you call yourself is your choice. But you are the first of our kind, the most ancient of us all. Therefore, we pay you homage.'

I couldn't hide the shudder that went through my wings. Badrick's words sank deep into my chest, even as I tried to dismiss them. I nodded back at him, but the gesture was the only thing I could think to do. The gargoyles dropped back and took up positions behind me.

Hugo and Zindelo opened the doors.

Ezzie fell into step next to Badrick as we walked into the sanctuary. My chest tightened immediately. My brother was right. It looked like a storm had hit the room. Pews were overturned. Statues of saints were toppled and cracked. Several stained-glass windows were shattered. A chandelier lay in pieces in the middle of the aisle.

Outcasts Gypsies were everywhere. Some were tending to injuries. Others were picking up broken glass and chunks of statues, trying to clean up the mess. Several groups mingled tightly together, talking in hushed voices. The dead had been carried out of the room, back to the Court of Shadows, I assumed. Marksmen went in and out of the side doors. I saw them through the broken windows, tending to the stone shadowen corpses outside on the lawn.

Josephine stood in front of the altar. Despite everything around me, my stomach fluttered at the sight of her. Even with dirt smearing her face and gravel stains across her skirt, she looked like a painting come to life.

She saw us enter and motioned us to join her.

Everyone followed her movement and riveted on us. My mouth went dry. Once, I thought nothing could be worse than the day I was introduced to the entire Circe de Romany by Nicolas. This was that moment, times one hundred. I kept walking, planting one foot firmly in front of the other. I had almost made it to the front without incident. Until I saw Katie Lewis.

Our eyes met. She left Kris' side and maneuvered around a broken pew until she reached the aisle. I set my shoulders. 'Hey, Katie.'

She hesitated, her eyes running a thorough scan of me from head to toe. 'Hey.'

'I'm glad you're okay,' I said quickly. I ran a hand through my hair, feeling awkward in a completely different way. 'And thanks for, you know, trying to rescue me and everything.'

She blinked up at me, and we stared at each other for one long moment. Then Katie rushed in and wrapped her arms around me. The scent of her thick, fruity perfume slammed into me, hitting me with so many memories that tears sprang to my eyes. I hadn't realized how tense I was until she hugged me, how much I'd been dreading what would happen to our friendship. The warmth of her embrace took all that away. My shoulders relaxed, and I felt my wings droop to the floor.

When she let me go, her eyes were glistening like bright blue stars. 'You should know, you're still a ridiculous social disaster,' she said, punching me on the shoulder. 'And an idiot.'

'Guilty as charged,' I replied.

The Corsis were suddenly surrounding me, clapping me

on the back and crushing me in bear hugs like they used to do around the shop. Hugo beamed at me, with a smile bigger than I'd ever seen it. My tears broke loose, and I let them fall. I didn't care anymore.

A voice rang out. 'The Queen of the Outcast Gypsies speaks!'

An older Gypsy, wearing a green hat, stood on the top of the altar steps. At his words, silence fell, even among the ones treating the injured. My eyes searched frantically for Josephine's. Before I could form a panicked question in my head, a single thought from her buzzed in my brain.

Trust me, Sebastian.

I pushed down my skittering feelings and watched as Josephine stepped forward, drawing the attention of everyone in the room. She looked every bit like a queen as she opened her mouth and began to speak.

'My friends, we have overcome a great danger that threatened to wipe out our very existence. But this victory has come at a high cost. Beginning tomorrow, we will mourn for eight days, as is our custom, for the Marksmen and *bandoleers* who lost their lives. And for Thalia Romany, our Queen.'

She paused, letting the weight of the deaths settle over the sanctuary. 'I am Josephine Romany, daughter of Nicolas Romany. I didn't ask to be my aunt's successor, but I'm humbled to have been her choice. With your help, I will do everything I can to lead our *kumpania* into a better place. But to make things new, we must first bring justice to the wrongs that have been done.' She looked at me. 'Guardians of the Roma, I invite you to stand before me.'

I looked back at Ezzie and the other gargoyles. I continued down the aisle, and they followed after me. When I reached the bottom of the stairs, I stopped. Ezzie took her place on my right side, and the others fanned out on either side.

'From this point forward,' said Josephine, 'all gargoyles will be treated in the manner they deserve. Without them, we would not have been able to defeat the plans of the *marimé* Augustine.' Josephine looked at Badrick. 'You are no longer bound to any Roma, unless you choose to do so of your own free will.'

He bowed. 'You have our gratitude, *Kralitsa*.'

'Evil shadowen remain throughout our *kumpania*,' she continued, looking to each of us. 'And we will need our guardians in the days to come more than ever. Not as our servants, but as our allies. And, as our friends.'

Josephine lifted her head and surveyed the assembly of Gypsies. There were spoken agreements from throughout the room. I heard the Corsis over everyone else, and I smiled to myself. At last, Josephine raised her hand for quiet.

'Having taken care of these matters, I have one last issue to be resolved before we can move forward.' She nodded to a tall, thin Marksman at the bottom of the steps. 'Bring them in.'

A block of ice suddenly dumped into my stomach. Several armed Marksmen entered the room, escorting two men up the steps. The first was Donani. The other one was Quentin Marks.

Red slammed over my vision so fast I didn't have time to brace myself. A snarl ripped from my throat and I felt myself move forward. But just as my hands curled into fists, I felt something different.

Control.

The fierce emotions swirled inside me, but this time, a new revelation came with them. I knew I could manage them. I wasn't a slave to them anymore. I took a deep breath, and then, the anger in me simply died. My vision righted. And though protective instincts still pumped strong in my blood, I was able, for the first time, to focus on the Marksman with complete, steady calm.

Quentin stared mutely ahead. His arm was cradled in a sling. A deep gash over his right eye had swollen it shut. There was nothing arrogant or triumphant about the Gypsy standing in front of him. Instead, I saw a broken man, and little more.

The man with the green hat spoke. 'As neither of you had knowledge of Augustine's true intent to murder Outcast Gypsies, you cannot be held responsible for his crimes. However, for the treatment of guardians placed in your care, you are liable.'

'Donani Marks, of the Marks clan, your service to the Queen has always been commendable, but the new Queen no longer requires your services. You are stripped of your rank as the Queen's Head Guard, and you will be assigned to another clan in the northern part of our *kumpania*.'

Donani dropped his head in shame. 'As *Kralitsa* wishes.'

The man turned to Quentin. 'Quentin Marks, of the Marks clan, you aligned yourself with the traitor Augustine for your own personal gain, and you used your position to mislead other Marksmen into following your orders. But your most serious crime is against our guardians. Therefore, the Queen has ordered a sentence of *marimé* for the period of three years. At the end of that time, should you have chosen to live your life in a wise and productive manner, the Court will reconsider the reinstatement of your Roma blood. Until then, you are banished from any and every Outcast establishment, and should you violate these terms, the sentence will be death.'

Quentin turned bloodshot eyes to Josephine. 'Please, hear me out.'

Josephine looked away. The man in the green hat did the same. One by one, every Gypsy in the room turned away from Quentin Marks. I expected him to scream or protest. But he didn't do anything – except meet my gaze. As I stared into his eyes, I pitied him. Maybe it showed in my face, because he suddenly turned without another word and walked out.

Josephine took a shaky breath. I felt her emotions clinging to me, like a heavy blanket. She wiped her eyes quickly, and when she looked forward once again, she was the Queen.

'And now,' she said in a steady voice. 'Sebastian Grey. Please join me.'

My legs felt wobbly as I ascended the stairs, and I remembered the first time I stood next to Josephine. It was to read a passage from *A Midsummer Night's Dream*. I swallowed past the lump in my throat. I was even more nervous now than I had been then.

'Sebastian,' she said, looking straight into my eyes. 'As my guardian, I'm afraid the safety and protection of this *kumpania* will now fall on you.'

I managed to crack a smile. 'I sort of figured that went along with the territory.'

She laughed softly, that musical laugh I'd fallen in love with from the first moment I heard it. Then, her expression turned serious. 'Do you accept this role?'

I felt the stares of everyone in the room, but I only had eyes for her. My wings quivered against my back. From a whispered plea in the cave under the Sutallee Bridge, to this moment, standing next to the girl who'd turned my world upside down. And made me want to live every day by her side.

I took a deep breath.
'If you will have me, Josephine Romany.'
Her eyes shone like emeralds.
'Always,' she said.
And she pressed her lips to mine.

Epilogue – Sebastian

'So this is where you're going to live now?'

Hugo crossed his arms and glared skeptically around the small room I'd chosen in the right tower of the Cathedral of Saints. Thankfully, the bell tower on the opposite side hadn't been used in years, and I was safe from the noise. The room was large enough for several pieces of furniture and, most importantly, for my wings to stretch out to their full length.

'What's wrong with it?' I shrugged at Hugo. 'I think it has lots of charm.'

'I think it looks like something out of a bad movie. But okay.'

Hugo shook his head and set down the last of the boxes he'd brought back from Sixes containing my stuff. He wiped his brow and crossed to the window. He looked out over the city.

'And you have to admit,' I added. 'The view's pretty sweet.'

'Yeah, you're right about that.'

I reached into the box and retrieved my collection of Shakespeare books. I brushed them off and set them on the shelf next to the small desk we'd also brought up. I glanced over my shoulder at my brother.

'I wanted to say thanks, by the way.'

He turned around and his thick brows shot up. 'Thanks for what, exactly? For not telling you the truth at the beginning, or for branding you without your knowing? Or maybe for keeping you with our clan against your will and then almost getting you killed—'

'Well,' I said. 'When you put it that way.'

He thrust out his hand. 'How about we leave the past in the past?'

I wrapped my clawed hand around his in a shake. 'Already been done.'

Hugo ruffled my hair. 'You're still my little brother, though. And you better not forget it.'

'Never.'

I finished arranging my books across the shelf, separating them by category, and then I sorted through the rest of the things on my desk. Hugo picked up another box from the window and walked it over to me.

'I saw Nicolas Romany in town today,' he said.

I reached out to take the box. 'Yeah, all the Romanys arrived last week.'

'So how's he feel about having a gargoyle for a son-in-law?'

The box slipped from my hands and clattered to the floor. 'What? There's no ... I mean, I haven't ... we haven't talked about ... that's not—'

'Relax,' said Hugo, chuckling. 'I get it. There's a lot of navigating to do.'

He knelt and retrieved the box. I sat on the edge of the bed, folding my wings forward so they'd hang over the edge, and I clasped my hands in front of me. Hugo set my stuff aside and leaned against the desk, folding his arms across his chest, waiting patiently.

'With everything that happened after Augustine's attack and witnessing the way Josephine handled the aftermath, the High Council decided unanimously to allow her to keep the throne, even though her status is—'

'Unmarried?'

My cheeks burned, and I fumbled with a new rip in my jeans. 'She's an adult in the eyes of the Court now, so marriage doesn't have to … I mean, it's her choice … you know, if she ever wants to, but it doesn't … anyway, I don't even know if we … I mean, if it's even allowed. I'm definitely not a Gypsy.' I fanned my massive gargoyle wings for effect. 'Aren't Outcast rules pretty strict?'

'Well, I guess it's a good thing you're in love with the Queen.'

The warmth I felt radiating through my chest made any protests I had fizzle on my lips. I loved Josephine, and she loved me back. It still felt too amazing to be true. My wings shuddered against the bed. Hugo was still looking at me, an almost smug expression on his face.

'What about you?' I asked quickly. 'How are things going with you and Ezzie?'

'That,' he said, 'is none of your business.'

I smirked, but I kept my mouth shut. I knew better than to press my brother for details. I pushed myself off the bed and folded my wings tight against my back. Hugo took another survey of the room.

'So you're really going to stay here?' he asked, glancing out the window.

'For now,' I replied. 'I've got a room in the Court of Shadows, but it's going to take some getting used to. I've not been really fond of the whole underground thing, lately.'

'And what's Josephine got to say about it?'

I sniffed the air, catching a scent. 'Why don't you ask her?'

Josephine stepped into the room, brushing dust off her jeans. 'I don't mind. This place might make a great little getaway place, once it's fixed up right.' She smiled at me, and I felt my face grow ten degrees hotter.

Francis entered the room behind his sister, carrying an open box. 'Hey, Sebastian. I brought your stuff from the Circe like you asked.' He glanced around the room approvingly. 'Nice place. Better than the quarters they've got us in down at the Court.'

'Thanks.'

I shot Hugo an overly satisfied look, which he conveniently ignored.

'Well,' said Francis, dropping the box into the nearest corner. 'I've gotta run, but I'll see you guys at the banquet tonight, right?'

'I don't think we really have much choice,' said Josephine.

Francis grinned. 'See ya later, Your Majesty.'

He turned and headed back down the stairs without another word. I felt myself grinning after him. I'd really missed Francis and the rest of the Circe, even if some of them were still slow in coming around to me.

Suddenly, Josephine let out a loud sigh. 'I just realized, I forgot my bag at the bottom of the stairs.'

'I'm on it,' I said.

I got the image in my head, drew in deep breath, and summoned the shadows. They swirled around me in a cold, comforting mist. I was back in a matter of seconds, with Josephine's bag in my hands.

'Thank you,' she said, kissing me on the cheek.

Hugo huffed, impressed. 'So, no more problems with the whole mist thing? Ezzie told me shadowing made you sick as a dog.'

'Not anymore,' I said with a shrug. 'I guess thanks to the other guy.'

I still refused to name the creature that had somehow shared space with me for a while. Because, even two weeks later, the idea that he might return still haunted me at night.

'So the horns aren't the only thing he left you with,' Hugo commented.

My smile dropped. 'No.'

'There's something else?'

'I ... he ... you know we didn't destroy all the shadowen that night. All of them in Savannah, definitely. But there are more. They communicate to me, sometimes. Not words, just emotions, mainly. But I know they're out there.'

Hugo frowned. 'Could you control them?'

What remained of the creature inside me was still fresh, and though I mastered it now, I also realized it would never truly go away. 'I don't know. Maybe. It's not something I really want to try right now.'

'Fair enough.' Hugo shoved his hands in his pockets. 'Well, I'm going to run out and grab some dinner.' He lowered his brows at me. 'I won't even ask if you want anything.'

'I'll pay you back,' I said politely.

'Yeah right,' he replied. 'I won't lose any sleep over it. You two have fun with all this ... stuff. But just as a warning, Josephine, this guy sucked at cleaning back home.'

Hugo ducked out of the room, but not before I pegged him in the back of the head with a paperback copy of *Hamlet*. Josephine laughed, then opened her bag and pulled out a letter.

'Katie wrote me this week.'

'I'm not surprised.'

'I love it. I mean, nobody writes letters anymore. And she always decorates it with glitter and stickers—'

'Because she's five.'

'Because she's *creative*. Anyway, she told me she might be coming to Savannah to attend college.'

I felt a grin spread over my face. 'Really?'

'Yeah, really. Of course, it doesn't have anything to do with us. Kris Corsi's opening up a tattoo shop downtown.'

I rolled my eyes. 'Should've known.'

Josephine set the letter on my desk and took my hands. It never failed to send a shiver of electricity up my arms. Her smiled faded, but it was replaced with a look that made my heart want to explode inside my chest. She led me to the window and climbed onto the ledge. I moved beside her.

'This is nice,' she said, as she squeezed my hand and cast a sideways look in my direction. 'But promise me you won't spend too much time up here.'

I pulled from a memory, my first official day as her guardian.

I go where you go, Josephine.

The words tingled in my head as I thought them, and I watched her expression shift contentedly as she heard it in her own mind. The bond between us resonated like music. There was no need for us to try and understand it anymore. I'd never felt anything so natural in my life. She leaned her

443

head against my shoulder, and I pulled my wing close, wrapping around her protectively.

'Are you sure about this?' I asked hesitantly. 'About us, I mean.'

'Absolutely,' she replied, without a hint of doubt in her voice. Then, she paused. 'As for the future, well, I guess we'll just have to wait and see. Things won't be easy.'

'Whatever happens next, I'll face it at your side, Josephine.'

She looked up at me. 'Together.'

Josephine wrapped her arms around my neck and snuggled into my chest. I took in her scent, the exotic spices from a world that was no longer foreign to me, but smelled like home. 'It's a beautiful night,' I said, looking out at the expanse before us. 'Would you care for a short flight, *Kralitsa*?'

She beamed at me like sunlight. 'Ready when you are.'

I swept Josephine into my arms and leapt from the window.

Acknowledgements

To God, who makes all things possible. Proverbs 16:3

To Doug, Liam, Justin, my parents, my in-laws, my niece and nephews, and all my amazing family. Thanks for your continued love and support.

To the wonderful team at HarperCollins/HarperVoyager for bringing this series to life. Thank you Lily Cooper and Natasha Bardon for all your work! Thanks to Ben Gardiner for my beautiful cover and to Simon Fox for making my words better.

To my agent Jill Corcoran for always being in my corner.

To my incredible friends, who bring out the best in me.

To Rachel Winterbottom. Thank you.

To Trail Mix – the best critique group and friends I could ask for.

And finally, to all the people who've read these books so enthusiastically, spread the word so diligently, and written reviews so beautifully . . . your encouragement means more than you know. Thank you for sharing this world with me.

Christi

Printed by RR Donnelley at Glasgow, UK